Anne Rice

PRINCE
LESTAT

PRINCE LESTAT

The Vampire Chronicles

ANNE RICE

ALFRED A. KNOPF

New York

2014

THIS IS A BORZOI BOOK
PUBLISHED BY ALFRED A. KNOPF

www.aaknopf.com

Library of Congress Cataloging-in-Publication Data
Rice, Anne, [date]
  Prince Lestat / Anne Rice.
    pages cm — (The vampire chronicles)
  ISBN 978-0-307-96252-2 (hardcover) — ISBN 978-0-307-96253-9 (eBook)
  1. Vampires—Fiction.   I. Title.
PS3568.I265P86 2014
813'.54—dc23   2014009319

Jacket design by Abby Weintraub

Manufactured in the United States of America
First Edition

From my stone pillow I have dreamed dreams of the mortal world above. I have heard its voice, its new music, as lullabies as I lie in my grave. I have envisioned its fantastic discoveries, I have known its courage in the timeless sanctum of my thoughts. And though it shuts me out with its dazzling forms, I long for one with the strength to roam it fearlessly, to ride the Devil's Road through its heart.

—Allesandra,
yet unnamed in
The Vampire Lestat

Old truths and ancient magic, revolution and invention, all conspire to distract us from the passion that in one way or another defeats us all.

And weary finally of this complexity, we dream of that long-ago time when we sat upon our mother's knee and each kiss was the perfect consummation of desire. What can we do but reach for the embrace that must now contain both Heaven and Hell: our doom again and again and again.

—Lestat
in *The Vampire Lestat*

In the flesh all wisdom begins. Beware the thing that has no flesh. Beware the gods, beware the *idea*, beware the devil.

—Maharet to Jesse
in *The Queen of the Damned*

Contents

Blood Genesis

In the beginning were the spirits. They were invisible beings, heard and seen only by the most powerful sorcerers or witches. Some were thought to be malevolent; some were praised as good. They could find lost objects, spy upon enemies, and now and then affect the weather.

Two great witches, Mekare and Maharet, lived in a beautiful valley on the side of Mount Carmel, and they communed with the spirits. One of these spirits, the great and powerful Amel, could, in his mischief making, take blood from human beings. Tiny bits of blood entered the alchemical mystery of the spirit, though how no one knew. But Amel loved the witch Mekare and was ever eager to serve her. She saw him as no other witch ever had, and he loved her for it.

One day the troops of an enemy came—soldiers of the powerful Queen Akasha of Egypt. She wanted the witches; she wanted their knowledge, their secrets.

This wicked monarch destroyed the valley and the villages of Mekare and Maharet and brought the sisters by force to her own kingdom.

Amel, the furious familiar spirit of the witch Mekare, sought to punish the Queen.

When she lay dying, stabbed over and over by conspirators of her own court, this spirit Amel entered into her, fusing with her body and her blood and giving her a new and terrifying vitality.

This fusion caused a new entity to be born into the world: the vampire, the blood drinker.

From the blood of this great vampire queen, Akasha, all the other vampires of the whole world were born over the millennia. A blood exchange was the means of procreation.

To punish the twins who stood opposed to her and her new power, Akasha blinded Maharet and tore the tongue from Mekare. But before they could be executed, the steward of the Queen, Khayman, a newly made blood drinker himself, passed on to the twins the powerful Blood.

Khayman and the twins led a rebellion against Akasha, but they could not stop her cult of blood drinker gods. Eventually the twins were captured and separated—sent out as castaways—Maharet into the Red Sea and Mekare into the great ocean to the west.

Maharet soon found familiar shores and thrived, but Mekare, carried across the ocean to lands yet undiscovered and unnamed, vanished from history.

This was six thousand years ago.

The great Queen Akasha and her husband, King Enkil, went mute after two thousand years, maintained like statues in a shrine by elders and priests that believed Akasha contained the Sacred Core—and that if she should be destroyed, all the blood drinkers of the world would die with her.

But by the time of the Common Era, the story of the Blood Genesis was completely forgotten. Only a few elder immortals passed on the tale, though they did not believe it even as they told it. Yet blood gods, vampires dedicated to the old religion, still reigned in shrines throughout the world.

Imprisoned in hollowed-out trees or brick cells, these blood gods starved for blood until the holy feasts at which they were brought offerings: evildoers to judge and condemn and feast upon.

AT THE DAWN of the Common Era, an elder, a keeper of the Divine Parents, abandoned Akasha and Enkil in the desert for the sun to destroy them. All over the world young blood drinkers perished, burnt to death in their coffins, their shrines, or in their tracks as the sun shone on the Mother and Father. But the Mother and Father themselves were too strong to perish. And many of the very old ones survived as well, though badly burned and in pain.

A newly made blood drinker, a wise Roman scholar by the name of

Marius, went down to Egypt to find the King and Queen and protect them so that no holocaust would ever again ravage the world of the Undead. And thereafter Marius made them his sacred responsibility. The legend of Marius and Those Who Must Be Kept endured for almost two millennia.

In the year 1985, the story of this Blood Genesis was told to all the world's Undead. That the Queen lived, that she contained the Sacred Core, this was part of the story. It appeared in a book written by the Vampire Lestat, who also told the tale in song and dance in film and from the stage where he performed as a rock singer—calling the world to know and destroy his own kind.

Lestat's voice waked the Queen from millennia of silence and slumber. She rose with a dream: that she would dominate the world of human beings through cruelty and slaughter and become for them the Queen of Heaven.

But the ancient twins came forward to stop Akasha. They too had heard Lestat's songs. Maharet appealed to the Queen to stop her superstitious blood tyranny. And the long-lost Mekare, rising from the earth after untold aeons, decapitated the great Queen, and took the Sacred Core into herself as she devoured the dying Queen's brain. Mekare, under the protection of her sister, became the new Queen of the Damned.

Lestat once again wrote the story. He had been there. He had seen the passing of the power with his own eyes. He gave his testimony to everyone. The mortal world took no notice of his "fictions," but his tales shocked the Undead.

And so the story of origins and ancient battles, of vampire powers and vampire weaknesses, and wars for control of the Dark Blood became the common knowledge of the Undead tribe the world over. It became the property of old ones who'd been comatose for centuries in caves or graves, of young ones misbegotten in jungles or swamps or urban slums who had never dreamed of their antecedents. It became the property of wise and secretive survivors who had lived in isolation through the ages.

It became the legacy of all blood drinkers the world over to know they shared a common bond, a common history, a common root.

This is the tale of how that knowledge changed the tribe and its destiny forever.

Blood Argot

When the Vampire Lestat wrote his books, he used any number of terms taught to him by the vampires he had encountered in his life. And those vampires who added to his work, offering their memoirs and their experiences in written form, added terms of their own, some much more ancient than those ever revealed to Lestat.

This is a list of those terms, which are now common amongst the Undead throughout the world.

The Blood—When the word is capitalized it refers to vampiric blood, passed on from master to fledgling through a deep and often dangerous exchange. "In the Blood" means that one is a vampire. The Vampire Lestat had over two hundred years "in the Blood" when he wrote his books. The great vampire Marius has over two thousand years in the Blood. And so forth and so on.

Blood Drinker—The most ancient term for vampire. This was Akasha's simple term, which she later sought to supplant with the term "blood god" for those who followed her spiritual path and her religion.

Blood Wife or Blood Spouse—One's vampire mate.

Children of the Millennia—Term for immortals who have lived more than a thousand years and most specifically for those who have survived more than two.

Children of the Night—Common term for all vampires, or all those in the Blood.

Children of Satan—Term for vampires of late antiquity and after who believed they were literally children of the Devil and serving God through serving Satan as they fed upon humankind. Their approach to life was penitential and puritanical. They denied themselves all pleasure except drinking blood and occasional Sabbats (large gatherings) at which they danced, and they lived underground, often in filthy and dismal catacombs and enclosures. The Children of Satan have not been seen nor heard of since the eighteenth century, and in all likelihood the cult has died out.

The Coven of the Articulate—A modern slang term popular among the Undead for the vampires whose stories appear in the Vampire Chronicles—particularly Louis, Lestat, Pandora, Marius, and Armand.

The Dark Gift—A term for the vampiric power. When a master bestows the Blood on a fledgling, that master is offering the Dark Gift.

The Dark Trick—Refers to the act of actually making the new vampire. To draw out the fledgling's blood and to replace it with one's own powerful Blood—is to work the Dark Trick.

The Devil's Road—Medieval term among the vampires for the road each vampire takes through this world; a popular term of the Children of Satan who saw themselves as serving God through serving the Devil. To ride the Devil's Road was to live one's life as an immortal.

The First Brood—These are the vampires descended from Khayman who were in rebellion against Queen Akasha.

The Queens Blood—These are the vampires made by Queen Akasha to follow her path in the Blood and fight the rebels of the First Brood.

The Sacred Core—This refers to the residing brain or governing life force of the spirit Amel, which is inside the body of the vampire Mekare. Before it was in Mekare it was in the vampire Akasha. It is believed that every vampire on the planet is connected to the Sacred Core by some sort of invisible web or network of tentacles. If the vampire containing the Sacred Core were to be destroyed, all the vampires of the planet would die.

The Fire Gift—This is the ability of older vampires to use their telekinetic power to burn matter. They can, through the power of their minds, burn wood, paper, or any flammable substance. And they can burn other vampires as well, igniting the Blood in their bodies and reducing them to cinders. Only older vampires possess this power, but no one can say when and how a vampire acquires it. A very young vampire made by an ancient one may immediately possess the power. A vampire must be able to see that which he or she wants to burn. In sum, no vampire can burn another if he cannot see that vampire, if he is not close enough to direct the power.

The Cloud Gift—This is the ability of older vampires to defy gravity, to rise up and move in the upper atmosphere and to cover long distances easily, traveling the winds unseen by those below. Again, no one can say when a vampire might acquire this power. The will to have it may work wonders. All truly ancient ones possess it whether they know it or not. Some vampires despise the power and never use it unless forced.

The Mind Gift—This is a loose and imprecise term which refers to the preternatural powers of the vampiric mind on many levels. Through the Mind Gift, a vampire might learn things from the world above even when he is sleeping in the earth below. And consciously using the Mind Gift, he might telepathically listen to the thoughts of mortals and immortals. He might use the Mind Gift to pick up images from others as well as words. He might use the Mind Gift to project images into the minds of others. And finally he might use the Mind Gift to telekinetically open a lock, push open a door, or stop the progress of an engine. Again, vampires develop the Mind Gift slowly over time, and only the most ancient can rape the minds of others for information they do not wish to give, or send a telekinetic blast to rupture the brain and blood cells of a human being or another vampire. A vampire can listen to many the world over, hearing and seeing what others hear. But to destroy telekinetically, he or she must be able to see the intended victim.

The Spell Gift—This refers to the power of vampires to confuse, beguile, and spellbind mortals and sometimes other vampires. All vampires, even fledglings, have this power to some extent, though many don't know how to use it. It involves a conscious attempt to "persuade" the victim of the reality the vampire wants the victim to embrace. It doesn't enslave the victim. But it does confuse and mislead. It depends on eye contact. One can't spellbind anyone from a distance. In fact, it more often involves words as well as glances, and certainly involves the Mind Gift on some level.

Fledgling—A new vampire very young in the Blood. Also, one's own offspring in the Blood. For example, Louis is the fledgling of Lestat. Armand is the fledgling of Marius. The ancient twin Maharet is the fledgling of her twin, Mekare. Mekare is the fledgling of the ancient Khayman. Khayman is the fledgling of Akasha.

The Little Drink—Stealing blood from a mortal victim without the victim knowing it or feeling it, without the victim having to die.

Maker—Simple term for the vampire who brought one into the Blood. Being slowly replaced by the term "mentor." Sometimes the maker is also referred to as the "master." However, this has gone out of use. In many parts of the world it is considered a great sin to rise up against or seek to destroy one's maker. A maker can never hear the thoughts of a fledgling, and vice versa.

The Queen of the Damned—Term given to the vampire Mekare by her sister Maharet once Mekare had taken the Sacred Core into herself. It was ironic. Akasha, the fallen Queen who had sought to dominate the world, had called herself the Queen of Heaven.

The Savage Garden—A term used by Lestat for the world, fitting with his belief that the only true laws of the universe are aesthetic laws, the laws that govern the natural beauty we see all around us on the planet.

The Undead—Common term for vampires of all ages.

Part I

THE
VAMPIRE
LESTAT

I

The Voice

YEARS AGO, I heard him. He'd been babbling.

It was after Queen Akasha had been destroyed and the mute red-haired twin, Mekare, had become "the Queen of the Damned." I'd witnessed all that—the brutal death of Akasha in the moment when we all thought we would die, too, along with her.

It was after I'd switched bodies with a mortal man and come back into my own powerful vampiric body—having rejected the old dream of being human again.

It was after I'd been to Heaven and Hell with a spirit called Memnoch, and come back to Earth a wounded explorer with no appetite anymore for knowledge, truth, beauty.

Defeated, I'd lain for years on the floor of a chapel in New Orleans in an old convent building, oblivious to the ever-shifting crowd of immortals around me—hearing them, wanting to respond, yet somehow never managing to meet a glance, answer a question, acknowledge a kiss or a whisper of affection.

And that's when I first heard the Voice. Masculine, insistent, inside my brain.

Babbling, like I said. And I thought, Well, perhaps we blood drinkers can go mad like mortals, you know, and this is some artifact of my warped mind. Or maybe he is some massively crippled ancient one, slumbering somewhere nearby, and somehow I, telepathically, get to share in his misery.

There are physical limits to telepathy in our world. Of course. But then voices, pleas, messages, thoughts, can be relayed through other minds, and conceivably, this poor slob could be mumbling to himself on the other side of the planet.

As I said, he had babbled, mixing languages, ancient and modern, sometimes stringing a whole sentence out in Latin or Greek, and then lapsing into repetitions of modern voices . . . phrases from films and even songs. Over and over he begged for help, rather like the tiny human-headed fly at the end of the B-movie masterpiece, Help me, help me, as if he too were caught in a spiderweb and a giant spider were closing in on him. Okay, okay, what can I do, I'd ask, and he was quick to respond. Near at hand? Or just the best relay system in the Undead world?

"Hear me, come to me." And he'd say that over and over again, night after night, until it was noise.

I have always been able to tune him out. No problem. Either you learn to tune out telepathic voices when you are a vampire or you go straight out of your mind. I can tune out the cries of the living just as easily. Have to. No other way to survive. Even the very ancient ones can tune out the voices. I've been in the Blood for over two hundred years. They've been in the Blood for six millennia.

Sometimes he simply went away.

Around the early years of the twenty-first century he began to speak in English.

"Why?" I asked.

"Because you like it," he said in that crisp masculine tone of his. Laughter. His laughter. "Everybody likes English. You must come to me when I call you," he said. Then he was babbling again, in a mélange of languages, all about blindness, suffocation, paralysis, helplessness. And it devolved into "Help me" again with snatches of poetry in Latin and Greek and French and English.

This is interesting for maybe three-quarters of an hour. After that, it's repetitious and a nuisance.

Of course I did not even bother to say no.

At one point, he cried out "Beauty!" and babbled on incessantly, always getting back to "Beauty!" and always with an exclamation point I could feel like the jab of a finger against my temple.

"Okay, 'beauty,' so what?" I asked. He moaned, wept, went into dizzying incoherent reverie. I tuned him out for a year, I think. But I could feel him rumbling under the surface, and then two years after that—it might have been—he started addressing me by name.

"Lestat, you, Brat Prince!"

"Oh, get off it."

"No, you, Brat Prince, my prince, boy oh boy, Lestat. . . ." Then he ran those words through ten modern languages and six or seven ancient ones. I was impressed.

"So tell me who you are, or else," I said glumly. I had to confess when I was extremely lonely, I was happy to have him around.

And that was not a good year for me. I was wandering aimlessly. I was sick of things. I was furious with myself that the "beauty" of life wasn't sustaining me, wasn't making my loneliness bearable. I was wandering at night in jungles and in forests with my hands up to touch the leaves of the low branches, crying to myself, doing a lot of babbling of my own. I wandered through Central America visiting Maya ruins, and went deep down into Egypt to walk in the desert wastes and see the ancient drawings on the rocks on the way to the ports of the Red Sea.

Young maverick vampires kept invading the cities where I roamed—Cairo, Jerusalem, Mumbai, Honolulu, San Francisco—and I grew weary of disciplining them, punishing them for slaughtering the innocent in their misbegotten hunger. They'd get caught, thrown into human jails where they'd burn up when dawn came. Occasionally they'd fall into the hands of actual forensic scientists. Bloody nuisance.

Nothing ever came of it. But more on that later.

The mavericks multiplying everywhere were causing trouble for one another, and their gang fights and brawls have made life ugly for the rest of us. And they think nothing of trying to burn with fire or decapitate any other blood drinker who gets in their way.

It is chaos.

But who am I to police these preternatural nincompoops?

When have I ever been on the side of law and order? I'm supposed to be the rebellious one, *l'enfant terrible.* So I let them drive me away out of the cities, and even from New Orleans, I let them drive me away. My beloved Louis de Pointe du Lac left soon after, and from that time on lived in New York with Armand.

Armand keeps the island of Manhattan safe for them—Louis, Armand, and two young blood drinkers, Benjamin and Sybelle, and whoever else joins them in their palatial digs on the Upper East Side.

No surprises there. Armand has always been skilled at destroying those who offend him. He was after all for hundreds of years the coven master of the old Children of Satan in Paris, and he'd burn to ashes any blood drinker who didn't obey the vicious old rules of those miserable religious fanatics. He's autocratic, ruthless. Well, he can have that mission.

But let me add here that Armand isn't the moral cipher I once thought he was. So much of what I thought about us, our minds, our souls, our moral evolution or devolution, was just wrong in the books I wrote. Armand's not without compassion, not without a heart. In many respects, he's just coming into himself after five hundred years. And what do I really know about being immortal? I've been in the Blood since when, 1780? That's not very long. Not very long at all.

I've been to New York, by the way, to spy on my old friends.

I've stood outside their gorgeous Upper East Side dwelling on warm nights, listening to the young vampire Sybelle play the piano and Benjamin and Armand talking by the hour.

Such impressive dwellings—three townhouses attached to one another and made into one grand palazzo, each with its own Grecian portico and front steps and little decorative iron fencing. Only the central entrance was used, with the bronze name in script above the door: TRINITY GATE.

Benji's the vampire responsible for the radio talk show beaming out of New York night after night. In the first years, it was broadcast in the regular way, but now it's internet radio and reaches the Undead all over the world. Benji's clever in ways no one could have predicted—a Bedouin by birth, brought into the Blood at age twelve perhaps, so he'll be five feet two inches tall and small forever. But he's one of those immortal children whom mortals always take for a diminutive adult.

I can't "hear" Louis when I'm spying, of course, since I made him, and makers and fledglings are deaf to each other, but my preternatural ears have never been better. Outside their house, I easily picked up his rich, soft voice and the images of Louis in the minds of the others. I could see the vividly colored baroque murals on their ceilings through the billowing lace curtains. Lots of blue there—blue skies with rich rolling gold-tinged clouds. Why not? And I could smell those crackling fires.

The townhouse complex was five stories, *Belle Époque*, and grand. Basements underneath and, high up there, an immense attic ballroom with a glass ceiling open to the stars. They'd made it into a palace, all right. Armand has always been good at that, drawing on unimaginable reserves to pave his stunning headquarters in marble and antique plank and to furnish the rooms with the finest designs ever produced. And he always made them secure.

The sad little icon painter from Russia, kidnapped and plunged into the West, had long ago embraced its humanist vision utterly. Marius, his maker, surely must have seen this with some satisfaction a long time ago.

I wanted to join them. Always do want to join them and never do. In fact, I marveled at the way they lived—slipping out in Rolls-Royce limousines to attend the opera, the symphony, the ballet, wandering the museum openings together, so well integrated into the human world around them, even inviting mortals to those gilded salons for wine and refreshments. Having mortal musicians in to play. How splendidly they passed for human. I marveled that I had ever lived that way, ever been able to do it with such finesse a century or more ago. I watched them with the eyes of a hungry ghost.

The Voice rumbled and bellowed and whispered whenever I was there, rolling their names around in a stew of invective and rumination and demand. One evening, the Voice said, "Beauty is what drove it, don't you see? It was the mystery of Beauty."

A year later, I was walking along the sands of South Beach in Miami when he broke that one on me again. For the moment, the mavericks and rogues had been leaving me alone. They were afraid of me, afraid of all the old ones. But not enough.

"Drove what, dear Voice?" I asked. I felt it was only fair to give him a few minutes before shutting him down.

"You cannot conceive of the magnitude of this mystery." He spoke in a confidential whisper. "You cannot conceive of this complexity." He was saying these words as if he'd just discovered them. He wept. I swear it. He wept.

It was an awful sound. I don't glory in any being's pain, not even the pain of my most sadistic enemies, and here was the Voice weeping.

I was hunting, thirsting though I didn't need to drink, at the mercy of the craving, the deep agonizing lust for heated pumping human blood. I found a young victim, female, irresistible in her combination of filthy soul and gorgeous body, white throat so tender. I had her in the fragrant darkened bedroom of her own lodgings, lights of the city beyond the windows, having come over the roofs to find her, this pale woman with glorious brown eyes and walnut-shaded skin, black hair like the snakes of Medusa, naked between the white linen sheets, struggling against me as I sank my fangs right into the carotid artery. Too hungry for anything else. Give me the heartbeat. Give me the salt. Give me the Viaticum. Fill my mouth.

And then the blood erupted, roared. Don't rush this! I was the victim suddenly laid waste as if by a phallic god, slammed by the rushing blood against the floor of the universe, the heart pounding, emptying the frail form it sought to protect. And lo, she was dead. Oh, too soon. Crushed lily on the pillow, except she'd been no lily and I'd seen her grimy petty purple crimes as that blood made a fool of me, wasted me, left me warm, indeed hot, all over, licking my lips.

Can't bear to linger near a dead human. Out over the roofs again.

"Did you enjoy that, Voice?" I asked. I stretched like a cat under the moon.

"Hmmm," he replied. "Have always loved it, of course."

"Then stop all the weeping."

He drifted off then. That was a first. He left me. I hit him with one question after another. No answer. No one there.

Three years ago, this happened.

I was in a wretched state, down and out, disgusted and discouraged. Things were bad all over the vampire world, no doubt about it. Benji in his endless broadcasts was calling for me to come out of exile. And others were joining him in that appeal. "Lestat, we need you." Tales of woe abounded. And I couldn't find many of my friends anymore—not Marius, or David Talbot, or even the ancient twins. Time was when I could find any and all of them fairly easily, but no more.

"We are a parentless tribe!" Benji cried over the internet vampire radio station. "Young ones, be wise. Flee the old ones when you see them. They are not our elders, no matter how many years they have in the Blood. They have refused all responsibility for their brothers and sisters. Be wise!"

On this dreary cold night, I'd been thirsty, more thirsty than I could bear. Oh, I don't technically need the blood anymore. I have so much blood from Akasha in my veins—the primal blood from the old Mother—that I can exist forever without feeding. But I was thirsting, and I had to have it to stanch the misery, or so I told myself, on a little late-night rampage in the city of Amsterdam, feeding off every reprobate and killer I could find. I'd hidden the bodies. I'd been careful. But it had been grim—that hot, delicious blood pumping into me and all those visions with it of filthy and degenerate minds, all that intimacy with the emotions I deplore. Oh, same old, same old. I was sick at heart. In moods like this, I'm a menace to the innocent, and I know it only too well.

Around four in the morning, it had me so bad, I was in a little public park, sitting on an iron bench in the damp, doubled over, in a bad seedy part of the city, the late-night lights looking garish and sooty through the mist. And I was cold all over and fearing now that I simply wasn't going to endure. I wasn't going to "make it" in the Blood. I wasn't going to be a true immortal like the great Marius or Mekare or Maharet or Khayman, or even Armand. This wasn't living, what I was doing. And at one point the pain was so acute, it was like a blade turning in my heart and in my brain. I doubled over on the bench. I had my hands clasped on the back of my neck, and I wanted nothing so much as to die, simply to close my eyes on all of life and die.

And the Voice came, and the Voice said:

"But I love you!"

I was startled. I hadn't heard the Voice in such a long time, and there it was, that intimate tone, so soft, so utterly tender, like fingers touching me, caressing my head.

"Why?" I asked.

"Of all of them, I love you the most," said the Voice. "I am with you, loving you now."

"What are you? Another make-believe angel?" I said. "Another spirit pretending to be a god, something like that?"

"No," he said.

But the moment he'd started to speak, I had felt this warmth in me, this sudden warmth such as addicts describe when they are infused with the substance they crave, this lovely reassuring warmth that I'd found so fleetingly in the Blood, and I'd begun to hear the rain, hear it not as this dismal drizzle but as a lovely soft symphony of sounds on the surfaces that surrounded me.

"I love you," said the Voice. "Now, get up. Leave this place. You must. Get up. Start walking. This rain is not too cold for you. You are too strong for this rain and too strong for this sorrow. Come on, do as I tell you. . . ."

And I had.

I had gotten up and started walking and made my way back to the elegant old Hôtel de l'Europe where I was lodged, and I'd gone into the large exquisitely wallpapered bedroom and closed the long velvet draperies properly over the coming sun. Glare of white sky over the Amstel River. Morning sounds.

Then, I'd stopped. I'd pressed my fingers to my eyelids and buckled, buckled under the weight of a loneliness so terrible I would have chosen death then if only I'd had such a choice.

"Come now, I love you," said the Voice. "You're not alone in this! You never were." I could feel the Voice inside me, around me, embracing me.

Finally, I lay down to sleep. He was singing to me now, singing in French, singing some lyrics put to the beautiful Chopin étude "Tristesse" . . .

"Lestat, go home to France, to the Auvergne where you were born," he whispered, just as if he were beside me. "Your father's old château there. You need to go there. All of you human beings need a home."

So tender it sounded, so sincere.

So strange that he would say this. I did own the old ruined château. Years ago, I had set architects and stone masons to rebuild it, though why I did not know. I saw an image of it now, those ancient round towers rising from that cliff above fields and valleys, where in the old days so many had starved, where life had been so bitter, where I had been bitter, a boy bound and determined to run away to Paris, to see the world.

"Go home," he whispered.

"Why are you not winking out the way I am, Voice?" I asked. "The sun's rising."

"Because it is not morning where I am, beloved Lestat."

"Ah, then you are a blood drinker, aren't you?" I asked. I felt I'd caught him. I began to laugh, to cackle. "Of course you are."

He was furious. "You miserable, ungrateful, degenerate Brat Prince," he was muttering . . . and then he'd left me again. Ah, well. Why not? But I hadn't really solved the mystery of the Voice, not by a long shot. Was he just a powerful old immortal communicating from another part of the globe by bouncing his telepathic message off vampiric minds in between, like light bouncing from mirror to mirror? No, that wasn't possible. His voice was too intimate and precise for all that. You can send out a telepathic call to another immortal by that method, of course. But you can't communicate directly as he had been doing all along with me.

When I woke, it was of course early evening, and Amsterdam was filled with roaring traffic, whizzing bicycles, myriad voices. Scent of blood pumped through beating hearts.

"Still with me, Voice?" I asked.

Silence. Yet I had the distinct feeling, yes, the feeling that he was here. I'd felt wretched, afraid for myself, wondering at my own weakness, inability to love.

And then this happened.

I went to the full-length mirror on the bathroom door to adjust my tie. You know what a dandy I am. Well, even down and out, I was in a finely cut Armani jacket and dress shirt, and, well, I wanted to adjust this bright, flashing, beautifully hand-painted silk tie and—my reflection wasn't there!

I was there, but not my reflection. It was another me, smiling at me with triumphant glittering eyes, both hands up against the glass as if he were in a prison cell behind it. Same clothes, yes, and me down to the last detail of long blond curling hair and glittering blue-gray eyes. But not a reflection at all.

I was petrified. The dim echo of *doppelgänger* rose in my ears, and all the horror such a concept connotes. I don't know if I can describe how chilling this was—this figure of myself inhabited by another, leering at me, deliberately menacing me.

I remained sober faced, and I continued to adjust my tie, though I could see no reflection of what I was doing. And he continued to smile in that icy mocking way, as the laughter of the Voice rose in my brain.

"Am I supposed to like you for this, Voice?" I asked. "I thought you loved me."

He was stricken. His face—my face—crumpled like that of a little boy about to sob. He put his hands up as if to shield himself, fingers hovering, eyes quivering. The image vanished, to be replaced by a true reflection of me standing there, puzzled, faintly horrified, and not a little angry. I straightened my tie for the last time.

"I do love you," said the Voice sadly, almost mournfully. "I love you!" and he began to chatter, and roar, and discourse, and all those vocabularies were suddenly tumbling together, Russian, German, French, Latin. . . .

That night, when Benji began broadcasting from New York, he

said that things could not continue like this. He urged the young ones to flee the cities. He begged once more for the elders of the tribe to step up.

I went to Anatolia to escape it all. I wanted to see Hagia Sophia again, to walk under those arches. I wanted to wander the ruins of Göbekli Tepe, the oldest Neolithic settlement ever discovered. To Hell with the problems of the tribe. Whatever gave Benji the idea that we were a tribe?

2

Benji Mahmoud

I FIGURED THAT Benji Mahmoud was probably twelve years old when Marius made him a vampire, but no one knew for sure, including Benji. He'd been born in Israel to a Bedouin family, then hired and imported into the United States by the family of a young female piano player named Sybelle—who was clearly insane—so that he could be Sybelle's companion. Both young people met the Vampire Armand in New York in the mid-1990s but weren't inducted into the Blood till a little later, when Marius worked the Dark Trick on both of them as a gift to Armand. Of course Armand was furious, felt betrayed, deplored that the human lives of his charges had been cut short, etcetera, but Marius had done the only thing that could be done with two humans who were living for all practical purposes in Our World and fast losing taste for any other. Human wards like that are hostages to fortune. And Armand should have known that, that some vampire enemy or other was going to knock off one or the other or both of these two young people just to get at Armand. That's the way such things can too easily go.

So Marius brought them over.

I was not myself in those days. I was battered and broken thanks to my adventures with Memnoch, a spirit who claimed to have been "the Devil" of the Christian belief system, and I scarcely noticed all this, only knowing that I loved the music that Sybelle made and little more.

By the time I took real notice of Benji Mahmoud, he was living in New York with Armand and Louis and Sybelle, and he had invented the radio station. As I mentioned earlier, it was broadcast at first, but Benji was far too inventive to put up with the mortal world's constraints on him for long, and he soon operated the program as an internet radio stream out of the townhouse on the Upper East Side, often speaking to the Children of the Darkness nightly and inviting their phone calls from all over the world.

In the broadcast days, Benji had talked in a low voice, under Sybelle's music, a voice that without specific enhancement couldn't be heard by mortal ears, hoping that the vampires of the world would get the message. Trouble was, a lot of the vampires couldn't hear him either. So when Benji went to internet radio he dropped that trick. He just talked, talked to Us and paid no attention whatsoever to the vampire-fiction enthusiasts or little Goths who called the show, weeding them out by the timbre of their voices easily enough to devote his on-air time to real Children of Darkness.

Sybelle's exquisite piano music was a major part of the show, and sometimes they broadcast as much as five or six hours a night, and sometimes not at all. But Benji's message was soon heard from one end of the Earth to the other:

We are a tribe; we want to survive; and the elders aren't helping us.

Now when he first started to talk of this—of the parentless and the undefended haunting every city on Earth and the negligence and selfishness of the "elders," I thought surely somebody would take offense, shut him down, or at least set him back in some dramatic way.

But Benji was right about things. I was not. Nobody bothered to stop him because in fact nobody cared. And Benji went on talking to the mavericks and rogues and orphans who called his line at night about how to be careful, how to persevere, how to feed on the evildoer, and cover up the kill, and remember always that the world belongs to humans.

Benji gave the Undead everywhere an argot as well, peppering his commentaries with terms from the Vampire Chronicles, including some I hadn't used before, or ever heard perhaps, establishing a language for all to share. Interesting, that. Or at least I found it so.

A couple of times I went to New York just to spy on Benji. He'd developed a definite personal style by then. He wore expertly tailored three-piece suits, usually in gray- or brown-striped worsted wool, gorgeous pastel dress shirts, and flashing Brooks Brothers silk ties, and he always wore a black felt Italian-made fedora, the perfect gangster hat, and spick-and-span wing-tip shoes.

As the result, even with his small build, small bones, small round cheerful little face, and glittering black eyes, he didn't look like a child at all, but like a little man, and that had become his favorite pet name for himself. "Little Man." Little Man owned more than five galleries in Chelsea and SoHo, a Greenwich Village restaurant just off Washington Square, and an old-fashioned haberdashery shop where he bought his hats. He had legal papers galore, including a legal driver's license, plus credit cards, cell phones, a bicycle or two, and often drove his restored MG TD sports car in New York on summer nights, but mostly went about in a chauffeur-driven black Lincoln stretch limousine, and spent a lot of time in cafés and restaurants pretending to dine with mortals who found him fascinating. He and Sybelle hunted well in the back alleys. They both knew the art of the Little Drink and could satisfy themselves with any number of Little Drinks at nightclubs and charity balls without ever taking a life or disabling some innocent victim.

And whereas Sybelle was something of a remote and mysterious presence at his side—gorgeous in designer gowns and costly gems—Benji had scores of human friends, who thought of him as eccentric and amusing and delightful with his "vampire radio show," which they considered "performance art" of the most clever sort, assuming he supplied all the voices for the show, including the Japanese- and Chinese-speaking Children of the Night who called in and talked for hours in their native tongue, taxing Benji's preternatural powers to the max as he strove to keep up with them.

In sum, Benji was a wild success as a vampire. He had a website backing up the radio show and an e-mail address, and sometimes read e-mails over the air, so to speak, but it always came back to the same thing: We're a tribe, and as a tribe we need to stick together, have loyalty, care about one another, and figure on lasting in this world where immortals could be burnt up or decapitated like anybody else. The elders have sold us out!

And always, always, there was Benji's warning to the Undead: "Don't come to New York. Don't try to find me. I'm here for you by phone and by e-mail, but never set foot in this town, or you'll have to face Armand, and I wouldn't wish that on anyone." In fact, he was always warning them that no one city could really support the numbers of vampires being Born to Darkness now, and fledglings had to be clever, had to seek out new territories, and had to learn to live in peace with others.

On the phone, the callers spilled their woe. They were anxious and afraid; they deplored the brawls happening all over; and they were scared to death of the ancient ones who would burn you up on sight. In vain they searched for the great Lestat, the great Marius, the great Pandora, on and on and on.

Over and over Benji commiserated, advised, and sometimes just shared their grief. "They don't help us, do they?" Benji would declare. "Why did Lestat write his books! Where is the great scholar David Talbot, and what of the great Jesse Reeves, Born to Darkness in the arms of the ancient Maharet? What a selfish, self-centered, and self-obsessed bunch they are!"

And then he'd start with his "Lestat, where are you?"

Like I'm one of the elders? Come on, now, seriously!

Well, in terms of influence, yes. Of course. I wrote my autobiography. I became the famous rock star, like for five minutes! I wrote the story of how Akasha was destroyed and how the fount of power was taken out of her and into the vampire Mekare. I admit. I did all that. I wrote and published my account of the Body Thief and of Memnoch. Okay, okay. And yes, if my rock music and rock videos hadn't been loosed into the world, the old queen Akasha might never have risen from her throne and worked the Great Burning, in which vampires all over the planet were turned to ashes. My fault, okay, I admit it.

But I have what?—two hundred and thirty-three years in the Blood? Something like that. As I said before, I'm a brat by anybody's standards, a reckless kid!

The real elders, the ones he was always taunting, insulting, and deriding, were the Children of the Millennia—the great immortals—Marius, and Pandora, and the ancient twins, of course, Mekare and Maharet, and their companion Khayman. Benji made that clear enough.

"How can this Mekare be the Queen of the Damned if she does not rule?" Benji would ask. "Does not her twin, Maharet, care for us as a great vampire family? And where is Khayman, old as the twins are, and why does he not care for us as we struggle through the world seeking for answers? How is it that Jesse, young Jesse of our world, does not urge these ancient ones to listen to our voices?"

All this was amazing to me and scary to me, as I've explained. But even if no one moved to silence Benjamin, was it going to come to anything? Was it going to make anything happen?

And all the while, other things were happening, bad things. Really bad things. And some good things too perhaps.

Benji was not the only vampire doing something entirely new under the stars of Heaven.

There was Fareed, who had come along well before Benji. And I hadn't thought Fareed would last either.

3

Fareed and Seth

I MET FAREED AND SETH six years before the end of the last
century. This was after I'd met the Body Thief but before I'd
met Memnoch. And though I'd thought the encounter was an
accident at the time, I realized later it most certainly was not, as they'd
been searching for me.

It was in Los Angeles on a mild and lovely evening when I agreed
to talk to them in a garden café not far from where they'd approached
me on Sunset Boulevard—two powerful vampires, one ancient and
one young who was fueled by the powerful blood of the other.

Seth was the ancient one, and as always with those great survivors, I knew him by his heartbeat long before I ever saw him. They
can cloak their minds, these antique monsters, and they can pass for
human, yes, no matter how old they are, and they do. But they can't
stop an immortal like me from hearing that heartbeat and along with
it a faint sound like respiration. Only it sounds like an engine purr-
ing when it comes from them. And that's the signal of course to run
unless you want to be burnt to a fine black powder or a little grease
spot on a pavement.

But I don't run from anything, and I wasn't very sure I wanted to
be alive any longer back then. I'd lately burnt my skin to dark brown
in the Gobi Desert in a failed attempt to end it all, and to say I had a
devil-may-care attitude would have been an understatement.

Also I'd survived so much; well, wouldn't I survive an encounter
with another ancient one? I knew the twins firsthand, did I not? I
knew the reigning Queen. Did I not have their protection?

But I had known something else as well back then, even then.

And that was that my rock singing, my videos, and my waking of the Queen had waked a number of immortals around the globe, and who and what they were nobody really knew for certain. I just knew they were out there.

And so here I was walking down Sunset in the thick of the crowds, just loving it kind of, forgetting I was a monster, forgetting I was no longer a rock star, and pretending more or less to be the beautiful Jon Bon Jovi.

I'd just caught a Jon Bon Jovi concert a few months prior to this, and on my little Walkman, I was playing his songs over and over obsessively. And there I was, you know, strutting, flirting now and then, smiling at the pulchritudinous mortals drifting by, now and then lifting my rose-colored sunglasses to wink at this one or that, and letting my hair blow free in that eternal chilling West Coast breeze and just, well, having a good time and a bitter time, when there comes that heartbeat, that fatal heartbeat.

Well, Maharet and Mekare had not disappeared from the world entirely by that point, so I thought, What have I done now? And who's going to bother me about it, when I spy coming towards me these two remarkable blood drinkers, the shorter one a good six feet in height with magnificent golden skin and blue-black curling hair around his handsome and inquisitive face and enormous green eyes and well-formed lips in an open smile, clothes natty, I suppose, an English bespoke suit, if I was any judge, and beautiful narrow tan bespoke shoes, too, and the taller one, the thin giant very dark of skin too, but burnt, I could tell that, and ancient, his black hair very short all over his well-shaped skull and with almond-shaped eyes, and his clothes eccentric for the streets of West Hollywood, though not perhaps for the city of Cairo or Jetta—a white ankle-length linen *thawb* and white pants with open sandals.

What a pair, and before I'm five feet away, the shorter man, the young one, new in the Blood, extended his hand in welcome. At once he started speaking with a fluid and resonant Anglo-Indian voice, and saying he was Dr. Fareed Bhansali, and this was his "mentor," Seth, and they would so love to have the pleasure of my company at their favorite café nearby.

There surged in me some little excitement that almost brought me to tears, but I kept that locked away from them. I made my loneliness, didn't I? I'd started all the way back then, so why all the emotion?

The café was beautiful with tables draped in blue linen that was almost the color of the night sky with the endless illumination of the great sprawling metropolis bouncing off the layer of moist cloud. And there was a thin, sweet sitar music playing with melodic threads lacing in and out of my thoughts as we sat there, each of us now playing with our food and now and then lifting a forkful of curry to savor the aroma. And the wine was bright and glistening in the sheer glass goblets.

And then they astonished me.

See that building across the street? No, no, that one, well, that was their building and it housed their laboratory, and they'd welcome my cooperation in offering them a few biopsies that would not cause the least pain—skin tissue, hair, blood, that kind of thing.

Then the story unraveled of how, in Mumbai last year, Seth had come into Fareed's hospital room where Fareed lay dying, a brilliant research scientist and medical doctor in his prime, as the result of a plot on the part of his wife and a fellow medical researcher. Fareed, in a locked-in coma, had thought Seth a figment of his tortured imagination.

"And you know," he told me in that rippling and exquisite Anglo-Indian accent, "I thought the first thing I would do was take revenge on my wife and her lover. They'd stolen everything from me, including my life. But I forgot those things almost instantly."

Seth had been a healer in ancient times. When he spoke, his speech was accented too, but I couldn't place it, and how could I, since he'd been brought into the Blood at the dawn of history?

He was what people call rawboned, with wondrously symmetrical bones to his face, and even his hands with their huge wristbones and knucklebones were interesting to me, as well as the fingernails, like glass of course, and then there was the way his cold face would fire with expression when he spoke, and the masklike smoothness imposed by the Blood would be banished.

"I brought Fareed into the Blood to be a physician," Seth explained. "I can't understand the science of these times. And I do not understand why there is no physician or scientific researcher amongst us."

Now they had their laboratory complete with every conceivable machine that medical science had invented.

And I soon found myself in that building on those upper floors, following them through brightly lighted chamber after chamber, and marveling at the staff of young blood drinkers ready to make the MRI or the CAT scan, or draw my blood.

"But what are you going to do with this data?" I asked. "And how do you do all this, I mean, are you bringing over scientists into the Blood?"

"Have you never seriously thought of such a thing?" Fareed asked.

After the biopsies and vials of blood were taken, we were sitting in their rooftop garden, great banks of tempered glass separating us from the chill Pacific wind and the lights of downtown Los Angeles dazzling in the pretty mist.

"I don't understand," said Fareed, "a world in which the most outspoken and high-profile blood drinkers are all romantics, poets, who bring into the Blood only those whom they love for emotional reasons. Oh, I do so appreciate your writing, you understand, every word of it. Your books are scripture for the Undead. Seth gave them to me at once, told me to learn them. But have you never thought to bring over those whom you actually need?"

I admitted I was afraid of the very idea, as afraid as a mortal might have been of designing offspring genetically to enter certain branches of the arts or certain professions.

"But we are not human," said Fareed, who was immediately embarrassed by how obvious and foolish it sounded. He actually blushed.

"What if another bloody tyrant arises?" I asked. "Someone to make Akasha look like a schoolgirl with her fantasies of world domination? You do realize everything I wrote about her was true, do you not? She would have transformed the world if we hadn't stopped her, made herself into a goddess."

Fareed was speechless and then glanced at Seth with the most anxious expression on his face. But Seth was only regarding me with intense interest. He reached over with one of his enormous hands and gently laid it on Fareed's right hand.

"This is all well and good," he said to Fareed. "Please, Lestat, continue."

"Well, suppose such a tyrant rose amongst us again," I said, "and suppose that tyrant brought into the Blood the technicians and soldiers he needed to implement some true takeover. With Akasha, it was all primitive, her scheme, with a 'revealed religion' at the core that would have set the world back, but suppose with laboratories like this, a tyrant could create a vampire race of weapons makers, makers of mind-altering drugs, makers of bombs, planes, whatever is needed to wreak havoc on the existing technological world. What then? Yes, you are right, those of us who are known to everyone today are romantics. We are. We are poets. But we are individuals, with an immense faith in the individual and a love of the individual."

I broke off. I sounded far too much like someone who actually believed in something. Lestat, the dreamer. What did I believe? That we were an accursed race, and that we ought to be exterminated.

Seth picked up the thought, and at once responded. His voice was deep, slow, sharpened by that indefinable Eastern accent. "Why do you believe these things of us, you who have rejected the revealed religions of your world so thoroughly? What are we? We are muta-tions. But all evolution is driven, surely, by mutations. I don't claim to understand it, but was it not true what you wrote, about how Akasha was destroyed, and how the Core, the fount, whatever you call it, the root that animates us was transferred into the body and brain of Mekare?"

"Yes, it was all true," I said. "And they are out there, those two, and they are of the retiring kind, I assure you, and if they think we have any right to exist as a species, they've never made it known to the rest of us. If they find out about this laboratory they will destroy it—perhaps."

I hastened to add that I wasn't certain about that at all.

"Why would they do that when we can offer them so much?" asked Fareed. "For I can fashion immortal eyes for Maharet, the blind one, so that she no longer must use human eyes, ever changing them as they die in her eye sockets? It is a very simple matter to me to make these immortal eyes with the proper blood protocols. And the mute Mekare, I could determine whether there is any brain left to her which will ever fully awaken."

I must have smiled bitterly. "What a vision."

"Lestat, don't you want to know what your cells are made of?" he asked. "Don't you want to know what chemicals are in the blood that's keeping senescence in your body completely at bay?"

"Senescence?" I didn't know quite what the word meant. We are dead things, I was thinking. You are a physician for the dead.

"Ah, but Lestat," Fareed said. "We're not dead things. That's poetry, and it's old poetry, and it will not endure. Only good poetry endures. We're very much alive, all of us. Your body's a complex organism playing host to another predatory organism that is some-how transforming it little by little year by year for some distinct evolutionary purpose. Don't you want to know what that is?"

These words changed everything for me. They were light dawn-ing, because I saw then a whole realm of possibility that I'd never seen before. Of course he might do things like that. Of course.

He talked on and on then, scientifically and I suppose brilliantly, but his terminology became thicker and more foreign. Try as I might, I'd never been able to fathom modern science at all. No amount of preternatural intelligence allowed me to really absorb medical texts. I had only the layman's smattering of the words he was using—DNA, mitochondria, viruses, eukaryotic cell tissue, senescence, genome, atoms, quarks, whatever. I pored over the books of those who wrote for the popular audience, and retained little or nothing but respect and humility and a deepening sense of my own wretchedness at being outside of life when life itself involved such magnificent revelations.

He sensed it was useless.

"Come, let me show you a very small part of what I can do," said Fareed.

And down we went into the laboratories again. Almost all the blood drinkers were gone, but I caught the faint scent of a human. Maybe more than one human.

He offered me a tantalizing possibility. Did I want to feel erotic passion, the same way I'd known it when I was a young man of twenty in Paris, before I died? Well, he could help me achieve this. And if he did, I would produce semen, and he would like to take a sample of that.

I was stunned. Of course, I wasn't about to turn this down. "Well, just how are we going to collect this semen?" I asked, laughing, and even blushing in spite of myself. "Even when I was alive, I preferred to carry out all my erotic experiments with others."

He offered me a choice. Behind a glass wall there sat, on a large soft bed, a young human female, clad only in a white flannel sleeping shirt, reading a thick hardcover book under a dim lamp. She couldn't see us through the one-way glass. She couldn't hear us. I figured her to be perhaps thirty-five or -six, which was quite young for these times, though it would not have been two hundred years ago, and I had to confess to myself, she looked familiar to me. Her hair was thick and long and wavy and distinctly blond though rather dark blond, and she had deep-set blue eyes that were a little too pale perhaps to be beautiful, and well-balanced features and a rather innocent-looking but generous mouth.

The room was like a stage set with its blue toile wallpaper and bedding, and frilly shaded lamps, and even a picture on the wall that one might find in a common bedroom, of an old nineteenth-century English village street. Geese and a creek and a bridge. Only the medical texts on the bedside table and the heavy book in the woman's hands seemed out of place.

She looked luscious in her white flannel shirt, with high firm breasts and long well-shaped legs. She was marking something in her book with a pen.

"You may couple with her, in which case I shall take the sample from her," Fareed explained. "Or you may take the sample for me yourself as you desire in the old solitary way." He made a gesture with his right hand opening his five fingers.

I didn't ponder for long. When I'd slipped into a human body thanks to the machinations of the Body Thief, I'd enjoyed the company of two beautiful women, but that had not been in this body, my body, my vampiric body.

"The woman is well paid, respected, at home here," said Seth. "She is a doctor herself. You will neither surprise her nor horrify her. She has never been a part of such an experiment before, but she is prepared for it. And she will be well rewarded when it's over."

Well, if no harm comes to her, I thought. How clean and pretty she was, with that well-scrubbed American look to her, and those shiny blue eyes, and her hair the color of fields of grain. I could almost smell her hair. In fact, I could smell it, a lovely fragrance of soapsuds or shampoo and sunshine. She looked delectable, and irresistible. I wanted every single drop of her blood. Could erotic feeling override that?

"All right, I'll do it."

But just how exactly could these gentlemen make a dead body like mine actually produce seed as if it were living?

The answer came swiftly with a series of injections and indeed an intravenous line that would continue throughout the experiment to deliver a powerful elixir of human hormones into my blood, overriding the vampiric body's natural tendency to resist senescence long enough for the desire to develop, the sperm to be produced, and then ejaculated.

I thought it was hilariously funny.

Now I could write an essay of five hundred pages on how this experience unfolded, because I did feel biological erotic desire again, and I fell on the young woman about as mercilessly as any greedy aristocrat of my time ever fell on a milkmaid in his village. But it was precisely as my beloved Louis had said a long time ago, "the pale shadow of killing," that is, the pale shadow of drinking blood, and it was over almost at once, it seemed, and then the passion was gone, back into the depths of memory once more as if it had never been aroused, the pinnacle, the ejaculation forgotten.

I'd felt strangely awkward afterwards. I was sitting on the bed beside this blond-haired fair-skinned human female, my back to a nest of sweet-smelling linen-covered pillows, and I felt I ought to talk to her, ask her how she came to be here, and why she was here.

And then quite suddenly, as I sat there, wondering if this was proper or even wise, she told me.

Her name was Flannery Gilman, she said. In a clear fresh West Coast American voice, she explained that she'd been studying "us" since the night I'd appeared on the stage as a rock star outside San Francisco, and so many of our kind had died as the result of my great scheme to be a mortal performer. She'd seen vampires that night with her own eyes, and had no doubt of their existence. She'd seen them immolated in the parking lot afterwards. Indeed, she'd scraped up samples of their burnt and oozing remains from the asphalt. She'd gathered burnt vampiric bones in plastic sacks, and she'd developed hundreds of photographs later of what she'd witnessed and captured on film. She'd spent five years studying and writing up her various specimens, preparing a thousand-page document to prove our existence and counter every objection she could anticipate from her medical colleagues. She'd gone broke because of her obsession.

What had it all come to? Utter ruin.

Even though she'd connected with at least two dozen other doctors who claimed to have seen and experimented upon vampires—perusing their samples, reviewing their material, and referencing it—she had found the doors of every reputable medical association in the world slammed in her face.

She was laughed at, ridiculed, denied grant money, and ultimately denied admission to conventions and conferences, and pointed out publicly as a laughingstock by those who ostracized her and advised her to "get psychological help."

"They destroyed me," she said calmly. "They ruined me. They

did it to all of us. They cast us out along with the believers in ancient astronauts, pyramid power, ectoplasm, and the lost city of Atlantis. They sent me into the wilderness of crackpot websites and New Age conventions and fringe gatherings where we were welcomed only by enthusiasts who believed in everything from Ouija boards to Bigfoot. My license to practice medicine was revoked in California. My family turned against me. I was for all practical purposes dead."

"I see," I said dismally.

"I wonder if you do," she said. "There's abundant evidence in the hands of science all over the planet that you exist, you know, but nobody's ever going to do a damned thing about it. At least not as things are now."

I was speechless. I should have known.

"I used to think that once a vampire fell into the hands of doctors, it would be over."

She laughed.

"It's happened many times," she said. "And I can tell you exactly what takes place. The vampire, having been taken captive in some sheltered place by day, wakes up at sundown to destroy his captors and lay waste their jail or their laboratory or their morgue. If he or she is too weak to do that, then the captors are generally spellbound and befuddled into releasing the victim, and retribution soon follows with all photographic or medical evidence immolated along with the witnesses. Sometimes other blood drinkers come to help free the captive. Sometimes an entire lab facility goes up in flames and almost everyone on the premises is killed. I documented at least two dozen accounts that fit this pattern. Every single one had a series of official 'rational' explanations of what happened attached to it, with marginalized survivors ridiculed and ultimately ignored. Some survivors have wound up in mental hospitals. You don't have to worry about a thing."

"And so you work now with Fareed."

"I have a place here," she said with a gentle smile. "I'm respected here for what I know. You could say I've been reborn. Oh, you cannot imagine the little fool I was that night when I saw you on the stage, so certain I was going to take the medical world by storm with all those pictures."

"What did you want to happen? I mean what did you want to happen to us?"

"I wanted to be believed, first and foremost, and then I wanted you to be studied! The very thing that Fareed's doing here. There is no rhyme or reason to what is actually studied 'out there.'" She gestured as if the mortal world were on the other side of the wall. "Doesn't matter anymore to me," she added. "I work for Fareed."

I laughed under my breath.

The warm natural erotic feeling was long gone. What I wanted to do now again, of course, was drain every drop of blood out of her precious, adorable, curvaceous, hot little body. But I settled for kissing her, snuggling up to her, and pressing my lips against her warm throat, listening to that thunder of blood in the artery.

"They've promised to bring you over, haven't they?" I asked.

"Yes," she said. "They're honorable. That's more than I can say for my colleagues in American medicine." She turned to me, drawing close enough to kiss me quickly one more time on the cheek. I didn't stop her. Her fingers went up to my face and she touched my eyelids.

"Thank you," she said. "Thank you for these priceless moments. Oh, I know you didn't do this for me. You did it for them. But thank you."

I nodded and I smiled. I held her face in my hands as I kissed her now with a fervor that came from the Blood. I could feel her body warming, opening like a flower, but the moment was gone, and I took my leave.

Later, Fareed and Seth told me they meant to keep that promise. She wasn't the only crazy vampire-obsessed doctor or scientist they'd invited in. As a matter of fact, they went out of their way to recruit these poor "loonies" whom the world had ostracized. It was easier after all to invite into our miracle those whose human lives were already ruined.

Well before dawn, the three of us hunted together. Sunset Boulevard was a mob scene, as they say, and the Little Drink was everywhere to be had, and so were a couple of despicable rogues whom I fed on with cruel abandon in the backstreets.

I think the medical experiments had left me desperately thirsting. I was letting the blood fill my mouth and holding it like that for a long time before swallowing, before feeling that great wash of warmth through my limbs.

Seth was a ruthless killer. The ancient ones almost always are. I watched him drain a young male victim, watched the body shrivel as

Seth drew quart after quart of the vital fluid. He held the dead boy's head against his chest. I knew he wanted to crush the skull, and then he did, tearing open the hairy wrapping around it and sucking the blood from the brain. Then he'd composed the corpse almost lovingly on piles of refuse in the alley, folding the arms across the chest, closing the eyes. He'd even reshaped the skull and smoothed the torn scalp over it, and stepped back from it as if he were a priest inspecting a sacrifice, murmuring something under his breath.

Seth and I sat in the roof garden as the morning was coming. The birds had begun to sing, and I could feel the sun, smell the trees welcoming the sun, smell the jacaranda blossoms opening far below.

"But what will you do, my friend," I said, "if the twins come? If the twins don't want this grand experiment to continue?"

"I am as old as they are," Seth answered quietly. He raised his eyebrows. He looked elegant in the long white *thawb* with its neat collar, rather priestly in it in fact. "And I can protect Fareed from them."

He seemed completely sure of it.

"Long centuries ago," he said, "there were two warring camps, as the Queen told you. The twins and their friend Khayman, they were known as the First Brood, and they fought the cult of the Mother. But I was made by her to fight the First Brood, and I have more of her blood in me than they ever had. Queens Blood, that is what we were aptly called, and she brought me for one very important reason: I was her son, born to her when she was human."

A dark chill ran through me. For a long time I couldn't speak, couldn't think.

"Her son?" I finally whispered.

"I do not hate them," he said. "I never wanted even in those times to fight them, really. I was a healer. I did not ask for the Blood. Indeed I begged my mother to spare me, but you know what she was. You know how she would be obeyed. You know as well as anyone from those times knows those things. And she brought me into the Blood. And as I said, I do not fear those who fought against her. I am as strong as they are."

I remained in awe. I could see in him now a resemblance to her, see it in the symmetry of his features, the special curve of his lips. But I couldn't sense *her* in him at all.

"As a healer, I traveled the world in my human life," he said, responding to me, to my thoughts. His eyes were gentle. "I sought to learn all I could in the cities of the two rivers; I went far into the northern forests. I wanted to learn, to understand, to know, to bring back with me great healers to Egypt. My mother had no use for such things. She was convinced of her own divinity and blind to the miracles of the natural world."

How well I understood.

It was time for me to be taking my leave. How long he could withstand the coming dawn, I didn't know. But I was about spent, and it was time to seek shelter.

"I thank you for welcoming me here," I said.

"You come to us anytime that you wish," he said. He gave me his hand. I stared into his eyes, and I felt strongly again that I did see his resemblance to Akasha, though she had been far more delicate, far more conventionally beautiful. He had a fierce and cold light in his eyes.

He smiled.

"I wish I had something to give you," I said. "I wish I had something to offer you in return."

"Oh, but you gave us much."

"What? Those samples?" I scoffed. "I meant hospitality, warmth, something. I am passing through. I've been passing through for the longest time."

"You did give us both something else," he said. "Though you do not know it."

"What?"

"From your mind we learned that what you wrote of the Queen of the Damned was true. We had to know if you described truthfully what you saw when my mother died. You see, we could not entirely fathom it. It is not so easy to decapitate one so powerful. We are so strong. Surely you know this."

"Well, yes, but even the oldest flesh can be pierced, sliced." I stopped. I swallowed. I couldn't speak of this in such a crude and unfeeling way. I couldn't think of that spectacle again—her severed head, and the body, the body struggling to get to the head, arms reaching.

"And now you do know," I said. I took a deep breath and banished all that from my mind. "I described it precisely."

He nodded. A dark shadow passed over his face. "We can always be dispatched in that way," he said. He narrowed his eyes as if reflecting. "Decapitation. Surer than immolation when we're speaking of the ancient ones, of the most ancient. . . ."

A silence fell between us.

"I loved her, you know," I said. "I *loved* her."

"Yes, I do know," he said, "and, you see, I did not. And so this doesn't matter to me very much. What matters much more is that I love you."

I was deeply moved. But I couldn't find words to say what I wanted so much to say. I put my arms around him, and kissed him.

"We'll see each other again," I said.

"Yes, that's my devout wish," he whispered.

Years later, when I came searching for them again, hungering for them, desperate to know if they were all right, I couldn't find them. In fact, I never actually found them again.

I didn't dare to send out a telepathic call for them. I had always kept my knowledge of them tightly locked in my heart, out of fear for them.

And for a long time I lived in terror that Maharet and Mekare had destroyed them.

Sometime later, a few years into the new century, I did something that was rather unusual for me. I'd been brooding over how Akasha died, thinking about the mystery of how we could so easily be destroyed by decapitation. I went into the shop of a specialist in antique armor and weaponry and hired him to make a weapon for me. This was in Paris.

I'd designed the weapon myself. It looked on paper like a medieval horseman's ax, with a narrow two-foot handle and a half-moon blade with a length of maybe twelve inches. I wanted the handle to be weighted, as heavy as the craftsman could make it. And that blade, it had to be weighted too but deadly sharp. I wanted the sharpest metal on earth, whatever it was. There was to be a hook and a leather thong on the end of the handle, just like in medieval times, so I could wear that thong around my wrist, or carry the ax blade down beneath one of my long frock coats.

The craftsman produced a beauty. He warned me it was too heavy for a man to comfortably swing. I wasn't going to like it. I laughed. It was perfect. The gleaming crescent-shaped blade could slice a piece of ripe fruit in half or a silk scarf blowing in the breeze. And it was heavy enough to destroy a tender tree in the forest with one powerful swing.

After that, I kept my little battle-ax near at hand, and often wore it, hung from a button inside my coat, when I went out roaming. Its weight was nothing to me.

I knew I wouldn't have too much of a chance against the Fire Gift from an immortal like Seth or Maharet or Mekare. But I could use the Cloud Gift to escape. And in a face-to-face confrontation with other immortals, with this ax I'd have a terrific advantage. If used with the element of surprise it could probably take down anyone. But then how do you surprise the very ancient ones? Well, I had to try to protect myself, didn't I?

I don't like being at the mercy of others. I don't like being at the mercy of God. I polished and sharpened the ax now and then.

I worried a lot about Seth and Fareed.

I heard tell of them once in New York, and another time in New Mexico. But I couldn't find them. At least they were alive. At least the twins hadn't destroyed them. Well, maybe then the twins would not.

And as the years passed, there were more and more indications that Maharet and Mekare thought little or not at all about the world of the Undead, which leads me now into my meeting with Jesse and David two years ago.

4

Trouble in the Talamasca
and in the Great Family

B ENJI HAD BEEN broadcasting for quite a long while by the
time I finally met Jesse Reeves and David Talbot in Paris.

I'd overheard David's telepathic plea to the vampire Jesse
Reeves to come to him. It was something of a coded message. Only
someone who knew that both blood drinkers had once been members
in the ancient Order of the Talamasca would have understood it—
David calling to his red-haired fellow scholar to please meet with her
old mentor, if she would be so kind, who'd been searching for her in
vain, with news to share of their old compatriots. He'd gone so far
as to reference a café on the Left Bank for a meeting, a place they'd
known in earlier years, "those sunny times," and vowed he'd be on the
watch for her nightly until he saw her or heard from her.

I was shocked by all this. In my wanderings, I'd assumed always
that Jesse and David were fast companions, still studying together
in the ancient archives of Maharet's secret jungle compound, which
she shared with her twin sister in Indonesia. It had been years since
I'd visited the compound, but I had had it in my mind to go there
sometime soon due to the troubles I was suffering in my heart, and
my general doubts about my own stamina to survive the misery I was
now enduring. Also, I'd been very concerned that Benji's persistent
broadcasts to "the vampire world" might eventually rile Maharet and
draw her out of her retreat to punish Benji. Maharet could be provoked. I knew that firsthand. After my encounter with Memnoch, I'd

provoked her and drawn her out. I worried about that more than I cared to admit to myself. Benji, the nuisance.

And now this, David searching for Jesse as if he hadn't seen her in years, as if he no longer knew where Maharet or Mekare could be found.

I had half a mind to go looking for the twins first. And finally I did.

I took to the skies easily enough and went south, discovering the spot and discovering that it had long been abandoned.

It was chilling to walk through the ruins. Maharet had once had many stone rooms here, gated gardens, screened-in areas where she and her sister could roam in solitude. There had been a bevy of native mortal servants, generators, satellite dishes, and even cooling machines, and all the comforts the modern world could provide in such a remote spot. And David had told me of the libraries, of the shelves of ancient scrolls and tablets, of his hours of speaking to Maharet about the worlds she'd witnessed.

Well, it was ruined and overgrown, and some of the rooms had been intentionally knocked down, and there were old tunnels down into the earth which were now half caved in with rocks and dirt, and the jungle had swallowed a wilderness of rusted electrical equipment. All traces of human or vampiric habitation had been obliterated.

So that meant the twins had vanished from here and not even David Talbot knew where they were, David, who had been so fascinated and fearless with the twins, so eager to learn what they had to teach.

And now David was calling to Jesse Reeves and begging for a meeting in Paris.

Red-haired confidante, I must see you, I must discover why it is I cannot find you.

Now understand I made David a vampire, so I can't hear his telepathic messages directly, no, but I caught them from other minds as so often happens.

As for Jesse, she was a fledgling vampire, yes, made the night of my travesty of a rock concert in San Francisco some decades before. But she'd been made by her beloved aunt Maharet, a true ancestor of hers, and a vampiric guardian, whom as I've explained had some of the oldest and most potent Blood in the world. So Jesse was no ordinary fledgling by any means.

David's call was going out over and over again, with the intelligence that he'd haunt the Left Bank till Jesse showed up there.

Well, I decided I'd haunt it too until I found David or both of them.

I headed for Paris to a suite I'd maintained for years, in the gorgeous Hôtel Plaza Athénée in the Avenue Montaigne, the closets stocked with a splendid wardrobe (as if that was going to hide the crumbling ruin which I had become), and I prepared to stay in residence and search until David and Jesse appeared. The safe in that suite held all the usual papers, plastic bank cards, and currency I'd need for a comfortable stay in the capital. And I brought with me a cell phone I'd recently had my attorneys obtain for me. I didn't want to greet Jesse or David as the ragged, dusty, windblown suicidal vagabond. I really was no longer that in spirit, and though I had scant interest in all things material, I felt more at ease in the capital as a member of human society.

It was good to be back in Paris, better than I expected, with all that dizzying life around me, and the magnificent lights of the Champs-Élysées, to be drifting through the galleries of the Louvre again in the early hours of the morning, or haunting the Pompidou or just walking the old streets of the Marais. I spent hours in Sainte-Chappelle, and in the Musée de Cluny loving the old medieval walls of the place, so like the buildings I had known when I was a living boy.

Over and over I heard the misbegotten blood drinkers near at hand, warring with one another, playing cat and mouse in the alleyways, harassing and torturing their mortal victims with a viciousness that astonished me.

But they were a cowardly bunch. And they did not detect my presence. Oh, now and then they knew an old one was passing. But they never got close enough to confirm their suspicions. In fact they fled at the sound of my heartbeat.

Over and over, I got those disconcerting flashes of olden times, my times, when there had been bloody executions in the Place de Grève, and even the most popular thoroughfares had run with mud and filth, and the rats had owned the capital as surely as humankind. Gasoline fumes owned it now.

But mostly, I had to admit I felt good. I even went to the grand Palais Garnier, for a performance of Balanchine's *Apollo*, and wandered the magnificent foyer and stairway at my leisure, loving the marble, the columns, the gilt, the soaring ceilings as much as the music. Paris, my capital, Paris, where I'd died and been reborn, was buried beneath the great nineteenth-century monuments I beheld around me, but it was still Paris where I'd suffered the worst defeat of my immortal life. Paris where I might live again every night if I could overcome my own tiresome misery.

I didn't have long to wait for Jesse and David.

The telepathic cacophony of the fledglings let me know that David had been seen in the streets of the Left Bank, and within hours they were singing songs of Jesse as well.

I was tempted to send out a warning blast to the fledglings to leave the pair entirely alone, but I did not want to break the silence I'd maintained for so long.

It was a chilly night in September, and I soon spotted the pair behind glass, in a noisy crowded brasserie called the Café Cassette in the Rue de Rennes. They had just seen each other as Jesse approached David's table. I stood concealed in a dark doorway across the way, spying on them, confident they knew someone was out there, but not me.

Meanwhile the fledglings were darting up, photographing them apparently with cell phones that looked like the slab of glass given to me by my attorneys, and then tearing away as fast as they could, without David or Jesse giving them the slightest acknowledgment.

This sent a stab through me, as I knew I'd be photographed too the moment I made my approach. This is the way it is with us now. This was what Benji had been talking about. This was what was happening with the Undead. There was no avoiding it.

I continued to listen and watch.

Now David isn't a vampire in the body into which he was born. The notorious Body Thief I encountered years ago was largely responsible for that, and when I brought David over into Darkness, as we so quaintly put it, he was a seventy-four-year-old man inhabiting a young, robust, dark-haired, and dark-eyed male body. So that is how he looks and how he will always look, but in my heart of hearts he remains David—my old mortal friend, once the gentle gray-haired Superior General of the Talamasca, and my partner in crime, my ally in my battle against the Body Thief—my forgiving fledgling.

As for Jesse Reeves, Maharet's near-incomparable blood had made her a formidable monster. She was a tall, thin woman, with bones like a bird, and rippling light red hair down to her shoulders, whose fierce eyes always regarded the world from an uncommitted remove and a deep isolation. She had an oval face, and looked far too chaste and ethereal to be what anyone would call beautiful. In fact, she had the neuter-gender quality of an angel.

She had come to the meeting in refined safari wear with pressed khaki jacket and pants, and there sat David beaming when he saw her, the British gentleman in gray Donegal tweed with a brown suede vest and elbow patches. He rose to take her in his arms, and at once they fell to confiding in one another in hushed whispers that I could easily hear from my shadowy hiding place.

Well, I could stand this for maybe three minutes. Then the pain was just too much. I almost fled. After all, I'd given up on all this, had I not?

But then I knew I had to see them, had to hold them each in my arms, had to put my heart close to their hearts. So I plunged across the rainy street and into the café and sat down right beside them.

There was a sudden rush of paparazzi blood drinkers from door-ways here and there, and they massed beyond the glass to take the inevitable pictures—*It's Lestat*—. And then they vanished.

David and Jesse had seen me before I was halfway there and David rushed to meet me and threw his arms around me. Jesse hugged both of us. I was lost for a moment to the beating of their hearts, to the subtle scents rising from their hair and skin, and the sheer softness of affection emanating from the firmest of touches. *Mon Dieu, why had I ever thought this was a good idea!*

Now came all the tears and recriminations, along with more embraces of course, and the tender fragrant kisses, and Jesse's lovely soft hair against my cheek again and David's strict disapproving eyes fixing me mercilessly even though there were blood tears on his face and he had to wipe at them with one of his perfect linen handkerchiefs.

"Okay, we're getting out of here," I said, and headed for the door with both of them struggling to keep up with me.

The hovering paparazzi vampires shot away in all directions, except for one intrepid young female with an actual camera flashing away as she danced backwards in front of us.

I had a car waiting to take us to the Plaza Athénée, and we were silent for the short trip, though it was the strangest and most sensuous experience to be with them, so close, in the backseat of the car, pressing on through the rain with the dim lights blurred in the downpour and the paparazzi following us. I felt pain, being so close to them, and so glad of it. I didn't want them to know how I felt; indeed, I didn't want anyone to know how I felt; *I* didn't want to know how I felt. So I grew hard and quiet and stared out the windows as Paris was rolling by, with all the endless undying energy of a great capital around us.

Halfway home, I threatened the paparazzi streaking on both sides with immolation if they didn't scatter now. And that did it.

The sumptuous wallpapered living room of my suite was a perfect sanctuary.

We were soon settled under the soft electric lights in the bland but comfortable mélange of eighteenth-century and modern-style sofas and chairs. I loved the comfort of these sturdy furnishings and relished the cabriole legs and bits of brass ormolu and the satin gloss of fruitwood tables and chests.

"Look, I'm not making any excuses for being in exile," I said at once, speaking my usual rough brash brand of English. "I'm here now and that's enough and if I want to tell you what I've been doing all these years, well, I'll write a damned book about it." But I was so glad to be with them. Even yelling at them was a sublime pleasure, instead of merely thinking about them and missing them and longing for them and wondering about them.

"Of course," David said sincerely, his eyes suddenly rimmed in red. "I'm simply glad to see you, that's all. The whole world's glad to know you're alive. You'll know that soon enough."

I was about to say something sharp and unkind when I realized that indeed "the whole world" would know soon enough with all those mavericks out there disseminating their iPhone images and videos. The initial telepathic blast must have been like a meteor crashing into the sea.

"Don't underestimate your own fame," I said under my breath.

Well, we'd be gone from here soon enough. Or I'd tough it out and go on enjoying Paris in spite of the little pests. But Jesse was talking now in that cool American-British voice of hers, drawing me back into the room.

"Lestat, it's never been more important," Jesse said, "that we come together." She looked like a nun with a ragged red veil of hair.

"And why is that?" I demanded. "How can we change what's happening out there? Wasn't it always like this, more or less, I mean what has changed really? It must have been this way before."

"A great deal has changed, apparently," she replied, but not argumentatively. "But there are things I must confide in you and in David, because I don't know where else to go or what to do. I was so glad when I realized David was looking for me. I might never have had the courage to come to you on my own—either of you. David, let me speak first, while I have the courage. Then you can explain what it is you want to tell me. It's about the Talamasca, I understand. But for now the Talamasca is not our greatest concern."

"What is it then, dearest?" David asked.

"I'm torn," she said, "because I have no leave to discuss these things, but if I don't . . ."

"Trust in me," David said reassuringly. He took her hand.

She sat on the edge of her chair, small shoulders hunched, her hair tumbled down around her in that veil of waves.

"As you both know," she said, "Maharet and Mekare have gone into hiding. This began some four years ago with the destruction of our sanctuary in Java. Well, Khayman is still with us, and I come and go as I please. And nothing's been said to forbid me from coming to you. But something's wrong, deeply wrong. I'm afraid. I'm afraid that our world may not continue . . . unless something is done."

Our world. It was perfectly plain what she meant. Mekare was the host of the spirit that animated us. If Mekare were destroyed, we would all be destroyed as well. All blood drinkers the world over would be destroyed, including that riffraff out there encircling this hotel.

"There were early signs," Jesse said hesitatingly, "but I didn't notice them. Only in retrospect did I come to realize what was going on. You both know what the Great Family meant to Maharet. Lestat, you weren't with us when she told the story, but you knew and you wrote the entire account of this accurately. David, you know all of this as well. My aunt's human descendants have kept her alive through the millennia. In every generation she reinvented a human persona for herself so that she might care for the Great Family, care for the genealogical records, distribute the grants and the trusts, keep branches and clans in touch with one another. I grew up in this family. Long before I ever dreamed there was any secret surrounding my aunt Maharet, I knew what it was like to be part of it, the beauty of it, the richness of the heritage. And I knew even then what it meant to her. And I know well enough now that this was the vocation that maintained her sanity when everything else failed.

"Well, sometime before we left the Java compound, she'd succeeded in making the Great Family entirely independent of herself. She confessed to me that the process had taken years. The family's huge; branches exist in almost every country in the world; she'd spent most of the first decade of the new millennium sitting in law offices and bank offices and building libraries and archives so that the family would survive without her."

"But all this is quite understandable," said David. "She's tired, perhaps. Perhaps she wants a rest. And the world itself has changed so dramatically in the last thirty years, Jesse. What with computers now it is entirely possible to unite and strengthen the Great Family in a way that simply wasn't possible before."

"All that's true, David, but let's not forget what the Great Family meant to her. I didn't like to see the weariness. I didn't like to hear it in her voice. I asked her many times if she would keep watch as she'd always done, even though she no longer had to play an official role."

"Surely she will," David offered.

"She said no," Jesse responded. "She said that her time with the Great Family was over. And she reminded me that it was her interfering in my life, as she called it, her coming to me as my beloved aunt Maharet, that eventually resulted in my being inducted, as she put it, into our world."

All this was true obviously. It had been Maharet's custom to visit many of her mortal descendants. And she'd been particularly drawn to the young Jesse. And the young Jesse had been kept too long in the company of blood drinkers not to realize that something profoundly mysterious set these "people" apart from others. So Maharet was right.

"I didn't like it," Jesse continued. "I feared it, but when I pressed her, she said this had to be. She said we were living in an internet age when scrutiny made impossible the secrecy of the past."

"Well, I think she's right about that too," David said.

"She said that the information age was creating a crisis of unbelievable dimensions for any race or group or entity that had depended on secrecy. She said that people alive today were not realizing just how grave the crisis was."

"Once again, she's right about that too," said David.

I didn't want to admit it, but I agreed. The great international Roman Catholic Church was being brought to its knees by the internet or information age. And that was only one such institution.

Benji's incessant broadcasts, websites, and blogs; maverick blood drinkers with picture-capturing iPhones; satellite mobiles that were better than telepathy at reaching individuals at any time in any part of the world—all were revolutionary beyond imagining.

"She said the time was past when an immortal could shepherd a network of human beings as she'd done with the Great Family. She said the ancient records wouldn't even have survived modern investigation if she had not done what she did. Understand, she said, no one would ever really catch on as to who she was and what she'd done with the Great Family. That was a story for us to understand; human beings would always believe it was fictive nonsense even if they read it in Lestat's books. But sooner or later new and enterprising members of the family would begin researching with exhaustive depth. Had she not withdrawn and covered her tracks, the whole endeavor would have become mired in unanswerable questions. The Great Family itself would have been hurt. Well, she said, she'd taken care of it. It had taken six years, but she'd done it and now everything was finished and she could be at peace."

"At peace," David repeated respectfully.

"Yes, well, I sensed a deepening sadness in her, a melancholy."

"And at the same time," David offered, "she showed little interest in anything else."

"Precisely," said Jesse. "You are so exactly right. For hours on end, she's listened to Benji's broadcasts out of New York, Benji's complaining that the tribe was parentless, that blood drinkers were orphans, and she said time and again that Benji was correct."

"So she wasn't angry with him," I said.

"Never," said Jesse. "But I've never known her to be angry with anyone. I've known her only to be sad."

"And what about Mekare in all this?" I asked. "How has it been with Mekare since Akasha was killed? That's the question tormenting me most of the time though I don't particularly want to admit it. How goes it with the one who is the true Queen of the Damned?" I knew well enough that Mekare had from the beginning seemed unchangeable, uncommunicative, mute in soul as well as mute in body, a mysterious thing that obviously loved one person and one person only, her twin, Maharet.

"Has there been no change in her over these years?" I pushed.

Jesse didn't respond. She looked at me in silence and then her face broke. I thought she'd break down completely but she pulled herself up.

She looked at David. David sat back on the sofa, and took a deep breath. "Mekare has never shown any sign of understanding what in fact happened to her," David said. "Oh, in the beginning, Maharet had hopes."

"If there's a true mind there," said Jesse, "no one can reach it. How long it took for my aunt to resign herself to this I can't say."

I wasn't surprised, but I was horrified. And anytime in my life I'd been in contact with Mekare, I'd been uneasy, as if dealing with something that looked human but was in no way human anymore. Now, all blood drinkers truly are human; they never cease being human. They may talk of being more or less human, but they are human, with human thoughts, desires, human speech. Mekare's face had never been more expressive than that of an animal, as mysterious and unreachable as the face of an animal, a thing that seems intelligent yet is not intelligent in the way we are at all.

"Oh, she knows she's with her sister and she shows love to her sister," said David, "but beyond that, if any thought, any coherent verbal thought, has ever emanated from Mekare, I've never heard it, and neither has Jesse. And neither has Maharet as far as I ever knew."

"But she remains docile, manageable," I said. "She always seemed that way, utterly compliant. Isn't that so?"

Neither replied. Jesse was looking uneasily at David and then she turned to me as if just hearing my question. "It certainly did seem that way," she said. "In the beginning, Maharet would spend nights, weeks even, talking with her, walking with her, taking her about the jungle compound. She sang to her, played music for her, sat her down before the television screens, playing films for her, brilliant colorful films full of sunlight. I don't know if you remember how large it was, the compound with all those salons, or how much of an enclosed area it provided for solitary walks. They were always together. Maharet was obviously doing everything in her power to draw Mekare out."

I did remember those massive overarching screened enclosures, with the jungle exploding against the steel mesh. Orchids, the wild screeching South American birds with their long blue and yellow feathers, the vines dripping pink or yellow blossoms. Had there not been tiny Brazilian monkeys chattering in the upper branches? Maharet had imported every small colorful tropical creature or plant imaginable. It had been marvelous to roam the paths discovering secretive and picturesque stone grottoes, streams, and little waterfalls—to be in the wilderness and yet somehow safe from it at the same time.

"But I knew early on," said Jesse, "that Maharet was disappointed, almost brutally disappointed, only of course she'd never say. All those long centuries searching for Mekare, certain that Mekare could be alive somewhere, and then Mekare appearing to fulfill her curse against Akasha, and then this."

"I can imagine it," I said. I remembered Mekare's masklike face, those eyes as empty as the paperweight eyes of a French doll.

Jesse went on, a frown creasing her smooth forehead, her reddish-blond eyebrows catching the light.

"There was never a mention, never a declaration or a decision. But the long hours of talking stopped. No more reading aloud, or music, or films. And after that there was simple physical affection, the two walking arm in arm, or Maharet at her reading with Mekare sitting motionless on a bench nearby."

And of course, I thought to myself, the horrifying thought that this thing, this motionless, thoughtless being, contained the Sacred Core. But then was it so bad? Was it so bad for the host of the Sacred Core to be without thought, without dreams, without ambition, without designs?

Akasha, when she had risen from her throne, had been a monster. "I would be the Queen of Heaven," she'd said to me as she slew mortals, and urged me to do the same. And I, the consort, had done her bidding all too easily, to my everlasting shame. What a price I'd paid for the powerful Blood she'd given me, and the instructions. No wonder I kept to my refuge now. When I looked back over my myriad adventures sometimes all I saw was shame.

Maharet had rightfully described her sister as the Queen of the Damned.

I stood up and went to the window. I had to stop. Too many voices out there in the night. Benji in faraway New York was already broadcasting of the appearance of Lestat in Paris, with David Talbot and Jesse Reeves. His amplified voice poured forth from countless devices out there, warning the fledglings: "Children of the Night, leave them alone. For your own safety, leave them alone. They will hear my voice. They will hear me begging them to speak to us. Give them time. For your own safety, leave them alone."

I went back to the couch. David was patiently waiting, and so was Jesse. Surely their preternatural hearing was as acute as mine.

"And then there was the time when Marius came to her," said Jesse, looking at me eagerly.

I nodded for her to continue.

"You know these things. Marius came wanting Maharet's permission to put an end to Santino, the vampire who'd done so much to harm him over the centuries, the vampire who brought the Children of Satan against him in Venice."

David nodded, and so did I. I shrugged.

"She had hated that she was asked to sit in judgment, that Marius wanted her to convene a court of sorts, to give permission for what he wanted to do. She refused permission to Marius to harm Santino, not because she didn't believe he should but because she did not want to be the judge. And she did not want a murder beneath her roof."

"That was clear," said David.

Marius had recounted this story in his memoir. Or somebody had recounted it. The memoir might have been polished up by David for all I knew. Probably was. Pandora and Armand had been present for this court or tribunal when Marius had come before Maharet with his request, wanting vengeance on Santino but forswearing it if Maharet would not give her blessing. And somebody had brought Santino there, but who precisely had done that? Maharet?

It was Marius who'd said somebody has to rule. It was Marius who had raised the entire issue of authority. What were we to expect from someone who came into the Blood during the age of the great Pax Romana? Marius had forever been the rational Roman, the believer in reason and law and order.

And then it had been another blood drinker, Thorne, an ancient fledgling of Maharet, an old Norseman, red-haired, romantic, newly emerged from the blessed solitude of the earth, who had destroyed Santino for reasons of his own. An ugly violent scene it had been with Santino burnt by Thorne right before Maharet's eyes. Maharet had wept. Her outrage had not been that of a queen so much as the mistress of a household defiled. And Thorne had followed this act of disobedience and defiance by offering Maharet a precious gift: his preternatural eyes.

Maharet had been blind all her long life as a blood drinker. Blinded by Akasha before she came into the Blood, she'd used the eyes of her mortal victims; but they had never endured very long. Thorne had given her his vampire eyes. He'd asked the mute and impassive Mekare to take his eyes from him and give them to her sister. And that Mekare had done. Thorne had remained in the compound after that for all anyone ever knew, a prisoner of the twins, blind, suffering, maybe content.

When I'd read that account in Marius's memoir, I'd thought back on Fareed's promise to achieve permanent preternatural eyes for Maharet. Had he ever had the opportunity?

"That broke something inside of her," said Jesse, "that awful trial. Not Thorne's rebellion, you understand. She loved and forgave Thorne. She kept Thorne with us after. But simply the fact of Marius appealing to her, saying that there had to be a law amongst us, that somebody had to have authority. That broke her. That made it all too plain that she was no sovereign for the Undead."

This had never occurred to me. I had assumed that one so old and so powerful had simply gone on, pursuing a path well beyond our various disputes.

"I think it was after that that she began to obliterate all contact with the Great Family, and I saw her slipping ever deeper into her own silence."

"But she'd summoned young ones from time to time, didn't she?" I asked. "And David, you were still coming and going. . . ."

"Yes, she did continue to invite others to the archives," said David. "She was especially tolerant of me. But I think I disappointed in those early years too. There were times when I could not bear the archives, and all the secret knowledge there that the outside world would never see. She knew how I felt. She knew that reading of lost cities and empires only made me feel less human, less vital, less purposeful. She saw all that. She knew."

"But she told me once we go through cycles, all of us," I protested. "I'm in a bad cycle now. That's why I so wanted to talk to her for a little while. I thought she was the great expert on cycles of despair and cycles of confidence. I thought she had to be. I thought she was the strongest of us all."

"She's a fallible being ultimately," said David, "just as you or I. Very likely her gift for survival depends on her limitations. Isn't that always the way it is?"

"How the Hell do I know!" I said crossly, but he only smiled as if he was on to my bad behavior and had always been. He waved it away and looked to Jesse.

"Yes, she did bring young ones to the compound," Jesse said, picking up the thread. "But only a few. Then four years ago something completely unexpected happened."

She took a deep breath, and sat back again, putting the sole of her boot up against the coffee table. Small delicate brown leather boot.

David was waiting, and from the world beyond I heard the voice of Benji broadcasting out of New York: "If you don't want disaster, I tell you leave them alone. Play my voice. Let my voice plead with them to come to us, to speak to us, yes, but do not approach them. You know their power. You know what they can do."

I closed my mind to the voices.

"All right," said Jesse as if she'd won an exhausting argument with herself. She sat up straight again, crossing her legs rather gracefully, and stretching her left arm along the back of the chair. "This was four years ago, as I said. And she'd been visited by a very strange blood drinker, perhaps the strangest blood drinker I'd ever encountered or heard of, and he took her completely by surprise. His name was Fareed Bhansali, and if you can believe it, he is a physician and a research scientist. This was something that Maharet had in particular always feared—a scientist blood drinker, a blood drinker who might use knowledge that she viewed as magical to take power in the world."

I was about to protest that I knew Fareed, had known him well, though we'd only met once, when I perceived that she understood this, understood it from my thoughts, and David was signaling that he knew Fareed as well. Very well. The story of Seth and Fareed was out there.

"But Fareed Bhansali would never seek to use power unwisely or wrongly," David said. "I've met him, sat with him, talked to him, talked to Seth, his mentor." ("Mentor," it seemed, had become interchangeable with the word "maker," which was fine with me.)

"Well, that's what she came to discover soon enough. He told her he could easily restore Thorne's eyes to Thorne and provide her with eyes from a blood drinker that would last her for eternity. He said he could implant these new eyes for her with surgical delicacy so that they would endure forever. He explained that he knew how to override the Blood in us and stop its relentless war on change long enough to make the alterations in tissue required for a true wedding of nerves and biological threads." Jesse sighed. "I didn't understand most of it. I don't think Maharet did either. But he was brilliant, undeniably brilliant. He explained he was a true physician for our kind. He said he'd recently attached a full-functioning vampiric leg to an ancient vampire named Flavius who had lost the limb before he was ever brought into the Blood."

"Of course, Flavius," said David. "Pandora's Flavius, her Athenian slave. But this is marvelous."

I knew that story as well. I smiled. Of course, Fareed could do such a thing. But what else might he do?

Jesse continued.

"Well, Maharet took him up on the offer. She did not like the idea that a young fledgling would be blinded for these purposes. But he soon got around this ethically, telling her to choose a victim for herself, one upon whom she thought it entirely proper and just to feed. He would take that victim, render him or her unconscious, and then infuse the body with the vampiric blood. When he'd removed the eyes, he would do away with the victim. She might be present at all stages if she wished. And once again, he emphasized that the placement of the eyes would involve his skills as a surgeon with more infusions of vampiric blood to perfect the result. Her eyes would be her eyes forever. She had only to pick the victim, as he said, from all those within her hearing, all those with the proper-color eyes."

That sent a chill through me: "the proper-color eyes." Brought back flashes of something horrible, but I didn't want to see exactly what it was. I shook myself all over and fastened my attention on Jesse.

"She took him up on it," said Jesse. "But she took him up on more than that. He wanted to welcome her and Mekare both to his laboratory in America. He had a huge place, apparently a mad scientist's dream. I believe it was in New York at that time. They'd tried a number of locations. But Maharet wouldn't risk trying to take Mekare to this place. Instead she spent a king's ransom bringing all Fareed's staff and equipment to us. She had everything flown into Jakarta, and brought out by truck to the compound. Electricians were brought in, new generators purchased and installed. When it was finished Fareed had what he needed to do every kind of test known to modern science on Mekare."

Again, she broke off.

"You're talking about magnetic imaging," I said, "CAT scans, all of it."

"Yes, exactly," said Jesse.

"I should have known. And all these years, I've been afraid for Fareed, afraid that she'd done away with him, blasted him and his staff off the planet."

"And how could she have done that with Seth protecting Fareed?" asked David. "When you met Fareed, surely you met Seth."

"She might have made a considerable dent in operations," I said. "She could have burned them both out. But you're saying"—I looked at Jesse—"you're saying, they're all friends."

"Allies," said Jesse.

"Did Mekare submit to the tests?"

"Completely," said Jesse. "Meekly. Mekare has never balked at anything that I was ever aware of. Nothing. And so they did the tests. There were these physician fledglings with them, and Seth was always working with Fareed. It was frightening to me to meet Seth. It was frightening to Khayman to meet him. Khayman had known Seth when Seth had been a human child. When Seth had been the Crown Prince of Kemet. Sometime after the Blood came into Akasha, she'd sent Seth away. Khayman had never had any knowledge of Seth being made into a blood drinker. He feared him, feared some old blood tie between mother and son that he said might be more powerful than our Blood. Khayman didn't care for anything that was happening, for these scientists taking tissue samples and X-rays, and sitting around with Maharet until early morning, discussing all the properties of our bodies, the properties of the force that makes us what we are."

"I've given up on scientific language," I said. "I never thought I'd need it. And now I wish I had been there, and understood everything they'd said." But this wasn't entirely true. I'd left Fareed and Seth of my own accord years ago when I might have asked to remain indefinitely. I'd fled from the intensity of both of them and what they might discover about us.

"So what the Hell was the upshot of all of it?" I said suddenly, unable to contain myself. "What the Hell did they find out?"

"They said Mekare was mindless," said Jesse. "They said the brain in her head was atrophied. They said there was so little indication of brain activity that she was like a human in a coma, kept alive by the brain stem alone. Apparently she'd been entombed so long, possibly in a cave, no one knew, that even her sight had been affected. The powerful Blood has actually hardened the atrophied tissue over time. I couldn't fathom it. Of course they took some three nights to say this with incredible disclaimers, qualifiers, and tangents, but that was the gist."

"And what about the other?" I asked.

"What other?" Jesse said.

I glanced at David and then back at her. They both appeared sublimely puzzled. This surprised me.

"What about the Sacred Core?" I asked.

Jesse didn't respond.

"So what you're asking is," David interjected, "could these various diagnostic instruments detect the Sacred Core?"

"Well, of course that's what I'm asking. Good grief. Fareed had the Mother in his clutches, didn't he? You don't think Fareed would be looking for evidence of a parasite inside her with some sort of cerebral activity of its own?"

They continued to stare at me as if I were mad.

"Fareed told me," I went on, "that this thing, Amel, was a creature just as we are creatures, that it has cellular life, boundaries, is knowable. Fareed made all this clear to me. I simply couldn't understand all his deductions, but he made it clear that he was obsessed with the physical properties of the Sacred Core."

Oh, why hadn't I listened more? Why had I been so pessimistic about the future of Fareed? Why did I have such a grim apocalyptic mind-set?

"Well, if he detected anything," said Jesse, "I heard nothing of it." She reflected for a long moment, and then asked: "What about you?"

"What about me when?"

"When you drank from Akasha," she pushed gently. "When you held her in your arms. Did you hear anything, detect anything? You were in direct contact with the Sacred Core."

I shook my head. "No, nothing that I could identify. She showed me things, visions, but they all came from her, always from her. As far as I know, from her." But I had to admit, that was an interesting question.

"I'm no Fareed," I muttered. "I had only the vaguest and most religious ideas, I confess, about the Sacred Core."

My mind traveled back and back to my memories of Maharet describing the genesis of the vampires. Amel had gone into the Mother and then Amel was no more. Or so the spirits had told Maharet. This thing that was Amel, invisible yet huge, was now diffused amongst more blood drinkers than ever before in history. It was a root planted in the earth from which myriad plants have sprung so that the root has lost its shape, its boundaries, its "rootness."

Even after all these years, I didn't like to speak of that intimacy with Akasha, being the Queen's lover, drinking her thick and viscid and magnificent blood. I didn't like to think of her dark eyes, and shining white skin, her curling smile. What a face, what a picture of innocence in one who would conquer the human world, in one who wanted to be the Queen of Heaven.

"And Mekare," I said. "Have you never drunk from her?" I asked.

Jesse regarded me again for a long moment as if I'd said something shocking and unpleasant and then she simply shook her head. "I'm not aware that anyone has ever approached her for her blood. I've never seen Maharet drink Mekare's blood or offer her blood to Mekare. I'm not sure they'd ever do such a thing, or ever did—that is, after the very first encounter."

"I have a deep suspicion that if anyone ever did try to drink her blood," said David, "she'd regard it as vile and she'd destroy that person, perhaps in some crude way, as with her fist."

Her fist. The six-thousand-year-old fist. Something to consider. A six-thousand-year-old immortal could destroy this hotel with her fist if she had a mind to do it, and the time.

Mekare had destroyed Akasha in a crude and simple way, that was certain, throwing her back against a plate-glass window with such force that she broke the glass. I saw that again, saw that great jagged sheet descending like the blade of a guillotine to sever her head. But I hadn't seen everything. Perhaps nobody really had except Maharet. How had the skull of Akasha been broken? Ah, the mystery of it: the combination of vulnerability and overwhelming strength.

"I never knew Mekare to have any sense of her powers," said David, "any sense of the Cloud Gift or the Mind Gift or the Fire Gift. From all you've told me, she came against Akasha with the certainty of an equal, nothing more."

"Thank the gods for that," said Jesse.

When she'd risen to kill the Queen, Mekare had come over land, walking night after night through jungle and desert, over mountain and valley, until she'd reached the Sonoma compound where we had all come together, guided by what images, what voices, we never knew. Out of what grave or cave she'd come we were never to know either. And I understood now the full implications of all that Jesse had been telling us: There never would be answers to our questions about Mekare. There never would be a biography of Mekare. There never would be a voice speaking on behalf of Mekare. There would never be a Mekare typing away on a computer to pour out her thoughts to us.

"She doesn't know she's the Queen of the Damned, does she?" I asked.

Jesse and David stared at me.

"And did Fareed offer to make for her a new tongue?" I pushed.

Again my question shocked both of them. Obviously it was extremely hard for all of us to deal with the implications of the existence and knowledge of Fareed. And the power and mystery of Mekare. Well, we were here to talk, weren't we? The question of the tongue seemed obvious to me. Mekare had no tongue. Her tongue had been ripped out before she was brought into the Blood. Akasha was guilty. She'd blinded one and ripped the tongue from the other.

"I think that he did make this offer," Jesse explained, "but there was no way to communicate this to Mekare or to make her cooperate. I'm only surmising. I'm not sure. They're all deaf to each other's thoughts, these ancient ones, as you know. But as usual, I heard nothing emanating from Mekare. I'd accepted the idea that she was mindless. She was willing enough to be the passive victim of tests, that was no problem. But beyond that, whenever he drew near to her or tried to examine her mouth, she stared at him as if she were watching the falling rain."

I could well imagine how frightening that must have been even for the intrepid Fareed.

"Was he able to narcotize her?" I asked.

David was clearly shocked. "You know you really are past all patience," he muttered.

"Why, for not putting it poetically?"

"Only for very short intervals," Jesse said, "and only a few times. She grew tired of the needles and stared at him like a statue come to life. He didn't try again after the first three times."

"But he took her blood," I said.

"That he did before she quite realized what was happening," said Jesse, "and of course Maharet was assisting and coaxing her and stroking her hair and kissing her and begging her permission in the ancient tongue. But Mekare didn't like this. She stared at the vials with a kind of revulsion as if she were looking at a loathsome insect feeding on her. He managed to take scrapings of her skin, samples of her hair. I don't know what else. He wanted everything. He asked us for everything. Saliva, biopsies of organs—biopsies he could take with needles, you understand—bone marrow, liver, pancreas, whatever he could get. I gave all that to him and so did Maharet."

"She liked him, respected him," I said.

"Yes, loves him," she hastened to say, emphasizing the present tense, "respects him. He did provide the eyes of a blood drinker for her, and restore to Thorne his eyes, the eyes he'd given Maharet. He did all that, and took Thorne under his wing when he left, took Thorne with him. Thorne had been languishing in the compound for years, but Thorne had been slowly restored over that time. Thorne wanted to find Marius again and Daniel Malloy, and Fareed took Thorne away with him. But Maharet loved Fareed, and she loved Seth also. We all loved Seth." She was rambling now, repeating herself, reliving it.

"Seth had been there the night long ago in ancient Kemet when Akasha had condemned Mekare and Maharet to death," Jesse said. She was picturing it. I was picturing it. "As a boy, he'd seen Mekare's tongue torn out and seen Maharet blinded. But Seth and Maharet spoke together as if this old history had no claim on them. None whatsoever. They agreed on many things."

"Such as what?" I prodded.

"Would you try to be polite, just try!" David whispered.

But Jesse answered me without stopping.

"They agreed that whatever they discovered on our behalf, they must never seek to interfere with human life in this world. That no matter what they achieved for us, they must never offer it to the human world. There might come a time, Maharet said, when a science of the vampires would be their greatest defense against persecution, but that time was in the remote future, and likely might never come at all. The human world must be respected. They agreed on all that. Fareed said he had no ambitions anymore in the realm of human beings, that we were his people. He called us that, his people."

"Benji would love him," I remarked. But I was hugely relieved to hear all this. More relieved than I could say.

"Yes," Jesse said sadly. "Surely Benji would. Fareed had a way of referring to us as 'the people' and the 'Blood People' and 'the People in the Blood.'"

"Our people, our tribe," I said, echoing Benji.

"So what did happen, dearest," asked David, "to make you all abandon the old compound?"

"Well, it was like this. Seth told Maharet of other ancient ones. He told her what I'm sure won't surprise anyone here, that there were ancient ones everywhere who'd survived Akasha's Time of Burning, who'd observed it but never feared it. And then he told her of ancient ones roused by it as he'd been. Seth had been in the earth for a thousand years when he heard your music, Lestat, and when he heard his mother's voice answering yours. Seth said that Maharet was not aware of how much Lestat's rock music and the Mother's rise had changed the vampiric world. She had no inkling of how these events had not only awakened old ones, but brought others to a global consciousness."

"*Mon Dieu*, a global consciousness," I said. "So I'm going to be blamed one way or another for everything?"

"Well, that may be the least important aspect of all this," David said, reaching out and taking my hand. "Whether you're blamed or not isn't the point, is it? Please, stop being the Brat Prince for five minutes, and let's listen to Jesse."

"Yes, Professor," I said. "Don't I always end up listening?"

"Not enough, I would say." He sighed and looked back to Jesse.

"Well, Maharet wanted to find one of these ancient ones—not one newly risen but one especially wise in Seth's estimation, and that was a blood drinker living now in Switzerland on the shores of Lake Geneva, a being with a powerful footprint in the human world. He'd maintained something of a vampire family since late antiquity. In fact, the vampire Flavius was the trusted friend and follower of this ancient one."

"What name does he use with us?" I asked.

"She never told me precisely," said Jesse. "But I do know his vast wealth is associated with pharmaceutical corporations and investments. I remember Seth saying as much. To continue, she went off to Switzerland to find him. She called me often while she was there."

"By phone?"

"She's never been a stranger to phones, computers, mobiles, whatever," said Jesse. "Remember she was my aunt Maharet in the world before I ever knew her true secret. She was the mentor of the Great Family for centuries. She's always functioned well in the world."

I nodded.

"Turns out she loved this ancient one in Geneva, loved the life he'd built for himself and for those under his care. She did not reveal herself to him. She was spying upon him, through the minds of his loved ones. But she loved him. When she called me, she wouldn't disclose his name or location by phone for obvious reasons, but all her reports were jubilant. This blood drinker had been brought over by Akasha to fight rebels like Maharet and Mekare and Khayman. Where they were called the First Brood, this vampire had been the Captain of the Queens Blood. But none of the old hatred mattered anymore to her, or so she said. And several times over the phone she told me that observing this creature had taught her all sorts of things, that his enthusiasm for life was contagious. I assumed all this was good for her."

I could see David knew nothing of this being either and he was fascinated.

"And this is only one of a number of immortals of which we don't know?" he asked gently.

Jesse nodded. "She said further that this Geneva blood drinker was tragically in love with Lestat." She looked at me. "In love with your music, your writings, your musings—tragically convinced that if he could talk with you about all the ideas in his head, he would find a soul mate in you. Apparently, he loves his devoted family of blood drinkers—but they tire of his relentless passion for life and his endless speculations on the tribe and the changes we experience. He feels you'd understand him. She never said whether she agreed with him on that or not. She wanted to approach the being. She was strongly considering it. It seemed to me that she wanted to bring you all together with him at some point. But she left without approaching him. And what she had wanted, well, all this soon changed."

"So what happened? Why didn't she do this?" I pressed. I'd never doubted that Maharet could find me wherever I was. I figured this great and powerful blood drinker in Geneva could find me too. I mean I'm not all that hard to find, really.

"Oh, yes, you are," Jesse said in answer to my thoughts. "You're very well hidden."

"Well, so what!"

"But back to the story, please," said David.

"It's what happened at the compound while she was gone," said Jesse. "I'd remained behind with Khayman and Mekare, and several young blood drinkers who'd been studying in the archives. I'm not sure who these young ones were. Maharet had brought them there before leaving, and all I knew was that she had approved of each of them and given them access to the old records. Well, Khayman and I shared the responsibility of maintaining the hearth, as you might say. And for two nights I went into Jakarta to hunt and left things to Khayman.

"When I came back, I discovered that half the compound had been burnt down, some of the young ones—maybe all of them—had obviously been immolated, and Khayman was in a state of confusion. Maharet had also returned. Some instinct had told her to return. The devastation was horrific. Many of the screened courtyards were burnt out, and some of the libraries burnt to the ground. Old scrolls, tablets, had been lost, but the truly hideous sight was the remains of those who'd apparently been burnt to death."

"Who were they?" I demanded.

"I honestly don't know," Jesse said. "Maharet never told me."

"But hadn't you met these young blood drinkers?" I pushed. "Surely you remember something about them."

"I'm sorry, Lestat," she said. "I don't remember them, except to say that I didn't know them by name or appearance. They were young, very young. There were always young ones coming and going. Maharet would bring them there. I don't know who perished. I simply don't know."

David was clearly shocked. He'd seen the ruins just as I'd seen the ruins but hearing about it had a fresh effect.

"What did Khayman have to say about all this?" David asked.

"That's just it. He couldn't remember what had happened. He couldn't remember where he'd been or what he'd done or what he'd seen during my absence. He was complaining of confusion and physical pain, actually physical pain in his head, and worse, he was drifting in and out of consciousness right in front of us, sometimes talking in the ancient tongue, and sometimes talking in other tongues I'd never heard before. He was babbling. And at times he seemed to be talking to someone inside his head."

I noted this and locked my mind like a vault.

"He was obviously suffering," Jesse said. "He asked Maharet what he could do for the pain. He appealed to her as a witch to heal the pain as if they were in ancient Egypt again. He said something was in his head hurting him. He wanted someone to take it out. He asked if that vampire doctor, Fareed, could open up his head and take this thing out. He kept reverting to the ancient tongue. I caught the most unbelievable and vivid cascade of images. And sometimes I think he did think they were back in those times. He was injured, crazy."

"And Mekare?"

"Almost the same as ever. But not quite." Jesse stopped.

"What do you mean?" I asked.

She wiped the images from her mind before I could catch them. She went for words.

"There's always been a demeanor to Mekare," said Jesse. "But when I first entered the compound, when I first saw all the burnt timber and the collapsed roofing, well, I came on Mekare standing in one of the passageways, and she was so altered, so different, that for a moment I felt I was looking at a stranger." Again she paused, looking away and then back to us. "I can't explain it. She was standing there, arms at her sides, and leaning against the wall. And she was looking at me."

Now the image did blaze up. I saw it. Surely David saw it.

"Now I know that doesn't sound remarkable at all," said Jesse, her voice having dropped to a murmur. "But I tell you, I'd never seen her look at me in that way before, as if suddenly she knew me, recognized me, as if some intelligence had flared in her. It was like encountering a stranger."

I could see it, all right. I'm sure David could too. But it was subtle.

"Well, I was afraid of her," said Jesse. "Very afraid. I don't fear other blood drinkers for obvious reasons. But in that moment I feared her. The expression on her face was so uncharacteristic. At the same time she was merely staring at me. I was petrified. I thought, This creature has powers enough to have done this, burned this place, burned those young ones. This creature can burn me. But then of course Khayman had that power too, and I didn't know yet that he couldn't remember anything.

"Maharet appeared, and she put her arm around Mekare, and then it seemed Mekare was Mekare again, drifting, eyes serene, eyes almost blind, standing upright and softening all over, and resuming her old characteristic grace—walking with the old simple movements, her skirts flowing around her, her head slightly bowed, and when she looked at me again her eyes were empty. Empty. But they were her eyes, if you follow me."

I said nothing. The image continued to blaze in my mind. I felt a chill all over.

David wasn't speaking. I wasn't speaking.

"And Maharet dismantled the compound and we left there," said Jesse. "And she never left Mekare alone after that, not for very long. No young ones were ever invited again to visit with us. No one was ever invited. In fact, she told me we must seal ourselves off from the world. And as far as I know she never contacted the Geneva blood drinker, though I can't be too sure of that.

"When we established our new refuge she set up more technical equipment than in the past, and she used the computers regularly for all manner of things. I thought she went into a new level of involvement with the age. But now I wonder. Maybe she simply didn't want to leave again. She had to communicate by computer. I don't know. I can't telepathically read my maker. And Maharet can't read Khayman or Mekare. The First Brood can't read each other. All too close. She told me she couldn't read this Geneva blood drinker either. Queens Blood or First Brood, the really old ones can't read each other's thoughts. I suppose technically that Seth is Queens Blood. Queens Blood were the true heirs of Akasha's blood drinker religion. First Brood remained the rebels, and First Brood gave the Blood without rules or codes to those they enlisted over the centuries. If one could trace the lineage of most of the blood drinkers of this era, I suspect they'd go back to First Brood."

"Probably right," I said.

"What happened with Khayman?" asked David. "How is it with Khayman?"

"Something is very wrong with him," said Jesse. "Wrong with him to this very moment. He disappears for nights on end. He doesn't remember where he goes or what he does. Most of the time he sits silent staring at old movies on the flat screens in the compound. Sometimes he listens to music all night. He says that music helps the pain. He watches your old rock videos, Lestat. He turns them on for Mekare and he watches and I suppose in some way she watches them too. Other times he doesn't do much of anything. But he always comes back to the pain in his head."

"But what about Fareed, what does Fareed say about this pain?" I asked.

"That's just it, Maharet has never invited Fareed again to visit us. She's never invited anyone, as I've said. If she e-mails Fareed, I know nothing of it. Her involvement with the computer is actually part of her withdrawal if you follow me. I've come here to tell you these things because I think you should know, both of you. And you should share this with Marius, and with the others, however you want to do it." She sat back. She gave a long sigh as if to say to herself, Well, now it is done, you've confided and it cannot be undone.

"She's protecting all the others from Mekare now," David said in a soft voice. "That's why she's hidden herself."

"Yes. And there is no connection at all anymore with her human family as I've said. We live from night to night in peace and contentment. She does not ask where I go when I leave, or where I've been when I come back. She advises me in a multitude of small things, just as she's always done. But she doesn't confide in me about the deepest things! To tell the truth, she behaves like someone who's being watched, monitored, spied upon."

Neither David nor I spoke, but I knew perfectly well what she meant. I pondered. I was not prepared to share with them any of my vague and troubling suspicions as to what was happening. Not at all prepared. I was not sharing my suspicions with myself.

"But still," said David, "it might have been Khayman who burnt the archives and destroyed the young ones."

"It might have been, yes," Jesse said.

"If she really thought it was Khayman, she'd do something," I said. "She'd destroy him if she felt she had to. No, it's Mekare."

"But how can she destroy Khayman? Khayman's as strong as she is," David said.

"Nonsense. She could get the jump on him," I said. "Any immortal can be decapitated. We saw that with Akasha. She was decapitated by a heavy jagged piece of glass."

"That's true," Jesse said. "Maharet herself told me this when she first brought me into the Blood. She said I'd grow so strong in the future that fire couldn't destroy me and the sun couldn't destroy me. But the sure way to murder any immortal was to separate the head from the heart and let the head and the body bleed out. She told me that even before Akasha came to the Sonoma compound with you. And then that's just what happened with Akasha, only Mekare took Akasha's brain and devoured it before the head or the heart bled out."

We all reflected for a long time in silence.

"Again, there's never been the slightest sign," said David gently, "that Mekare knows her own powers."

"Correct," said Jesse.

"But if she did this, she must know her own powers," David continued. "And Maharet is there to be a check upon her every waking moment."

"Perhaps."

"So where is all this going?" I asked. I tried not to sound exasperated. I loved Maharet.

"I don't think she will ever destroy herself and Mekare," said Jesse. "But I don't know. I do know she listens all the time to Benji's broadcasts out of New York. She listens to them on her computer. She sits back and listens for hours. She listens to all those young blood drinkers who call Benji. She listens to everything that they have to say. If she were going to bring the tribe to an end, I think she would warn me. I simply don't think she means to do it. But I think she agrees entirely with Benjamin. Things are in a very bad way. Things have changed. It wasn't only your music, Lestat, or Akasha rising. It's the age itself, it's the accelerated rate of technological advancement. She said once, as I believe I told you, that all institutions which depended upon secrecy are now threatened. She said that no system based on arcana or esoteric knowledge would survive this age. No new revealed religion could take hold in it. And no group that depended upon occult purpose could endure. She predicted that there would be changes in the Talamasca. 'Human beings won't fundamentally change,' she said. 'They'll adapt. And as they adapt they'll explore all mysteries relentlessly until they have found the fundamentals behind each and every one.'"

"My thoughts on the matter exactly," I offered.

"Well, she's right," said David. "There have been changes in the Talamasca, and that's what I wanted to tell you. That's why I sent out the call for you. I wouldn't have dared to disturb Maharet when she obviously did not want to be disturbed, but I have to confess I was hoping for news of her when you surfaced, and now I'm a bit stunned. What's been happening with the Talamasca of late doesn't mean so very much."

"Well, what has been happening?" I asked. I wondered if I was becoming a nuisance. But without my goading them, these two would have lapsed into long periods of silence and meaningful stares, and frankly, I wanted information.

Information age. I guess I'm part of it, even if I can't remember how to use my iPhone from week to week, and have to learn how to send e-mails all over again every couple of years, and can't retain any profound technological knowledge about the computers I sometimes use.

"Well, the answer to all that," Jesse said, responding to my thoughts, "is to use the technology regularly. Because we know now that our preternatural minds don't give us any superior gift for all knowledge, only the same kinds of knowledge we understood when we were human."

"Yes, right. That is certainly true," I confessed. "I'd thought it was different, because I'd learned Latin and Greek so easily in the Blood. But you're absolutely right. So on to the Talamasca. I assume they've digitized all their records by now?"

"Yes, they completed that process several years back," said David. "Everything's digitalized; and relics are in museum-quality environments under the Motherhouses in Amsterdam and in London. Every single relic has been photographed, recorded on video, described, studied, classified, etcetera. They had begun all that years ago when I was still Superior General."

"Are you talking to them directly?" asked Jesse. She herself had never wanted to do that. Since she came into the Blood, she'd never sought to contact her old friends there. I'd brought David over. She had not. For a while, I'd harassed the Talamasca, baited them, engaged now and then with their members, but that was now a long time ago.

"No," said David. "I don't disturb them. But I have occasionally visited those old friends of mine on their deathbeds. I have felt an obligation to do that. And it's simple enough for me to get into the Motherhouses and get into those sickrooms. I do that because I want to say goodbye to those old mortal friends, and also I know what they're experiencing. Dying without so many answers. Dying without ever having learned anything through the Talamasca that was transformative or transcendent. What I know now of the present state of the Talamasca I know from those encounters and from watching, simply watching and listening and prowling about, and picking at the thoughts of those who know someone is listening, but not who or what." He sighed. He looked weary suddenly. His dark eyes were puckered and there was a tremor in his lips.

I saw his soul so clearly now in the new youthful body that it was as if the old David and the new David had completely fused for me. And indeed his old persona did shape the expression of his youthful face. A multitude of facial expressions had reshaped the piercing black eyes of this face. Even his old voice sounded now through the newer vocal cords as if he had retuned them and refined them merely by using them for all those softly spoken, unfailingly polite words.

"What's happened," he said, "is that the mystery of the Elders and the origins of the Order have been buried in a new way."

"What do you mean?" asked Jesse.

David looked at me. "You're familiar with this. We never knew our origins really. You know that. We always knew the Order had been founded in the mid–eighth century, and we knew there was unaccountable wealth somewhere which financed our existence and our research. We knew the Elders governed the Order but we didn't know who they were or where they were. We had our hard-and-fast rules: observe but do not interfere, study but do not ever seek to use the power of a witch or a vampire for one's own gain, that sort of thing."

"And this is changing?" I asked.

"No," he replied. "The Order's as healthy and virtuous as ever. If anything they're thriving. There are more young scholars coming in today who know Latin and Greek than before, more young archaeologists—like Jesse—who are finding the Order attractive. The secrecy has been preserved, in spite of your charming books, Lestat, and all the publicity you so generously heaped on the Talamasca, and as far as I know there have been few scandals in recent years. In fact none whatsoever."

"So what's the big problem?"

"Well, I wouldn't call it a problem," said David. "I'd call it a deepening of the secrecy in a new and interesting way. Sometime in the last six months newly appointed Elders started introducing themselves to their colleagues and welcoming communication with them."

"You mean Elders actually chosen from the ranks," said Jesse with a bit of an ironic smile.

"Precisely.

"Now in the past," David went on, "we were always told that the Elders came from the ranks, but once they were chosen they became anonymous except to other Elders, and their location was never revealed to anyone. In olden times they communicated by letter, sending their own couriers to deliver and retrieve all correspondence. In the twentieth century, they moved to fax communication and computer communication, but again, they themselves remained anonymous and their location unknown.

"Of course the mystery was this; no one ever knew personally any member called to be an Elder. No one ever encountered personally anyone who claimed to be an Elder. So it was strictly a matter of faith that the Elders were chosen from the ranks, and as early as the Renaissance, as you know, members of the Talamasca had suspicions about the Elders, and were profoundly uncomfortable with not knowing who they really were or how they passed their power on to succeeding generations."

"Yes, I remember all this," I said. "Of course. Marius talked about it in his memoir. Even Raymond Gallant, his friend in the Talamasca, had asked Marius what he knew about the origins of the Talamasca, as if he, Raymond, were uneasy with not knowing more."

"Correct," said Jesse.

"Well, now it seems everybody knows who the new Elders are," said David, "and where their meetings will take place, and all are invited to communicate with these new Elders on a daily basis. But obviously, the mystery of the Elders before this time remains. Who were they? How were they chosen? Where did they reside? And why are they handing off power now to known members?"

"Sounds like what Maharet's done with the Great Family," I said.

"Exactly."

"But you never seriously thought they were immortals, did you?" asked Jesse. "I never did. I simply accepted the need for secrecy. I was told the Talamasca was an authoritarian order when I joined. I was told it was like the Church of Rome, in that its authority was absolute. Never expect to know who the Elders are or where they are or how they know what they know."

"I've always thought they were immortals," said David.

Jesse was shocked and a little amused. "David, you're serious?"

"Yes," said David. "I've thought all my life that immortals founded the Order to spy on and record the goings-on of other immortals—spirits, ghosts, werewolves, vampires, whatever. And of course we were to spy on all those mortals who can communicate with immortals."

I was reflecting. "So the Order's collected all this data over the centuries, while the central mystery—the origins—remains unexplored."

"Exactly. And if anything this change moves us farther away from the central mystery," said David. "Within a few generations the entire mystery might well be forgotten. Our shadowy past will be no more intriguing than the shadowy past of any other ancient institution."

"That does seem to be what they want," I said. "They're bowing out before any serious investigation is mounted, either within or without the Order, to find out who they are. Another decision prompted by the information age? Maharet was right."

"What if there's a deeper reason?" David asked. "What if the Order was indeed founded by immortals, and what if these immortals are no longer interested in pursuing the knowledge they wanted so badly? What if they've abandoned their quest? Or what if they've found out what they wanted to know all along?"

"What could that possibly be?" Jesse asked. "Why, we know no more about ghosts, witches, and vampires than we ever did."

"That's not true," David said. "What have we been discussing here? Think."

"Too many unknowns," I said. "Too many suppositions. The Talamasca has an amazing history, no doubt about that, but I don't see why it couldn't have been founded by scholars and maintained by them, and what any of this proves. On the surface of it, the Elders have simply changed their method of interacting with the members."

"I don't like it," said Jesse softly. She appeared to shiver. She rubbed the backs of her arms with her long white fingers. "I don't like it at all."

"Has Maharet ever told you anything about the Talamasca, anything entirely personal that she alone knew?" asked David.

"You know she hasn't," Jesse responded. "She knows all about them; she thinks they're benign. But no, she's confided nothing. She's not terribly interested in the Talamasca. She never has been. You know that. David, you asked her these questions yourself."

"There were legends," said David, "legends we never discussed. That we were founded to track the vampires of the Earth, and all the rest of the research was essentially unimportant, that the Elders themselves were vampires."

"I don't believe that," I said, "but then you lived with all the talk, I didn't."

"It used to be said that when you died within the Order, the Elders came to you right before death and revealed themselves. But who started that old tale I never knew. And as I kept watch with one dying colleague after another in my time, I came to know this wasn't true. People died with many unresolved questions about their life's work, and its value." David looked at me. "When we first met, Lestat, I was a disillusioned and burnt-out old man. You remember that. I wasn't sure all my work studying the supernatural had come to anything."

"Whatever the case, the mystery remains unresolved," I said. "And maybe I should try to find the answer. Because I think this new development does have something to do with the crisis our kind is facing." But I broke off, uncertain of what more I could say.

They sat there in silence.

"If it's all connected, I don't like it," I muttered. "All this is too apocalyptic," I said. "I can live with the notion that this world is a Savage Garden, that things are born and die for random reasons, that suffering is irrelevant to the great brutal cycle of life. I can live with all that. But I don't think I can live with great overarching connections between things as enduring as the Great Family and the Talamasca and the evolution of our tribe. . . ."

Fact was, I simply couldn't put it all together. So why act like the idea of it was frightening me? I wanted to put it all together, didn't I?

"Oh, well, then you do admit there is a crisis," David said with a trace of a smile.

I sighed. "All right. There's a crisis. What I don't understand is why, exactly. Oh, I know, I know. I woke up the Undead world with my songs and videos. And Akasha awoke and went on a rampage. All right. I get it. But why are all those mavericks everywhere now? They weren't before. And what's the impact of these ancient ones rising, and why do we need a Queen of the Damned in the first place? So Mekare and Maharet don't care to rule. So what? Akasha never ruled. Why didn't things simply lapse back to the way they'd always been?"

"Because the whole world was changing," said David impatiently.

"Lestat, don't you see, what you did in 'coming out' as a vampire to the public was part of the zeitgeist. No, it didn't change the mortal world in any way, of course not, but how can you underestimate the effects of your books, your words, all of it on all the blood drinkers in existence? You gave the inchoate masses out there an origin story, a terminology, and a personal poetry! Of course this waked old ones. Of course this invigorated and charged apathetic ones. Of course this roused from torpor wanderers who'd given up on their own kind. Of course this emboldened mavericks to make other mavericks using the famous Dark Trick, Dark Gift, Dark Blood, etcetera!"

None of this was said with contempt, no, but it was said with a kind of scholar's fury.

"And yes, I did my part, I know that," David continued. "I published the stories of Armand, Pandora, and finally Marius. But the point I'm trying to make is this: you gave a legacy and a definition to a population of shrinking, self-loathing predators who had never dared to claim any such collective identity for themselves. So yes, it changed everything. It had to."

"And then the human world gave them computers," said Jesse, "and more and better planes, trains, and automobiles, and their numbers have grown exponentially and their voices have become a chorus heard by all from sea to shining sea."

I got up off the couch and went to the windows. I didn't bother to pull back the loose filmy curtains that covered them. The lights of all the surrounding towers were magnificently beautiful through this cloud of white gauze. And I could hear the fledglings out there, milling, pondering, covering the various entrances of the hotel, and reporting to one another, variations of "No action here. Keep watching."

"You know why this disconcerts you so very much?" David said. He drew up beside me. He was angry. I could feel the heat coming off him. In this strong, stout-chested young body he was my height, and those intense black eyes fixed me with David's soul. "I'll tell you why!" he said. "Because you never admitted to yourself that what you did in writing your books, in writing your songs, in singing your songs . . . you never admitted that it was all for us. You always pretended it was some great gesture to humankind and for their benefit. 'Wipe us out.' Really! You never admitted that you were one of us, talking to the rest of us, and what you did, you did as part of us!"

I was suddenly furious. "It was for me that I did it!" I said. "All right. I admit it. It was a disaster, but it was for me that I did it. There was no 'us.' I didn't want the human race to wipe us out, that was a lie, I admit it. I wanted to see what would happen, who would show up for that rock concert. I wanted to find all those I'd lost . . . Louis, and Gabrielle, and Armand and Marius, maybe Marius most of all. That's why I did it. Okay. I was alone! I didn't have any grand reason! I admit it. And so goddamned what!"

"Exactly," he said. "And you affected the entire tribe and you never took one ounce of responsibility for having done so."

"Oh, for the love of Hell, are you going to preach vampire ethics from a pulpit?" I said.

"We can have ethics and we can have honor and we can have loyalty," he insisted, "and every other key virtue we learned as humans." He was roaring at me under his breath, as the British so often do it, with a veneer of silvery politeness.

"Oh, preach it in the streets," I said disgustedly. "Go on Benji's radio show. Call in and tell him and all of them out there. And you wonder why I go into exile?"

"Gentlemen, please," said Jesse. She sat there still in her armchair looking small, fragile, shaken, shoulders hunched as if against the blast of our argument.

"Sorry, dearest," said David. He returned to his chair beside her.

"Look, I need the remaining time before dawn," she said. "Lestat, I want you to give me your iPhone, and you, David, let me give you all the numbers too. E-mail, mobile numbers, everything. We can stay connected with one another. You can e-mail Maharet and me. You can call us. Please, let's share all our numbers now."

"So what, the reigning Queen in hiding is willing to share her mobile number?" I asked. "And e-mails?"

"Yes," said Jesse. David had complied with her request and she was tapping away on the shiny little device, fingers fluttering over it with such speed they were a bit of a blur.

I came back, flopped heavily on the sofa, and threw down my iPhone as if it were a gauntlet on the coffee table. "Take that!"

"Now, please, share with me all the information you're willing to share," she said.

I told her again what I'd told Maharet years ago. Contact my attorneys in Paris. As for my e-mails, well, I changed them all the time as

I forgot how to use them and tried to learn all over again with some new and superior service. And I always forgot or lost the old devices or the old computers and then had to begin again.

"All the info's in the phone," I said. I unlocked it for her and gave it to her.

I watched as she brought the devices up to date. I watched as she shared my information with David, and David's information with me, and I was ashamed to admit that I was glad I had these ephemeral numbers. I'd shoot a record of all this to my attorney and he'd keep it through thick and thin, even when I'd forgotten how to access it online myself.

"Now, please," Jesse said finally. "Spread the word. Express my concerns to Marius, to Armand, to Louis, to Benji, to everyone."

"It will drive Benji out of his gourd to have 'secret intelligence' about the twins perhaps immolating themselves," David said. "That I will not do. But I will indeed try to find Marius."

"Surely there are old ones in Paris," I said, "old enough to have spied on us here tonight." I wasn't speaking of the riffraff.

Yet I had the feeling Jesse didn't care. Let the riffraff hear it, for all Jesse cared. Let the old ones hear it. Jesse was frayed from conflict and anxiety. And even confiding in us had not eased her pain.

"Were you ever happy in the Blood?" I asked suddenly.

She was startled. "What do you mean?"

"In the beginning, during those first years. Were you happy?"

"Yes," she said. "And, I know that I will be happy again. Life is a gift. Immortality is a precious gift. It shouldn't be called the Dark Gift. That's not fair."

"I want to see Maharet in person," said David. "I want to go with you home."

Jesse shook her head. "She won't allow it, David. She knew what I meant to say when I found you. She allowed this. But she will not receive anyone now at home."

"Do you still trust in her?" asked David.

"In Maharet?" Jesse asked. "Always. Yes, in Maharet."

That was significant. She didn't trust the other two.

She was backing away from us towards the double doors to the hallway.

"I've given you what I have to give for now," she said.

"And what if I want to find that vampire in Geneva?" I asked.

"That would be your decision. He's in love with you. I can't imagine him hurting you. Does anyone ever try to hurt you?"

"Are you joking?" I asked bitterly. Then I shrugged again. "No, I don't guess anyone ever does anymore."

"You're the one they look to . . . ," she said.

"So Benji says!" I muttered under my breath. "Well, there's no reason for them to look to me. I may have started it but I sure as Hell can't finish it."

She didn't answer.

David sprang up suddenly and went to her and took her in his arms. They held each other silently for a moment and then he went with her to the doors.

I knew she was as good at the Cloud Gift as I was, what with all that ancient blood. She'd leave the hotel by the roof so fast she might as well have been invisible.

David closed the doors behind her.

"I want to go walking," I said. My voice was thick, and suddenly I realized I was weeping. "I want to see that old district where the markets used to be, and the old church. Haven't been there since . . . Will you come with me?" I had half a mind to flee now, just go. But I didn't.

He nodded. He knew what I wanted. I wanted to see the area of Paris where once les Innocents, the ancient cemetery, had existed— beneath which, in torch-lit catacombs, Armand and his Children of Satan coven had held court. It was there that, orphaned by my maker, I'd discovered with shock the others of our kind.

He embraced me and kissed me. This was David whom I knew intimately in this body. This was David's powerful heart against me. His skin was silken and fragrant with some subtle male perfume, and his fingers were thrilling me vaguely as he took my hand. Blood of my Blood.

"Why do people want me to do something about all this?" I asked. "I don't know what to do?"

"You're a star in our world," he said. "You made yourself that. And before you say anything rash or angry, remember. That's what you wanted to be."

We spent hours together.

We moved over the rooftops far too fast for the fledglings below to track us.

We drifted through the streets of les Halles, and through the darkened interior of the great old church of Saint-Eustache with its paintings by Rubens. We sought out the little Fontaine des Innocents in the Rue Saint-Denis—a tiny relic of the olden times—which had once stood beside the wall of the vanished cemetery.

This made my heart both glad and anguished. And I let the memories come back to me of my battles with Armand and his followers who believed so fervently we were anointed servants of the Devil. Such superstition. Such rot.

Eventually some of the paparazzi vampires found us. They were persistent. But they kept their distance. We didn't have much time.

Pain, pain, and more pain.

No trace remained of the old Théâtre des Vampires or where it had once stood. Of course I'd known that but had to visit the old geography anyway, confirm that the old filthy world of my time had been paved over.

Armand's magnificent nineteenth-century house—which he'd built in Saint-Germaine-de-Prés—was shut up and maintained by unwitting mortals, full of murals, carpets, and antique furniture covered in white sheets.

He'd refurbished that house for Louis right before the dawn of the twentieth century, but I don't think Louis had ever been at home in it. In *Interview with the Vampire* he did not so much as even mention it. The *fin de siècle* with its glorious painters, actors, and composers had meant nothing to Louis, for all his pretensions to sensitivity. Ah, but I couldn't blame Louis for shunning Paris. He'd lost his beloved Claudia—our beloved Claudia—in Paris. How could he be expected ever to forget that? And he'd known Armand was a jungle wildcat among revenants, hadn't he?

Still . . . Paris . . . I'd suffered here too, had I not? But not at the hands of Paris, no. Paris had always fulfilled my dreams and expectations. Paris, my eternal city, my home.

Ah, but Notre Dame, the great vast cathedral of Notre Dame was as always Notre Dame, and there we spent hours together, safe in the cold shadows in that great forest grove of arches and columns where I'd come more than two hundred years ago to weep over my transformation, and was in some way weeping over it even now.

David and I walked the narrow quiet streets of the Île Saint-Louis talking together. The fledgling paparazzi were within blocks of us but dared not come closer. The grand townhouse in which I'd made my mother, Gabrielle, into a Child of Darkness was still there.

Gradually we fell to talking again, naturally. I asked David how he had come to know Fareed.

"I sought out Fareed," David said. "I'd heard plenty of whispers of this mad vampire scientist and his ancient guardian angel, and their 'evil' experiments, you know, the gossip of the misbegotten. So I went to the West Coast and looked for him till I found him."

David described the new compound where Seth and Fareed were now, safe and secure in the wastes of the California desert, beyond the city of Palm Springs. Out there, they had built the perfect facilities for themselves—isolated and protected by two sets of high walls and mechanical gates, with tunnels for emergency evacuation and a heliport. They ran a small clinic for mortal incurables, but their real work took place in secure laboratories in sprawling three-story buildings. They were close enough to other medical facilities for their activities to attract little or no attention and far enough away from everything else to have the isolation and land they had needed but could not have in Los Angeles.

They'd welcomed David immediately. Indeed they'd been so hospitable that one could not imagine them being anything but that to everyone.

David had pressed Fareed on a very special issue: how was his mind and his soul anchored now in this body in which he had not been born, his own body being in a grave in England?

Fareed had done every conceivable test that he could on David. He could find no evidence that any "intelligence" existed inside him that was not generated by and expressed through his own brain. As far as he could see, David was David in this body. And his connection with it was utterly secure.

"Before you came into the Blood," Fareed had told David, "very possibly you could have exited this body. You could have been some sort of discarnate entity, a ghost, in other words, capable of possessing other susceptible bodies. I don't know. I can't know. Because you are in the Blood now and very likely this Blood has more securely than ever bound you to your physicality."

Speculation. But David had been comforted.

He too felt that Fareed and Seth would never seek to use their scientific knowledge against humans.

"But what about their underlings?" I asked. "They were already bringing doctors and scientists into the Blood when I met them."

"Be assured. They pick and choose carefully. The vampire researchers I encountered were like idiot savants of their profession, obsessed, focused, completely devoid of any grand schemes, in love with studying our blood under microscopes."

"And that is his central project, is it not?" I asked. "To study our blood, the Blood, so to speak?"

"It's a frustrating proposition from what I understand, as whatever the Sacred Core is physically, we cannot see it. If it's made of cells, the cells are infinitely smaller than the cells that we can see. So Fareed's working with properties."

David rambled on, but it was science poetry again, and I couldn't absorb it.

"Do you think they're still there, in that same location?"

"I know they are," David said. "They tried a number of others first that did not work out."

Perhaps that was when I was searching for them.

"They're there. You can easily find them. In fact, they would be overjoyed if you would come to see them."

The night was rolling to an end. The paparazzi had retreated to their coffins and lairs. I told David he could keep my suite at the hotel as long as he liked, and I had to head home soon.

But not quite yet. We'd been walking in the Grand Couvert of the Tuileries—in tree-shrouded darkness. "I'm thirsting," I said aloud. At once he suggested where we might hunt.

"No, for your blood," I said, pushing him backwards against the slender but firm trunk of a tree.

"You damnable brat," he seethed.

"Oh, yes, despise me, please," I said as I closed in. I pushed his face to one side, kissing his throat first, and then sinking my fangs very slowly, my tongue ready for those first radiant drops. I think I heard him say the single word, "Caution," but once the blood struck the roof of my mouth, I wasn't hearing clearly or seeing clearly and didn't care.

I had to force myself to pull back. I held a mouthful of blood as long as I could until it seemed to be absorbed without my swallowing, and I let those last ripples of warmth pass through my fingers and toes.

"And you?" I asked. He was slumped there against the tree, obviously dizzy. I went to take him in my arms.

"Get away from me," he growled. And started off walking, fast away from me. "Stick your filthy droit du seigneur right through your greedy heart."

But I caught up with him and he didn't resist when I put my arm around him and we walked on together like that.

"Now, that's an idea," I said, kissing him quickly though he stared forward and continued to ignore me. "If I was 'King of the Vampires,' I'd make it the right of every maker to drink from his fledgling anytime he chose. Maybe it would be good to be king. Didn't Mel Brooks say, 'It's good to be the king'?"

And then in his droll cultured British voice he said with uncharacteristic brashness, "Kindly shut up."

Seems I heard *other* voices in Paris; seems I sensed things. Seems I might have paid a little more attention, and not so cavalierly lumped all intrusions on my mind with the paparazzi vampires.

There was a point right after that when we were walking near the old catacombs, where the bones of the old eighteenth-century cemetery, Les Innocents, had been gathered, that I heard something, something distinct and plaintive, the voice of an old immortal singing, laughing, murmuring, "Ah, young one, you are riding the Devil's Road in such glory." I knew that voice, knew that timbre, that slow lilting tone. "And with your venerable battle-ax beneath your splendid raiment." But I closed my ears. I wanted to be with David just then, and only David. We made our way back to the Tuileries. I didn't want complications, or new discoveries. I wasn't ready yet to be open as I'd once been to the mysteries surrounding me. And so I ignored that strange rumbling song. I never even knew if David could hear it.

And finally I told David I had to go back now into exile, I had no choice. I assured him that I was not in danger of trying to "end it," just not ready at all to come together with others or to think about the horrific possibilities that had alarmed Jesse. He was all mollified by then and didn't want me to vanish on him.

Yes, I have a safe refuge, I insisted. A good refuge. Be assured. Yes, I will use the iPhone magic to communicate.

I had turned to leave him when he took hold of me. His teeth went into the artery before I could think what was happening, and his arms went tight around my chest.

His pull was so strong that I swooned. Seems I turned and put my arms around him, catching his head in my left hand, and struggled with him, but the visions had opened up, and I didn't know one realm from the other for a moment, and the manicured paths and trees of the Tuileries had become the Savage Garden of all the world. I'd fallen into a divine surrender, with his heart pounding against my heart. There was no restraint in him, no caution such as I'd shown in feeding on him.

I came to myself on the ground, my back to the trunk of a young chestnut tree, and he was gone. And the mild balmy night had turned to a gray winter dawn.

Home I went—to my "undisclosed location," only minutes away on the currents of the wind, to ponder what I'd learned from my friends because I couldn't do anything else.

The next night on rising, I caught the scent of David on my jacket, even on my hands.

I fought off the desire for him and forced myself to relearn how to use my powerful computer, and to obtain yet another e-mail address through another service, and then I sent a long missive to Maharet. I asked if I might visit her, wherever she was, and if not, would she communicate with me in this way? I let her know that I was aware of how things were changing for us, and how Benji's pleas for leadership on the part of the older ones echoed the feelings of many, but I myself did not know how to respond. I asked for her thoughts.

Her communication was brief. I must not try to find her. Under no circumstances approach her.

Of course I asked why.

She never replied.

And six months later, her numbers were disconnected. E-mail no longer valid.

And in time I forgot again how to use the computer. The little iPhone rang a number of times. It was David. We'd talk, it would be brief, and then I'd forget to recharge the little thing. He did tell me he'd found Marius in Brazil and he was heading there to talk with him. He told me that Daniel Malloy, Marius's companion, was in very good spirits and that Daniel was taking him to Marius. But I didn't hear from him again.

Truth was, I lost the little iPhone. And went back to calling my attorneys in Paris and New York now as I had always done, with an old-fashioned landline phone.

A year passed.

I was lodged now in my father's château in the mountains of the Auvergne—in my special hiding place in "plain sight," so to speak, and where no one thought to look for me—the renovations on it now almost complete.

And the Voice came again.

"Have you no desire to punish those fledglings in the capital?" he asked. "Those vermin who chased you out of Paris last time you were roaming there?"

"Ah, Voice, where have you been?" I asked. I was at my desk drawing up plans for the new rooms that would soon be added to this old château. "Have you been well?"

"Why did you not destroy them?" he asked. "Why do you not go there and destroy them now?"

"Not my style, Voice," I said. "Too often in the past I've taken life, both human and preternatural. I have no interest now in doing such things."

"They drove you out of your city!"

"No, they didn't," I said. "Goodbye, Voice. I have things to do."

"I was afraid you would take this attitude," he said. "I should have known."

"Where are you, Voice? Who are you? Why do we always meet like this in audial encounters at odd moments? Aren't we ever going to meet again face-to-face?"

Ah, what a blunder. No sooner were the words out of my mouth than I looked to the great eighteenth-century mirror over the mantelpiece, and there he was of course in the guise of my reflection, down to the old bag-sleeve shirt I wore, and my loose hair, only he wasn't reflecting me otherwise, but rather peered at me as if he were trapped in a glass box. Lestat's face twisted with anger, almost petulant, childish.

I studied the image in the mirror for a moment and then I used my considerable powers to force it to disappear. That felt extremely good. Subtle and good. I could do that now. I knew. And though I could hear a low rumbling in my head, I was able to sink it down, down below the lovely music, the music of Sybelle playing the piano that came from my computer, Sybelle broadcasting from New York.

The simple fact was, I wasn't interested in him anymore. I didn't even bother to thank him for advising me to come home here, home to these stone rooms in which I'd been born, home to the quiet of this mountaintop. Why didn't I do that? It was he who'd put the idea in my head, he who'd guided me back to the old fields and forests, to this sublime rural quiet, this breathtaking and familiar solitude where I felt so safe, so content.

I didn't care enough to thank him.

Oh, it would have been nice to identify him before banishing him forever. But we don't always get what we want.

Part II

THE OPEN HIGHWAY THROUGH THE SAVAGE GARDEN

5

The Story of Rose

THE FIRST TIME Rose saw Uncle Lestan, he carried her up into the stars. That's how she remembered it and nothing ever weakened the conviction that he'd scooped her up from the terrace by the seawall and carried her straight through the clouds and towards the Heavens. Rose remembered always the chill of the wind and those stars above her, millions of stars fixed in the black sky like myriad burning lights. She remembered Uncle Lestan's arms around her, and the way he whispered to her not to be afraid, the way he brought his coat close to protect her.

They were on another island when Rose learned her mother had died in the earthquake. Everyone had died. The entire little island had gone down into the sea, but this island would not, Uncle Lestan said. She was safe with him here. He'd find her people in America. He gave her a beautiful doll with long blond hair and a pink dress and bare feet. It was made of vinyl and would never break.

This was in a beautiful house with rounded windows and big balconies over the sea, and two very gentle ladies took care of Rose though she couldn't understand a word they said. Uncle Lestan explained they were Greek ladies, but he wanted Rose to remember: What was her last name? What was her mother's name?

Rose said her mother's name was Morningstar Fisher. She had no father. Her grandparents didn't like her because they didn't know who her father was and they wouldn't give money anymore to Morningstar. Rose remembered seeing her grandmother and grandfather in Athens, Texas. "We don't know who her father is," the old man had said. Rose's mom had given up, and carried Rose out of the little brick house and across a big field, and they'd hitched a ride to the airport in Dallas and flown away with Mom's new friend, JRock, who had money from his band to live in Greece for at least a year.

"They don't want me," Rose said. "Can't I stay with you?"

Uncle Lestan was so kind to Rose. He had darkly tanned skin and the most beautiful blue eyes Rose had ever seen. When he smiled, Rose loved him.

Uncle Lestan said, "I'll be with you, Rose, as long as you need me."

She woke in the night crying for her mother. He held her in his arms. He felt so strong, so powerful. They stood on the edge of the patio, looking up at the cloudy sky. He told her that she was sweet and good and beautiful, and he wanted her to be happy.

"When you grow up, Rose, you can be anything you want," Uncle Lestan said. "Remember that. This is a magnificent world. And we are blessed with the gift of life in it." He sang to her in a low voice. He told her this was "Serenade" from an operetta called *The Student Prince*. The song made her cry, it was so beautiful.

"Remember always," he said, "that nothing is as precious to us as the magnificent gift of life. Let the moon and the stars always remind you of this—that though we are tiny creatures in this universe, we are filled with life."

Rose felt she knew what magnificent was as she looked out over the shining waters below, and then up once more at those stars twinkling beyond the mist. Uncle Lestan's left fingers touched the flowering vines that covered the railing, and he tore off a small handful of petals for Rose, and said that she was as soft and precious as these petals, a "precious living thing."

When Rose thought back on it, she remembered seeing him several times before the night the island sank into the sea. He'd been roaming around on that island. He was a tall man with beautiful blond hair, just the most beautiful hair. It was long and full and he wore it back, tied at the back of his neck with a little black string. He always wore a velvet coat, just like Rose's best velvet dress which had been in her suitcase. He had walked around the island looking at things. He wore shiny black boots, very smooth without buckles. Not cowboy boots. And whenever he happened to pass Rose, he smiled at her and he winked.

Rose hated Athens, Texas. But he took her there, though she could not clearly remember the trip. Just waking up in the Dallas airport with a nice lady to take care of her, and a porter collecting their bags. Uncle Lestan showed up the next night.

The old woman and the old man didn't want her. They sat in a lawyer's office on "the town square" at night, and the old man said that they didn't have to make this appointment after dark, that he didn't like to drive at night when he didn't have to, that this was "disruptive" and he and his wife could have explained all this on the telephone. The old woman just shook her head as the old man explained: "We didn't have anything to do with Morningstar, you see, what with the musicians and the drugs. We don't know this child."

The lawyers talked on and on, but Uncle Lestan became angry. "Look, I want to adopt her," he said. "Make it happen!"

That was the first time Rose had ever heard someone say, "Make it happen." And it was the first and last time she ever saw Uncle Lestan angry. He'd dropped his angry voice to a whisper but he'd made everybody in the room jump, especially Rose, and when he saw this, he took Rose in his arms and carried her outside the building, for a walk around the little town.

"I'll always take care of you, Rose," he said. "You're my responsibility now and I'm glad of it. I want you to have everything, Rose, and I'll see to it that you do. I don't know what's wrong with those people that they don't love you. I love you."

Rose went to live in Florida with Aunt Julie and Aunt Marge in a beautiful house blocks from the sea. The sand on the beach was as white and fine as sugar. Rose had her own room with flowered wallpaper and a canopy bed, and dolls and books that Uncle Lestan sent to her. Uncle Lestan wrote her letters in the most beautiful handwriting and black ink on pink paper.

Aunt Marge drove Rose to a private school called the Country Lane Academy. The school was a wonderland of games to play and projects to do, and computers on which to write words, and bright-faced eager teachers. There were only fifty students in the whole school and Rose was reading Dr. Seuss in no time. On Tuesdays, the whole school spoke Spanish and only Spanish. And they went on trips to museums and zoos and Rose loved all this.

At home Aunt Marge and Aunt Julie helped Rose with her homework, and they baked cakes and cookies, and when the weather was cool, they cooked barbecue outdoors and drank lemonade mixed with iced tea with lots of sugar. Rose loved swimming in the gulf. For her sixth birthday, Aunt Marge and Aunt Julie gave a party and invited the whole school to come, even the older kids, and it was the best picnic ever.

By the time Rose was ten, she understood that Aunt Julie and Aunt Marge were paid to take care of her. Uncle Lestan was her legal guardian. But she never doubted that her aunts loved her, and she loved them. They were retired schoolteachers, Aunt Julie and Aunt Marge, and they talked all the time about how good Uncle Lestan was to all of them. And they were all happy together when Uncle Lestan came to visit.

It was always late in the evening when he arrived, and he brought presents for everyone—books, clothes, laptop computers, and wonderful gadgets. Sometimes he came in a big black car. Other times he just appeared, and Rose laughed to herself when she saw how mussed his hair was, because she knew he'd been flying, flying like that first time, when the little island had sunk into the sea and he had carried her up into the Heavens.

But Rose never told anyone about that, and as she got older she came to think that it just couldn't have happened.

She'd gone from the Country Lane Academy to the Willmont School some fifty miles farther away, and there she was really getting into the most fascinating subjects. She loved literature and history best of all, and after that music, and art appreciation and French. But she did all right in science and math because she felt she had to. Everybody would be so disappointed if she did not do well. But what she really wanted was to read all the time, and her happiest times at school were in the library.

When Uncle Lestan called, she told him all about it, and they talked of books he loved and that she loved, and he reminded her: "Rose, when you grow up, remember, you can be anything you want. You can be a writer, a poet, a singer, a dancer, a teacher, anything."

When Rose turned thirteen, she and her aunts went on a tour of Europe. Uncle Lestan wasn't with them but he had paid for everything. This was the greatest time of Rose's life. They spent three whole months traveling together, and went to all the great cities of the world in what Uncle Lestan called "the Grand Tour." And they visited Russia too, spending five days in Saint Petersburg and five days in Moscow.

For Rose it was all about the most beautiful old buildings, palaces, castles, cathedrals, ancient towns, and the museums filled with the paintings she'd read about and saw now with her own eyes. Above all else, Rose loved Rome, Florence, and Venice. But everywhere she turned, Rose was enchanted by new discoveries.

Uncle Lestan surprised her when they were in Amsterdam. He had a secret key to the Rijksmuseum because he was a patron and he took Rose through it in the evening hours so they could be alone and linger as long as they wanted before the great Rembrandt paintings.

He arranged after-hours showings like that for them in many cities. But Amsterdam had a place in Rose's heart, because there, Uncle Lestan had been with her.

When Rose was fifteen, she got into trouble. She took the family car without permission. She didn't have a driver's license yet, and it was her plan to get the car back before either Aunt Julie or Aunt Marge woke up. She'd only wanted to drive for a few hours with her new friends, Betty and Charlotte, and none of them thought anything bad would happen. But they got into a fender bender on the highway, and Rose ended up in juvenile court.

Aunt Julie and Aunt Marge sent word to Uncle Lestan, but he was traveling and no one could find him. Rose was glad. She was so shamed, so miserable, so afraid that he would be disappointed in her.

The judge who heard the case shocked everyone. He let off Betty and Charlotte because they had not stolen the car, but he sentenced Rose to Amazing Grace Home for Girls for the period of one year due to her criminal behavior. He gave a dire warning to Rose that if she did not behave well at Amazing Grace, he would extend her stay till she was eighteen and possibly even longer. He said Rose had been in danger of becoming an addict with her antisocial behavior and possibly even a street person.

Aunt Marge and Aunt Julie were frantic, begging the judge not to do this. Again and again, they argued, as did the lawyers, that they were not pressing charges against Rose for stealing the car, that this had been a prank and nothing more, that the child's uncle must be contacted.

It did no good. Rose was handcuffed and taken as a prisoner to the Amazing Grace Home for Girls somewhere in southern Florida.

All the way there, she sat quiet, numb with fear, while the men and women in the car talked of a "good Christian environment" where

Rose would learn the Bible, and learn how to be "a good girl" and come back to her aunts "an obedient Christian child."

The "home" exceeded Rose's worst fears.

She was met by the minister Dr. Hays and his wife, Mrs. Hays, both of whom were well dressed and smiling and gracious.

But as soon as the police were gone and they were alone with Rose, they told her that she must admit all the bad things she'd done or Amazing Grace wasn't going to be able to help her. "You know the things you've done with boys," Mrs. Hays said. "You know what drugs you've used, the kind of music you've been listening to."

Rose was frantic. She'd never done anything bad with boys, and her favorite music was classical. Sure she did listen to rock music but—. Mrs. Hays shook her head. Denying who and what she had done was bad, said Mrs. Hays. She did not want to see Rose again until Rose had had a change of attitude.

Rose was given ugly shapeless clothes to wear, and escorted everywhere around the grim sterile buildings by two older students who stood guard over her even when she had to use the bathroom. They would not give her a minute of privacy. They watched her when she performed the most delicate of bodily functions.

The food was unbearable, and lessons were reading and copying Bible verses. Rose was slapped for making eye contact with other girls, or with teachers, or for trying to "talk," or for asking questions, and made to scrub the dining room on her hands and knees for failing to show a "good attitude."

When Rose demanded to call home, to talk to her aunts about where she was, she was taken to "a time-out room," a small closet with one high window, and there she was beaten with a leather belt by an older woman who told her that she had better show a change of attitude now, and that if she didn't she'd never be allowed a phone call to her "family."

"Do you want to be a bad girl?" asked the woman sorrowfully. "Don't you understand what your parents are trying to do for you here? Your parents don't want you now. You rebelled, you disappointed them."

Rose lay on the floor of that room for two days, crying. There was a bucket and a pallet there and nothing else. The floor smelled of chemical cleaners and urine. Twice people came in with food for her. An older girl crouched down and whispered, "Just go along with it.

You can't win against these people. And please, eat. If you don't eat, they'll keep giving you the same plate over and over until you do eat the food, even if it's rotting."

Rose was furious. Where were Aunt Julie and Aunt Marge? Where was Uncle Lestan? What if Uncle Lestan knew what had happened and he was angry and disgusted with her? She couldn't believe it. She couldn't believe he'd turn his back on her like that, not without talking to her. But she was consumed with shame for what she'd done. And she was ashamed of herself now in the shapeless clothes, her body unwashed, her hair unwashed, her skin itching and feverish.

She felt feverish all over and her system had locked up. In the bathroom, before the watchful eyes of her guardians, she could not move her bowels. Her body ached and her head ached. In fact, she was feeling the worst pain she'd ever known in her stomach and in her head.

Rose was surely running a temperature by the time she was taken to the first group session. Without a shower or bath, she felt filthy.

They put a paper sign on her that said I AM A SLUT and told her to admit that she had used drugs, that she'd listened to satanic music, that she'd slept with boys.

Over and over Rose said that she had not slept with anyone, that she had not done drugs.

Again and again, other girls stood before her screaming at her: "Admit, admit."

"Say it: 'I am a slut.'"

"Say it: 'I am an addict.'"

Rose refused. She started screaming. She'd never done drugs in her life. No one at the Willmont School did drugs. She'd never been with a boy except to kiss at a dance.

She found herself down on the floor with other girls sitting on her legs and her arms. She couldn't stop screaming until her mouth filled with vomit. She almost choked on it. With all her soul, she struggled, screaming louder and louder, spitting vomit everywhere.

When Rose awoke, she was alone in a room and she knew she was more than just a little sick. She was hot all over and the pain in her stomach was unbearable. Her head was on fire. Over and over when she heard another person passing she asked for water.

The answer came back, "Faker."

How long did she lie there? It seemed like days, but soon she was half dreaming. Over and over she prayed to Uncle Lestan. "Come get me, please, come get me. I didn't mean to do it, please, please forgive me." She couldn't imagine that he would want her to suffer like this. Surely Aunt Julie and Aunt Marge had told him what was happening. Aunt Marge had been hysterical by the time they took Rose away.

At some point, Rose realized something. She was dying. All she could think of now was water. And every time she drifted off, it was a dream that someone was giving her water; then she'd wake and there was no water; and there was no one there; no one passing; no one saying "faker," and no one saying "admit."

A strange calm came over Rose. So this is how her life would end, she thought. And maybe Uncle Lestan just didn't know or didn't understand how bad it was. What would it matter?

She slept and she dreamed but she kept shivering and waking with a jolt. Her lips were cracked. And there was so much pain in her stomach and chest and her head that she could feel nothing else.

Sliding in and out, dreaming of cold clear water in glasses from which she could drink, she heard sirens go off. They were loud screeching sirens far away but coming closer, and then alarms within this place itself went off, blasting with horrific volume. Rose could smell smoke. She could see the flicker of flames. She heard the girls screaming.

Right before her, the wall broke apart and so did the ceiling. The whole room blew apart with chunks of plaster and wood flying in all directions.

Wind swept through the room. The screams around her grew louder and louder.

A man came towards Rose. He looked like Uncle Lestan, but it wasn't Uncle Lestan. It was a dark-haired man and a beautiful man with the same bright eyes that Uncle Lestan had, except this man's eyes were green. He scooped Rose up from her pallet and wrapped her in something warm and close, and then they went upwards.

Rose saw flames all around as they rose. The entire compound was burning.

The man carried her up and up into the sky just as it had happened long years ago above the little island.

The air was marvelously cold and fresh. "Yes, the stars . . . ," she whispered.

When she saw the great sweep of diamond-bright stars, she was that little child again in Uncle Lestan's arms.

A gentle voice spoke in her ear, "Sleep, Rose, you're safe now. I'm taking you to your uncle Lestan."

Rose woke in a hospital room. She was surrounded by people in white coats and masks. A kindly female voice said, "You're going to be all right, darling. I'm giving you something to make you sleep."

Behind the nurse stood that man, that dark-haired man with the green eyes, who'd brought Rose here. He had the same darkly tanned skin as Uncle Lestan had, and his fingers felt like silk as he stroked Rose's cheek now.

"I'm your uncle's friend, Rose," he said. "My name is Louis." He pronounced it the French way, Louie. "Believe me, Rose, your uncle will be here soon. He's on his way. He'll take care of you, and I'll be here until he comes."

Next time she opened her eyes, she felt completely different. All the pain and pressure were gone from her stomach and chest. They'd evacuated all the waste from her body, she realized that. And when she thought of how revolting that must have been, fingers prying into her unwashed flesh, removing all that filth, she felt ashamed again and sobbed against the pillow. She felt to blame and miserable. The tall dark-haired man stroked her hair and told her not to worry any-more. "Your aunt Julie is on the way. Your uncle is on the way. Go back to sleep, Rose."

Though she was groggy and confused, she could see she was being given fluids and something white, some sort of IV nourishment. The doctor came. She said it would be about a week before Rose could leave, but the "danger" was past. It had been touch and go there for a while, all right. But Rose would be fine. The infection was under control; Rose was hydrated now. The man named Louis thanked the doctor and the nurse.

Rose blinked through her tears. The room was filled with flowers. "He's sent you lilies," said Louis. He had a soft deep voice. "He's sent you roses, too, all colors of roses. Your flower, Rose."

When Rose started to apologize for what she'd done, Louis wouldn't hear of it. He told her the people who'd taken her were "evil." The judge had gotten kickbacks from the Christian home to send perfectly decent teenagers there for incarceration. The school bilked the parents of the children and the state for exorbitant pay-ments. He said that the judge would soon be in jail. As for the home, it was gone, burned down, shut up, and lawyers would see that it never opened again.

"It was wrong what they did to you," he whispered.

In his soft unhurried voice, he said there would be many lawsuits against the home. And the remains of two bodies had been found buried on the grounds. He wanted Rose to know these people would be punished.

Rose was amazed. She wanted to explain about the car, that she had never meant to hurt anybody.

"I know," he said. "It was a little thing. It was nothing. Your uncle is not angry with you. He would never be angry with you over such a thing. Sleep now."

By the time Uncle Lestan came Rose was home with Aunt Marge in a Miami Beach apartment. She had lost weight and felt frail and jumped at the slightest noise. But she was much better. Uncle Lestan took her into his arms, and they went out to walk along the beach together.

"I want you to go to New York," said Uncle Lestan. "New York is the capital of the world. And I want you to go to school there. Aunt Marge is going to take you. Aunt Julie will stay behind. Florida is her home and she can't adjust to the big city. But Aunt Marge will take care of you, and you're to have other companions now, good, decent security guards who'll keep you both safe. I want you to have the finest education." He went on, "Remember, Rose, whatever you've suffered, no matter how bad it's been, you can use that, use that to be a stronger person."

For hours they talked, not about the horrid Christian home but about other things, Rose's love of books, her dreams of writing poetry and stories someday, and her enthusiasm about New York, and how she so wanted to go to a great university like Harvard or Stanford or who knows where?

Those were wonderful hours. They'd stopped at a café on South Beach, and Uncle Lestan sat there quietly, leaning on his elbows, beaming at her as she poured out all her thoughts and dreams and questions.

The new apartment in New York was on the Upper East Side, about two blocks from the park in a venerable old building with spacious rooms and high ceilings. Aunt Marge and Rose were both overjoyed to be there.

Rose went to a marvelous day school which had a curriculum far superior to that of the Willmont School. With the help of several tutors, mostly college students, Rose soon caught up and was deep into her school work preparing to go to college.

Though Rose missed the beautiful beach in Florida and the lovely warm sweet rural nights, she was ecstatic to be in New York, loved her schoolmates, and was secretly happy that Aunt Marge was with her and not Aunt Julie, as Aunt Marge had always been the adventurous one, the mischievous one, and they had more fun together.

Their household soon included a permanent housekeeper and cook, and the security-guard drivers who took them everywhere.

There were times when Rose wanted to strike out on her own, meet kids on her own, take the subway, be independent.

But Uncle Lestan was adamant. Rose's drivers went where Rose went. Embarrassed as Rose was by the big stretch Lincoln limousine that dropped her off at school, she came to depend on this. And these drivers were all past masters of double parking anywhere in Midtown while Rose shopped, and thought nothing of carrying twenty and thirty bundles and even braving the checkout lines for Rose, or running errands for her. They were young mostly, cheerful guys, and kind of like guardian angels.

Aunt Marge was frank about enjoying all this completely.

It was a new way of life, and it had its charms, but the real lure of course was New York itself. She and Aunt Marge had subscription tickets to the symphony, the New York City Ballet, the Metropolitan Opera. They attended the latest musicals on Broadway, and plenty of off-Broadway plays. They shopped at Bergdorf Goodman and Saks; they roamed the Metropolitan Museum for hours on Saturdays and often spent weekends visiting the galleries in the Village and SoHo. This was *life*!

Over the phone, Rose talked endlessly to Uncle Lestan about this or that play she'd seen, or concert, or what was happening with Shakespeare in the Park, and how they wanted to go to Boston this weekend, just to see it, and perhaps visit Harvard.

The summer before Rose's senior year, she and Aunt Marge met Uncle Lestan in London for a marvelous week of visiting the most wonderful sites after hours and with private guides. Then Aunt Marge and Rose went on to Rome, and to Florence and to a whole string of other cities before returning to New York just in time for school to start.

It was sometime just before her eighteenth birthday that Rose turned to the internet to research the ghastly Amazing Grace Home for Girls where she'd been imprisoned. She had never told anyone she knew about what actually happened to her there.

The news reports confirmed everything Louis had told her long ago. The judge who'd sent Rose there had gone to prison. And two lawyers had gone with him.

On Rose's last night there, apparently, a boiler had exploded, setting fire to the entire establishment. Two other explosions had destroyed outbuildings and stables. Rose had never known there were stables. Local firefighters and police had converged on the school to find girls wandering the grounds dazed and incoherent from the shock of the blast, and many had had visible welts and bruises from being beaten. One or two had shaved heads; and two had been taken to local emergency rooms due to malnutrition and dehydration. Some girls had the words SLUT and ADDICT written on them with felt-tip pen. Newspaper stories reflected contempt and outrage. They railed against the school as a racket, part of the unregulated religious Troubled Teen Industry in which parents were bilked out of thousands of dollars to pay for "reformation" of teen girls they feared were in danger of becoming druggies or dropouts or suicides.

Everybody connected with the place had been indicted for something, it seemed; but charges eventually were dropped. There was no law requiring regulation of religious schools in Florida, and the owners and "faculty" of the place dropped out of the record.

But it was easy to trace Dr. Hays and Mrs. Hays. They had both died within months in a fiery home invasion. One of the other more notorious teachers had drowned off Miami Beach. And yet another had been killed in a car wreck.

Rose hated to admit it but this gave her a great deal of satisfaction. At the same time, something about it bothered Rose. A terrible feeling crept over her. Had someone punished these people for what they'd done, done to Rose and to others? But that was absurd. Who would do such a thing? Who *could* do such a thing? She put it out of her mind, and it was dreadful, she told herself, to be glad these people were dead. Rose did a little more reading on the Troubled Teen Industry and other scandals besetting these unregulated Christian schools and homes, but then she couldn't endure another moment of thinking of it all. It made her too angry, and when she became angry, she became ashamed, ashamed that she'd ever—. There was no end to it. She closed the book on that brief and horrid chapter of her life. The present beckoned.

Uncle Lestan wanted Rose to follow her own star when it came to college. He assured her nothing was off-limits.

She and Marge flew to California to visit Stanford and the University of California at Berkeley.

Stanford, near beautiful Palo Alto, California, was Rose's final choice, and Rose and Marge moved the July before school started.

Uncle Lestan met Rose in San Francisco for a brief holiday in August. Rose fell in love with the city, and had half a mind to live there and commute. Uncle Lestan had another suggestion. Why not live near campus as planned, and have an apartment in San Francisco? It was soon arranged, and Rose and Marge moved into a spacious modern condo walking distance from Davies Symphony Hall and the San Francisco Opera House.

Their small house on a tree-lined street in Palo Alto was charming. And though the change of coasts meant a new housekeeper, and two new drivers, Rose was soon settled in and loving the California sunshine.

After her first week of classes, Rose was in love with her literature professor, a tall, wiry, and introspective man who spoke with the affectation of an actor. Gardner Paleston was his name; he'd been a prodigy of sorts, publishing four volumes of poetry as well as two books on the work of William Carlos Williams before he was thirty. At thirty-five, he was brooding, intense, bombastic, and utterly seductive. He flirted openly with Rose, and told her over coffee after class that she was the most beautiful young woman he'd ever seen. He e-mailed her poems about her "raven hair" and "inquisitive eyes." He took her to dinner at expensive restaurants and showed her his large, old Georgian-style home in old Palo Alto. His mother and father were dead, he said. His brother had died in Afghanistan. And so he haunted the house, now, what a waste, but he couldn't bear to give it up, filled as it was with the "rag-and-bone shop of my childhood."

When Uncle Lestan came to visit, he took Rose walking through the quiet leafy streets of Palo Alto. He remarked on the magnolia trees and their hard, rustling green leaves, and how he loved them from his time "in the South."

He was mussed and dusty all over and Rose realized that she'd often seen Uncle Lestan this way, exquisitely dressed, but dusty.

It was on the tip of her tongue to tease him about flying about in the stars, but she didn't. His skin was more darkly tanned than usual and looked almost burned, and his beautiful thick hair was almost white.

He wore a dark blue blazer and khaki pants and black shoes shined to look like glass, and he talked in a low, gentle voice telling her that she must always remember: she could do absolutely anything in this world that she wanted. She could be a writer, a poet, a musician, an architect, a doctor, a lawyer, whatever it was, that she wanted. And if she wanted to marry and make a home for her husband and her children that was fine, too. "If money can't buy you the freedom to do anything you want, well, what is the good of it?" he asked. He sounded almost sad. "And money you have, Rose. Plenty of it. And time. And if time can't give us freedom to do what we want, what good is time?"

Rose felt a terrible pain. She was in love with Uncle Lestan. Beside Uncle Lestan, all thoughts of her teacher, Gardner Paleston, simply faded into nothingness. But Rose didn't say a word. On the verge of tears, she only smiled, and explained that yes, she knew this, that he'd told her this long ago when she'd been a little girl, that she could be and do anything she wanted. "The trouble is I want to do everything!" she said. "I want to live and study here, and live and study in Paris, and in Rome and in New York; I want to do everything."

Uncle Lestan smiled and told her how proud of her he was. "You've grown into a beautiful woman, Rose," he said. "I knew you'd be pretty. You were pretty when I first saw you. But you're beautiful now. You're strong and healthy and, well, you're beautiful. There's no point mincing words about it." And then he turned suddenly into a tyrant, telling her that her driver had to go with her wherever she went, that he even wanted her driver sitting in the back of her college classrooms when there was room, or right outside of them. Rose argued. She wanted freedom. But he wouldn't hear of it. He had become an overzealous and intensely European guardian, it seemed to Rose, but how could Rose really argue? When she thought of all Uncle Lestan had done for her, she fell silent. All right. Her driver would go everywhere with her. He could carry her books. That would be nice, though these days with iPads and Kindles, she didn't have to carry many books.

Six months after that visit, Rose received a letter from Uncle Lestan saying that she would not be hearing from him so often anymore but that he loved her, and he needed this time to be alone. Be assured of his love, and be patient. He would eventually come round. And in the meantime she was entirely safe and must ask his attorneys for whatever her heart desired.

That had always been the way, really. And how could she ask for more?

A year passed without her hearing from Uncle Lestan.

But she had been so busy with other things. And then another year, but it was all right. It would have been wicked and ungrateful to complain, especially when his attorney in Paris called regularly every month.

Two weeks into her junior year, Rose was hopelessly in love again with Gardner Paleston. She was in three of his classes and certain that she could become a great poet someday if she listened to every single word he said. She'd gone to the campus clinic and gotten the information and pills she needed to prevent any accidental pregnancy, and she was just waiting for the time to be perfect for them to be together. Gardner Paleston called her every evening and talked to her for an hour. She had more potential than any other student he'd ever had, he said.

"I want to teach you all I know, Rose," he said. "I've never felt that way about anyone before. I want to give you all that I can, do you understand what I'm saying, Rose? Whatever I know, what I've learned, whatever I have to pass on, I want to give it to you." It sounded as if he was crying on the other end of the line. Rose was overcome.

She wanted desperately to talk with Uncle Lestan about Gardner but that was not to be. She wrote long letters and sent them to the attorney in Paris, and received the most touching little gifts in response. Surely they came from the attorney, she thought, but then each arrived with a gift card signed by Uncle Lestan, and these cards were more precious to her than the pearl necklaces or amethyst brooches they accompanied. Surely Uncle Lestan would one day see Gardner's exceptional talent, his passion, his genius, for what it was.

As she sat dreaming in class, Gardner Paleston became the most sensitive and brilliant being Rose had ever imagined. He was not as beautiful as Uncle Lestan, no, and he looked older actually, perhaps because he didn't have Uncle Lestan's health, she couldn't know. But she came to love everything about Gardner including his hawklike nose, his high forehead, and the long fingers with which he gestured dramatically as he strode back and forth before the classroom.

How disappointed he was, he declared, how crushed, he said bitterly, that "not a single student in this room understands a tenth of what I'm saying here!" He bowed his head, eyes closed, fingers pressed to the bridge of his nose, and trembled. Rose could have cried.

She sat on the grass under a tree reading over and over William Carlos Williams's poem: "The Red Wheelbarrow." What did it mean? Rose wasn't sure she knew! How could she confess this to Gardner? She burst into tears.

Before Christmas, Gardner told Rose the time had come for them to be together. It was the weekend. He'd carefully prepared everything.

Rose had a big fight with her favorite driver, Murray. Murray was young and dedicated, and fun really, but just as obnoxious as all the other paid guardians. "You stay two blocks behind us," said Rose. "Don't let him see that you're following! I'll be spending the evening with him, you understand, and you can wait outside, quietly, unobtrusively. Now, Murray, don't ruin this for me."

Murray had his doubts. He was a small muscular man, of Russian Jewish descent, who'd been a San Francisco policeman for ten years before getting this job, which paid him three times what he'd made before. He was also a very honest, straightforward, and decent guy, like all the drivers, and he let it be known he didn't approve of "this professor." But he followed Rose's orders.

Gardner picked up Rose about six o'clock that evening and drove her to the mysterious old Georgian mansion in old Palo Alto, following a curved drive through the manicured garden up to a porte cochere that couldn't be seen from the street.

Rose was wearing a simple lilac cashmere dress for this blessed evening, with black stockings and black leather shoes, her hair free down her back, with a small diamond clasp over one ear. The soft leafy grounds of Gardner's house were beautiful to her in the gathering darkness.

It had been a splendid place once, that was obvious, with old creaking hardwood floors, richly paneled walls, and a broad central stairway. But now it was littered with Gardner's books and papers, the huge dining room table a glorified desk with his two computers and various notebooks strewn about.

Up the stairs they crept, over old worn red carpet, and down the long dark hall to the master bedroom. A fire blazed in a stone fireplace, and candles burned everywhere. Candles on the mantel, candles on the old high-mirrored dressing table, candles on the night tables. The bed itself was a delicate antique four-poster, with an old "rice design," Gardner explained, which his mother had inherited from her mother.

"Just a full bed, a small bed," he said. "They didn't make queen and king beds in those days, but this is all we need."

Rose nodded. On a long coffee table before an old red-velvet couch sat trays of French cheese, crackers, black caviar, and other choice tidbits. There was wine there, uncorked, waiting for them.

This was Rose's dream, that this, her first experience, would be one of the highest love, and that everything would be perfect.

"I take Holy Communion," whispered Gardner as he kissed her, "my innocent one, my sweet and gentle one, my flower."

They had taken it slowly, kissing, tumbling under the white sheets, and then it had been rough, almost divinely rough, and then it was over.

How could anything have been so perfect? Surely Aunt Marge would understand—that is, if Rose ever told her. But perhaps it was best to tell no one ever. Rose had kept secrets all her life, kept them close, sensing that to divulge a secret could be a terrible thing. And perhaps she would keep this night secret all her life.

They lay together on the pillow, Gardner talking about all that Rose had to learn, all that he wanted to share with her, how much hope he had for her. Rose was just a child, a blank slate, he said, and he wanted to give Rose all he could.

It made Rose think of Uncle Lestan. She couldn't help it. But what would Uncle Lestan have thought had he known where she was now?

"Can I tell you things?" Rose said. "Can I tell you things about my life, about the mysteries of my life that I've never told anyone?"

"Of course you can," Gardner whispered. "Forgive me that I haven't asked you more. Sometimes I think you're so beautiful that I can't really talk to you." This actually wasn't true. He talked all the time to her. But she sensed what he meant. He hadn't said much about wanting to hear her talk.

She felt close to him as she'd never felt close to anyone. Lying beside him felt so perfect. She could not tell whether she was sad or supremely happy.

And so she told him what she'd never told her friends ever. She told him about Uncle Lestan.

She started talking in a low voice, describing the earthquake and that sudden ride up into the stars, and into the Heavens. And she went on to describe him, and the mystery that he was, and how her life had been guided by him. She said a little about the horrid Christian home, skipping quickly to the night she was rescued—again, the dramatic ascent, the wind, the clouds, and those stars again above her in the naked sky. She spoke of Louis and Uncle Lestan and her life since . . . and how she sometimes thought about her mother of long ago, and that island, and what an accident it was that Uncle Lestan had saved her, loved her, protected her.

Quite suddenly Gardner sat up. Reaching for a white terrycloth robe, he stood, wrapped it around him, and walked away towards the fireplace. He stood there with his head bowed for a long moment. He put his hands on the mantel and he let out a loud groan.

Cautiously, Rose sat back against the pillows, pulling the sheet up to cover her breasts. She could hear him continuing to groan. Suddenly he cried out, and as she watched, he rocked back and forth on his bare feet with his head thrown back. Then came his low, angry voice:

"This is so disappointing, oh, so disappointing! I had such hopes for you, such dreams!" he said. She saw him trembling. "And you give me this, this stupid, ridiculous cheap high school vampire babble!" He turned around and faced her, his eyes wet and glittering. "Do you know how you've disappointed me? Do you know how you've let me down?" His voice grew louder and louder. "I had dreams for you, Rose, dreams of what you might be. Rose, you have such potential." He was roaring at her. His face had grown red. "And you feed me this foolish, pedestrian schoolgirl trash!"

He turned to the left, then to the right, and then went towards the bookcase on the wall, his hands moving like big white spiders over the books. "And for God's sakes, get the damned names right!" he said. He drew a large hardcover book down from the shelf. "It's Lestat, damn it," he said, coming towards the bed, "and not Lestan! And Louie is Louis de Pointe du Lac. If you're going to tell me ridiculous childish stories, get it straight, damn it."

He hurled the book at her. Before she could duck, the spine caught her in the forehead. A fierce stabbing pain spread through her skin and gripped her head.

She was stunned. She was maddened by the pain. The book fell down on the comforter. *The Vampire Lestat* was the title. It was old, and the paper jacket was torn.

Gardner had gone back to the mantelpiece, and once again he moaned. Then he began again. "This is so disappointing, so disappointing, and on this night of all nights, Rose, this night. You can't begin to know how you've failed me. You can't begin to know how disappointed I am. I deserve better than this, Rose. I deserve so much more!"

She sat there shaking. She was in a rage. The pain went on and on in her head and she felt a silent fury that he had hurled this book at her, hurled it right at her face, and hurt her in this way.

She slipped out of the bed, her legs wobbling. And in spite of her trembling hands, she pulled on her clothes as quickly as she could.

On and on he spoke, down into the crackling fire, crying now. "And this was to be a beautiful night, such a special night. You cannot imagine how you have disappointed me! Vampires carrying you up into the stars! Good Lord in Heaven! Rose, you don't know how you've hurt me, how you've betrayed me!"

She grabbed her shoulder bag and tiptoed out of the room, rushing down the stairs, and out of the house. She had her iPhone out before she hit the long dark driveway, calling for Murray.

The headlights soon appeared in the deserted street as the big limousine coasted up to her. She had never been so glad to see Murray in all her life.

"What's the matter, Rose!" Murray demanded.

"Just drive," she said. In the big black leather backseat of the car, she put her head down on her knees and cried. Her head was still aching from the blow, and when she rubbed her forehead she felt the soreness there.

She felt stupid suddenly for ever trusting this man, for ever thinking that she could confide in him, for ever allowing herself to be intimate with him. She felt like a fool. She felt ashamed and she never, never wanted anyone ever to know about it. For the moment, she couldn't understand the things he'd said. But one thing was clear. She'd trusted him with the most precious secrets of her life, and he'd accused her of borrowing stories from a novel. He'd hurled that heavy book at her, not giving a damn whether he hurt her with it. When she thought of herself naked beside him in that bed, she shuddered.

The following Monday, Rose dropped Professor Gardner Paleston's classes, giving family problems as a reason for having to cut her schedule. She never intended to see him again. Meanwhile, he was calling her constantly. He came by her house twice, but Aunt Marge agreeably explained that Rose wasn't home.

"If he comes again," Rose told Murray, "ask him please to stop bothering me."

It was a week later, on a Friday night, in a bookstore downtown, that Rose saw a paperback book with the title: *The Vampire Lestat.*

As she stood in the aisle examining the book, she saw that it was number 2 in some sort of series of novels. Quickly, she found several others. These books were called the Vampire Chronicles.

Halfway home, she was so upset thinking about Gardner again that she was tempted to throw the books away, but she had to admit she was curious. What were these books about? Why did he think she was repeating stories from them?

Since that awful night, Rose had been in a kind of a daze. She'd lost all appetite for school, for friends, for everything. She'd been moving around the campus as if in a half sleep, scared to death of running into Gardner anywhere or everywhere, and her mind kept circling back over what had happened. Maybe it would do her good to read these books and see just how unfair to her Gardner had been.

Rose read the entire weekend. On Monday, she cut class and continued reading, complaining to Marge of an upset stomach. Sometime around Wednesday, she heard voices outside the little house and looked down to see Murray arguing with Gardner Paleston at the curb. Murray was clearly angry, but then so was Gardner. Finally the professor turned and walked off, shaking his head, his hand flung out before him, clawing at the air, and he appeared to be murmuring to himself.

By Friday of that week, Rose felt remarkably calm about the situation. Whatever she was thinking no longer had much to do with Gardner. She was thinking of the books she'd been reading and she was thinking of Uncle Lestan.

She knew now why Gardner had made his distasteful and hostile accusations. Yes, she could see it quite clearly. Gardner was a self-centered and inconsiderate man. But she knew now why he had said what he had said.

Uncle Lestan's physical description perfectly matched that of "the Vampire Lestat," and his friend and lover, "Louis de Pointe du Lac" was certainly a dead ringer for the Louis who'd rescued Rose from Amazing Grace Home for Girls. Dead ringer. Now that was a good pun.

But what did it mean that this was the case?

Not for one moment did Rose believe in vampires. Not for one second. She no more believed in vampires than she believed in werewolves, or Bigfoot, or the Yeti, or aliens from outer space, or little winged fairies living in gardens, or elves capturing people in dark woodlands and transporting them to Magonia. She didn't believe in ghosts, or astral travel, or near-death experiences, or psychics or witches or sorcerers either. Well, maybe she believed in ghosts. And well, maybe she believed in "near-death experiences," yes. She had known a number of people who had those.

But vampires?

No. She did not believe in them. Whatever the case, she was intrigued by this series of fictional stories about them. And there was not a single description in any of them of the Vampire Lestat, or a single line of dialogue spoken by him, that did not check completely with her vision of Uncle Lestan. But that was sheer coincidence, surely. As for Louis, well, the character with the similar name was indeed exactly like him, yes, but that was sheer coincidence, too, wasn't it? Well, it had to be! There was no other explanation.

Unless they belonged to some organization, her uncle and this man, in which they engaged in role-playing games of some sophisticated sort modeled after the characters in these novels. But that was ridiculous. Playing roles was one thing. How in the world could anyone make himself look the way Uncle Lestan did?

She felt a strange embarrassment at the very thought of asking Uncle Lestan whether or not he'd read these books. It would be insulting and demeaning to do this, she thought, rather like Gardner insulting her when he threw the book at her face, and went on with his accusations.

But the entire problem began to obsess Rose. Meanwhile she read every last word of every book she could find with these characters.

And the stories in truth amazed her, not only by their complexity and depth, but by the peculiar dark turns they took, and the chronology they laid out for the main character's moral development. She realized that she was now thinking of Uncle Lestan as that main character. He'd been wounded, shocked, the victim of a series of disasters and adventures. He'd become a wanderer in these books. And his skin was tanned because he kept letting himself suffer the effects of sunlight in a painful attempt to mask his preternatural identity.

No, this is impossible.

She barely noticed when Marge told her that Gardner had gotten hold of their home number and she had had to change it. Rose keyed the new number into her cell and forgot about it. She didn't use the landline much, but of course it was the principal way to reach Marge. So she had to have that number.

"Do you want to tell me what's the matter?" Marge asked. "I know something happened."

Rose shook her head. "Just reading, thinking," she said. "I'm better now. I'm going back Monday. I have a lot of catching up to do."

In class, she could barely keep her mind on the lecture. She kept drifting off, thinking about that long-ago night when Uncle Lestan had caught her in his arms and carried her up and up from that island. She saw him in that dim, shadowy little lawyer's office in Athens, Texas, saying, "Make it happen!"

Well, there had to be some explanation. And then it struck her. Of course. Her uncle knew the author of these books. Her uncle had perhaps inspired them. It was so simple she almost laughed out loud. That had to be it. He and his friend Louis had inspired this fiction. And when she'd tell him she'd found the books, of course, he would laugh and explain how they'd come to be written! He'd probably say he'd been honored to be the inspiration of such bizarre and romantic ramblings.

Sitting in the back of a history class, oblivious to the teacher's words, she slipped *Interview with the Vampire* out of her purse and checked the copyright: 1976. No, that couldn't be right. If her uncle had been a grown man by that time, well, now he'd be nearly sixty. No way was Uncle Lestan that old. That was positively ridiculous. But then . . . how old was he? How old had he been when he'd rescued her from that island earthquake? Hmmm . . . this wasn't adding up. Maybe he'd been just a boy, then, when he'd rescued her and he'd looked like a grown man to her—a boy of what, sixteen or seventeen, and now he was what, forty? Well, that was possible. But hardly likely. No, this did not add up, and overshadowing it all was her vivid conviction of his demeanor, his charm.

Class was over. Time to shuffle on, and go through the motions someplace else, to drift until she saw Murray waiting for her on some curb somewhere. . . . But surely there was a logical explanation.

Murray drove her away from the campus to a restaurant she particularly liked where Marge was to meet her for an early dinner.

It was getting dark. They had a regular table and she was glad that she had a little while to sit there alone, enjoy a badly needed cup of black coffee, and just think to herself.

She was looking out the window, paying very little attention to much of anything, when she realized someone had sat down opposite her.

It was Gardner.

She was badly startled.

"Rose, do you realize what you've done to me?" he asked. His voice was deep and tremulous.

"Look, I want you to leave," she started. He reached across the table and tried to take hold of her hand.

Drawing it back, she stood up and stumbled away from the table, running towards the back of the restaurant. She hoped and prayed the one small ladies' room would be empty.

Gardner came pounding after her, and when she realized her mistake, it was too late. He'd grabbed hold of her wrist and was dragging her out of the back exit into an alleyway. Murray was all the way around front, parked at the curb.

"Let go of me!" she said. "I mean it, I'll scream," she said. She was as angry as she had been when the book had struck her.

Without a word, he dragged her right off her feet and down the alleyway towards his car, and threw her in the passenger side, slamming the door and locking it with his remote.

When he went to open the driver's side, he unlocked only that door. She beat on the windows. She screamed. "Let me go!" she said. "How dare you do this to me?"

He started the car, backed out of the alley, and took off down the side street, away from the main boulevard where Murray was no doubt waiting to pay for Marge's taxi.

Down a quiet street, he drove the car at reckless speed, oblivious to the squeal of the wheels or enjoying it.

Rose beat on the windshield, on the side window, and when she could see no one anywhere around, she reached for the key in the ignition.

With a resounding blow he sent her backwards against the passenger door. For a moment she didn't know where she was, then it came back to her completely and horribly. She struggled to sit up, reaching into her purse and quickly finding the iPhone. She sent the SOS message to Murray. Then Gardner grabbed the purse from her and, buzzing down his window, hurled it out, phone and all.

By now the car was speeding through traffic, and she was being thrown from one side to the other as it swerved around one intersection after another. It was making for old Palo Alto, the neighborhood where Gardner lived. And soon the streets would once again be deserted.

Again, Rose banged on the windows, gesturing frantically to passing cars, to people on the sidewalk. But no one seemed to notice her. Her screams filled the car. Gardner grabbed her by her hair and pulled her head away from the window. The car slammed to a stop.

They were in some side street now with big trees, those big beautiful dark green magnolias. He turned her around and held her face in the vise of his thin fingers, his thumb biting painfully into her jaw.

"Who the Hell do you think you are!" he breathed at her, his face dark with rage. "Who the Hell do you think you are to do this to me!"

These were exactly the words she wanted to speak to him, but all she could do was glare at him, her entire body soaked in sweat. She grabbed at his hair with both her hands and yanked it as he'd yanked hers. He hurled her back against the window again and slapped her repeatedly, until she was gasping uncontrollably.

The car drove on, tires screaming, and as she struggled to sit up again, her face burning, she saw the driveway in front of her, and the old Georgian house looming over her.

"You let me go!" she screamed.

He dragged her from the car, pulling her out the driver's side, and dragging her onto her knees on the concrete.

"You don't begin to know what you've done to me!" he roared. "You miserable stupid girl! You don't begin to grasp what your fun and games have done."

He dragged her through the door and hurled her across the dining room so that she hit the table hard and sank to the floor. When he lifted her up, she'd lost one of her shoes, and blood was pouring from her face down onto her sweater. He hit her again, and she went out. Out.

Next thing Rose knew, she was in the bedroom. She was on the bed, and he was standing over her. He had a glass in his hand.

He was talking in a low voice, saying once more how she'd broken his heart, how she'd disappointed him. "Oh, this has all been the disappointment of my life, Rose," he said. "And I wanted it to be so different, so very different, with you, Rose, of all the flowers of the field, you were the fairest, Rose, the fairest of all."

He came towards her as she struggled to get up.

"Now we will drink this together."

She tried to scurry backwards, away from him, off the bed, but his right hand caught her wrist while, with his left hand, he held the glass of liquid high out of her reach.

"Now, stop it, Rose." He growled between his clenched teeth. "For the love of God, do this with dignity."

Suddenly a pair of headlamps sent their beams over the master-bedroom windows.

Rose began to scream as loud as she could. It was nothing like those nightmares in which you try to scream and you can't. She was shrieking. The screams just erupted uncontrollably.

He dragged her towards him as he went on and on, shouting over her screams: "You are the most dreadful disappointment of my life," he cried, "and now as I seek to make all things new, to make all things whole, for you and for me, Rose, you do this to me, to me!"

With the back of his hand, he slammed her into the pillow. Out. When she opened her eyes, a foul burning fluid was in her mouth. He had her nose pinched between his fingers. She gagged, and bucked and struggled to scream. The taste was ghastly. Her throat was burning. So was her chest.

He thrust the half-full glass at her and the liquid inside it splashed on her face, burning her. The smell was acrid, chemical, caustic. It burned into her cheek and neck.

Twisting around as she struggled against his grip, she vomited on the bed. She kicked at him with both feet. But he wouldn't let go. He threw the liquid at her and she turned with all her strength, feeling it splash against her face. It went into her eyes. It blinded her. Her eyes were on fire.

Murray's voice sounded from the hallway door.

"Let her go."

And then she was free, screaming, crying, grabbing for the covers to wipe the burning liquid off her face, and from out of her eyes.

The men were scuffling and the furniture was breaking. There was a loud crash as the mirror on the dresser broke.

"I've got you," said Murray as he grabbed up Rose and carried her out of the room, running down the steps with her.

She could hear sirens approaching. "Murray, I'm blind!" she sobbed. "Murray, my throat is on fire."

Rose woke up in the ICU. Her eyes were bandaged, her throat was aching unbelievably, and her hands were strapped so that she couldn't move.

Aunt Marge and Murray were with her. Desperately, they were trying to reach Uncle Lestan. They would not give up trying. They would find him.

"I'm blind now, aren't I?" Rose wanted to ask, but she couldn't talk. Her throat wouldn't open. The pain in her chest was grinding.

Gardner Paleston was dead, Murray assured her. He'd died from a blow to the head in the fight with Murray.

It was an open-and-shut case of attempted murder-suicide. The bastard, as Murray called him, had already posted his suicide note online fully describing his plan to give Rose "the burning hemlock," along with an ode to their mingled decomposing remains. She heard Aunt Marge begging Murray to stop talking.

"We're going to find Uncle Lestan," Marge said.

Terror engulfed Rose. She couldn't speak. She couldn't see. She couldn't beg for reassurance; she couldn't even tell them about the pain, the unrelenting pain. But Uncle Lestan was coming. He was coming. Oh, what a fool she'd been, such a fool, to have loved Gardner, to have trusted Gardner. She was so ashamed, ashamed as she'd been years ago lying on the floor of Amazing Grace Home, so ashamed.

And all the confusion about the books, those books which had affected her so deeply that for days she'd lived in them, imagining Uncle Lestan to be the hero, rising with him, in his arms, towards the stars. *Give me the stars.*

She lapsed back into sleep because there was no place else to go.

There was no day or night, only an alternating rhythm of activity and noise. More commotion in the room, and in the corridor beyond, more voices near at hand yet muffled, indistinct.

Then a doctor was talking to her.

He was close by her ear. His voice was soft, deep, resonant, sharpened by an accent she didn't know.

"I am caring for you now," he said. "I will make you well."

They were in an ambulance moving through traffic, and she could feel every bump of the road. The siren was distant but steady. And when she woke next she knew she was on a plane. She could hear Marge talking softly to someone, but it wasn't Murray. She couldn't hear Murray.

Next time she woke she was in a new bed, a very soft bed, and there was music playing, a lovely song from Romberg's *The Student Prince*. It was the "Serenade" that long ago Uncle Lestan had sung to her. If her eyes had not been wrapped tight, they would have filled with tears. Maybe they did fill with tears.

"Don't cry, precious dear," said the doctor, the doctor with the accent. She felt his silken hand on her forehead. "Our medicines are healing you. By tomorrow this time, your vision will be restored."

Slowly it dawned on her that her chest no longer hurt. There was no pain in her throat. She swallowed freely for the first time in so long.

She was dreaming again, and a soft tenor voice, a rather deep voice, was singing Romberg's "Serenade."

Morning. Rose opened her eyes very slowly, and she saw the light of the sun coming in the windows, and gradually the deep sleep left her, falling away from her as if veils were being drawn back, one after another.

It was a beautiful room. A wall of glass looked out on the distant mountains, and between here and there was the desert, golden in the burning sun.

There was a man standing with his back to her. At first the image of him was indistinct against the bright distant mountains and the deep blue sky.

She sighed deeply and turned her head easily back and forth on the pillow.

Her hands were free and she brought them up to touch her face. She touched her lips, her moist lips.

The young man came into focus. Broad shoulders, tall, maybe six feet tall, with luxuriant blond hair. Could it be Uncle Lestan?

Just as his name rose to her lips, the figure turned to face her and came towards the bed. Oh, how completely he resembled Uncle Lestan, but he was younger, definitely younger; he was the image of Uncle Lestan in a young boy.

"Hello, Rose," he said, smiling down at her. "I'm so glad you're awake."

Suddenly her vision dimmed, blurred, and a pain shot through her temples and her eyes. But it was gone, this pain, as quickly as it had come, and she could see again. Her eyes were only dry and itching. She could see perfectly.

"Who are you?" she asked.

"I'm Viktor," said the boy. "I'm here to be with you now."

"But Uncle Lestan, is he coming?"

"They're trying to find him. It's not always easy to find him. But when he finds out what happened to you, I promise you, he will come."

The young boy's face was cheerful, fresh, his smile generous and almost sweet. He had large blue eyes so like Uncle Lestan's, but it was the hair and the shape of his face more than anything that locked in the resemblance.

"Precious Rose," he said. In a soft even voice, an American voice that had nevertheless a kind of crisp enunciation to it, he explained that Aunt Marge could not be here now in this place. But Rose was safe, completely safe, from all harm, and he, Viktor, would see to that. And so would the nurses. The nurses would take care of her every need.

"You've had surgery after surgery," Viktor said, "but you're improving wonderfully and soon you'll be fully yourself again."

"Where is the doctor?" Rose asked. When he reached for her hand, she clasped his.

"He'll come tonight, after sunset," said Viktor. "He can't be here now."

"Like a vampire," she said, musing, laughing softly under her breath.

He laughed with her, gently, softly. "Yes, very like that, Rose," he said.

"But where is the Prince of the Vampires, my uncle Lestan?" Never mind that Viktor would never in a thousand years understand her mad humor. He would ascribe it to the sedatives that were making her loopy and almost content.

"The Prince of the Vampires will come, I assure you," Viktor answered. "As I said, they are searching for him now."

"You're so like him," she said dreamily. There came that pain again to her eyes and that blurring vision, and it seemed for one instant that the window was on fire. She turned her head away in a panic. But the pain stopped and she could see clearly all the objects of this room. What a pretty room, painted a cobalt blue and with bright white enameled moldings, and on the wall a brilliant painting of roses, wild, exploding roses against a backdrop of a darker blue.

"But I know that painting, that's my painting," she said. "That's from my bedroom at home."

"All your things are here now, Rose," said Viktor. "Just tell me whatever you want. We have your books, your clothes, everything. You'll be able to get up in a few days."

A nurse came into the room, soundlessly, and appeared to be checking the equipment that surrounded the bed. For the first time, Rose saw the glistening plastic sacks of IV fluid, the slender gleaming silver cords that ran to the needles taped to her arms. She really was drugged. One moment she thought her mind was clear and the next she was astonished or confused. Clothes. Get up. Books.

"Any pain, darling?" asked the nurse. She had soft brown skin and large sympathetic brown eyes.

"No, but whatever it is, give me more of it." She laughed. "I'm floating. I believe in vampires."

"Don't we all?" asked the nurse. She made some adjustment in the IV feed. "There now," she said, "you'll be sleeping again soon enough. When you sleep you heal, and that's what you must do now. Heal." Her shoes made a soft squeaking noise as she left the room.

Rose drifted and then she saw Viktor again smiling down at her. Well, Uncle Lestan never wore his hair that short, did he? And never did he wear that kind of sweater vest, even if it was cashmere, or a pink shirt like that open at the neck.

"You look so like him," she said.

In the distance she heard the "Serenade" again, that plaintive, painful music, trying to describe beauty, pure beauty, and so heart-breakingly sad. "But he sang that to me when I was little. . . ."

"You told us this," said Viktor, "and that's why we're playing it for you now."

"I could swear, you look more like him than any human being I've ever seen in my life."

Viktor smiled. Why, it was that same smile, that same infectious and loving smile.

"That's because I'm his son," said Viktor.

"Uncle Lestan's son?" she said. She was so drowsy. "Did you say you were his son?" She sat up, staring at him. "My God in Heaven! You are his son. I had no idea that he had a son!"

"He doesn't have any idea either, Rose," said Viktor. He bent over her and kissed her forehead. She put her arms around him, the wires streaming from their needles. "I've been waiting such a long time," he said, "to tell him myself."

6

Cyril

HE SLEPT FOR MONTHS at a time. Sometimes years. Why not? In a cave on Mount Fuji, he had slept for centuries. There were years when he slept in Kyoto. Now he was in Tokyo. He didn't care.

He was thirsty and crazed. He'd been having bad dreams, dreams of fire.

He crawled from his hiding place and went out into the teeming nighttime streets. Rain, yes, cooling rain. Didn't matter to him much who the victim was, as long as it was young and strong enough to survive that first bite. He wanted hearts that would pump the blood into him. He wanted that blood being pumped by another heart through his heart.

As he walked deeper and deeper into the Ginza district of the city, the neon lights delighted him and made him happy. Lights flickering, dancing, racing up and down and across on the borders of great moving pictures. Lights! He decided to take his time.

Strange it was that when he emerged from his hiding places, he always knew the languages and the ways of the people who were nearest to them. He was never surprised so much as delighted by their goings-on. Rain couldn't stop the crush of people here, the beautiful, fresh-faced, scrubbed, and scented children of this century, so rich, so innocent, so willing to provide him with draught after draught of their blood.

Drink because I want you. I have much for you to do.

Ah, there was that nagging voice, that being talking inside his head. Who was this arrogant blood drinker shogun who thought he could tell Cyril what to do?

He wiped his lips with the back of his hand. Human beings were staring at him. Well, let them stare. His brown hair was filthy, of course, and so were the rags he wore, but he accelerated his pace, skillfully, moving fast away from prying eyes. Then he looked down. He was barefoot. And who's to say that I can't be barefoot? He laughed under his breath. After he'd fed, he would bathe, wash himself properly, and make himself "blend in."

However did he get here, to this country? he wondered. Sometimes he could remember and sometimes he could not.

And why was he seeking out this particular place—a narrow building that he kept seeing in his mind?

You know what I want of you.

"No, I don't," he said aloud, "and there's no telling I'll do it."

"Oh, yes, you will," came the answer very distinctly right inside his brain. "If you do not do what I wish I will punish you."

He laughed. "You think you can?"

Other blood drinkers had been threatening to punish him ever since he could remember.

Long ago on the flank of Mount Fuji, an ancient blood drinker had said to him, "This is my land!" Well, guess what happened to him? He laughed when he thought of it.

But long before that, he'd been laughing at threats from those around him—those blood drinker priests of *her* temple, always threatening to punish him if he didn't do *her* will. He had marveled at the timidity of the blood gods who submitted to her inane rules. And when he'd brought his fledglings right into the temple to drink her blood, those cowardly priests had backed off, not daring to challenge him.

The last time he'd brought that pretty girl, that Greek girl, Eudoxia, and told her to drink from the Mother. Those priests had been in a rage.

And what about the Mother? She'd been nothing more than a statue full of the Blood by that time. So much for stories of divinity and high calling and reasons to suffer and sacrifice and obey.

Even if he went way back, as far as he could recall, to the very first time he'd been in her presence, brought there by the elder to drink from her and become a blood god, he'd thought it was foolishness, lies. He'd been sly enough to do what they told him. Ah, that blood had felt so good. And what had life been for him before that, backbreaking labor, hunger, his father's constant bullying. All right, I'll die and be reborn. And then I'll smash in your faces with my new godly fists! He knew a blood god was infinitely stronger than a human being. You want to give me that power? I'll bend the knee. But you'll regret it, my sanctimonious friends.

"Drink," said the being talking in his head. "Now. Choose one of the victims the world offers you."

"You don't have to tell me how to do it, you fool," he said, spitting the words into the rain. He'd stopped and they were staring at him and then he did this feint he had perfected, falling down on his knees, then rising, head bowed, as he staggered into a deep but small shop in a narrow building, where only one serving girl waited for a customer, and came towards him with arms out, asking if he were ill.

It was so simple to force her into the storage room behind the little emporium and hold her tight in one arm as he sank his fangs into her neck. She shuddered and shivered like a bird in his grasp, words strangled in her throat. The blood was sweet with innocence, with deep convictions of harmony amongst all the creatures of the planet, with some exalted sense that this encounter now which clouded her mind and ultimately paralyzed her must have meaning. Else how could such a thing happen to her?

She lay on the floor at his feet.

He was reflecting on the quality of the blood. So rich, so healthy, so filled with exotic flavors, so different from blood in the time he'd been made. Ah, these robust and powerful modern humans, what a world of food and drink they enjoyed. The blood was sharpening his vision as it always did, and calming something in him for which he had no name.

He snapped off the electric lights in the storage room and waited. Within seconds a pair of customers had come into the shop, a big gawky boy and a pale emaciated European girl.

"Back here," he said, beckoning to them, smiling at them, focusing his precious power right on their eyes, glancing from one to the other. "Come."

This was his favorite way to do it, with a tender throat in each hand, taking one and then the other, suckling, lapping, sloshing the hot salty blood around in his mouth, then going at it again, and then the first victim again, letting both weaken at the same gentle speed until he was satisfied. He could drink no more. Three deaths now had passed through him in wrenching spasms. He was hot and tired and he felt like he could see through walls as well as walk through them. He was full.

He took the boy's shirt, white and fresh and clean, and he put that on. The dungarees were all right too. And the leather belt fit. The shoes were big and soft and laced up, and they felt loose to him, but it was better than being stared at, better than having to fight with some little gang of mortals and then flee them, though it was easy enough to do.

Now with the young European woman's hairbrush he cleaned all the dust and soil from his brown hair. And with her dress, he wiped off his face and hands. It made him sad to look at them dead, the three of them, his victims, and he had to admit it always did.

"What sentimental nonsense," said the being talking inside him.

"You shut up, what do you know!" he said aloud.

He walked through the brightly lighted store and back out into the throng in the streets. The lighted towers rose on either side of him; the lights were so beautiful to him, so magical, climbing higher and higher into the sky—strips of blue and red and yellow and orange, and all that artful lettering. He liked their lettering, the Japanese. It made him think of the writing of the old times when people had carefully painted their words on papyrus and on walls.

Why did he turn off the beautiful thoroughfare? Why did he leave behind the crowds?

There it was, the little hotel he'd been seeking. That's where they hid from the world, the pesky young ones, the foolish and blundering blood drinker riffraff.

Ah, yes, and you will burn them now, burn them all. Burn the building. You have the power to do it. The power is inside you here with me.

Was that really what he wanted to do?

"Do as I have told you to do," said the angry voice now in words.

"What do I care about all those blood drinkers hiding in there?" he said aloud. Weren't they simply lost and lonely and dragging themselves through eternity just as he was? Burn them? Why?

"The power," said the being. "You have the power. Look at the building. Let the heat collect in your mind, focus it, then send it forth."

It had been so long since he'd attempted something like that. It was tempting to see if he could do it.

And suddenly he was doing it. Yes. He felt the heat, felt it as if his own head would explode. He saw the façade of the little hotel waver, heard it crackle, and saw the flames erupting everywhere.

"Kill them as they come out!"

Within seconds the hotel was a tower of flame. And they were rushing right towards him, right into the path of the one who was burning them. It was like a game, throwing the beam at one and then another and another. They were each individual torches for an instant, dying quickly to the rainy pavement.

His head ached. He staggered backwards. A woman stood by the entrance sobbing, reaching out to one of the young ones who'd been burnt to the ground. She was old. It would take such heat to burn her. I don't want to. I don't want to do any of this.

"Ah, but you do! Now, lift her out of her pain and her suffering. . . ."

"Yes, such pain and such suffering . . ."

He sent the blast at her with all his strength. Throwing up her arms, she threw a blast of her own towards him but her face and arms were already turning black. Her clothes were on fire. Her legs gave out. Another blast and she was finished and then another and another and only her bones gave off smoke as they melted.

He had to be quick. He had to get those who had escaped from the back.

Through the burning building he ran, easily picking them out when he reemerged into the rain.

Two, three, then a fourth, and there were no more.

He sat slumped against a wall, and the rain soaked through his white shirt.

"Come," said the dictatorial voice. "You are dear to me now. I love you. You have done my will and I will reward you."

"No, get away from me!" he said disgustedly. "I don't do anyone's will."

"Oh, but you have."

"No," he said. He got to his feet, the cloth shoes wet and heavy. Disgustedly he tore them off his feet and threw them away. He walked on and on. He was walking out of this immense city. He was walking away from all this.

"I have work for you in other places," said the being.

"Not for me," he said.

"You betray me."

"Weep by yourself over that. It's nothing to me."

He stopped. He could hear other blood drinkers in the night in far-distant places. He could hear voices screaming. Where were these dreadful cries coming from? He told himself he didn't care.

"I will punish you," said the being, "if you defy me." His voice was angry again. But very soon, as Cyril walked on and on, the creature fell silent. The creature was gone.

Well before morning, he'd reached the open countryside, and he dug deep into the earth to sleep for as long as he could. But the nagging voice had come back to him at sunset. "There isn't much time. You must go to Kyoto. You must destroy them."

He ignored the orders. The voice grew angrier and angrier as it had last night. "I will send another!" the voice threatened. "And some night soon I will punish you."

On he slept. He dreamed of flames but he didn't care. He wasn't doing that anymore, no matter what happened. But sometime during the night he saw the old vampire refuge in Kyoto burning. And he heard those awful screams again.

I will punish you!

In a perfect imitation of American slang, which he'd come to love, he answered, "Good luck with that."

7

The Story of Antoine

H E HAD DIED at the age of eighteen, Born to Darkness in weakness and confusion, beaten, burned, and left for dead along with his maker. In his fragile short human life, he'd played the piano only, studying at the Conservatoire de Paris when he was but ten years old. A genius he'd been called, and, oh, the Paris of those times. Bizet, Saint-Saëns, Berlioz, even Franz Liszt—he'd seen them, heard their music, known them all. He might have become one of them. But his brother had betrayed him, fathering a child out of wedlock, and selecting him—a third son, aged seventeen—to take the blame for the scandal. Off to Louisiana he'd been shipped with a fortune that funded his ruin through drink and his nightly attendance at the gambling tables. Only now and then did he vengefully attack the piano in some fashionable parlor or hotel lobby, delighting and confusing happenstance audiences with a riot of broken and violent riffs and incoherent melodies. Taken up by whores and patronesses of the arts alike, he traded upon his looks: jet-black wavy hair, very white skin, and famously deep blue eyes and a baby Cupid's bow mouth that others liked to kiss and touch with their fingertips. He was tall but gangly, fragile looking, but notoriously strong, able to land a punch with ease to break the jaw of anyone who might try to harm him. Fortunately he had never broken his precious piano fingers doing such things, but knowing it well might happen, he'd taken to carrying a knife and a pistol, and he was no stranger either to the rapier and attended, a few times, at least, a fashionable New Orleans fencing establishment.

Mostly, he fell apart, disintegrated, lost things, woke up in strange bedrooms, got sick with tropical fever, or from bad food, or from drinking himself into a stupor. He had no respect for this raw, mad, essentially colonial town. It wasn't Paris, this disgusting American place. It might as well have been Hell for all he cared. If the Devil kept pianos in Hell, what did it matter?

Then Lestat de Lioncourt, that paragon of fashion, who lived in the Rue Royale with his trusted friend Louis de Pointe du Lac and their little ward Claudia, had come into his life with his fabled generosity and swaggering abandon.

Those days. Ah, those days. How beautiful they seemed in retrospect, and how raw and ugly they had been in fact. That crumbling city of New Orleans, the filth of it, the relentless rains, the mosquitoes and the stench of death from the soggy graveyards, the lawless riverfront streets, and that enigmatic gentleman in exile, Lestat, sustaining him, putting gold in his hands, luring him away from the bars and the roulette wheels and urging him to pound the nearest keyboard.

Lestat had purchased for him the finest pianoforte that he could find, a magnificent Broadwood grand, shipped from England, and played at one time by the great Frédéric Chopin.

Lestat had brought servants to clean up his flat. Lestat had hired a cook to see that he ate before he drank, and Lestat had told him that he had a gift and that he must believe in it.

Such a charmer, Lestat in his elegant black frock coats and glossy four-in-hands, marching up and down on the antique Savonnerie carpet, urging him on with a wink and a flashing smile, his blond hair bushy and rebellious down to his crisp white collar. He smelled of clean linen, fresh flowers, the spring rain.

"Antoine, you must compose," Lestat had told him. Paper, ink, everything he needed for his writing. And then those ardent embraces, shrill and chilling kisses when oblivious to the silent and devoted servants they lay in the big cypress four-poster bed together beneath the flaming red silk tester. So cold Lestat had seemed yet so rampantly affectionate. Hadn't those kisses now and then hurt with a tiny sting like an insect biting into his throat? What did he care? The man intoxicated him. "Compose for me," he'd whispered in Antoine's ear, and the command imprinted itself on Antoine's heart.

Sometimes he composed for twenty-four hours without stopping—

never mind the endless noise from the crowded muddy street outside his windows—then fell down from exhaustion to sleep over the piano itself in a stupor.

Then Lestat in those shining white gloves and with that glistening silver walking stick was there blazing before him, face moist and cheeks ruddy.

"Here, get up now, Antoine. You've slept enough. Play for me."

"Why do you believe in me?" he'd asked.

"Play!" Lestat pointed to the piano keys.

Lestat danced in circles as Antoine played, looking up into the smoky light of the crystal chandelier. "That's it, more, that's it : . ."

And then Lestat himself would flop down into the gold fauteuil behind the desk and begin writing with superb speed and accuracy the notes that Antoine was playing. What had happened to all those songs, all those sheets of parchment, all those leather folders of music?

How lovely it had been, those candlelight hours, curtains blowing in the wind and sometimes people gathered on the banquette below to listen to his playing.

Until that awful night when Lestat had come to demand his allegiance.

Scarred, filthy, dressed in rags that reeked of the swamp, Lestat had become a monster. "They tried to kill me," he'd said in a harsh whisper. "Antoine, you must help me!"

Not the precious child, Claudia, not the precious friend, Louis de Pointe du Lac! You cannot mean this. Murderers, those two, the picture-perfect pair who glided through the early evenings as if in some shared dream as they walked the new flagstone pavements?

Then as this ragged and crippled creature had fastened itself to Antoine's throat, Antoine had seen it all in visions, seen the crime itself, seen his lover savaged again and again by the monster child's knife, seen Lestat's body dumped into the swamp, seen him rise. Antoine now knew everything. The Dark Blood had rushed into his body like a burning fluid exterminating every human particle in its path. The music, his own music, rose in his ears in dizzying volume. Only music could describe this ineffable power, this raging euphoria.

They had been defeated, both of them, when they went against Claudia and Louis—and Antoine had been hideously burned. That is how Antoine learned what it meant to be Born to Darkness. You could suffer burns like that and endure. You could suffer what should have meant death for a human being, and you could go on. Music and pain, they were the twin mysteries of his existence. Even the Dark Blood itself did not obsess him as did music and pain. As he lay on the four-poster beside Lestat, Antoine saw his pain in bright flashing colors, his mouth open in a perpetual moan. I cannot live like this. And yet he didn't want to die, no, never to die, not even now, not even with the craving for human blood driving him out into the night though his body was nothing but pain, pain scraped by the fabric of his shirt, his trousers, even his boots. Pain and blood and music.

For thirty mortal years, he'd lived like a monster, hideous, scarred, preying on the weakest of mortals, hunting in the crowded Irish immigrant slums for his meals. He could make his music without ever touching the keys of a piano. He heard the music in his head, heard it surge and climb as he moved his fingers in the air. The mingled noises of the rat-infested slums, the roaring laughter from a stevedore's tavern, became a new music to him, caught in the low rumble of voices to the right and to the left, or the cries of his victims. Blood. Give me blood. Music I will possess forever.

Lestat had gone to Europe, chasing after them, those two, Claudia and Louis, who had been his family, his friends, his lovers.

But he had been terrified to attempt such a journey. And he had left Lestat at the docks. "Goodbye to you, Antoine." Lestat had kissed him. "Maybe you will have a life here in the New World, the life I wanted." Gold and gold and gold. "Keep the rooms, keep the things I've given you."

But he hadn't been clever like Lestat. He'd had no skill for living like a mortal among mortals. Not with these songs in his head, these symphonies, and the blood ever beckoning. His own legacy he'd squandered, and Lestat's gold was gone too at last, though where or how he could never remember. He had left New Orleans, journeying north, sleeping in the cemeteries as he made his way.

In St. Louis he'd begun to actually play again. It was the strangest thing. Most of his scars were gone by then. He no longer looked infected and contagious with some disfiguring disease.

It was as if he'd waked from a dream, and for years the violin was his instrument, and he even played for money at mortal gatherings, and managed to become a gentleman again, with clean linen and a small apartment with paintings, a brass clock, and a wooden closet of fine clothes. But all that had come to nothing. He felt loneliness, despair. The world seemed empty of monsters like himself.

He'd wandered out west, why he didn't know. By the 1880s, he'd been playing the piano in the Barbary Coast vice dens of San Francisco and hunting the seamen for blood. He worked his way up from the sailors' saloons to the fancy melodeons and the French and Chinese parlor houses, glutting himself on the riffraff in dark streets where murder was rampant.

Gradually he came to realize the quality parlor houses loved him, even the finest of them, and he was soon surrounded by admiring ladies of the evening, who were a comfort to him, and therefore immune from his murderous thirst.

In the Chinatown brothels, he fell in love with the sweet tender exotic slave girls who delighted in his music.

And finally, in the great music halls, he heard applause for the songs he wrote on the spot, and his dizzying improvisations. He was back in the world again. He was loving it. Dressed like a dandy, he put pomade in his dark hair, clenched a small cheroot between his teeth, and lost himself in the ivory keys, intoxicated by the adulation all around him.

But other vampires crept into his bloody paradise—the first he'd seen since Lestat set sail from the New Orleans docks.

Powerful males, clad in brocade vests and fancy frock coats, obviously using their skills to cheat at cards and dazzle their victims, cast a cold eye on him and threatened him before fleeing themselves. In the dark streets of Chinatown he ran up against a Chinese blood drinker in a long dark coat and black hat who threatened him with a hatchet.

Though he longed desperately to know these vampire strangers—though he longed to trust them, talk with them, share the story of his journey with them—he left San Francisco in terror.

He left behind the pretty waiter girls and courtesans who'd sustained him with their sweet friendship and the easy pickings of the drunken men.

From city to city he'd moved, playing in the small raucous orchestras of theaters wherever he got work. It never lasted very long. He was a vampire after all; he merely looked human; and a vampire cannot pass indefinitely as human in the same close group of humans. They begin to stare, to ask questions, then to veer away, and finally there is some fatal aversion as if they've discovered a leper in their midst.

But his many mortal acquaintances continued to warm his soul. No vampire can live on blood and killing; all vampires need human warmth, or so he thought. He made deep friends now and then, those who allowed it and never questioned his eccentricities, his habits, his icy skin.

The old century died; the new century was born, and he shied away from the electric lights, keeping to the back alleys in blessed darkness. He was completely healed now; there was no sign of his old wounds at all, and indeed, it seemed he'd grown stronger over the years. Yet he felt ugly, loathsome, unfit to live, existing from moment to moment like an addict. He gravitated to the crippled, the diseased, the bohemian, and the downtrodden when he wanted an evening of conversation, just a little cerebral companionship. It kept him from weeping. It kept him from killing too brutally and indiscriminately.

He slept in graveyards when he could find a large and secret crypt, or in coffins in cellars, and now and then almost trapped by the sun he dug straight down into the moist Mother Earth, uttering a prayer that he would die there.

Fear and music and blood and pain. That was still his existence.

The Great War began. The world as he'd known it was coming to an end.

He couldn't clearly remember coming to Boston, only that it had been a long journey and he'd forgotten why he had ever chosen that city. And there for the first time, he'd gone underground for the long sleep. Surely he would die in the earth, buried as he was, week after week, month after month with only the memory of blood bringing him back now and then to uneasy consciousness. Surely this would be the finish. And the inevitable and total darkness would swallow mercilessly any question or passion that had ever obsessed him.

Well, he didn't die, obviously.

Half a century passed before he rose again, hungry, emaciated, desperate, but surprisingly strong. And it was music that brought him forth, but not the music he had so loved.

It was the music of the Vampire Lestat—his old maker—now a rock-star sensation, with music carried on airwaves, blasted from television screens, music seeping from tiny transmitters no bigger than a pack of playing cards to which people listened through plugs in their ears.

Oh, what sweet glory to see Lestat so splendidly restored! How his heart ached to reach him.

The Undead were everywhere now on the new continent. Maybe

they had always been here, spreading, breeding, creating fledglings as
he'd been created. He couldn't guess. He only knew his powers were
greater now; he could read the minds of mortals, hear their thoughts
when he didn't want to hear them, and he could hear that relentless
music, and those strange eerie stories that Lestat told in his little
video films.

We had come from ancient parents out of darkest Egypt: Akasha
and Enkil. Kill the Mother and the Father and we all die, or so the
songs said. What did the Vampire Lestat want with this mortal persona: rock star, outcast, monster, gathering mortals to a concert in
San Francisco, gathering the Undead?

Antoine would have gone out west to see Lestat on the stage. But
he was still struggling with the simplest difficulties of life in the late
twentieth century when the massacres began.

All over the world, it seemed, the Undead were being slaughtered,
as coven houses and vampire taverns were burnt to cinders. Fledglings and old ones were immolated as they fled.

All this Antoine learned from the telepathic cries of brothers and
sisters whom he'd never known in places he'd never been.

"Flee, go to the Vampire Lestat, he will save us!"

Antoine could not fathom it. He played for coins in the subways
of New York, and once set upon by a gang of mortal cutthroats for
his earnings, he slew them all and fled the city making his way south.

The voices of the Undead said it was the Mother, Akasha, who'd
been slaughtering her children, that ancient Egyptian Queen. Lestat
had been taken prisoner by her. Elders were gathering. Antoine, like
so many others, was prey to strange dreams. Frantically he played
his violin in the streets to surround himself with a solitude he could
manage and sustain.

And then the immortal voices of the world fell silent.

Some catastrophe had emptied the planet of blood drinkers.

It seemed he was the last left alive. From city to city he went
playing his violin for coins on street corners, sleeping once again in
graveyards and abandoned cellars, emerging hungry, dazed, longing for some refuge that seemed beyond his reach. He slipped into
crowded taverns or nightclubs in the evening, just to feel human
warmth around him, bodies brushing against him, to swim in the
sound of happy human voices, and the aroma of blood.

What had become of Lestat? Where was he, that shining Titian in his red-velvet frock coat and lace, who had roared with such confidence and power from the rock music stage? He did not know, and he wanted to know, but more acutely he wanted to survive, consciously, in this new world, and he set out to accomplish this.

In Chicago, he managed actual lodgings, and realized reasonable sums from his street-corner playing, and soon a band of mortals gathered to greet him when he appeared each evening. It was a simple matter to move to bars and restaurants again, and once more he found himself seated at the piano in a darkened nightclub with the twenty-dollar bills filling the brandy snifter beside the music stand.

In time he leased an old three-story white frame house in a suburb called Oak Park that was made up of such beautiful structures, and he bought an old steamer trunk in which to sleep by day, and his own piano. He liked his mortal neighbors. He gave them money to hire the gardener or the cleaning lady for him that they recommended. Sometimes he even swept the sidewalks himself in the very early hours of the morning with a big yellow broom. He liked that, the scrape scrape of the broom, and the leaves piled up, curling and brown, and the pavement so clean. Must we disdain all mortal things?

The streets of Oak Park with their great trees were soothing to him. Soon he was shopping in brightly lighted emporiums for decent clothes. And in his comfortable parlor from midnight till dawn he watched television, learning all about this modern world in which he'd emerged, how things were done, how things had to be. A steady stream of dramas, soap operas, news broadcasts, and documentaries soon taught him everything.

He lay back in his large overstuffed easy chair marveling at the blue skies and the brilliant sun he saw before him on the large television screen. He watched sleek and powerful American automobiles speeding on mountain roads and over prairies. He watched a somber, bespectacled teacher speak in sonorous tones of "the ascent of man."

And then there were the films of symphony performances, the full-scale operas, the unending virtuoso concerts! He thought he'd go mad with the beauty of it—witnessing in living color and mesmerizing detail the London Philharmonic play Beethoven's Ninth Symphony, or the great Itzhak Perlman racing through the Brahms Concerto with an orchestra surrounding him.

Going into Chicago to hunt, he now purchased tickets to see splendid performances in the immense opera house, marveling at its size and luxury. He was awake to the wealth of the world. He was awake to an age that seemed made for his sensibilities.

Where was Lestat in this world? What had happened to him? In the music stores, they still sold his old album. You could buy a video of the single concert to which he'd drawn a capacity crowd. But where was the being himself—and would he remember his once-beloved Antoine? Or had he made a legion of followers since those long-ago southern nights?

Hunting was harder in these great times, yes. One had to seek far and wide to find the detestable human vermin who in ages past had been infinitely more numerous and more at hand. He could find no metropolitan cesspools like the old Barbary Coast. But he didn't mind that. He didn't "love" his victims. He never had. He wanted to feed and be done with it.

Once he'd spotted a victim, he was relentless. There was no way for that man or woman to hide. He slipped easily into darkened houses and caressed his mark with rough and eager hands. *Let blood be blood.*

He was soon playing the piano for a salary in a fine restaurant and making plenty of money from tips on top of that. And he learned to hunt more skillfully among the innocent—drinking from one victim after another on crowded dance floors until he had had enough—without killing or crippling anyone. This took discipline, but he could do it. He could do what he had to do to survive now, to be part of this age, to feel vital and resilient and, yes, immortal.

Ambition began to grow in him. He needed papers to live in this world; he needed wealth. Lestat had always had papers to live in the world. Lestat had always had great wealth. In the old nights so long ago, Lestat had been a respected and highly visible gentleman, for whom tailors and shopkeepers had kept late hours, a patron of the arts, a common figure nodding to those he passed in Jackson Square or on the steps of the Cathedral. Lestat had had a lawyer who handled his affairs of the world; Lestat came and went as he chose. "These matters are nothing," said Lestat. "My fortune is divided in many banks. I will always have what I need."

Antoine would do this. He would learn. Yet he had no real knack for it. Surely someone could forge papers for him, he must focus on this. He had to have some safety in this world, and he wanted a vehicle, yes, a powerful American car, so that he could travel miles and miles in one night.

The voices came again.

The Undead were returning, and appearing in great numbers in the cities of North America. And the voices were talking, the voices spoke of the population spreading throughout the world.

The old Queen had been destroyed. But Lestat and a council of immortals had survived her, and the new Mother was now a red-haired woman, ancient as the Queen had been, Mekare, a sorceress, who had no tongue.

Silent this new Queen of the Damned. Silent those immortals who'd survived with her. No one knew what had become of them, where they'd gone.

What was it to Antoine? He cared but he did not care.

The voices spoke of vampire scripture, a canon, so to speak. The Vampire Chronicles. There had been two, and now there were three, and this canon told of what had happened to Lestat and the others. They told of the "Queen of the Damned."

Walking boldly into a brightly lighted bookstore, Antoine bought the volumes, and read them over a week of strange nights.

In the pages of the first book, published long ago, he found himself, nameless, "the musician," with not so much as a physical description except that he'd been a "boy," a mere footnote to the life and adventures of his maker as told by the vampire Louis, that one whom Lestat had so loved, and feared to anger. "Let him get used to the idea, Antoine, and then I'll bring you over. I can't . . . I can't lose them, Louis and Claudia." And they had turned on him, sought to kill him, dumped Lestat's body in the swamp. And after that final battle in flames and smoke when he had fought with Lestat to punish them, Antoine had never been mentioned again.

What did it matter? Claudia had died for it all, unjustly. Louis had survived. The books were filled with stories of other older and more powerful beings.

So where were they now, these great survivors of Queen Akasha's massacre? And how many like Antoine were roaming the world, weak, afraid, without comrades or the consolation of love, clinging to existence as he did?

The voices told him there was no dream coven of elders. They spoke of indifference, lawlessness, a retreat of the ancient ones, of wars for territory that always ended in death. There were notorious vagabond masters who turned mortals into vampires every night until their stamina ran out, and the Dark Trick no longer worked when they attempted it.

Not six months passed before a gang of maverick vampires came after Antoine.

He'd just finished the latest book in the vampire scripture, Lestat's *Tale of the Body Thief.* It was in the back alleys of downtown Chicago. In the early hours they surrounded him with long knives, pasty-faced gangster vampires with sneering lips, and flaming hair, but he was too strong for them, too quick. He found in himself a reserve of the telekinetic power described in the Chronicles, and though he was not strong enough to burn or kill them, he drove them back, slamming them into walls and pavements, bruising and shocking them senseless. That gave him the time he needed to use their long knives to cut off their heads. He had barely time to conceal their bloody remains in garbage heaps before making for his lair.

Voices told him such skirmishes and deaths were occurring in American cities everywhere, and indeed in the cities of the Old World and in Asia.

Things couldn't go on like this with him in such a world. This could mean discovery. This could mean battles of vengeance. Chicago was too rich a plum for the Undead certainly, and Antoine's refuge in Oak Park was too close.

One night his house, his beautiful old graceful white frame house with its rambling porches and gingerbread eaves, was burnt to the ground while he was hunting.

They finally got him in St. Louis.

They called themselves a "coven." They surrounded him and doused him with gasoline and set him on fire. Down into the earth he went to smother the flames and then up again. They came after him. He ran, burnt, in agony, over the miles, outdistancing them easily and burying himself again.

Many things had happened in the world since then.

But not very much of it to him.

In the earth he slept, healing, his mind in a feverish realm of semiconsciousness in which he dreamed he was in New Orleans again and Lestat was listening to his music, Lestat was whispering to him that he had a great talent, and then there were flames.

And then he heard distinctly through his dreams a young vampire speaking to him, and not to him alone but to all the Children of the

Night everywhere. It was a vampire who called himself Benji Mahmoud broadcasting from New York, and how many nights Antoine listened before he rose, he could not say. A lovely rippling piano flooded his ears as Benji spoke, and Antoine knew, absolutely knew, that this was the music of a vampire like himself, that no mortal could have created such intricate, bizarre, and perfect melodies. The vampire Sybelle was her name, said Benji Mahmoud. And sometimes his voice dropped away for her music to take over the airwaves.

Benji Mahmoud and Sybelle prompted Antoine to come to the surface once more and face the bright dangerous electric nights of the new century.

It was the year 2013. This fact alone astonished him. Over twenty years had passed and his burnt flesh was healed. His strength was greater than before. His skin was whiter, his eyes sharper, his ears ever more sensitive.

It was all true what the vampire scripture had said. One healed in the earth, and one grew strong from pain.

The world was filled with sound, waves and waves of sound.

How many other blood drinkers heard Benji Mahmoud and Sybelle's piano? How many other minds transmitted it? He did not know. He only knew that he could hear it, thinly but certainly, and he could hear and feel *them* everywhere, the Children of the Night, too many, surely, listening to the voice of Benji Mahmoud. And they were frightened, these others.

Massacres had started again. Massacres like the Burnings done by Akasha—massacres of vampires in the cities on the other side of the world.

"It is coming for us," said the voices of the frightened ones. "But who is it? Is it the mute Mother, Mekare? Has she turned on us the way Akasha turned? Or is it the Vampire Lestat? Is he the one trying to wipe us out for all our crimes against our own kind, our bickering, our quarreling?"

"Brothers and Sisters of the Night," declared Benji Mahmoud. "We have no parents. We are a tribe without a leader, a tribe without a credo, a tribe without a name." The piano music of Sybelle was masterly, rippling with preternatural genius. Ah, how he loved this. "Children of the Night, Children of Darkness, the Undead, the Immortals, Blood Drinkers, Revenants, why don't we have an honorable and graceful name?" demanded Benji. "I implore you. Do not fight. Do not seek to hurt one another. Band together now against the forces that would wipe us out. Find strength in one another."

Antoine moved with renewed purpose. I am alive again, he thought. I can die a thousand deaths like any coward and come back to life again. He hunted on the margins as before, struggling for clothes, money, lodgings, a new age flaming into color around him. In a small hotel room, he studied his new Apple computer, determined to master it, soon connecting with the website and radio program of Benji Mahmoud.

"Vampires have been slaughtered in Mumbai," declared Benji. "The reports have been confirmed. It is the same as in Tokyo and Beijing. Havens and sanctuaries burnt to the ground and all who fled immolated in their tracks, only the swiftest and the most fortunate surviving to give us the word, the pictures."

A frantic vampire calling from Hong Kong poured out her fears to Benji.

"I appeal to the old ones," said Benji. "To Mekare, Maharet, Khayman, speak to us. Tell us why these immolations have happened. Is a new Time of Burning begun?"

Caller after caller begged for permission to come to Benji and Louis and Armand for protection.

"No. This is not possible," Benji confessed. "Believe me, the safest place for you is where you are. But avoid known coven houses, or vampire bars and taverns. And if you witness this horrific violence, take shelter. Remember those who strike with the Fire Gift must see you in order to destroy you! Don't flee in the open. If you possibly can, go underground."

Finally after many nights, Antoine broke through. In an anxious whisper he told Benji he'd been made by the great Vampire Lestat himself. "I am a musician!" he pleaded. "Allow me to come to you, I beg you. Confirm for me where you are."

"I wish I could, brother," said Benji, "but alas, I cannot. Don't seek to find me. And be careful. These are dreadful times for our kind."

That night late, Antoine went down in the darkened hotel dining room and he played the piano for the small, weary night staff who stopped only now and then to listen to him as he poured his soul out on the keys.

He would call again, from some other number. He would beg Benji to understand. Antoine wanted to play music like Sybelle played music. Antoine had this gift to offer. Antoine was telling the truth when he spoke of his maker. Benji had to understand.

For two months, Antoine worked on his music nightly, and during that time he read the later books of vampire scripture, the memoirs of Pandora, Marius, and Armand.

Now he knew all about the Bedouin, Benji Mahmoud, and his beloved Sybelle—Benji, a boy of twelve when the great vampire Marius had brought him over, and Sybelle, the eternal gamin who had once played only Beethoven's *Appassionata* over and over again, but who now went through the repertoire of all the greats Antoine knew and recent composers of whom he had not dreamed.

Deviled and driven by her playing, Antoine strove for perfection, assailing pianos in bars, restaurants, deserted classrooms and auditoriums, piano stores, and even private homes.

He was now composing music of his own again, breaking piano keys in his fervor, breaking strings.

Another terrible Burning took place in Taiwan.

Benji was plainly angry now as he appealed to the elders to shed light on what was happening to the tribe. "Lestat, where are you? Can you not be our champion against these forces of destruction? Or have you become Cain the slayer of your brothers and sisters yourself!"

At last Antoine had the money to purchase a violin of good quality. He went into the countryside to play under the stars. He rushed into Stravinsky and Bartók, whose work he'd learned from recordings. His head teemed with the new dissonance and wailing of modern music. He understood this tonal language, this aesthetic. It spoke for the fear and the pain, the fear that had become terror, the pain that had become the very blood in his veins.

He had to reach Benji and Sybelle.

More than anything it was critical loneliness that drove Antoine. He knew he'd end up in the earth again if he didn't find someone of his own kind to love. He dreamed of making music with Sybelle.

Am I an elder now? Or am I a maverick to be killed on sight?

One night Benji spoke of the hour, and of the weather, confirming surely that he was indeed broadcasting from the northern East Coast. Filling a leather backpack with his violin and his musical compositions, Antoine started north.

Just outside Philadelphia, he encountered another vagrant blood drinker. He almost fled. But the other came to him with open arms—a lean big-boned vampire with straggly hair and huge eyes, pleading with Antoine not to be frightened and not to hurt him, and they came together, all but sobbing in each other's embrace.

The boy's name was Killer and he was little more than a hundred years old. He'd been made, he said, in the very early days of the twentieth century in a backwater town in Texas by a wanderer like himself who charged Killer to bury his ashes after he'd burnt himself up.

"That's the way a lot of them did it in those days," said Killer, "like the way Lestat describes Magnus making him. They pick an heir when they're sick of it all, give us the Dark Blood, and then we have to scatter the ashes when they're gone. But what did I care? I was nineteen. I wanted to be immortal, and the world was big in 1910. You could go anywhere, do anything at all."

In a cheap motel, by the glimmering light of the muted television, as if it were the flicker of a fireplace, they talked for hours.

Killer had survived the long-ago massacre of Akasha the great Queen. He'd made it all the way to San Francisco in 1985 to hear the Vampire Lestat onstage, only to see hundreds of blood drinkers immolated after the concert. He and his companion Davis had been fatally separated, and Killer, sneaking into the slums of San Francisco, had found himself the next night one of a tiny remnant fleeing the city, thankful to be alive. He never saw Davis again.

Davis was a beautiful black vampire, and Killer had loved him. They'd been members of the Fang Gang in those times. They even wore those letters on their leather jackets and they drove Harleys and they never spent more than two nights in any one place. All over, those times.

"The Burning now, it has to happen," Killer told Antoine. "Things can't go on the way they are. I tell you, before Lestat came on the scene in those days, it wasn't like this. There just weren't so many of us, and me and my friends, we roamed the country towns in peace. There were coven houses then, havens like, and vampire bars where anyone could enter, you know, safe refuge, but the Queen wiped all that away. And with it went the last of vampire law and order. And since those times, the tramps and the mavericks have bred everywhere, and group fights group. There's no discipline, no rules. I tried to team up with the young ones in Philadelphia. They were like mad dogs."

"I know that old story," Antoine said, shivering, remembering those flames, those unspeakable flames. "But I have to reach Benji and Sybelle. I have to reach Lestat."

In all these years, Antoine had never told the story of his own life to anyone. He had not even told it to himself. And now, with the lamp of the Vampire Chronicles illuminating his strange journey, he poured it out to Killer unstintingly. He feared derision, but none came.

"He was my friend, Lestat," Antoine confessed. "He told me about his lover, Nicolas, who had been a violinist. He said he couldn't speak his heart to his little family, to Louis or Claudia, that they would laugh at him. So he spoke his heart only to me."

"You go to New York, my friend, and Armand will burn you to cinders," said Killer. "Oh, not Benji or Sybelle, no, and maybe not even Louis . . . but Armand will do it and they won't bat an eye. And they can do it too. They have Marius's blood in their veins, those two. Even Louis's powerful now, got the blood of the older ones in him. But Armand is the one who kills. There are eight million people in Manhattan and four members of the Undead. I warn you, Antoine, they won't listen to you. They won't care that Lestat made you. Least I don't think they will. Hell, you won't even have a chance to tell them. Armand will hear you coming. Then he'll kill you on sight. You do know they have to see you to burn you up, don't you? They can't do it unless they can see you. But Armand will hunt you down and you won't be able to hide."

"But I have to go," Antoine said. He burst into tears. He wrapped his arms tight around himself and rocked back and forth on the edge of the bed. His long black hair fell down over his face. "I have to get back to Lestat. I have to. And if anyone can help me find him, it's Louis, isn't it?"

"Hell, man," said Killer. "Don't you get it? Everybody's looking for Lestat. And these Burnings are happening now. And they're moving west. No one's seen hide nor hair of Lestat in the last two years, man. And the last sighting in Paris could have been bogus. There's lots of swaggering dudes walking around pretending to be Lestat. I was down in New Orleans last year and there were so many fake Lestats swaggering around in pirate shirts and cheap boots, you wouldn't believe it. The place is overrun. They drove me out of the city after one night."

"I can't go on alone," said Antoine. "I have to reach *them*. I have to play my violin for Sybelle. I have to be part of them."

"Look, old buddy," said Killer, softened and sympathetic and putting his arm around Antoine. "Why don't you just come out west with me? We both rode out the last Burning, didn't we? We'll ride this one out too."

Antoine couldn't answer. He was in such pain. He saw the pain in bright explosive colors in his mind as he had when he was so badly burned years and years ago. Red and yellow and orange was this pain. He took up the violin and began to play it, softly, as softly as you can play a violin, and he let it mourn with him for all he'd ever been or might have been and then sing of his hopes and dreams.

The next night after they'd hunted the country roads, he told Killer of his loneliness over the centuries, of how he'd grown to love mortals the way Lestat had once loved him, and how he'd pulled away from them finally, always afraid that he couldn't make another, as Lestat had made him. Lestat had been badly wounded when he'd made Antoine. It hadn't been easy. It was nothing like the majestic procedure of the Dark Trick described in the pages of Marius's memoir, *Blood and Gold*. Marius made it sound like the giving of a sacrament when he'd made Armand in the 1500s in those Renaissance rooms in Venice, filled with Marius's paintings. It had been nothing like that at all.

"Well, I can tell you as a fact," said Killer, "that lately it's not been working at all. Right before these massacres started, they were all talking about it, how hard it was to bring somebody over. It was like the Blood was played out. Too many in the Blood. Think about it. The power comes from the Mother, from that demon, Amel, who entered into Akasha and then passed into Mekare, the Queen of the Damned. Well, maybe Amel really is an invisible creature with tentacles just like Mekare once said, and those tentacles have stretched just as far as they can. They just can't stretch forever."

Killer sighed. Antoine looked away. He was obsessed.

"I'm going to tell you something horrible I hate to tell anybody," said Killer. "Last two times I tried to bring somebody over, it flat-out failed. Now it was never like that before, I can tell you." Killer shook his head. "I tried to bring over the most beautiful little girl I ever saw in one of those towns back there, and it just did not work. It just didn't work. Come dawn, I did the only thing I could do—chop off her head and bury her, and I'd promised her eternal life and I had to do that. She was a zombie thing, and she couldn't even talk and her heart wasn't beating, but she wasn't dead."

Antoine shuddered. He'd never had the courage to try. But if this was true, if he did not have the slightest hope of ever ending this loneliness by making another, well, then, that was all the more reason to press on.

Killer laughed under his breath. "It used to seem so easy," he said, "back when I was making members of the old Fang Gang, but now the filth and the rabble and the trash are everywhere, and even if you make them, they'll turn on you, rob you, betray you, and take off with someone else. I tell you these massacres have to come. They have to. There's bad dudes selling the Blood. Can you believe? Selling the Blood. Least they were. I expect they're played out too and running for their lives now like everybody else."

Again Killer begged Antoine to stay with him.

"For all we know, Armand and Louis and Lestat are all in this together," Killer said. "Maybe they're all doing it, the big heroes of the Vampire Chronicles. But these things have to happen, like I said. I know this is what Benji thinks, but he won't say it. He can't. But this is worse than before. Can you hear them, the voices? There was a Burning last night in Kathmandu. Think about it, man. It's going to move across India, whoever's doing it, and then into the Middle East. It's worse than the last time. It's being more thorough. I can sense it. I remember. I know."

Tearfully, they parted a short way southeast of New York. Killer wouldn't go any farther. Benji's broadcast the night before had confirmed Killer's worst fears. There had been no direct witnesses to the Burning when it hit Kolkata. Vampires for hundreds of miles caught images of the immolation. They were fleeing west.

"All right, if you're determined to go through with this," said Killer. "I'll tell you what I know. Armand and the others live in a mansion on the Upper East Side half a block from Central Park. It's three townhouses linked together, and each one's got a door to the street. There are little Greek columns on each little porch and big limbed trees growing out front surrounded by little skirts of iron.

"These townhouses are maybe five stories high and they've got these fancy little iron balconies up high on the windows that aren't balconies at all."

"I know what you mean," said Antoine gratefully. He was picking up the images from Killer's mind, but it seemed rude to say so.

"It's gorgeous inside," said Killer, "like a palace, and they leave all those windows open on nights like this, you know, and they'll see you long before you ever see them. They could be anywhere up in those high windows looking out long before you even get close. The mansion's got a name, Trinity Gate. And a lot of blood drinkers can tell you, it's the gate of death to us if we go there. And remember, my friend, it's Armand who's the killer. Back years ago, when Lestat was down and out in New Orleans—after he'd met Memnoch the Devil—it was Armand who kept the trash away from him. Lestat was sleeping kind of in this chapel in this old convent. . . ."

"I remember from the books," said Antoine.

"Yeah, well, it was Armand who cleared the town. Antoine, please don't go there. He'll blast you right off the face of the Earth."

"I have to go," said Antoine. How could he ever explain to this simple survivor that existence was unbearable to him as it was? Even this blood drinker's company had not been enough to fill the gnawing emptiness inside him.

They embraced before parting. Killer repeated that he was headed out to California. If the massacres were moving west, well, he'd move west too. He'd heard tell of a great vampire physician who lived in Southern California, an immortal named Fareed, who actually studied the Dark Blood under microscopes and sometimes sheltered roamers like Killer, if they would donate some tissue and some blood for experiments.

Fareed had been made with ancient blood by a vampire named Seth, who was almost as old as the Mother. And nobody could hurt Seth or Fareed. Well, Killer was going to look for that doctor in California because he figured that was his only hope. He begged Antoine to change his mind and come with him. But Antoine could not.

Antoine wept afterwards. Alone again. And as he lay down to sleep that morning, he heard the voices wailing, powerful ones crying out, conveying the word. The Burning was annihilating the vampires of India. A great sense of doom filled Antoine. When he thought of all the years he'd roamed and slept in the earth he felt he had wasted the gift Lestat gave him. Waste. He had never thought of it as precious. It had been only a new kind of suffering.

But that's not what it was for Benji Mahmoud. "We are a tribe and we should think like one," Benji said often. "Why should Hell have dominion over us?"

Antoine was bound and determined to continue. He had a plan.

He wouldn't try to speak to these powerful Manhattan vampires. He would let his music speak for him. Hadn't he done that all his long life?

Outside the city—before he stole a car to drive into Manhattan—he had his black hair cut and trimmed modern style by a precious little girl in a salon full of perfume and lighted candles, and then outfitted himself in a fine Armani suit of black wool with a Hugo Boss shirt and a gleaming Versace silk tie. Even his shoes were fancy, made of Italian leather, and he carefully rubbed his white skin with oil and clean paper ash to make himself look less luminescent in the bright city lights. If all these blandishments gave them a moment's pause he would use that pause to make the violin sing.

At last he was on foot on Fifth Avenue, having ditched the stolen car on a side street, when he heard the wild unmistakable music of Sybelle. And there, yes, was the great townhouse complex described by Killer, Trinity Gate, facing downtown with its many warmly lighted windows, and he could all but hear the powerful heart of Armand.

As he dropped the violin case at his feet, and tuned his instrument rapidly, Sybelle broke off the long turbulent piece she'd been playing and suddenly moved into the soft beautiful Chopin étude "Tristesse."

Crossing Fifth Avenue, he moved towards the doors of the mansion, already playing with her, following her as he glided into the soft sweet unmistakably sad melody of the étude and racing with her into the more violent phrasing. He heard her hesitate and then her playing moved on, slowly again, and his violin sang with it, weaving high above her. The tears rolled down Antoine's cheeks; he couldn't stop them, though he knew they would be tinged with blood.

On and on he went with her, moving beneath her into the deepest and darkest notes he could make on the G string.

She stopped.

Silence. He thought he would collapse. In a blur he saw mortals gathered around him, watching him, and suddenly he brought down his bow, ripping away from the gentle caressing music of Chopin into the strong full melodies of Bartók's Concerto for Violin, playing both orchestra lines and the violin lines in a torrent of wild, dissonant agonized notes.

He saw nothing suddenly, though he knew the crowd had thickened and no music answered him from the keyboard of Sybelle. But this was his heart, his song now, as he plunged deeper and deeper into the Bartók, his tempo speeding up, becoming almost inhuman, as on and on he went.

His soul sang with the music. It became his own melodies and glissandi as his thoughts sang with it.

Let me in, I beg you, let me in. Louis, let me in. Made by Lestat, never having had a chance to know you, never meant to harm you or Claudia, those long-ago times, forgive me, let me in. Benji, my guiding light, let me in. Benji, my consolation in unending darkness, let me in. Armand, I beg you, find a place in your heart for me, let me in.

But soon his words were lost, he was no longer thinking in words or syllables but only in the music, only in the throbbing notes. He was swaying wildly as he played. He no longer cared whether or not he looked or sounded human, and deep in his heart he was aware that if he were to die now, he would not revolt against it, not with any molecule of his being, because the death sentence would come upon him by his own hand and for what he truly was. This music was what he truly was.

Silence.

He had to wipe the blood from his eyes. He had to, and slowly, he reached for his handkerchief and then held it trembling, unable to see.

They were close. The mortal crowd meant nothing to him. He could hear that powerful heart, that ancient heart that had to be Armand's heart. Cold preternatural flesh touched his flesh. Someone had taken the handkerchief from him, and this one was blotting his eyes for him, and wiping the thin streaks of blood from his face.

He opened his eyes.

It was Armand. Auburn hair, face of a boy, and the dark burning eyes of an immortal who'd roamed for half a millennium. Oh, this truly was the face of a seraph right off the ceiling of a church.

My life is in your hands.

On all sides of him, people were applauding, men and women clapping for his performance—just innocent people, people who didn't know what he was. People who didn't even notice these blood tears, this fatal giveaway. The night was bright with streetlamps, and rows and rows of yellow windows, and the daytime warmth was coming up from the pavements, and the tall tender saplings shed their very tiny leaves in a warm breeze.

"Come inside," said Armand softly. He felt Armand's arm around him. Such strength. "Don't be afraid," said Armand.

There stood the incandescent Sybelle smiling at him, and beside her the unmistakable Benji Mahmoud in a black fedora with his small hand extended.

"We'll take care of you," said Armand. "Come inside with us."

8

Marius and the Flowers

FOR HOURS, he'd been painting furiously, his only light in the old ruined house an old-fashioned lantern.

But the lights of the city poured in the broken-out windows, and the great roar of the traffic on the boulevard was like the roar of a river, quieting him as he painted.

His left thumb hooked into an old-fashioned wooden palette, his pockets filled with tubes of acrylic paint, he used only one brush until it fell to pieces, covering the broken walls with brilliant pictures of the trees, the vines, the flowers he'd seen in Rio de Janeiro and the faces, yes, always the faces of the beautiful Brazilians he encountered everywhere, walking through the nighttime rain forest of Corcovado, or on the endless beaches of the city, or in the noisy garishly lighted nightclubs he frequented, collecting expressions, images, flashes of hair or shapely limbs as he might have collected pebbles from the frothy margin of the ocean.

All this he poured into his feverish painting, rushing as if at any moment the police would appear with the old tiresome admonitions. "Sir, you cannot paint in these abandoned buildings, we have told you."

Why did he do it? Why was he so loath to interfere with the mortal world? Why didn't he compete with those brilliant native painters who spread their murals out in the freeway underpasses and on crumbling favela walls?

Actually, he would be moving on to something much more challenging, yes, he had been giving it a lot of thought, wanting to move to some godforsaken desert place where he might paint on the rocks and the mountains confident that all would restore themselves in time as the inevitable rains would wash away all that he'd created. He wouldn't be competing with human beings there, would he? He wouldn't hurt anybody.

Seemed for the last twenty years of his life, his motto had been the same as many a doctor had taken in this world: "First, do no harm."

The problem with retiring to a desert place was that Daniel would hate it. And keeping Daniel happy was the second rule of his life, as his own sense of well-being, his own capacity to open his eyes each evening with some desire to actually rise from the dead and celebrate the gift of life, was connected to and sustained by making Daniel happy.

And Daniel was certainly happy now in Rio de Janeiro. Tonight Daniel was hunting in the old Leda section of Rio, feasting slowly and stealthily among the dancing, singing, partying crowds, drunk no doubt on music as well as on blood. Ah, the young ones with their insatiable thirst.

But Daniel was a disciplined hunter, master of the Little Drink in a crowd, and a slayer of the evildoer only. Marius was certain of that.

It had been months since Marius had touched human flesh, months since he'd lowered his lips to that heated elixir, months since he'd felt the fragile yet indomitable pulse of some living thing struggling consciously or unconsciously against his remorseless hunger. It had been a heavy, powerful Brazilian man whom he stalked into the darkened woods of Corcovado, flushing him deeper and deeper into the rain forest and then dragging him from his hiding place for a long slow repast.

When had it happened that arterial blood was not enough, and he must rip out the heart and suck it dry also? When had it started that he had to lick the most vicious wounds for the little juice they would yield? He could exist without this, yet he couldn't resist it, and so he sought—or so he told himself—to make the very most of it when he feasted. There had been but a mangled mess of remains to bury afterwards. But he'd kept a trophy, as he so often did—not just the thousands in American dollars in drug money that the victim had been carrying, but a fine gold Patek Philippe watch. Why had he done that? Well, it seemed pointless to bury such an artifact, but timepieces had of late begun to fascinate him. He had become faintly superstitious about them and knew it. These were remarkable times, and timepieces themselves reflected this in intricate and beautiful ways.

Let it be for now. No hunting. No hunting needed. And the watch was secure on his left wrist, a surprising ornament for him, but so what?

He closed his eyes and listened. Out of his hearing the traffic of the boulevard died away, and the voices of Rio de Janeiro rose as if the sprawling metropolis of eleven million souls were the most magnificent choir ever assembled.

Daniel.

Quickly, he locked in on his companion: the tall thin boyish young man with the violet eyes and the ashen hair whom Lestat had so aptly called "the Devil's Minion." It was Daniel who had interviewed the vampire who was Louis de Pointe du Lac, thereby giving birth unwittingly and innocently enough decades ago to the collection of books known as the Vampire Chronicles. It was Daniel who'd captured the damaged heart of the Vampire Armand and been brought over by him into Darkness. It was Daniel who had languished for many a year—shocked, deranged, lost, unable to care for himself—in Marius's care until only a couple of years ago when his sanity, ambition, and dreams had been restored to him.

And there he was, Daniel, in his tight white short-sleeved polo shirt and dungarees, dancing wildly and beautifully with two shapely chocolate-skinned women under the red lights of a small club, the floor around them so packed that the crowd itself appeared to be one writhing organism.

Very well. All is well. Daniel is smiling. Daniel is happy.

Earlier that evening, Daniel and Marius had been to the Teatro Municipal for a performance of the London Ballet, and Daniel had pleaded in appealing gentlemanly fashion for Marius to join him as he haunted the nightclubs. But Marius couldn't bring himself to give in to that request.

"You know what I have to do," he'd said, heading for the old pastel-blue ruined house he'd chosen for his present work. "And you stay away from the clubs the blood drinkers frequent. You promise me!"

No wars with those little fiends. Rio is vast. Rio is surely the greatest hunting ground in the world with its teeming masses, and its high star-spangled skies, its ocean breezes, its great drowsy green trees, its endless pulse from sunset to sunrise.

"At the slightest sign of trouble, you come back to me."

But what if there really were trouble?

What if there were?

Was Benji Mahmoud, broadcasting out of New York, right about the coven house in Tokyo having been deliberately burnt to the ground, and all those fleeing from it burnt in their tracks? When a "vampire refuge" in Beijing had burned the next night, Benji had said, "Is this a new Burning? Will this Burning be as fearful as the last? Who is behind this horror?"

Benji hadn't been born when the last Burning happened. No, and Marius was not convinced that this was indeed another Burning. Yes, coven houses in India were being destroyed. But all too likely it was simply war amongst the scum, of which Marius had seen enough in his long life to know that such battles were inevitable. Or some ancient one, sick of the intrigues and skirmishes of the young, had stepped forth to annihilate those who had offended him.

Yet Marius had told Daniel tonight, "Stay away from that coven house in Santa Teresa." He sent the message telepathically now to Daniel with all the force he could put behind it. "You see another blood drinker, you come back here!"

Was there a response? A faint whisper?

He wasn't sure.

He stood still, the palette in his left hand, the brush lifted in his right, and the strangest most unexpected idea came over him.

What if he himself went to the coven house and burnt them out? He knew where it was. He knew there were twenty young blood drinkers who called it a safe haven. What if he were to go now, and wait until the early hours came, when they'd be returning home, slinking back to their filthy makeshift graves beneath the foundations, and then burn them out, down to the last one, slamming the rafters with the Fire Gift until the structure and its inhabitants were no more?

He could see it as if he were doing it! He could all but feel the Fire Gift concentrating behind his forehead, all but feel that lovely burst of strength when the telekinetic force leapt out like the tongue of a serpent!

Flames and flames. How gorgeous were these flames, dancing against his imagination as if in cinematic slow motion, rolling, expanding, rollicking upwards.

But this was not something he wanted to do. This was not something he had ever in all his long existence wanted to do—destroy his own kind for the sheer pleasure of it.

He shook himself all over, wondering how in the world he had even thought of such a thing.

Ah, but you do want to do it.

"I do?" he asked. Again, he saw that old colonial house burning, that multistoried mansion in its gardens in Santa Teresa, white arches engulfed in flames, the young blood drinkers spinning in flame like whirling dervishes.

"No." He spoke it aloud. "This is a repulsive ugly image."

For one moment he stood stock-still. He listened with all his powers for the presence of another immortal, some unwelcome and intrusive being who might have drawn closer to him than he should ever have allowed.

He heard nothing.

But these alien thoughts had not originated with him, and a chill passed through him. What force outside himself was powerful enough to do this?

He heard faint laughter. It was close, like an invisible being whispering in his ear. Indeed it was inside his head.

What right has that trash to threaten you and your beloved Daniel? Burn them out; burn the house down around them; burn them as they escape.

He saw the flames again, saw the square tower of the old mansion engulfed, saw the adobe tiles of the roofs cascading into the flames and again the Blood Children running. . . .

"No," he said quietly. He lifted the brush in a brave show of nonchalance and caught up a thick daub of Hooker's green on the wall before him, shaping it almost mechanically into an explosion of leaves, ever more detailed leaves. . . .

Burn them. I tell you. Burn them before they burn the young one. Why are you not listening to me?

He continued to paint, as if he were being watched, determined to ignore this outrageous intrusion.

It grew louder suddenly, distinct, so loud it seemed to be not in his head but in this long shadowy room. "I tell you burn them!" It was almost a sobbing voice.

"And who are you?"

No answer. Simply the quiet suddenly of the old predictable noises. Rats scurrying about in this old house. The lantern giving off a low sputter. And that waterfall of traffic that never stopped, and a plane circling above.

"Daniel," he said aloud. *Daniel.*

The noises of the night enveloped him suddenly, deafening him. He threw down the palette and took his iPhone from his coat pocket, quickly stabbing in Daniel's number.

"Come home now," he said. "I'll meet you there."

He stood stranded in the room for a moment, looking at the long spread of color and figure that he had created in this anonymous and unimportant place. Then he snuffed out the lantern and left it behind.

In less than an hour, he walked into his penthouse suite at the Copacabana Hotel to find Daniel lying on the moss-green velvet couch, ankles crossed, head propped on the arm. The windows were open to the white balustraded veranda, and beyond sang the shining ocean.

The room was dark, illuminated only by the bright night sky over the beach and an open laptop computer on the polished coffee table from which the voice of Benji Mahmoud was holding forth on the sorrows of the Undead around the planet.

"What's the matter?" Daniel said, at once getting to his feet.

For a moment, Marius couldn't answer. He was staring at the bright, youthful, and sensitive face, at the appealing eyes, and the fresh young preternatural skin, and he could hear nothing but the beating of Daniel's heart.

Slowly the voice of Benji Mahmoud penetrated. ". . . reports of young vampires immolated in Shanghai, and in Taiwan, in Delhi . . ."

Respectfully, patiently, Daniel waited.

Marius moved past him in silence and went through the open doors to the white railing and let the ocean breeze wash over him as he looked up at the pale and luminous Heavens. Below, the beach was white beyond the traffic moving on the avenue.

Burn them! How can you look at him and think of their hurting him? Burn them, I tell you. Destroy that house. Destroy them all. Hunt them down. . . .

"Stop it," he whispered, his words lost in the breeze. "Tell me who you are."

Low laughter rolling into silence. And then the Voice was against his ear again. "I would never hurt him or you, don't you know that? But what are they to you but an offense? Were you not glad, secretly, when Akasha hunted them down in the streets and the back alleys and in the woods and in the swamps? Were you not exultant to have stepped forth on Mount Ararat above the world, unharmed, with your mighty friends?"

"You're wasting my time," said Marius, "if you don't identify yourself."

"In time, beautiful Marius," said the Voice. "In time, and oh, I have always so loved the flowers. . . ."

Laughter.

The flowers. There flashed into his mind the flowers he'd painted tonight on the cracked and chipped wall of the abandoned house. But what could this mean? What could this conceivably mean?

Daniel was standing next to him.

"I don't want you to leave me again," Marius said under his breath, still staring out at the shining horizon. "Not just now, not tomorrow, not for I don't know how many nights. I want you at my side. Do you hear me?"

"Very well," Daniel said agreeably.

"I know I try your patience," said Marius.

"And haven't I tried yours?" asked Daniel. "Would I be here or anywhere if it wasn't for you?"

"We'll do things," said Marius as though placating a restless spouse, a demanding spouse. "We'll go out tomorrow; we'll hunt together. There are films we should see, I don't remember the names now, I can't think—."

"Tell me what's the matter?"

From the living room came the voice of Benji Mahmoud. "Go to the website. See the images for yourselves. See the photographs being posted hourly. Death and death and death to our kind. I tell you it is a new Burning."

"You don't believe all that, do you?" Daniel asked.

Marius turned and slipped his arm around Daniel's waist. "I don't know," he said frankly. But he managed a reassuring smile. Seldom had another blood drinker ever trusted in him so completely as this one, this one salvaged so easily and so selfishly from madness and disintegration.

"Whatever you say," said Daniel.

I have always so loved the flowers.

"Yes, humor me for now," said Marius. "Stay close . . . where . . ."

"I know. Where you can protect me."

Marius nodded. Again he saw painted flowers, but not the flowers of tonight in this vast tropical city but flowers painted long ago on another wall, flowers of a green garden in which he'd walked in his dreams, right into the shimmering Eden that he had created. Flowers. Flowers shivering in their marble vases as if in some church or shrine . . . flowers.

Beyond the banks of fresh and fragrant flowers in the lamp-lit shrine sat the immovable pair: Akasha and Enkil.

And around Marius there formed the gardens he had created for their walls, resplendent with lilies and roses and the twining of green vines.

The twining of vines.

"Come inside," said Daniel gently, coaxingly. "It's early. If you don't want to go out again, there's a film I want you to see tonight. Come on, let's go in."

Marius wanted to say yes, of course. He wanted to move. But he stood still at the railing staring out, this time trying to find the stars beyond the veil of the clouds. *The flowers.*

Another voice was talking from the laptop on the coffee table behind him, a young female blood drinker somewhere in the world pleading for reassurance over the wires or airwaves as she poured out her heart. "And they say it happened in Iran, a refuge there up in smoke, and nobody survived, nobody."

"But then how do we know?" asked Benji Mahmoud.

"Because they found it like that the next night and all the others were gone, dead, burned. Benji, what can we do? Where are the old ones? Are they the ones doing this to us?"

9

The Story of Gregory

GREGORY DUFF COLLINGSWORTH STOOD watching and listening in Central Park. A tall male of compact and well-proportioned build, with very short black hair and black eyes, he stood in the deep fragrant darkness of a thicket of trees, listening with his powerful preternatural ears and seeing with his powerful preternatural eyes all that was taking place—with Antoine and Armand and Benji and Sybelle—inside of the *Belle Époque* mansion in which Armand's family now lived.

In his English bespoke gray suit and brown shoes, and with his darkly tanned skin, Gregory looked very much like the corporate executive that he had been for decades. Indeed his pharmaceutical empire was one of the most successful in the international marketplace right now, and he was one of those immortals who had always been highly capable at managing wealth "in the real world."

He had come from Switzerland not only to attend to business in his New York offices, but to spy upon the fabled coven of New York at close hand.

He'd picked up the raging emotions of the young blood drinker Antoine as the boy had driven into the city this evening, and if Armand had tried to destroy Antoine, Gregory would have intervened, instantly and effectively, and taken the boy away with him. This he would have done out of the goodness of his heart.

Decades ago, outside the Vampire Lestat's one and only rock concert in San Francisco, Gregory had intervened to save a black blood drinker named Davis, carrying him up and away from the carnage wreaked upon his hapless cohorts by the Queen of Heaven, who gazed pitilessly upon the scene from a nearby hill.

In the case of this complex and interesting young blood drinker, Antoine, Gregory could easily have deflected any blast of the Fire Gift coming directly at the fledgling, especially from one so young and inexperienced as the notorious Armand.

Not that Gregory had anything against Armand. Quite the opposite. He was as eager to meet him in some ways as he was to meet any blood drinker on the planet, though in his heart of hearts he nourished the precious dream of meeting Lestat above all other hopes. Gregory had come here this very evening to spy on the Upper East Side vampires because he thought surely Lestat had come to join them by now. If Lestat had been there, which he was not, Gregory would have come knocking at the door.

Benji Mahmoud's broadcasts had Gregory's understanding and sympathy and he had wanted to assure himself once again that Benji was not the dupe of powerful brothers and sisters, but in fact an authentic soul putting forth the idea of a future for the blood drinker tribe. He had been assured. Indeed Benji was not only the genuine article but something of a rebel in the house, as arguments Gregory had overheard easily proved.

"Oh, brave new world that hath such blood drinkers in it," Gregory sighed, pondering whether he should make himself known right now to the refined and erudite vampires of the residence in the middle of the block before him or hold back.

Whenever he did reveal himself, the secretive existence he'd guarded for well over a thousand years would be inalterably influenced, and he was not in fact ready for the measures that would have to be taken when that occurred.

No, best for now to hang back, to listen, to try to learn.

That had always been his way.

Gregory was six thousand years old. He'd been made by Queen Akasha and was very likely only the fourth blood drinker to be created by her, after the defection of her blood drinker steward Khayman and the accursed twins, Mekare and Maharet, who became the rebels of the First Brood.

Gregory had been in the royal palace the night that the vampire race was born. He hadn't been called Gregory then, but Nebamun, and that was the name he'd used in the world until the third century after Christ—when he took the name of Gregory and began a new and enduring life.

Nebamun had been a lover of Akasha, chosen from the special guard she'd brought with her from the city of Nineveh into Egypt, and as such, Nebamun had not expected to live very long. He was nineteen years old, robust and healthy, when the Queen selected him for the bedchamber and just twenty years old the night the Queen became a blood drinker and brought King Enkil over with her into the curse.

He'd been hiding helpless inside a huge gold-plated chest, the lid propped so that he might see the full horror of the conspirators stabbing the King and the Queen on that night—unable to protect his sovereign. Then with fearful and horrified eyes, he'd seen a swirling cloud of blood particles above the dying Queen, and seen that cloud drawn down into her, seemingly through her many obviously fatal wounds. He'd seen her rise, eyes like the painted orbs of a statue, her skin flashing white in the lamplight. He'd seen her sink her teeth into the neck of the dying Enkil.

Those memories were as vivid to him now as ever—he felt the desert heat, the cooling breeze off the Nile. He heard the cries and whispers of the murderous conspirators. He saw those gold-threaded curtains tied back to the blue-painted columns, and he saw even the distant indifferent and brilliant stars in the black desert sky.

Like a loathsome thing she'd been when she crawled atop her husband's body. To see him jerked into life by the mysterious blood as he drank from her wrist had been a frightful sight.

Nebamun might have gone mad after that, but he was too young, too strong, too optimistic by nature for madness. He had laid low, as they say now. He had survived.

But he'd been living with a death sentence for quite some time. Everyone knew that to please her jealous King Enkil, Akasha did away with her lovers in a matter of months. The King was said not to mind a steady stream of consorts in and out of his Queen's bedroom in the cool of the evening, but he feared any one rising in power, and though Nebamun had been reassured a hundred times by Akasha's affectionate whispers that he was not to be put to death anytime soon, Nebamun knew otherwise, and he had lost all skill at pleasing her, and spent many hours merely thinking about his life, and the meaning of life in general, and getting drunk. He'd had a great passion for life ever since he could remember, and did not want to die.

Once the Queen and King had been infected by the demon Amel, the Queen seemed utterly to have forgotten about Nebamun.

He'd gone back into the guard, defending the palace against those who called the King and Queen monsters. He told no one what he had witnessed. Again and again, he pondered that eerie cloud of bloody particles, that living swirling mass of tiny gnatlike points that had been sucked into the Queen as if by an intake of breath. She'd tried to make a new cult of it, believing firmly that she was now a goddess, and the "will of the gods" had subjected her to this divine violence because of her innate virtue and the needs of the land she ruled.

Well, that was, as they say these days, a load of bunk. Yes, Nebamun had believed in magic, and yes, he'd believed in gods and demons, but he had always been practical in a ruthless way, like many of his time. Besides, gods even if they did exist could be capricious and evil. And when the captive witches Mekare and Maharet explained how this seeming "miracle" had happened, that it was no more than the caprice of a vagrant spirit, Nebamun had smiled.

Once the rebels were born under the rule of the renegade blood drinker Khayman, with Mekare and Maharet to spread "The Divine Blood" with them, Nebamun had been called back into the Queen's presence, and made into a blood drinker without explanation or ceremony until he'd risen thirsting and half mad, and dreaming only of draining human victims of all the life and blood they contained.

"You are now the head of my blood army," the Queen had explained. "You will be called the 'Guard of the Queens Blood,' and you will hunt down the rebels of the First Brood as they dare to call themselves and all the misbegotten blood drinkers made by them who have dared to rebel against me and my King and my laws."

Blood drinkers were gods, the Queen had told Nebamun. Now he too was a god. And at that point, he'd actually started to believe it. How else to explain what he saw now with the new vision of the Blood? His heightened senses bedeviled and tantalized him. He fell in love with the song of the wind, with the rich colors that pulsed all around him in the flowers and drowsy palm trees of the palace gardens, with the chanting pulse of those succulent humans upon whom he fed.

For a thousand years he'd been the dupe of superstition. The world had seemed a grim and unchangeable place to him, full of folly and misery and injustice, and blood drinker fighting blood drinker as incessantly as human fought human, when he'd finally sought the refuge of Mother Earth as so many others had done.

He knew with an aching heart what young Antoine had suffered. Only one blood drinker in existence claimed to have never known such burial and rebirth, and that was the great indominable Maharet.

Well, maybe the time had come for him to make himself known to Maharet, and to talk of those olden times. *You've always known that it was I, Captain of the Queen's soldiers, who separated you aeons ago from your sister—who put the two of you in coffins, and sent you off on rafts in different seas.*

Was not the world of the Undead poised for destruction if old secrets and old horrors were not confronted and examined by those who knew the stories from the earliest nights?

In truth, Gregory was no longer the Captain of the hated "Queens Blood" who had done those things. He remembered those times, yes, but not the force of personality or attitude behind the memories, or the means by which he'd survived those endless nights of war and bloodshed. Who was Maharet? He did not really know.

When he rose in the third century of the Common Era, a new life for him had begun. Gregory was the name he'd chosen for himself in those nights, and he had been Gregory ever since, acquiring names and wealth over the millennia as he needed them, never again resorting to madness, or the earth, but slowly building a realm for himself with wealth and love. The wealth was easy to acquire, so easy in fact that he marveled at beggar mavericks like Antoine and Killer—and his beloved Davis—who tramped through eternity, and the love of other blood drinkers had been easy to acquire as well.

His Blood Wife of all these centuries was named Chrysanthe, and it was she who'd educated him in the ways of the Christian era and the waning Roman Empire when he'd brought her from the great Arab Christian city of Hira—a shining capital on the Euphrates—to Carthage in North Africa, where they'd lived for many years. There she'd taught him Greek and Latin, offering the poetry, the histories, and the philosophies of cultures unknown to him when he'd gone into the earth.

There she explained to him the marvels he'd embraced the moment he'd risen, and how the world had actually changed, changed when he had thought the world unchanging, as did all those with whom he had once shared humanity and the Blood.

He came to love Chrysanthe as he had once loved his first Blood Wife of long ago, the lost pale-eyed and yellow-haired Sevraine.

Ah, such wonders he'd discovered in those early years as the great Roman Empire came tumbling down around him—a world of metals, monuments, and art that had been inconceivable to his Egyptian mind.

And ever since the world had been changing, each new miracle and invention, each new attitude, ever more astonishing than those which had come before.

He had been on an upwards trajectory ever since those early centuries. And he held close to him the very same companions he'd acquired in those first few hundred years.

Very soon after he and Chrysanthe had taken up residence in their palace by the sea in Carthage, they'd been joined by a comely and dignified one-legged Greek named Flavius who told of being made by a powerful and wise female blood drinker named Pandora, consort of a Roman blood drinker, Marius, the keeper of the King and Queen.

Flavius had fled the household of Marius because Marius had never consented to his making, and when he'd come upon the household of Chrysanthe and Gregory in Carthage, he'd thrown himself on their mercy, and they had gladly taken him in—worthy to be Blood Kin. He'd lived in Athens as well as Antioch, in Ephesus and in Alexandria, and had visited Rome. He knew the mathematics of Euclid and the Hebrew scriptures in their Greek translation, and spoke of Socrates and Plato and the Meditations of Marcus Aurelius and the natural history of Pliny and the satire of Juvenal and Petronius, and the writings of Tertullian and Augustine of Hippo who had only lately died.

What a marvel Flavius had been.

No one in the courts of the old Queen would have dared to give the Blood to one marked with deformity. Not even to the ugly or the badly proportioned was the Blood given. Indeed every human offered to the remorseless appetite of the spirit of Amel had been a lamb without blemish and indeed with beauty and gifts of strength and talent that his maker must witness and approve.

Yet here was Flavius crippled in his mortal years but burning brightly with the Blood, a meditative and well-spoken Athenian reciting the tales of Homer by memory as he played his lute, a poet and a philosopher who'd understood law courts and judgments, and who had memorized whole histories of peoples of the Earth he'd never known or seen. Gregory had imbibed so much from Flavius, sitting at his feet by the hour, prodding him with questions, committing to memory the stories and songs that came from his lips. And how grateful had been this honorable scholar. "You have my loyalty for all time," he'd said to Gregory and Chrysanthe, "as you have loved me for what I am."

And to think, this gracious blood drinker knew the very location of the Mother and the Father. He had seen them in the eyes of Pandora who made him; he had lived beneath the very roof of Marius and Pandora where the Divine Pair were kept.

How amazed Gregory—Nebamun of old—had been by Flavius's stories of King Enkil and Akasha, now mute and blind living statues who never showed the slightest sign of sentience as they sat on a throne above banks of flowers and fragrant lamps in a gilded shrine. And it was Marius, the Roman, who had stolen the unresisting King and Queen out of Egypt, from the old blood drinker priesthood that had thrived there for four thousand years. The elders of the priesthood had sought to destroy the Mother and the Father, as they had come to be called, by placing them in the killing rays of the sun. And indeed—as the King and Queen had suffered this blasphemous indignity—countless blood drinkers around the world had perished in flames. But the oldest had been doomed to continue, though their skin was darkened, even blackened, and their every breath was taken in pain. Akasha and Enkil had only been bronzed by this foolish attempt at immolation and indeed the elder himself had survived to share the torture of those he had hoped would all be burnt to death.

But priceless as this history was to Gregory—that his old sovereign endured without power—it was not the Blood history that mattered to him, but the new Roman world.

"Teach me, teach me everything," Gregory had said over and over again to Flavius and to Chrysanthe, and wandering the busy streets of Carthage, filled now with a mélange of Romans and Greeks and Vandals, he struggled to explain to his two devoted teachers how astonishing was the wealth of this world which they took for granted, where common people had gold in their pockets, and plenty to eat on their tables, and spoke of "eternal salvation" as belonging to the most humbly born.

In his time, so very long ago, only the royal court and a handful of nobles had lived in rooms with floors. Eternity had been the property of only that same handful of persons living and breathing under the stars.

But what did it matter? He didn't expect Chrysanthe and Flavius to understand him. He wanted to understand them. And as always he drew knowledge from his victims, feeding on their minds as surely as he fed on their blood. What a vast world the common people inhabited, and how small and arid had been that geography belonging to him so very long ago.

Less than two hundred years had passed before two more blood drinkers joined his Blood Kindred at Gregory's invitation. Carthage was no more. He and his family lived then in the Italian city of Venice. These newcomers had also known the infamous Marius, keeper of the King and Queen, as had Flavius. Their names were Avicus and Zenobia and they came from the city of Byzantium and were glad of Gregory's invitation to find safety and hospitality beneath his roof.

Avicus had been a blood god of Egypt same as Gregory, and indeed Avicus had been told tales of the great Nebamun and how he'd led the Queens Blood to drive the First Brood from Egypt, and they had much to talk about of those dark and dreary times and the torture of being blood gods encased within stone shrines, forced to dream and starve between great feast days when the faithful would bring them blood sacrifice and ask them to look into hearts and judge the innocent from the guilty with their blood drinker minds. How could the Queen have doomed so many to such misery and drudgery, such wretched heartbreaking isolation? Nebanum had had his own taste of that "Divine Service" in the end.

No wonder Marius, forced into the priesthood, had stolen the Mother and the Father—rejecting out of hand the ancient superstition—and returned to a willful, rational Roman life of his own.

Avicus was Egyptian, tall, dark skinned, and half mad still after a thousand years of serving the old blood cult. He had been a slave to the old religion right into the Common Era, whereas Nebamun had fled it thousands of years before. His Blood Wife, Zenobia, was a delicately built female with voluminous black hair and exquisite features; she brought into the house a universe of new learning, having been brought up in the palace of the Emperor of the East before being brought into the Blood by a wicked female named Eudoxia who had made war on Marius and ultimately lost.

Zenobia had been left to the mercy of Marius, but he'd loved her, making her Blood Kin, and he had taught her how to survive on her own. He had approved her love for Avicus.

Zenobia cut her long hair nightly, and went forth in the garb of a man. Only in the quiet sanctuary of the home did she revert to female garments and let her black hair flow over her shoulders.

Both would never lift a finger against Marius, or so they told their new mentor. Marius was the sworn protector of the Mother and the Father. He maintained them in a magnificent shrine, filled with flowers, and lamps, its walls painted with verdant gardens.

"Yes, he's the clever and educated Roman all right," said Flavius. "And a philosopher of sorts, and every ounce the patrician. But he has done all in his power to make existence bearable for the Divine Parents."

"Yes, I have come to understand all this," Gregory had told them. "The story of this Marius becomes ever more clear. Nothing evil must ever befall him. Not while he protects the Divine Parents. But one thing I vow, my friends, and do listen. I will never ask that you bring harm to any blood drinker, unless that blood drinker seeks to bring direct harm to us. We hunt the evildoer, and we seek to feed as well upon the beauty we see all around us, the marvels we are privileged to witness, don't you understand?"

It took years for them to fully comprehend Gregory's approach to life and how little it mattered to him, the wars of blood drinkers against one another.

But he loved his only family, his own Blood Kin.

Century after century, they had remained together, sustaining one another on wondrous tales and shared learning and unquestioned loyalty and love, Gregory's ancient blood giving strength to those under his wing. From time to time other blood drinkers did join them but only for a while and never to be Blood Kindred. Yet they generally came and went in peace.

After Venice, they had moved by the year 800 into northern Europe, and finally into the area now known as Switzerland. They continued to greet others with kindness, making war on them only in defense of themselves.

By then, Gregory had become a great scholar of the Undead, writing down many theories of blood drinkers and how they changed over time. The changes in himself, both great and small, he chronicled meticulously, and he observed also the sometime pain and alienation of his companions, their reasons for wandering, or drifting away for a spell, and the reasons why they always came home. Why did the ancient ones so avoid the company of other ancient ones and seek to learn from the much-younger children of different eras, and why did a creature such as himself not set out to find those he remembered from those grim times when he knew that surely some of them had persevered? These questions obsessed him. He filled leather-covered journals with his thoughts.

The Vampire Chronicles and the happenings in the vampire world from 1985 when Lestat woke Queen Akasha until now had deeply fascinated Gregory, and he had pored over the pages of the books, forever interested in the deep current of psychological observation that united these works. Never in all these centuries had he encountered poetic souls among the Undead such as Louis de Pointe du Lac and Lestat de Lioncourt, or even Marius whose own memoir reeked of the same profound romanticism and melancholy as their works. Patrician Roman he might have been, Gregory mused, but he was certainly the embodiment of the Romantic Man of Sensibility now finding solace in his inner strength and attachment to his own values.

Of course this thing called romanticism was nothing new, but Gregory thought he understood why the world of the eighteenth and nineteenth centuries had defined and explored it so thoroughly, thereby shaping generations of sensitive human beings to believe quite fully in themselves in a way no human or vampire had before.

But Gregory had existed since the beginning of recorded human history and he knew full well that "romantic souls" had always existed as well and were but one kind of soul among many. In sum, there have always been romantics, poets, outsiders, outcasts, those who sang of alienation whether they had a clever word for it or not.

What had really given birth to the Romantic Movement in the history of human ideas was affluence—an increase in the number of people who had plenty enough to eat, enough education to read and write, and time to ruminate on their own personal emotions.

Why others did not see this, Gregory could not quite grasp.

He had seen the growth of affluence since the dawn of the Christian era. Even coming out of the Egyptian desert, a ragged half-crazed remnant, he'd been astonished at the abundance of the people of the Roman Empire—that common soldiers rode horses in battle (an unthinkable advantage for a being of Gregory's time), that Indian and Egyptian fabrics were sold over the whole known world, that female peasants had their own great looms, and that solid Roman roads bound together the empire, replete with caravansaries for travelers every few miles, and plenty to eat for everyone. Why, these enterprising Romans had actually invented a liquid stone with which they built not only roads but aqueducts to carry water over miles to their ever-growing cities. Exquisitely made pots, jugs, amphora were imported to the remotest towns for sale to the common people. In fact all manner of practical and fancy goods traveled Roman roads and waterways from roof tiles to popular books.

Yes, there had been great setbacks. But despite the wholesale collapse of the Roman Empire, Gregory had seen nothing but "progress" ever since with the early inventions of the Middle Ages—the barrel, the mill wheel, the stirrup, the new harnesses that did not choke the oxen in the fields, the ever-spreading taste for ornate and beautiful clothes, and the building of soaring cathedrals in which the common people could worship right along with the richest and most privileged among them.

What a far cry from the great churches of Rheims or Amiens were the crude temples of ancient Egypt reserved entirely for their gods and a handful of priests and rulers.

Yet it fascinated him and intrigued him that it had taken the romantic era to produce vampires bound and determined to make themselves known to history and in such melancholy and philosophical literature as those books.

There was another key aspect to this that greatly puzzled Gregory as well. He felt with all his soul that this was the greatest age for the Undead that he had ever known. And he did not understand why the poetic authors of the Vampire Chronicles never addressed this obvious fact.

Ever since public lighting had been introduced into the cities of Europe and America, the world had gotten better and better for the Undead. Did they not grasp the miracle of the gas lamps of Paris, the arc lighting that could bring virtual daylight to a park or plaza anywhere in the world, the miracle of electricity that penetrated homes as well as public places bringing the brilliance of the sun into cottages and palaces alike? Did they have no inkling of how the advances in lighting had affected the behavior and the minds of people, what it meant for the tiniest hamlet to have its brilliantly lighted drugstores and supermarkets, and for people to wander at eight o'clock of an evening with the same energetic curiosity and eagerness for work and experience that they enjoyed during the sunlight hours?

The planet had been transformed by lighting and by the sheer magic of television and computers, leveling the playing field for blood drinkers as never before.

Well, he could understand if Lestat and Louis took such things for granted; they'd been born during the Industrial Revolution whether they knew it or not. But what about the great Marius? Why didn't he go into raptures about the brightly lighted modern world? Why didn't he cherish the huge upsurge in human freedom and physical and social mobility in modern times?

Why, these times were perfect for the Undead. Nothing was denied to them. They could be privy to every aspect of daylight and daylight activity through television and film. They were no longer really Children of Darkness at all. Darkness had been essentially banished from the Earth. *It had become a choice.*

Oh, how much he wanted to discuss his views of things with Lestat. How must this be affecting the destiny of the world's blood drinkers? And now that the internet had embraced the planet, wasn't Benji Mahmoud's radio broadcast out of his very own house just the beginning?

When would we see the data banks enabling blood drinkers everywhere, regardless of age and isolation, to find their lost ones, their loved ones, immortals who had been mere legend to them for too long?

And what about glass? Look at what had happened to the world through the invention, evolution, and perfection of glass? Spectacles, telescopes, microscopes, plate glass, walls of glass, palaces of glass, towers of glass! Why, the architecture of the modern world had been transformed by the use of glass. Science had advanced in dramatic and mysterious ways due to the availability and use of glass!

(It struck him as highly ironic and perhaps meaningful that the great Akasha had been decapitated because of a great sheet of broken glass. After all, a six-thousand-year-old immortal is a very strong and resilient creature, and Gregory was not sure that a simple ax could have decapitated the Queen, or that a simple ax could decapitate him.

But an enormous shard of plate glass had been sharp enough and heavy enough to separate head from body so that Akasha's death was in fact accomplished. An accident yes, but a very strange one, indeed.)

All right, so the "Coven of the Articulate" as they were called had not been made up of social or economic historians. But surely romantics as sensitive as Marius and Lestat would be interested in Gregory's notions of progress, and particularly his theory that this was the Age of the Vampire, so to speak. This ought to be a Golden Time, to use Marius's phrase, for all the Undead.

Oh, the time must come when he would meet them.

But even as he told himself that some of this longing and enthusiasm was childish and naïve and even ridiculous, Gregory was drawn almost obsessively to Louis and Lestat. Particularly Lestat.

Louis was a damaged pilgrim, and though he'd been recovering now for the last decade or so, Lestat was indeed the "lion heart" that Gregory wanted to know with his whole soul.

It seemed at times that Lestat was the immortal for whom Gregory had been waiting all this time, the one with whom he could discuss his myriad observations of the Undead and the human stream of history they had followed through six thousand years. Gregory actually fell in love with Lestat.

He knew that he had, and when Zenobia and Avicus teased him about this, or Flavius said it "worried" him, Gregory did not deny it. Nor did he seek to defend it. Chrysanthe understood. Chrysanthe always understood his obsessions. And Davis understood, Davis, his gentle black companion, rescued from the massacre following Lestat's concert, Davis understood too.

"He was like a god on that stage," said Davis of Lestat at the concert. "He was the one vampire we all loved! It was as if nothing could stop him, and nothing ever would."

But something had stopped Lestat most definitely or certainly slowed him down. Demons of his own making perhaps or spiritual exhaustion. Gregory longed to know, longed to sympathize, longed to lend support.

Secretly, Gregory had searched the world for Lestat, and come very close to him many times, spying on him, and divining Lestat's immense anger and great need to be alone. Always, Gregory had backed off, unable to force himself on the object of his obsession, retreating silently in disappointment and a kind of shame.

Two years ago in Paris, he had drawn close enough to see Lestat in the flesh, rushing there from Geneva at the first word of Lestat's appearance, yet he had not dared to reveal himself. Only love could create such conflict, such longing, such fear.

Now Gregory felt the very same reluctance to make himself known to the New York coven of Trinity Gate. He could not make an overture. He could not yet extend himself and risk rebuff. No. These creatures meant too much to him. The time was not yet right, no.

Indeed, only one blood drinker in recent years had brought him out of anonymity and that had been Fareed Bhansali, the physician vampire in Los Angeles, who had sufficiently fascinated him to cause him to reveal himself, and this for very specific reasons. For this Fareed was as unique in his own way—if unique can be compared—as the romantic poet vampires Louis and Lestat, in that Fareed was the only modern blood drinker physician known to Gregory.

Oh, in the distant past there had been some, surely, but they were rudimentary healers and alchemists who when they came into the Blood lost all interest in their scientific explorations, and with reason, for there had been a limit for thousands of years to what could be known scientifically.

Magnus, the great Parisian alchemist, had been a perfect example. In his old age, stooped and deformed by the natural wasting of his bones, Magnus had been denied the Blood by the vain Rhoshamandes, who at that time quietly ruled the Undead of France, never allowing their numbers to become unmanageable. Bitter, angry, and not to be outdone, Magnus had managed to steal the Blood from a young acolyte of Rhoshamandes known as Benedict. Binding Benedict and draining his body of blood right at sunset, Magnus had become a full-fledged blood drinker lying stunned on the comatose body of his maker, who found himself upon waking too weak to break his bonds, too weak even to call for help. What shocks this clever theft of the Blood had sent through the entire Undead world. How many would dare to imitate the bold Magnus? Well, precious few ever did. Precious few blood drinkers were ever as careless or stupid as gentle Benedict had been, entrusting the location of his resting place to a mortal "friend."

And then Magnus, this truly revolutionary thinker, had turned his back entirely on the medical and alchemical knowledge of his human life, holed himself up in a tower near Paris, and devoted himself to the most bitter reflections until he went mad in the end, his only real achievement being the capture and making of the Vampire Lestat. To Lestat, he bequeathed his blood, his property, and his wealth.

Ah, such dreadful failures.

And where was Rhoshamandes now? Where were his fine progeny—the beautiful Merovingian Allesandra, daughter of Dagobert the First, or the disgraced and ever contrite Benedict? Had Allesandra really immolated herself on a pyre in the catacombs under Les Innocents, only because the Vampire Lestat had come marching through her world and destroyed the old Children of Satan who had long kept her mind and her soul and her body prisoner? A pyre might have been enough to destroy the body of Magnus, yes; but Allesandra had been old before Magnus came into existence, though her own age and experience had been lost to her in madness more than once.

Gregory had known little of Rhoshamandes during those centuries but he'd observed much from afar. And why not? Hadn't Rhoshamandes been his own fledgling? Well, no. The Mother had made Rhoshamandes for the Queens Blood, then given him to Gregory (her devoted Nebamun) to instruct and train.

There were many he hoped to find in the future, including his long-lost Blood Wife, Sevraine. She'd come as a slave into Egypt thousands of years ago, her hair and eyes as fair as those of the red-haired witches, and he, Gregory or Nebamun, Captain of the Queens Blood, had so loved her that he'd brought her over without the Queen's blessing and almost paid for this the ultimate price. Somewhere out there in the great bright world, Sevraine lived. Gregory was sure of it. And perhaps one dark side of all this misery of late was that the old ones would come together. Even Rhoshamandes would surface, and some of his strong progeny like Eleni and Eugénie, once captives of the Paris Children of Satan. And where was Hesketh? Gregory could not forget about her.

The tragic Hesketh had been the most malformed blood drinker that Gregory had ever encountered, made and loved by the old renegade blood god Teskhamen, who had escaped the Druids who'd worshipped him and sought to put an end to him on their pyre. Gregory had encountered Hesketh and Teskhamen in the wilds of France in the 700s of the Common Era when Rhoshamandes had still ruled in those parts, and later in the far north. Teskhamen had tales to tell, but didn't they all? Surely those as wise and hearty as Hesketh and Teskhamen still survived.

But the point was, this Fareed Bhansali, a physician vampire, had fascinated Gregory enough to cause him to reveal himself. This Fareed Bhansali appeared unique.

And as word had spread through the world that a blood drinker doctor had indeed appeared "on the scene" in Los Angeles and in fact set up an entire clinic in a medical office tower for the study of the Undead, and that this doctor was powerful and brilliant and had been an accomplished Mumbai surgeon and researcher before being Born to Darkness, Gregory set out to observe this man at close hand.

Indeed, he hurried. He feared that the awful twins—Mekare and Maharet—who now had control of the spirit Amel and the primal fount of the Blood, might burn to ashes this upstart, and Gregory wanted to be there to stop it and whisk away the bold Fareed Bhansali to safety in his own house in Geneva.

Why this doctor did not do anything to hide himself, Gregory couldn't understand. But Fareed didn't. Indeed there were times when he seemed positively eager to advertise his presence, seeking mavericks and riffraff everywhere for his research.

But Gregory had another motive for finding Fareed.

For the first time in seventeen hundred years, Gregory was wondering: could Flavius's missing leg be somehow replaced by some clever device of plastic and steel such as the humans of this age had perfected? Now there was a vampire doctor to provide the answer.

It took some persuading to get Flavius to agree to this experiment, or even to the idea of making the crossing from Europe to America, but when that was finished, Gregory found Fareed at once.

As soon as Gregory came upon Fareed walking in the tree-darkened streets of West Hollywood on a radiant summer evening, Gregory realized his worries for Fareed's safety had been in vain. Beside him walked a vampire nearly as old as Gregory, and indeed this one was none other than Seth, the son of the ancient Mother.

How strange to see him here, removed by aeons from that long-ago time, this one, standing on the pavements of this modern city, lean and tall as he had always been with powerful shoulders and slender fingers, and a large well-shaped head and those dark almond-shaped eyes. His dark skin had faded over the aeons and he had a pale Oriental cast to him with short black hair and the courtly demeanor of olden times.

The old crown prince.

Seth had been a boy when his mother, Queen Akasha, had been infected with the demon blood, and sent away for his own safety to Nineveh, but as the wars between Queens Blood and First Brood had raged on, the Mother out of concern for him, lest he fall into the wrong hands, had sent for him and brought him over as a young man into the Blood.

Now this Seth had been a healer, true, though Gregory had forgotten it, or so the old stories of those times went. He had been a dreamer and a wanderer who traveled the cities of the two rivers searching for other healers from whom he sought to increase his knowledge, and he had not wanted to return to his mother's mystery-shrouded court in Egypt. Far from it. He'd been brought by force.

Akasha had given Seth the Blood in a great and pompous ceremony within the royal palace. He must become for her, she said, the greatest leader the Queens Blood had ever known. But Seth had disappointed his mother and his sovereign, and had disappeared into the sands of the desert and the sands of oblivion never to be heard of by anyone ever again.

Now it was Seth—Seth the healer—who walked with Fareed. It was Seth's powerful ancient blood that fired the veins of Fareed. Of course. The ancient healer had made the vampire doctor.

Fareed was almost as tall as his maker and guardian, with flawless honey-brown skin and ink-black wavy hair. His eyes were green. Something like an Indian Bollywood idol, thought Gregory to himself, with that luxuriant hair and those glittering green eyes. Green eyes had been so very rare in ancient times. One could live a human lifetime back then and never gaze on a being who had blue or green eyes. Their pale-red hair and blue eyes had rendered the witches Mekare and Maharet all the more suspicious and fearsome to the Egyptians, and the beautiful northern slave, Gregory's beloved Sevraine, had been feared.

As late as the Common Era, when Flavius, a Greek, had come to him, Gregory had been dazzled by the seeming miracle of that golden hair and those blue eyes.

How formally, how courteously, Gregory and Seth had greeted one another. *Why, Seth, my friend, it has been six thousand years!*

Even the Mother, Mekare, who now housed the demon, could not have burnt or destroyed this powerful doctor as long as Seth was at his side. And each night of their lives—Gregory came to know—Seth gave more of his ancient blood to Fareed.

"Give yours to him and we will gladly do anything to help Flavius," said Seth, "for yours is pure as well."

"Is it so very pure?" Gregory asked as he marveled.

"Yes, my friend," said Seth. "We drank from the Mother. Those who drink from the Mother possess a power like no other."

And the Vampire Lestat drank from the Mother as well, thought Gregory to himself. And so had Marius, the wanderer. The fledglings of Marius, Pandora, and Bianca, had drunk from the Mother. And so had Gregory's own Avicus and Zenobia, yes. And Khayman, poor Khayman, was he really a simpleton under the protection of the twins? He had drunk from the Mother as well. How many others had drunk directly from the Mother?

Back in the luxurious bedroom of Fareed's high-rise living quarters and clinic, Gregory had taken this brilliant doctor into his arms and sunk his needlelike teeth into the man's soul and his dreams. *I shall take your blood and you will drink of my blood and we will know each other and love each other and be brothers now for all time. Blood Kin.*

A beautiful being was Fareed. Like many a blood drinker, his morals had been forged in the crucible of his human experience, and they would not give way now to the blandishments of the Blood. He would be forever a servant of vampires, yes, but respecting of all living things, and never engage in that which would harm anyone unless somehow that being had fallen beneath the bar of his concern by being an unspeakable monster of some sort.

What this meant was that Fareed could do no evil, not to vampires or to human beings. Whatever the course of his scientific discoveries they would never be perverted or abused.

But of incorrigible, inveterate, unredeemable evildoers he had had enough in his life, and therefore he could and would pluck from the rampant vampire herd a real bad, no-count, filthy, degenerate bully from whom he could take a leg for Flavius to have grafted on as his own. Indeed, he had taken more than one such vampire body for his experiments. He was candid about that. No, he would never do this to a human, but to a cruel and relentlessly destructive vampire, yes, he could do it. And he did it to get Flavius the leg. A true and living leg that became part of Flavius's immortal body!

Ah brave new world . . .

Those nights with Fareed and Seth had been like nothing Gregory had ever experienced, given over to endless scientific talks and visions and experiments. "If either of you gentleman wants to feel the passion of biological men once more, I can arrange this simply with hormonal injections," said Fareed, "and indeed would like very much if you would yield to me in this and allow me to harvest the seed from the experiments."

"Are you saying that a living seed can come forth from us again?" asked Flavius.

"Yes," answered Fareed. "I have achieved this in one case, but the case was not ordinary." He had indeed infused an eighteenth-century vampire with these powerful hormones and the vampire's seed had indeed fathered a son. But it had not been simple. Indeed the magic connection had been made in a dish, and the son was more a clone than an offspring, birthed through a biological mother.

Gregory was stunned. So was Flavius.

But what shocked Gregory to the core was not that this had worked, this bit of cellular razzle-dazzle, but that it had worked with a vampire that Gregory had been stalking the world over. Fareed struggled to keep the vampire's identity secret. But when next Gregory drew the doctor to himself to drink his blood and give his own in return, he reached for deeply buried images and answers and brought them to himself.

Yes, the great rock singer–poet Lestat de Lioncourt had fathered a son.

Then on a bright screen in a dark room Fareed finally revealed to him images of this young human boy, the "spitting image" of his father down to the smallest particular, containing the full packet of his father's DNA.

"And Lestat knows this?" asked Gregory. "And he has acknowledged this boy?" He realized how ridiculous these words sounded as soon as he'd uttered them, and he knew the answer as well.

Lestat, wherever he was, knew nothing of the existence of young Viktor.

"I don't think Lestat guessed for a moment," said Fareed, "that I would attempt such a thing."

Seth sat in the shadows beside his beloved Fareed as all this was discussed, his narrow angular face impassive, but surely he and Gregory were thinking the same thing. Seth, the Mother's human son, had once been the most sought-after hostage by her enemies; that's why the great Queen had sent for him and given him the Blood, to keep him from her enemies who might have tortured him unendingly to demand concessions or surrender from her.

Could not this same fate befall this human boy?

"But what if his enemies have already destroyed Lestat?" asked Flavius. "No one has heard one word from him for so long."

"He's alive, I know he is," said Gregory. Fareed and Seth had not responded.

That had been years ago, that meeting.

The boy must now be eighteen or nineteen years old, a man for all practical purposes, and nearly the same age his father had been when Magnus raped him and made him a vampire.

Before Gregory and Flavius had taken their leave, Seth had assured them both that he had no ancient grudge against the twins for the slaying of his mother.

"The twins know we're here," said Seth. "They have to know. And they don't care. That's the secret of the reigning Queen of the Damned. She does not care and her sister does not care. Well, I care. I care about everything under the sun and the moon, and that's why I made Fareed. But I don't care about revenge against the twins or about ever seeing them eye to eye. This is of no importance to me."

Seth had been right of course that Maharet knew, but Gregory had not known it at the time. He had not learned it until much later. And Seth had been merely speculating then. He and Fareed and Maharet had not yet met.

"I understand, I so understand," said Gregory softly. "But have you never wanted, yourself, to take the demon out of Mekare and into your own body? Have you never felt that simple urge, to dispatch her in exactly the same way that she dispatched the Mother?"

"You mean *my* mother," said Seth. "And no. Why would I want the demon in me? What, you think as her son, I see myself as Akasha's heir to this demon?" He was plainly disgusted.

"Not so much that," said Gregory, politely backing off. "But so that the threat of our annihilation doesn't belong to another. So that you have the fount safe within yourself."

"And why would it be safer with me than anyone else?" asked Seth. "Have you ever wanted to take the Sacred Core into your body?"

They had been in the large drawing room of Fareed's personal quarters when they had this last discussion. The chill Los Angeles night had warranted a fire, and they were gathered by the hearth in leather chairs. Flavius had this new and functioning leg laid across a leather ottoman, gazing at it from time to time in wonder. Beneath his gray wool trousers, only his sock-covered foot was visible. From time to time he flexed the toes as if to convince himself he possessed this limb fully and completely.

Gregory pondered that question.

"Until the night Mekare slew the Queen I had no idea any force on Earth could take the Sacred Core from Akasha and move it into anyone," he confessed.

"But now you do know," said Seth. "Have you, yourself, thought of trying to steal it?"

Gregory had to confess the thought had never occurred to him, not in any form. Indeed, when he reviewed the scene in his mind—which he had not witnessed, which he had seen only in telepathic flashes from remote points, which he had read described in Lestat's books—he saw it as mythic.

"I still don't know how they achieved it," he said. "And no, I would never attempt such a thing and I would not want to have the Sacred Core within me."

He thought for a long moment, allowing his thoughts to be totally readable by the others, though only Fareed and Flavius, it seemed, could read them.

He was a mystery to Seth, and Seth was a mystery to him—common enough to the early generation.

"Why would anyone want to be the host of the Sacred Core?" Gregory asked.

Seth didn't immediately answer. Then in a quiet distinct voice he spoke.

"You suspect me of conniving, don't you? You think our work here is reducible to some simple plot to gain power over the source."

"No, that's not true," Gregory said. He'd been astonished. He might have been insulted, but it wasn't his way ever to be insulted.

Seth was staring at him, staring at him as if he loathed Gregory. And Gregory realized that he was at a significant turning point.

He could loathe Seth now as well, if he chose to do it. He could fear him, give in to jealousy of his age and power.

He didn't want to do this.

He had thought sadly then of how he had dreamed of encounters such as this, dreaming of making himself known to the great Maharet simply to talk to her, talk and talk and talk, the way he was always talking to his beloved little family who never really understood what he was talking about.

He had looked away.

He would not despise Seth. And he would not seek to intimidate him. If he had learned one thing from his long time in this world, it was that he could intimidate others beyond his wildest intentions to do it.

When a statue talks to you, a statue that can breathe and move, it's faintly horrible.

But with Fareed and Seth, Gregory had wanted something warm, something vital.

"I want us to be brothers," he had said to Seth in a low voice. "I wish there were a good word for brothers and sisters the world over, something more specific than 'kindred.' But you are my kindred, both of you. I've exchanged blood with you, and that makes you my special kindred. But we are all kindred."

He had stared helplessly at the ornamental fireplace. Black-veined marble. French gilt. Flashing gold andirons. He let his preternatural hearing rise; he heard the voices beyond the glass, the voices of millions, in soft undulating waves, punctuated by the music of cries, prayers, laughter.

Fareed began to talk then, talk of his immediate work and how Flavius would now have to use this "living" leg he had affixed so skillfully. And on he went about the fine points of the long surgery during which the leg had been attached, about the nature of the Blood, how it behaved so distinctly from human blood.

He used a multitude of Latin words which Gregory could not understand.

"But what is this thing, Amel?" Gregory said suddenly. "Oh, forgive me that I don't know what all these words mean. But what is this animating force inside us? How has it changed the blood to the Blood?"

Fareed seemed enjoyably absorbed in the question as he responded.

"This thing, this monster, Amel . . . it's made up of nanoparticles, how can I describe it, made up of cells infinitely smaller than the tiniest eukaryote cells known to us, but cells, you understand—it has a cellular life, dimensions, boundaries, some sort of nervous system, a brain or nucleus of some sort that governs its physicality and its etheric properties. It once had intelligence if we are to believe the witches. It once possessed a voice."

"You mean you can see these cells under a microscope?" Gregory asked.

"Not at all," said Fareed. "I can't. I know its properties by how they behave. When a creature is made into a vampire, it's as if a tentacle of this monster invades the new organism, hooking itself into the brain of the human being and then slowly beginning to transform it. Senescence is stopped forever. And then the alchemical blood of the creature works on the human blood, slowly absorbing it and then transforming what it does not absorb. It works on all the biological tissue; it becomes the sole source of cell development and change within the host. Are you following me?"

"Well, yes, I think I've always understood that," said Gregory.

"Now it needs more human blood to continue its work."

"And what's the goal of its work?" asked Flavius.

"To make us into perfect hosts for itself," said Fareed.

"And to drink blood, always to drink more blood," said Gregory. "To drive us to drink more blood. I remember how the Queen cried out in those early months. The thirst was unbearable. It wanted more blood. The red-haired witches told her that before they'd been given the Blood. 'It wants more blood.'"

"But I don't think that is its main goal," said Fareed. "Nor has it ever been. But I'm not sure that it is conscious of a goal! That is what I want to know more than anything. Is it self-conscious? Is it a conscious being living inside the body of Mekare?"

"But in the very beginning," Gregory said, "the spirits of the world told the twin witches that Amel, once fused with the Queen, was not conscious. They said, 'Amel is no more.' They said Amel was lost now inside the Mother."

Fareed laughed to himself and looked into the fire.

"I was there," said Gregory. "I remember it, when the twins said these things."

"Well, of course you were, but what amazes me is that after all the generations you've seen rise and fall, you still believe those spirits actually spoke to the witches."

"I know they did."

"Do you?" asked Fareed.

"Yes," said Gregory. "I do know."

"Well, you may be right and the spirits may be right, and the thing is mindless and subsumed, but I cannot help but wonder. I tell you, there are no discarnate entities. This thing, Amel, is not a discarnate entity but something of immense size and intricate organization, something that has now so thoroughly mutated its host and those connected to her. . . ." And suddenly his language ascended again into a vocabulary as opaque to Gregory as the syllables uttered by dolphins or birds.

Gregory tried to pierce the language with the finest abilities of his own mind, to see the pictures, shapes behind it. Design. But he saw something that resembled the stars in the night sky and their infinite and purely accidental patterns.

Fareed continued.

". . . I suspect these creatures, which we have for thousands of years called spirits or ghosts, these creatures draw their nourishment from the atmosphere, and just how they perceive us is impossible to know. There is a beauty to it, I suspect, a beauty as there is to all of nature, and they are part of nature. . . ."

"Beauty," Gregory said. "I believe there is beauty in all things. I believe that. But I must find the beauty and coherence in science or I'll never learn, never understand."

"Listen to me," said Fareed gently. "I was brought over because this is my field, my language, my realm, all this. You need not ever fully understand it. You can't understand any more than Lestat or Marius or Maharet can understand it, or millions of people out there who have no capacity to absorb scientific knowledge or use it any way other than the simplest and most practical. . . ."

"I am that crippled here," said Gregory, nodding.

"But trust in me," said Fareed. "Trust in me that I study for *us*, what I can study that no human scientist can possibly study, and don't think they haven't tried, they have."

"Oh, I know," said Gregory. He thought back on those long-ago nights in 1985, after Lestat's famous San Francisco rock concert, of the scientists who gathered up what they could of those burnt remains all over the parking lots surrounding the concert hall.

He'd watched that with the coldest detachment.

But nothing, absolutely nothing, had come of it, any more than anything ever came of the vampires who were now and then captured by scientists, imprisoned in labs, and studied until they made their spectacular escapes, or were spectacularly rescued. Nothing came of it. Except that now the world was inhabited by some thirty or forty frantic men and women of science who claimed there were real vampires out there and they had seen them with their own eyes—outcasts from their profession whom the world branded lunatics.

Time was when Gregory left the security of his Geneva penthouse to rescue any misbegotten little vampire who'd ended up in a laboratory prison under fluorescent lights gazed on by government officials. He'd hastened to break them out, destroy whatever evidence had been collected. But now he scarcely bothered. It didn't matter.

Vampires didn't exist and everybody knew that. All the amusing popular novels, television series, and motion pictures about vampires served to reinforce the common wisdom.

Besides, captured vampires almost always escaped. They were plenty strong. If caught in confusion and weakness, they collected themselves, bided their time, seduced their captives with cooperative speech, then shattered skulls, burnt laboratories, and scampered back off into the great and unending shadow world of the Undead, leaving behind not a scintilla of evidence that they had ever been lab rats.

Didn't happen very often anyway.

Fareed was aware of all this. He had to be.

Fareed—with or without their help—would find out everything.

Fareed laughed. He laughed easily and cheerfully with his entire face, his green eyes crinkled and his lips smiling. He'd been reading Gregory's mind. "You are so right," he said. "So very right. And some of those poor ostracized researchers, who scraped up the oily residue of mythic monsters from the asphalt, are working with me now in this very building. They make the most willing pupils of what Seth and I have to offer."

Gregory smiled. "That's not at all surprising."

He had never thought to bring such creatures into the Blood.

On that long-ago night in San Francisco, when Lestat's concert had ended in a flaming massacre, his one thought had been to rescue his precious Davis from the holocaust. Let the doctors of the human world do what they would with the bones and slime that dead blood drinkers had left behind.

He'd taken Davis in his arms, and gone up high into the Heavens before the Queen could fix him with her lethal eyes.

And only later had he returned, the boy safe now as the Queen had moved on, to watch from a distance those forensic workers gathering their "evidence."

He had thought of Davis then as he sat with Fareed in Los Angeles, thought of Davis's dark caramel skin and those thick black eyelashes, so common in males of African descent. Nearly twenty years had passed since the night of that concert, yet Davis was just now coming into himself, recovering from the deep wounds of his early exile in the Blood. He was again dancing as he had long ago in New York as a mortal boy—before intense anxiety had crushed his chances for the Alvin Ailey American Dance Theater and sent him into the awful mental decline in which he'd been made a vampire.

Ah, well, that was another story. Davis had taught Gregory things about this age which Gregory could have never divined on his own. Davis had a soft silky voice that always made his simplest statements sound like the most hallowed confidences, and a touch that was eternally gentle. And the gentlest gaze. Davis had become a Blood Spouse to Gregory as surely as Chrysanthe, and she too loved Davis.

In the severe and modern drawing room in Los Angeles, with its Impressionist paintings and French fireplace, Fareed had sat quiet for a long time, thinking to himself, shielding his ruminations perfectly.

At last he'd said gently, "You must tell no one about Viktor."

This was Lestat's biological son.

"Of course not, but they will know. They will all eventually know. Surely the twins know now."

"Perhaps they do," said Seth. "Perhaps they don't. Perhaps they are beyond caring what happens to us in this world." His voice was not cold or hostile. He spoke evenly and politely. "Perhaps they have not come to us because they are indifferent to what we do here."

"Whatever the case, you must keep the secret," Fareed thought. "We will be moving soon from this building to a safer, more remote compound. It will be safer there for Viktor."

"Has the boy no normal human life?" Gregory asked. "I don't mean to challenge your judgment. I am only asking."

"Actually much more than you might think. After all, by day he's quite safe with the bodyguards we provide for him, is he not? And again, what would anyone gain from making him a hostage? Someone has to want something before he takes a hostage. What has Lestat to give but himself, and whatever that is, it cannot be extorted."

Gregory nodded, somewhat relieved when he considered it in that light. It would have been rude to push for more information. But of course there was a reason to take him hostage—to demand Lestat's or Seth's powerful Blood. Better not to point this out.

He had to leave this mystery in their hands.

But he secretly wondered if Lestat de Lioncourt wouldn't be furious when he discovered the existence of Viktor. Lestat was known for having a temper almost as extreme as his sense of humor.

Before that night was finished, Fareed had made a few more statements about vampiric nature.

"Oh, if only I knew," he said, "whether that thing is truly unconscious, or whether it retains an autonomous life and whether or not it wants something. All life wants something. All life moves towards something. . . ."

"And what are we then?" Gregory had asked.

"We are mutants," Fareed answered. "We are a fusion of unrelated species, and the force in us which turns our human blood into vampire blood is making of us something perfect, but what that is, what that will be, what that must be, I do not know."

"He wanted to be physical," said Seth. "That was well known in olden times. Amel wanted to be flesh and blood. And he got what he wanted, and he lost himself in the process."

"Perhaps," said Fareed. "But does anyone really want to be mortal flesh and blood? What all beings want is to be immortal flesh and blood. And this monster has come closer to that perhaps than any spirit who temporarily possesses a child or a nun or a psychic."

"Not if he's lost himself in the process," said Seth.

"You speak as if Akasha possessed him," said Fareed. "But it was his goal to possess her, remember."

This had frightened Gregory and it had taught him something.

For all his protests of wanting to learn about all things, for loving and embracing the ever-evolving world, well, he was frightened of this new knowledge that Fareed was acquiring. Truly frightened of it. For the first time, he knew well why religious humans so feared scientific advances. And he discovered the heart of superstition in himself.

Well, he would suppress this fear; he would annihilate this superstition in himself and work diligently on his old faith.

The next night, they had embraced for the final time right after sunset.

Gregory had been surprised when Seth came forward and took Gregory in his arms. "I *am* your brother," he whispered, but this he said in the ancient tongue, the ancient tongue no longer spoken anywhere under the moon or the sun. "Forgive me that I've been cold to you. I feared you."

"And I feared you," Gregory confessed, the old language coming back to him in a flood of sorrow. "My brother." Queens Blood and Blood Kindred. No, something greater, infinitely greater. And brother does not betray brother.

"You are too much alike, you two," said Fareed gently. "You even resemble each other—same high cheekbones, same slightly slanted eyes, same jet-black hair. Oh, some night in the far future I will complete a DNA study of every immortal on the planet, and what will that tell us about our human ancestors as well as our Blood ancestors?"

Seth had embraced Gregory all the more warmly after that, and Gregory had returned the affection with all his heart.

Back in Geneva, he kept the secret of Viktor even from Chrysanthe. He kept it as well from Davis, Zenobia, and Avicus. Flavius kept the secret as well. Flavius learned to trust his new and perfect limb over the coming months until it was truly part of him.

Years had passed since then.

The Undead world knew nothing of Viktor. And Fareed had told no one of Gregory Duff Collingsworth or his preternatural clan.

And two years ago—when Gregory came to spy on Lestat with David and Jesse in Paris—he'd realized that Lestat still had no inkling of Viktor's existence. He'd also learned, as he eavesdropped on the three in their hotel-room confab, that Fareed and Seth were still thriving, though now in a new compound in the California desert, and that Maharet herself had gone to Fareed for his skills.

That had reassured him greatly. He did not want to think of the twins as creatures of ambition. He dreaded the very possibility. And it had greatly comforted him to learn that Fareed's scans and imaging equipment had detected no mind in the mute Mekare. Yes, that was better than a host of Akasha's ambitions and ultimate dreams.

But it had tormented him that night in Paris—as he eavesdropped—to hear Jesse Reeves talk of the little massacre in the library archive of Maharet's household, and of Khayman's confusion and pain. Khayman had always been on the edge of madness as far as Gregory was concerned. Every time Khayman had ever come across Gregory's path, he had been more or less out of his mind. In the age of Rhoshamandes, he'd been Benjamin the Devil, and eventually the Talamasca had studied him under that name. But then Gregory considered the Talamasca to be harmless as Khayman was harmless. He was the perfect vampire for their treatises. Imbeciles like Benjamin the Devil and fast talkers like Lestat kept them believing the Undead were harmless and more interesting alive than dead.

And to think, before that horrid massacre in Maharet's compound, the great one had actually been spying on him, on Gregory, in Geneva, and she had been contemplating a meeting involving them all! That intelligence, too, had deepened Gregory's excitement and his dread. How he would love to talk to Maharet now, if only . . . but his nerve had failed him two years ago when he had first heard of these things in his spying on Jesse Reeves, and his nerve failed him now.

Now, in the year 2013—as Gregory stood in Central Park in this warm September night, watching, listening, as inside the house called Trinity Gate, Armand and Louis and Sybelle and Benji gathered around their new companion, Antoine—all of this weighed on Gregory's heart.

Was Lestat still completely ignorant of Viktor's existence? And where were the twins at this very hour?

Gregory realized he'd not be joining Armand and Louis and the others tonight, even if the loveliest music on Earth was now coming from the townhouse, with Antoine playing his violin as Sybelle played the piano, both of them traveling the exhilarating crescendos of Tchaikovsky, effortlessly inflating the music with their own madness and charm.

But the time would certainly come when they must all meet.

And how many would die by fire before such a gathering took place?

He turned and headed deeper into the darkness of Central Park, walking faster and faster, his thoughts crowding in on him as he pondered whether to stay in this city or go home.

He had spent last night in his penthouse apartment on Central Park South and assured himself all was in order should he have to bring his family there. He was the owner of the building, and his basement crypts were as safe as those of Louis and Armand. No need to go back there now. He longed for Geneva, for his own lair.

Suddenly, without the conscious decision, he was ascending, and so rapidly that no mortal eye could have followed his progress, rising ever higher and turning eastward as the city of New York receded below him yet remained a wondrous and endless carpet of brilliant and pulsing lights.

Oh, what do the great electrified cities of this world look like to Heaven? What do they look like to me?

Perhaps these urban galaxies of electric splendor offered to the endless Heavens an homage, a mirror image of the stars.

Cutting higher and higher, he fought the wind that would stop him, until he had broken into the thinnest air beneath the vast canopy of silent stars.

Home, he wanted to go home.

A vague panic seized him.

Even as he moved eastward and out over the cold black Atlantic, he heard the voice of Benji Mahmoud broadcasting again. His brief visit with Antoine had apparently been interrupted by frightening intelligence.

"It has happened now in Amman. The vampires of Amman have been massacred. It is the Burning, Children of the Night. We are now certain of it. But we have reports of massacres in other places, random places. We are trying to confirm now whether shelters in Bolivia have been attacked."

Pushed to the limit of his strength, Gregory traveled faster towards the European continent, desperate suddenly to be at his own hearth. For the ancient ones, Chrysanthe, Flavius, Zenobia, and Avicus, he had little fear as Benji's frantic appeals faded into the roar of the wind, but what about his beloved Davis? Could it possibly be that his beloved Davis would once again suffer the hot breath of the Burning which had so nearly taken him from the Earth once before?

All was well when he arrived, but it was almost dawn. He'd lost half the night in traveling east, and he was weary to the core of his soul. There was time to embrace Flavius and Davis, but Zenobia and Avicus had already gone to the vaults beneath the ten-story hotel.

How fresh and beautiful Davis looked to him with his shining dark skin and liquid eyes. He had hunted that night in Zurich with Flavius and they'd only just returned. Gregory caught the scent of the human blood in him.

"And all's well with the people of Trinity Gate?" asked Davis. He was eager to return to New York, Gregory knew this, eager to revisit his old home in Harlem and the places where once as a young man he had sought to be a Broadway dancer. He was convinced the past could not hurt him now, but he wanted to put his hopes to the test.

In a hushed voice, Gregory told him that his old compatriot, Killer of the Fang Gang, was alive, that the young musician Antoine had met him on his journey to New York. This assuaged an old guilt in Davis, guilt that he had been rescued from Akasha's massacre after Lestat's concert, leaving Killer to perish.

"Maybe somehow a great good will come out of this," Davis said, searching Gregory's face. "Maybe somehow Benji's dream is possible, do you think, that we could all come together? In the old days, it was every gang for itself, it was back alleys and gutters and graveyards. . . ."

"I know," said Gregory. They had been over many times how the Undead had lived before Lestat had raised his voice and told them the story of their beginnings—vampire bars, swanky coven houses, and roving gangs, yes, all of that.

"Can there be a way for us to live in peace?" Davis asked. Obviously he felt so safe here under Gregory's watchful eye that the stories of the new Burnings did not frighten him, not at all, not the way they frightened Gregory. "Is it possible we could really embrace a future? You know, we never had a future in those nights. We just had the past and the now and then the outskirts of life."

"I know," said Gregory.

He kissed Davis and sent him away with only the gentlest warning. "Go nowhere without me, without Flavius, without one of us."

Davis, like all his little family, had never rebelled against him.

Gregory had only a few precious moments alone to look out on placid and lovely Lake Geneva, and the bright broad quay below, where early morning strollers were already out, and the vendors offering hot chocolate and coffee, and then to go upstairs as he did every morning to his own glass cell on the roof. Geneva was quiet. There had never been a coven house or refuge in Geneva. And as far as Gregory could tell, there were no Undead mavericks challenging him here. If there was a target for the Burning, however, it was this building where he and his beloved family lodged.

Tomorrow he'd strengthen all security systems, sprinklers, and examine the vaults to make certain that the thick stone-and-lead walls were unbreachable. He was no stranger to the Fire Gift. He knew what it could do and what it could not do. He'd foiled Akasha when she sought to burn Davis simply by carrying him upwards so swiftly her eyes could not follow the escape. And throughout the nighttime, from now on, he would keep the young and vulnerable Davis at his side.

Now he mounted the steel-lined stairway and pushed back the heavy-plated doors to his small open bedroom under the sky. In this roofless high-walled cell, under a high canopy of steel mesh, he would endure the paralysis of the daylight hours, exposing his six-thousand-year-old body to the burning rays of the sun.

When he woke each night, of course, he knew a slight discomfort from this exposure, but as the result of this process, his skin remained darkly tanned, helping him to pass for human, never to become the living white-marble statue that Khayman had become that would so frighten human beings.

As he lay down on his soft bed, the sky brightening above him, he picked up the book he'd been studying, *Glass: A World History* by Alan Macfarlane and Gerry Martin, and read for a few precious minutes from this engrossing text.

Some night soon, somehow he and Lestat would sit together somewhere, in a paneled library or a breezy open café, and they would talk together, talk and talk and talk, and Gregory would not be so alone.

Lestat would really understand. And Lestat would teach Gregory things! Yes. Surely that would happen, and that is what Gregory longed for more than anything else.

He was just sliding into unconsciousness when he heard dim telepathic cries from somewhere in the world. "The Burning." But that was someplace where the sun was not shining and the sun was indeed shining here and Gregory sank into sleep beneath its warm penetrating rays now because he could do nothing else.

10

Everard de Landen

H E WANTED no part of this, this "Voice" telling him to
burn the young ones. He wanted no part of wars or fac-
tions or covens or books about vampires. And certainly
he wanted nothing to do with any entity who said solemnly and telepathically, "I am the Voice. Do as I say."

The very idea. He had laughed!

"And why don't you want to slaughter them?" demanded the Voice.
"Have they not driven you out of Rome?"

"No, they haven't. And I do wish you'd go away."

Everard knew from bad experience that it was not in the vampire
nature to collect in groups except for evil, and that fighting other
blood drinkers was a foolish enterprise that ended only in ruin for
all involved. He had long chosen to survive alone. In the hills of Tuscany not far from Siena, he kept a small refurbished villa staffed by
mortals, and in the evenings the rooms were his alone. He was coldly
hospitable to the immortals who now and then called on him. But this
Voice wanted it to begin all over again, and he would not listen. He
went into Rome or Florence to hunt because they provided the only
really safe and rich hunting grounds, but he would not go into Rome
to burn.

Seven hundred years ago he'd been made in France by a great
vampire named Rhoshamandes who had created a line of de Landen
vampires, as he called them—Benedict, Allesandra, Eleni, Eugénie,
Notker, and Everard—most of which had no doubt perished over
the centuries, but Everard had survived. True he'd been captured

by the coven of the Children of Satan, those infamous superstitious vampires who made of their miserable existence a religion, and he'd served them, but only after he'd been tortured and starved. Sometime in the Renaissance years, he couldn't remember precisely when, he'd been sent by the vicious little Parisian coven master Armand to the Children of Satan in Rome to find out how the coven fared. Well, the coven had been in ruins, and Santino the coven master had been living a blasphemous existence in worldly clothes and jewels flouting all the rules he'd forced on others. And Everard saw his chance. He escaped the Children of Satan, striking out on his own, remembering the things that the powerful Rhoshamandes had taught him long ago before the Children of Satan drove him from France.

Since then Everard had survived many an encounter with others more powerful than himself. He'd survived the terrible Burning when Akasha passed over the world striking down Children of Darkness everywhere without regard to character, courage, merit, or mercy.

He'd even survived a brief and insulting mention in one of the Vampire Chronicles by Marius, who'd described Everard without naming him as "gaunt and big boned" with dusty clothes and dirty lace.

Well, he could endure the "gaunt and big boned." That was true, and he thought himself quite beautiful in spite of it, but the dusty clothes and dirty lace? It infuriated him. He kept his shoulder-length black hair and his clothes immaculate. If he ever ran into Marius again, he intended to smack his face.

But that was all foolishness really. If he played his cards right, he'd never run into Marius or anyone else, except to exchange a few kind words and then move on. The point was Everard lived with other blood drinkers at peace.

And now this inane Voice, this Voice that came right into his head, bedeviled him nightly with commands to kill and to burn and to rampage. And he could not shut this Voice out.

Finally, he'd resorted to music. Everard had started purchasing excellent systems for amplified music since the beginning of the twentieth century. Indeed the storerooms of his little villa were a veritable museum, as he hated to throw good things away. And so he had windup Victrolas, stacks of thick old black phonograph records that he had once played on them, as well as early electrical machines that had once given him "high fidelity" and "stereo" and now collected dust.

He'd moved on to compact discs, streaming, and the like and so forth, and so putting his iPhone into the little Bose dock that would amplify its music, he flooded the villa with the "Ride of the Valkyries" and prayed the Voice would go away.

No such luck. The imbecilic, bad-tempered, and childish little monster continued to invade his thoughts.

"You are not going to persuade me to burn anyone, you idiot!" Everard snarled with exasperation.

"I will punish you for this. You are young and weak and stupid," said the Voice. "And when I do accomplish my purpose I will send an ancient one to destroy you for your disobedience."

"Oh, stuff it up your chimney, you vain little nuisance," said Everard. "If you are so high and mighty and capable of doing this, why are you talking to me at all? And why aren't you blasting all the blood drinker tramps of Rome on your own?"

Who was this fool, some ancient one buried deep underground or walled up in some ruin somewhere desperately trying to control others and ultimately draw them to his prison? Well, he was doing a very bad job of it with all this incitement to war and idle threats.

"I shall make you suffer," said the Voice, "and turn off that infernal music!"

Everard laughed. He turned the volume higher, took the iPhone out of the dock, put it in his pocket, connected the earpiece, and went out for a walk.

The Voice fumed but he could hardly hear it.

It was a lovely route he took downhill to the walled city of Siena. And how Everard loved the place, with its tiny winding medieval streets that made him feel safe, made him think of his Paris.

The Paris of today terrified him.

He even loved the bright-faced and gentle tourists who flooded Siena, pretty much enjoying what Everard enjoyed—wandering, gazing into shopwindows, and sitting in the wine bars.

Everard liked the shops and wished more were open after dark. He often sent his mortal servants down to purchase stationery for him, on which to write his occasional poems, which he then framed and hung on his walls. And he purchased scented candles and bright silk neckties.

Like many of the old ones made in the Middle Ages, he favored ornate and big-sleeved shirts, tight-fitting pants that were almost like leggings, and fancy mostly velvet coats. And these things he ordered online with his big dazzling Mac computer. But the town had fine men's gloves, and golden cuff links and such. Lots of glittering accoutrements.

He had a lot of money, accumulated over the centuries in many ways. He wasn't hungry. He'd fed in Florence the night before, and it had been a long slow delicious feast.

And so on this cool and mild evening, under the Tuscan stars, he was happy even though the Voice grumbled in his ear.

He entered the town with a nod to the few people he actually knew who gave him a wave as he passed—"the gaunt one with the big bones"—and followed the narrow street in the direction of the Cathedral.

Soon he came to the café he liked the most. It sold newspapers and magazines, and had a few tables set out on the street. Most of the patrons were inside tonight, as it was just a little chilly for them, but for a vampire the weather was perfect. Everard sat down, switching the music feed from Wagner to Vivaldi, whom he liked much better, and waited for the waiter to bring him his usual, a cup of hot American coffee which of course he could not and would not drink.

Years ago, he used to go to great lengths to make it appear that he ate and drank. Now he knew it was a waste of time. In a world such as this where people consumed food and drink for amusement as well as nourishment, nobody cared if he left a mug full of coffee on a café table so long as he left a generous tip. He left huge tips.

He settled back in the little iron chair which was likely made of aluminum and began to hum with the Vivaldi violin music as his eyes passed over the darkly stained old façades that surrounded him, the eternal architecture of Italy that had survived so many changes, just as he had.

Quite suddenly his heart stopped.

In the café across from him, seated at an outdoor table with their backs to the tall building behind them, sat an ancient vampire and what appeared to be two ghosts.

Everard was too terrified to even take a breath. At once, he thought of the threat of the Voice.

And here sat this ancient one not fifty feet from him, the color of waxen gardenias with bright deep-set black eyes and short well-groomed snow-white hair, looking directly at Everard as if he knew him, and beside him these two ghosts, clothed in bodies of particles, though how he knew not, both staring at him too. These creatures appeared friendly. What was the chance of that?

These ghosts were magnificent. No doubt about that. Their bodies appeared wondrously solid, and appeared to be breathing. He could even hear their hearts. And they wore real clothes, these ghosts. So very clever.

But ghosts had been getting better and better at passing for human for centuries. Everard had been seeing them in one form or another ever since he was born. Few had been able to form particle bodies for themselves in those long-ago days, but now it was fairly common. He frequently glimpsed them in Rome in particular.

But of all the modern apparitions he'd seen on city streets throughout Europe, these two were absolutely the best.

One ghost, the nearest to the ancient vampire, appeared to be a man of perhaps fifty with wavy iron-gray hair and a somewhat-noble face. His bright eyes were crinkled with a friendly expression and he had an agreeable almost pretty mouth. Beside him sat the illusion of a man in his prime with short well-groomed ashen hair and gray eyes. All were neatly dressed in what anyone in this day and age would call fine and respectable clothes. The younger male ghost had a proud bearing and actually turned his head and looked about him as if he were enjoying these moments in the busy little street no matter why the trio had come here.

The vampire with the full well-groomed white hair gave a little nod to Everard, and Everard went silently crazy.

He sent the telepathic message, *Well, damn you, blast me if you intend to do it. I'm too frightened to be civil. Get on with it but first, first, I demand that you tell me why.*

He killed the music from the iPhone. He didn't want to die with a soundtrack. And he fully expected to hear the Voice raging and cackling exultantly. But the Voice was not there.

"Miserable coward," he muttered. "You order my death and decamp without even remaining here to witness it. And you wanted me to burn down the Roman Vampire Refuge in the Via Condotti. Well, you're ugly and you're mad."

The ancient vampire across the way rose to his feet and gestured in a decidedly friendly manner for Everard to join them. He was not overly tall and he was very delicate of build. He took a chair from a nearby table and placed it in their circle. He waited patiently for Everard's response.

It was as if Everard had forgotten how to walk. All his life in the Undead he'd seen vampires burned by others, seen that horrific spectacle of a living breathing creature going up in a personal inferno because some older more powerful vampire—like that contemptible, condescending Marius—had decided he or she should die. His legs were wobbling so badly as he crossed the street, he thought he would at any moment collapse. His narrow tailored leather jacket felt heavy and his boots pinched and he wondered inanely whether his blue silk tie had a stain on it, and whether the cuffs of his lavender shirt were sticking too far out of his coat sleeves.

His hands were shaking visibly as he reached to accept the hard icy hand of the old vampire. But he managed it. He managed to sit down.

The ghosts were smiling at him, and they were even more perfect than he'd thought. Yes, they breathed, they had internal organs, and yes, they were wearing real clothes. Nothing illusory about that dark worsted wool, or linen and silk. And no doubt all this superb "tissue" could vanish in a twinkling, and the costly clothes would drop to the ground on top of the empty shoes.

The old vampire placed a hand on Everard's shoulder. He had small but long fingers and he wore two stunning gold rings. This was a traditional way vampires greeted each other, not with embraces, not with kisses, but with the placing of the hand on the shoulder. Everard remembered that from times when he had lived amongst them.

"Young one," he said with the characteristic pomposity of the elder blood drinkers, "please, do not be afraid." He spoke in Parisian French.

Up close the ancient one's face was truly impressive, very fine of feature with exquisite black eyelashes and a serene smile. High cheekbones, a firm, discernible, yet narrow jaw. His skin did look like the petal of a gardenia in the moonlight, yes, and his white hair had a subtle silvery sheen. He hadn't been Born to Darkness with that hair. Rhoshamandes, Everard's maker, had long ago explained that when some of the ancient ones were badly burnt their hair was white forever after. Well, it was that kind of magnificent white hair.

"We know you've heard the Voice," said this ancient one. "I too have heard it. Others have heard it. Are you hearing it now?"

"No," said Everard.

"And it's telling you to burn others, isn't it?"

"Yes," said Everard. "I have never harmed another blood drinker. Never had to. Never want to. I've lived in this part of Italy for almost four hundred years. I don't go into Rome or Florence to fight with people."

"I know," said the ancient one. It was a pleasing voice, a gentle voice, but then all the old ones had good voices, at least as far as Everard had ever observed. What he remembered more than anything else about his maker, Rhoshamandes, was his seductive voice, and that voice luring him into the forest on the night he was Born to Darkness against his will. Everard had thought the lord in the castle was summoning him for an erotic encounter, that afterwards he'd be dismissed with a few coins if he'd managed to please, and that he would have tales of tapestry-covered walls and blazing fires and fine clothes to tell his grandchildren. Ha! He could remember Rhoshamandes talking to him as if it were last night: *You are surely one of the most beautiful young men in your village!*

"My name is Teskhamen," said this ancient one who was looking at him with such mild, gracious eyes. "I come from old Egypt. I was a servant of the Mother."

"Doesn't everyone say that these days, since the publication of the Vampire Chronicles?" asked Everard angrily before he could stop himself. "Do any of you ever cop to having been a renegade or some clever menace who wheedled the Blood from a Gypsy blood drinker in a ragged caravan?"

The ancient one laughed out loud. But it was a good-natured laugh. "Well, I see I have indeed put you at your ease," he said. "And that didn't prove to be hard after all." His face grew serious. "Do you have any idea who the Voice might be?"

"You're asking me?" Everard scoffed. "You must have two thousand years in the Blood. Look at you." He glared at the two ghosts. "Don't *you* know who he is?" He flashed back on Teskhamen. "That little monster's driving me crazy. I can't shut him out."

Teskhamen nodded. "I'm sorry to hear that, but it is possible to ignore him. It takes patience and skill, but it can be done."

"Oh, blah, blah, blah, blah, BLAH!" said Everard. "He sticks his invisible needle through my temple. He must be in the vicinity."

He glared again at the two ghosts. They didn't even shiver. Sometimes ghosts did that when you glared directly at them. The apparitions shivered or quivered, but not these two.

The one who appeared to be an older man extended his ghostly hand.

Everard took it, discovering it felt entirely human and that it was warm and soft.

"Raymond Gallant," said the ghost in English. "If you'll allow it, I'm your friend."

"Magnus," said the younger male ghost. His was a marvelous face for anyone, ghost or blood drinker, or mortal, for that matter. His eyes crinkled again agreeably as he smiled and he did indeed have a particularly beautiful mouth, what people call a generous mouth, as well formed as the Apollo Belvedere. His forehead was beautiful, and his hair moving back from it in waves of ashen blond was handsome.

Those names rang a bell, but Everard couldn't place them. Raymond Gallant. Magnus.

"I don't think the Voice is in the vicinity," said Teskhamen. "I think he can be anyplace that he wants to be, anywhere in the world, but it does seem he can only be in one place at a time and of course that 'place' is inside a blood drinker's mind."

"Which means what, exactly?" demanded Everard. "How's he doing it? Who is he?"

"That is what we would like to know," said Raymond Gallant. Again he spoke in British English.

Everard switched into English immediately. He liked the brashness of English, and he had become entirely used to it as the language of the world today. But Everard's English was American.

"What are you, a blood drinker, doing with two ghosts?" he asked Teskhamen. "No offense intended, believe me. It's only that I've never seen a blood drinker keep company with ghosts."

"Well, we do keep company," said the iron-haired apparition, the one who appeared to be an older man. "We have for a long time. But I assure you, we have no evil designs on you or anyone."

"Then why are you here and asking me questions about this Voice?"

"He's inciting violence all over the world right now," said Teskhamen. "Young blood drinkers are being slain in small towns and cities everywhere. This happened once before but we know the cause of that massacre. We don't know the cause of what's going on now. And blood drinkers are being quietly annihilated in out-of-the-way places and even in their private sanctuaries without anyone taking notice."

"Then how did you notice?" asked Everard.

"We hear things," said the ghost named Magnus. Deep, smooth voice.

Everard nodded.

"There's an American vampire out of New York broadcasting about it," said Everard with a faint sneer. There was something insufferably vulgar about those words, and he was mortified suddenly to have spoken them, but at once the three beings all confirmed agreeably that they already knew.

"Benji Mahmoud," said Teskhamen.

"He's as addle-brained as the Voice," said Everard. "The little numbskull thinks we're a tribe."

"Well, we are, aren't we?" asked the ancient one gently. "I always thought we were. We were in olden times."

"Well, not now," said Everard. "Listen, this Voice thing promised to destroy me if I didn't do its bidding. Do you think it has the power to do that? Can it do that?"

"It appears to work in a fairly simply way," said Teskhamen. "It rouses old ones to burn others, and young ones to burn their lairs. And I suspect it depends entirely on finding gullible and susceptible servants. It seems to have no other plan."

"Then it can rouse some gullible or susceptible one to stamp out me."

"We'll tell you what we can to prevent that," said Teskhamen.

"Why would you bother?" asked Everard.

"We truly are all one tribe," said the iron-haired ghost softly. "Human, vampire, spirit, ghost—we're all sentient creatures bound to this planet. Why can't we work together in the face of something like this?"

"And to what end?" asked Everard.

"To stop the Voice," said Teskhamen with just a trace of impatience. "To prevent it from hurting others."

"But we deserve to be hurt," said Everard. "Don't we?" He was surprised to hear this come out of his mouth.

"No, I don't think that we do," said Teskhamen. "That's the kind of thinking that has to change. That's the kind of thinking that will change."

"Oh, wait, don't tell me!" Everard declared. And in a mock-American voice he said, "'We are the change that we seek'! No? Tell me you believe that, and I'm going to fall off this chair and roll into the street laughing."

The three smiled at him, but he could sense that, polite as they were, they did not like being mocked, and he was suddenly sorry. It penetrated to him with amazing sharpness that these three had been nothing but kind and courteous and that he was behaving crossly and stupidly, wasting these moments, and for what?

"Why can't we come together," asked the younger male ghost, "to achieve some kind of peace for the realm we share?"

"And what realm is that?" asked Everard. "Since you're a ghost, my friend, and I'm flesh and blood, no matter how loathsome I am?"

"I was a human being once," said the younger ghost. "I was a blood drinker for centuries after that. And I am a ghost now. And my soul has been my soul in all three forms."

"Blood drinker," murmured Everard. He was marveling, studying the face of this ghost again and that generous, kindly mouth and the expressive eyes. "Magnus!" he said with a start. "Not Magnus the Alchemist."

"Yes, that's who I was," replied the ghost. "And I knew you in those old times, Everard. You were made by Rhoshamandes and I was made, so to speak, by Benedict."

Everard laughed out loud. "Methinks it was you who made Benedict all right," he said. "Stealing the blood from him and making him the laughingstock of blood drinkers everywhere. And so you've become a ghost, a ghost of a blood drinker."

"I don't think I'm the only one in this world," said Magnus, "but I've had help from my closest friends here, help in becoming what you see before you."

"Well, it bears no resemblance to the wicked old hunchback I knew," Everard said, but he was immediately sorry. He looked down and then up. "I regret those words," he whispered. "I beg your pardon."

But Magnus was smiling. "No need to be sorry. I was a frightening creature. One of the great advantages of being a ghost is that you can perfect the etheric body much more profoundly than ever you could the physical body even with the Blood. And so you see me as I had always wanted to look."

It was shaking Everard to his bones that this was Magnus, the Magnus he'd known, yes, and the Magnus who'd made the Vampire Lestat, the fledgling who'd changed vampiric history. And yes, he could somehow see through this dazzle and gloss the Magnus that he had known, that wise and brilliant alchemist who'd begged Rhoshamandes so eloquently for the Blood, that healer who'd worked miracles amongst the poor, and studied the stars with a bronze telescope before ever Copernicus had become famous for it.

This was Magnus, beloved of Notker of Prüm, later brought into the Blood by Benedict quite deliberately and lovingly. Notker was alive now somewhere, of that Everard was certain. Rhoshamandes had said that Notker's music would be heard in the snowy Alps when a thousand older blood drinkers had gone to their fiery graves.

Magnus a ghost now.

And the other? This Raymond Gallant, who had he been?

"Are you hearing the Voice now?" asked the ghost named Raymond Gallant.

"No," Everard answered. "He went silent right before I saw you. He's gone. I don't know how I know, but he's gone. I can sort of feel it when he's aiming his magic beam at me, as if it were some kind of laser."

He tried not to stare so much at these two. He glanced uneasily at Teskhamen.

"Has he never said anything to you about his ultimate purpose?" asked Teskhamen. "Has he offered you secrets?"

"Mostly threats," replied Everard. "He's so childish, so stupid. He tries to prey on my fears, my . . . my being so very alone of late. But I can see through his tricks. He speaks of unendurable pain, and near blindness, and that he is powerless to so much as lift a finger."

"He said those things? Used those words?" asked Raymond Gallant.

"Yes, he says he's helpless on his own, that he requires my loving assistance, my devotion, my trust in him. As if I should trust him! He says I have powers in me of which I don't dream, and he talks of blood drinkers hiding in Italy and wants me to burn them out. He's merciless."

"But you don't listen to him."

"Why should I?" asked Everard. "And what can I do if this is one of the ancient ones and if he wants to destroy me? What can I do!"

"You do know how to hide from the Fire Gift, don't you?" asked Teskhamen. "Your best way is to simply escape. Travel away from the spot as fast as you can, using the Cloud Gift if at all possible to simply get beyond the attacker's range. If you can go swiftly down into the earth, that's even better, because it cannot penetrate the earth. Whoever sends the Fire Gift has to see the victim, see the building, see the target. That's the only way it can work."

Everard was no expert on any of this. He was more grateful for this clarifying advice, frankly, than he could say. He had to admit Benji Mahmoud had been saying something similar, but he'd never trusted him any more than humans trusted televangelists.

And Everard had never been formally taught a thing about the higher gifts. He was not going to confess that all he knew of them he'd learned from the Vampire Chronicles, and that he'd been practicing his skills, if that's what they were, based on descriptions written by disreputable vampire authors like Lestat de Lioncourt and Marius de Romanus and so forth and so on. He let these thoughts roll where they might. Curse the Children of Satan and their rules and injunctions. They hadn't cared anything for vampiric gifts!

Now the great Rhoshamandes, his maker, that was another matter. What tales he'd told of riding the winds, and, oh, the spells he could cast, the visions he could arouse for Everard and others. Rhoshamandes in his burgundy-colored robes, fingers laden with rings, playing chess at his great inlaid-marble chessboard with those kings and queens and knights and bishops and pawns carved especially for him, to whom he'd given various names. Chess was his favorite game, he declared, because it pitted Mind Gift against Mind Gift.

"Yes," Magnus whispered. "I remember him so very well. And I often sat at that chessboard with him."

Everard would have blushed had he been human, to have had his thoughts read that easily, those images examined. But he didn't mind. He was too fascinated with this ghost of Magnus. So many questions came to his mind: "Can you eat, can you drink, can you make love, can you taste?"

"No," said Magnus, "but I can see very well, and I can feel hot and cold in a pleasurable way, and I have a sense of being here, being alive, occupying this space, being tangible, and having a tempo in time. . . ."

Ah, this was Magnus all right, this was Magnus talking, who could talk the night away with Rhoshamandes. How Rhoshamandes had loved him and respected him, throwing a veil of protection about him and forbidding all blood drinkers to harm him. Even after he'd stolen the Blood, Rhoshamandes had not hunted him down and sought to kill him.

"He has a great fascination for me," Rhoshamandes had said. "And Benedict is to blame for allowing it to happen. But let's see what he will do with the Blood, poor humpbacked and clever Magnus."

"Be very careful, Everard," said Magnus. He looked for all the world like a man of forty-five, or perhaps fifty in these healthy times of plenty and rampant good health, with glowing skin and hair truly the color of ashes. Why hadn't he made himself flamingly beautiful like the flashy Lestat with that leonine golden mane, and those violet-blue eyes? But as he gazed at Magnus, this seemed a stupid question. This was a splendid being here before him. They were both splendid, these ghosts. And they could change, couldn't they, anytime they wanted to.

"Yes, but we try not to do that," said Raymond. "We seek to perfect what we are, not to constantly alter it. We seek to find something that is a true expression of our soul with which to shape what makes up our form. But there's no need for you to trouble yourself over these things."

"Stay safe," said Teskhamen. "Be clever. And if this Voice provokes a gathering of the tribe, consider coming. We cannot stay the same in these times, because nothing now can stay the same, and we must needs meet the challenges as humans are meeting them."

Teskhamen took a small white card out of his pocket and handed it to Everard. A gentleman's calling card. On it was written the name TESKHAMEN in golden script, and beneath it was an e-mail very simple to memorize, actually, and a phone number.

"We're going now, friend," said Teskhamen. "But if you need us, contact us. We wish you luck."

"I think I'll survive this, same way I survived world wars and the earlier massacre, but thank you. And thank you for putting up with my . . . my disagreeable behavior."

"It's been a pleasure," said Teskhamen. "One last bit of advice. Keep listening to Benji. If there is to be a coming together, Benji will give the word."

"Hmmm." Everard shook his head. "A coming together? Like last time? A big showdown to stop the wicked Voice the way the wicked

Queen was stopped? How do you have a showdown with a Voice that can pop into the head of anyone at any time and can hear anything perhaps that I'm saying . . . or even thinking?"

"That's a good question," said Raymond Gallant. "It all depends, doesn't it, on what the Voice really wants."

"And what is that," said Everard, "other than to turn us against one another?"

The three creatures rose to their feet. Teskhamen extended his hand.

Everard also rose with obvious respect. "You make me think of better times, you really do," he murmured in spite of himself. Suddenly he was furious at himself for becoming so emotional.

"And what times were those?" asked Teskhamen kindly.

"When Rhoshamandes was still . . . Oh, I don't know. Hundreds of years ago before the Children of Satan destroyed his castle. Destroyed everything. That's what happens when blood drinkers unite, band together, believe things. We're evil. We've always been."

The three looked at him calmly without making the slightest response. Nothing in their expressions or demeanor suggested agreement. Or evil.

"And you have no idea at all where Rhoshamandes might be, do you?" asked Raymond Gallant.

"None," said Everard. And then he found himself confessing, "If I did, why, I'd go to him." Such strange words coming from him, who had such complete disregard for other blood drinkers, who scorned covens, havens, vampire hostels, and gangs. But he knew he had confessed the truth, that he'd travel the Earth to find Rhoshamandes. Actually, he never traveled anywhere much. But it was good to think he'd travel the Earth to find his old master. "He's long gone, dead, burned up, immolated, whatever!" he said sharply. "Has to be."

"You think?" asked Raymond Gallant.

A sudden pain tugged at Everard's heart. *He has to be dead or he would have found me by now, gathered me to him, forgiven me. . . .*

Rhoshamandes had abandoned the wild thick forests of France and Germany in the 1300s. Weary of battling the ever-increasing Children of Satan who had cannibalized his own fledglings to his eternal misery, he had simply left the ancient battlefield.

But Everard had never known the true story. The Children of Satan had had Everard by then, dragging him out nightly to scourge the innocent of Paris. They bragged that they'd driven the last great blasphemer from French land. Had they really? Magnus they had not feared as they had Rhoshamandes.

They told tales of Rhoshamandes's castle and lands burnt in the daylight hours by rabid monks and nuns driven to do it by the nightly whispers of Children of Satan pretending to be angels. Ah, those times. Those superstitious times when vampires could speak to gullible religious minds and play infernal games with them.

"Well, I can tell you this," Everard said, denying the pain. "If he's slumbering underground somewhere under some Merovingian ruin, the Voice won't get anywhere with him, no matter what state he's in. He's too wise for that, too powerful. He was . . . he was magnificent."

Sharp grinding memory. Everard going out in filthy rags with the Children of Satan to harry the Parisian poor, slinking into filthy hovels to feed on the innocent, and somewhere near the voice of Rhoshamandes calling: "Everard, break free. Come back to me!"

"Goodbye, Everard," said Teskhamen, and the three moved off together.

For a long moment, Everard watched them as they walked down the narrow street and disappeared around the corner.

Not a single human being would ever guess what they were. Their human poise was simply superb.

He leaned his elbow on the table and rested his chin in his hand. Was he glad they were gone? Or was he sorry?

Did he want to run after them and say, Don't leave me here! Take me with you. I want to stay with you.

Yes and no.

He did want to do that, but he simply could not do it. He didn't know how to do that, how to speak that honestly to them, how to implore them for their help or their companionship. He didn't know how to be anything but what he was.

Suddenly the Voice was there. He heard it sigh.

"They can't protect you from me," said the Voice. "They're devils."

"They didn't seem like devils to me," said Everard testily.

"They and their laughable Talamasca!" said the Voice. "Be damned!"

"Talamasca," whispered Everard in amazement. "Of course. Talamasca! That's where I heard that name Raymond Gallant before. Why, that man was known to Marius. That man . . ." Died about five hundred years ago.

It was amusing to him suddenly, very amusing. He'd always known about the Talamasca, the old Order of scholars of the supernatural. Rhoshamandes had warned him about them, and their old monastery in southern France. Yet his maker had urged him to respect them and leave them alone. He'd loved them the way he'd loved Magnus.

"For they are gentle scholars," he'd said in that deep seductive voice of his, "and they mean us no harm. Ah, but it is astonishing. They know as much of us as the Church of Rome, but they do not condemn us and they mean us no harm. They want to learn about us. Imagine it. They study us, and when have we ever studied ourselves? I rather like them for that. I do. You must never hurt them."

And so their membership included humans and ghosts, did it? And blood drinkers. Raymond Gallant, Teskhamen, and Magnus.

Hmmm. Did all of their human members become ghosts when they died? Well, that would never have worked, surely. There'd be thousands of spectral members floating around by now. That was absurd.

No. It was fairly easy to figure that it was a rare occurrence to recruit a dying member from their ranks to remain with them "in spirit" simply because it was so very rare for any dying person's spirit to remain behind. Oh, the planet had lots of ghosts, but they were an infinitesimal remnant of all those poor slobs who'd been born and died since the dawn of creation. But how blessed must be the ghosts inducted into the Talamasca with book-educated sorcerers to help them learn to materialize? That's what Magnus had been driving at. No wonder they'd been so good at it, those two, with their warm ruddy complexions and their shining moist lips.

But the vampire, Teskhamen. How in the world did he become part of them?

Everard ran a quick scan in his mind of what he'd learned about the Talamasca—from Lestat's writings, and Marius's memoir. Dedicated, honorable, committed to truth without religious suspicion, censure, or judgment, yes. If their ranks included vampires, the vast majority of the rank and file certainly had never guessed it.

Then there was the great mystery of who had founded the Talamasca. If it turned out to be a vampire, a mere blood drinker, such as Teskhamen, old as he was, well, that would be a crushing disappointment to the others, wouldn't it?

Hmmm. That was their problem.

He studied the little white card, and put it safely in his jacket.

"Contemptible," said the Voice. "In the end, I will burn them all as well. I will burn their libraries, their little museums, their retreat houses, their—."

"I get it!" said Everard angrily.

"You will rue the night you mocked me."

"Oh, yeah?" Everard said in a low American drawl. "If you're all that strong, Voice, why don't you give it a try? They've been around since the Dark Ages. And they don't appear to be afraid of you at all."

"You infuriating stupid disrespectful and foolish monster!" said the Voice. "Your time will come."

Everard was suddenly startled. A waiter stood beside him with a mug of coffee, the steam rising in the cool air.

"Talking to yourself again, Signore de Landen?" he said cheerfully.

Everard smiled, shook his head, and took out a couple of bills of big, pretty Italian currency and gave them to the young man.

Then he sat back and held the warm cup in both hands. Lestat did get that right in the Vampire Chronicles, he thought. It was nice to hold a hot mug of coffee in your two hands and let the steam rise into your face.

The only sounds around him were the predictable voices of the town. A motor scooter firing up somewhere far off and then belching as it went away into the country, and the low hum of conversations blossoming behind closed doors.

He was thirsting.

Suddenly he was thirsting, really thirsting, but he hadn't the energy to go far enough away from his home to satisfy his thirst. He left the coffee, and got up and made his way through the streets to the city gates.

Within moments he'd passed out of the illumination of the high-walled town and he was walking uphill fast in cool darkness and he felt like weeping and he didn't quite know why.

Was it conceivable that we are a tribe? Was it conceivable that we were beings who could love one another, be gentle with one another the way that Teskhamen had been with his spectral companions, the way Rhoshamandes had been with him so very long ago?

What if there had never been any Children of Satan in his existence, starving and torturing him and teaching him that he was a child of the Devil, that he had to be miserable and create misery for others, that he was a damned and loathsome thing?

What if there had only been mad Rhoshamandes in his crumbling old castle speaking of poetry and power and "splendor in the Blood"?

Human beings didn't buy all that old religious rot nowadays, did they? They didn't skulk about under the burden of Original Sin and concupiscence anymore, pleading for absolution for having bedded their wives the night before going to Holy Communion, cursing their anatomy for dooming them to Eternal Damnation, denouncing themselves as bags of stinking bones and flesh. No, quite the contrary. In this new century they were filled with hope and a new kind of innocence and strangely confident optimism that they could solve the problems confronting them, and cure all illness and feed the entire world. At least so it seemed in this clean and peaceful part of Europe which in the past had known so much suffering, so much misery, so much bloodshed and meaningless death.

What if such a bright and shining time had come for blood drinkers as well, even the most monstrous, as Everard had become? His thoughts drifted back in spite of himself to the last brother in the Blood he'd loved—such a fine, spirited young male vampire who, remembering little of his life before the Dark Gift, had seen life around him as miraculous, whispering of the Blood being a sacrament and singing long carefree songs of an evening to the moon and the stars.

But that one had been burnt to ashes by the great and terrible Queen Akasha when she passed over. Everard had seen that with his own eyes—all that sweet vitality extinguished in an instant, indifferently as fire engulfed the whole vampire hangout in Venice where so many others had perished as well. Why had Everard survived?

He shuddered. He didn't want to think of that. Best never to love another. Best to forget instantly those who winked out as if they'd never existed. Best to live for the pleasures of each night as they came.

But what if it were a time now for them all to come together, to be the tribe that Benji believed them to be, to approach others, old and young, without rage or fear?

Rhoshamandes had laughed at the very idea of the Children of Satan, and their sanctimonious ways. He used to say, "I was in the Blood before their god was even born."

Everard didn't want to think too much about all that either. Let it go. And never remember the satanic covens and their Sabbats. Forget forever those horrid hymns offered to the Prince of Darkness.

Ah, what if it were possible to come together, and worship not a Prince of Darkness but *a prince of us*?

He opened his iPhone and tapped the screen for the app that connected him directly to Benji's broadcast. The broadcast should be in full swing now in America.

Two hours before dawn.

He was dozing in his favorite leather chair, half dreaming.

Benji was still talking very low through the Bose speaker dock in which Everard had deposited his iPhone. But he was not hearing this.

The dream: Back in Rhoshamandes's castle in that big hollow hall with the fire blazing and Benedict, handsome Benedict with the pretty face, begging to make a vampire of the monk known as Notker the Wise, a creature of immense talent who wrote music night and day as one possessed, songs, motets, chants, and canticles. And Rhoshamandes considering it, nodding and moving his chess pieces about, and saying, "But you blood drinkers brought over from the Christian god, I simply do not know."

"Oh, but, Master, the only god Notker worships is music. Master, would that he could play his music forever."

"Shave off that monkly crown of hair from him first," Rhoshamandes had said, "and then you bring him over. Your blood, not my blood. But I will not have a tonsured blood drinker."

Benedict laughed. It was no secret that Rhoshamandes had locked Benedict up for months to allow his "monkly" hair to grow back all over his pretty head before he'd given him the Dark Blood, and Benedict had prepared for the Dark Gift as if it were a sacrament. Rhoshamandes demanded beauty in his fledglings.

Notker the Wise of Prüm was famously beautiful.

A noise awakened Everard.

It drew him abruptly back from that familiar old hall with its soaring beams and stone pavers.

He heard the sharp strike of a match. Flare of flames against his eyelids. There were no matches in this house! He used the Fire Gift to light his fires.

He shot out of the leather easy chair and found himself facing two wild-eyed and disheveled young blood drinkers—a male and a female in the typical vagabond dress of denim and leather. They were setting fire to the draperies in this room.

"Burn, you devil, burn!" shouted the male in Italian.

With a roar, Everard hurled the female through the window, shattering the glass, and yanked down the burning drapery and threw it over the male as he dragged him roughly through the opening and out into the dark garden.

Both were cursing and snarling at him. The male rolled out from under the heap of smoldering velvet with a knife in his hand and ran at Everard.

Burn.

Everard collected the Fire Gift with all his strength in the center of his forehead, then sent the blast against the fool. Flames shot up out of the boy's body, enveloping his arms and head, and his gasping screams were silenced by the roar of the blaze, the Blood burning as if it were petrol. The female had fled.

But Everard caught her as she mounted the wall, dragging her backwards as he sank his fangs into her throat. She screamed as he tore open the artery, the blood squirting into his mouth, against the back of his mouth, inundating his tongue.

At once the flood of images drugged him, her pounding heart driving them as it drove the blood: the Voice, yes, the Voice telling her to kill, telling them both to kill, lovers made in a filthy back alley in Milan by a scrawny bearded blood drinker who pushed them out to kill and steal, twenty years in the Blood maybe, dying, and then it broke down into bits and pieces of childhood, her white First Communion dress, incense, the crowded Cathedral, "Ave Maria," a mother's smiling face, a dress of checkered cloth, apples on a plate, taste of apples, the inevitable peace. He drank deeper, drawing every last drop he could from her, on and on, till there was nothing and the heart had stopped gasping like an open-mouth fish.

From the garden shed, he took a spade and chopped her head from her body. Then he slurped what blood now oozed from the torn neck tissues, the emptying vessels. Shimmer of consciousness. Ghastly! He dropped her head and brushed his hands clean.

With a gentle blast of the Fire Gift he incinerated her remains, the sightless staring head with the long straggly locks of black hair caught in her white teeth, the limp body.

The smoke died away.

The soft breeze of early fall caressed him and comforted him.

The silent garden glittered with fragments of broken glass on the tender grass. The blood had cleared his head, sharpened his vision, warmed him, and made the dark morning miraculous. Like jewels, this broken glass. Like stars.

He breathed in the scent of the lemon trees. All the night was empty around him. No dirges to be sung for this anonymous pair, these beings who might have survived for a thousand years if only they had not pitted themselves against one they could not hope to vanquish.

"Ah, so Voice," Everard said with contempt. "You won't leave me alone, will you? You haven't hurt me, you contemptible monster. You sent these two to their deaths."

But there was no answer.

With the spade he buried the pair, carefully smoothing down the earth, scraping the clods off the stepping-stones, off the path.

He was shaken. He was disgusted.

But one thing was certain. His gift for making fire was now stronger than ever. He had never actually ever used it against another blood drinker. But this had taught him what he could do if he had to do it.

Small consolation.

Then the Voice sighed. Ah, such a sigh. "That was my intention, Everard," said the Voice. "I told you I wanted you to kill them, the riffraff. And now you have made a start."

Everard made no reply.

He leaned on the handle of the spade and thought.

The Voice had gone.

Quiet the sleeping countryside. Not so much as a car moving on a country road. Only this clean breeze and the glistening leaves of the fruit trees around him, and the white calla lilies glowing against the walls of the villa, the walls of the garden. Fragrance of lilies. Miracle of lilies.

Across the sea, Benji Mahmoud was still talking. . . .

His voice suddenly drove a sword through Everard's heart.

"Elders of the tribe," Benji was appealing. "We need you. Come back to us. Come back to your lost children. Hear my cry on high, a mourning and a bitter weeping, I am Benji weeping for my lost brothers and sisters because they are no more."

11

Gremt Stryker Knollys

IT WAS an old colonial mansion, red with white trim, a sprawling building with deep verandas and peaked roofs, covered with
soft fluttering green vines and invisible from the winding road
on account of the massive bamboo and mango trees surrounding it.
A lovely place with palms swaying ever so gracefully in the breeze.
It appeared abandoned but it had never been. Mortal servants maintained it by day.

And this vampire Arjun had been sleeping beneath it for centuries.

Now he was weeping. He sat at the table, his face in his hands.

"In my time I was a prince," he said. He wasn't boasting. He was
merely reflecting. "And among the Undead I was a prince for so long.
I do not know how I came to this."

"I know all this is true," Gremt said.

The blood drinker was undeniably beautiful, with light golden-
brown skin so flawless it appeared unreal now, and large fierce black
eyes. He had a wealth of jet-black hair worthy of a lion. Made by the
wandering blood drinker Pandora in the days of the Chola dynasty
of southern India, he had indeed been a prince, and much darker of
skin than he was now and just as comely. The Blood had lightened his
skin, but not his hair, which was sometimes the case, though no one
knew why.

"I have always known who you were," said Gremt. "I knew you
when you traveled Europe with Pandora. I beg you, for both of us, tell
me simply in your own words what happened."

He withdrew a small white visiting card from his pocket, on which was written his full name in golden script: GREMT STRYKER KNOLLYS. Beneath it was his e-mail address and the numbers of his mobile phone.

But this blood drinker didn't even acknowledge this human gesture. He could not. And Gremt moved the card discreetly to the center of the teak table and put it halfway under the brass base of the small shaded candle that was flickering there, giving a little bit of light to their faces. A soft golden light also came from the open doors along this deep porch.

This was a beautiful place.

It touched Gremt that this battered soul, this creature in such distress, had taken such time to wash the dirt from his shining hair, and that he was clothed now in a long well-fitted and richly jeweled sherwani, and black silk pants, and that his hands were clean and scented with true sandalwood.

"But how could you have known me then?" asked the blood drinker in a plaintive voice. "What are you? You're not human, I know this. You are not human. And you are not what I am. What are you?"

"I am your friend now," said Gremt. "I've always been your friend. I've been watching you for centuries, not just you, but all of you."

Arjun was suspicious, of course, but more than anything he was horrified by what he'd done and he was warming piteously to Gremt's persuasive tone, to the warmth of Gremt's hand on his.

"All I wanted was to sleep," Arjun said. He spoke with the same accent that was familiar in Goa and India to this day, though his command of English was perfect. "I knew I would return. My beloved, Pandora, she knows that I am here. She's always known. I was safe here when the queen Akasha went on her rampage. She didn't find me beneath this house."

"I understand," said Gremt. "Pandora is coming to you."

"How can you know this?" Arjun asked. "Oh, truly I want to believe it. I need her so very much. But how do you know?"

Gremt hesitated. He gestured for Arjun to speak. "Tell me everything."

"Ten years ago, I sat on this veranda with Pandora, and we spoke," said Arjun. "I was still tired. I was not ready to join with her and her beloved friends. I told her I needed the sanctuary of the Earth and what we learn in the Earth, for we do learn when we sleep as if an umbilical cord connects us to the living world above."

"That's true," said Gremt.

"It was never my intention to wake now."

"Yes."

"But this Voice. It spoke to me. I mean it was in my mind at first and it seemed these were my own thoughts, but in my sleep I did not embrace these thoughts."

"Yes."

"And then it had a tone and a vocabulary all its own, this Voice, speaking to me in English sharply, telling me that I wanted to rise, I, Arjun, wanted to rise, to go into Mumbai and wipe them out, the young ones. It seemed so true to me, true! Why did I listen to this? I, who have never wanted trouble with my own kind, who stood my ground patiently centuries ago with Marius, telling him from my soul I would give up my maker to him if that's what he wanted, what she wanted. You understand? I fought my last battles when I was a mortal prince. What is this to me, murdering, massacring, burning young ones?" He hastened to answer his own question. "Is there something in the gentlest of us that longs to destroy? Something that dreams of annihilating other sentient beings?"

"Perhaps there is," said Gremt. "When did you realize that this was not what you wanted?"

"When it was happening!" confessed Arjun. "The buildings were in flames. They were screaming, pleading with me, going down on their knees. And these were not all fledglings, you understand. Some of them had been in the Blood hundreds of years. 'We survived the Queen to perish like this?' That's what they screamed as they put out their arms to me. 'What have we done to you?' But it was only slowly coming clear to me what I had started. It became a battle, their fighting me with the Fire Gift and I overriding their weaker power. It was . . . it was . . ."

"Pleasurable."

Tears of shame rose in Arjun's eyes. He nodded.

"Ah, you murder a human being," Arjun said, "and you steal a life, yes, and that is unspeakable. You murder a blood drinker and you steal eternity! You steal immortality!"

He laid his head down on his arm.

"What happened in Kolkata?"

"That was not me," he said at once. He sat back in the old rattan peacock chair, the broad woven back creaking against his weight. "I did not do it."

"I believe you," said Gremt.

"But why did I kill these children in Mumbai?"

"The Voice roused you for the purpose. It's done this in other places. It's done it in the Orient. It's doing it in South America. I've suspected from the beginning there was no one blood drinker enacting the Burning."

"But who is the Voice?" asked Arjun.

Gremt grew quiet. "Pandora is coming," he said.

Arjun rose to his feet, almost upsetting the big chair behind him. He looked from right to left, trying to see through the darkness.

When she emerged from the long thick bamboo hedge, he went into her arms, and for a long moment, they held one another, rocking back and forth, and then he broke the grip and covered her face with kisses. She stood very still, allowing this, a slender female with wavy brown hair wearing a long simple hooded cloak and robe, her pale-white hands stroking Arjun's hair, her eyes closed as she savored the moment.

Excitedly he brought her towards the veranda, and into the light coming from the rooms of the bungalow. "Sit here, please, sit here!" he said, bringing her to the teakwood table and the peacock chairs. Then, unable to stop himself, he embraced her again and sobbed silently against her shoulder.

She whispered to him in the tongue they'd shared when she'd wooed and wed him. She consoled him with her kisses.

Gremt had risen to his feet as any gentleman might in the presence of a woman. And this woman, Pandora, took his measure carefully, even as she suffered more kisses and embraces from Arjun. Her eyes were now fixed on him, and she was obviously listening to the beat of Gremt's heart, to the sound of his respiration, as she studied his skin, his eyes, his hair.

What did she see? A tall blue-eyed male with short black wavy hair and Caucasian skin and a face modeled on a Greek statue, a man with broad capable shoulders and slender hands, dressed in a plain long black silk *thawb* that covered him to his ankles, a garment that might have passed for a priest's cassock in another country. This was the body Gremt had perfected for himself over some fourteen hundred years. It might have fooled any human being on the planet. It could withstand the scrutiny of X-ray machines in modern airports. But it could not fool Pandora. It wasn't biologically human.

She was shocked to the soul, but Gremt knew full well she'd seen beings like him before. Many times. Powerful beings walking around in made-up bodies, so to speak. Indeed she'd seen Gremt many a time, though she had not always known that it was Gremt by any means. And the very first time he had ever seen her, he had been bodiless.

"I am your friend," Gremt said immediately. And he extended his hand to her, though she didn't lift her hand in response.

Arjun was now wiping away his tears with an old linen handkerchief. Carefully, he tucked this back into his pocket.

"I did not mean to do it!" he said frantically. He was imploring her to understand.

And Pandora as if wakened from a spell turned her eyes away from Gremt and back to him.

"I knew you didn't," she said. "I understood this completely."

"What you must think of me!" he persisted, his face stricken with shame.

"Ah, but it wasn't you at all, was it?" she said at once, taking his hand and then kissing him again and drawing back once more to look at Gremt. "It was a voice, wasn't it?"

"Yes, a voice," he said. "I was telling Gremt. Gremt understands. Gremt is a friend."

Very reluctantly, she sat down as Arjun urged her to do so, and he settled back into his chair to the left of her.

Only then did Gremt take his seat again.

"But you must have believed me guilty," Arjun said to Pandora, "or why else would you have come here to me?"

Pandora was again staring at Gremt. She was far too uncomfortable with the obvious mystery of Gremt to hear what Arjun wanted her to hear.

Gremt turned to Arjun and spoke softly. "Pandora knew because of the pictures, Arjun. When it happened there were witnesses snapping pictures, and those pictures went viral, as they say on the internet. These pictures were infinitely more detailed and clear than telepathic glimpses. These pictures don't fade as memory fades; they will circulate for all time. And in New York, a young blood drinker named Benjamin Mahmoud, made by Marius, posted the pictures on a website. And Pandora saw those pictures."

"Ahhh! Unspeakable disgrace," Arjun said, covering his face with his long fingers. "And so Marius and his children think I am guilty of this. And how many others believe it?"

"No, not so," said Pandora. "We're all coming to understand. Everyone is coming to understand."

"You must. You must know that it was the Voice." He looked helplessly to Gremt for confirmation.

"But Arjun is himself now," said Gremt. "And he is now perfectly capable of resisting the Voice. And the Voice has moved on to some other slumbering blood drinkers."

"Yes, that explains part of it," said Pandora, "but not all of it. Because it is now almost certain that the burnings happening in South America arc being done by none other than Khayman."

"Khayman?" said Arjun. "Gentle Khayman? But I thought he had become the consort and guard of the twins now!"

"That he is and has been for a long time," said Gremt. "But Khayman has always been a broken soul, and he is now apparently as susceptible to the Voice as some of the other old ones."

"And Maharet cannot control him?" asked Pandora. There was an edge to her voice. She wanted to talk of all this, wanted to know what Gremt knew, but she wanted most certainly to know more about Gremt, so she spoke with a tone that said, You are a stranger to me.

She narrowed her eyes. "Is Maharet herself the Voice?" she asked with obvious horror.

Gremt said nothing.

"Could it be her twin, Mekare?"

Still Gremt didn't answer.

"Unspeakable thought," whispered Arjun.

"Well, who else could guide gentle Khayman to such things?" Pandora murmured. She was thinking out loud.

Again Gremt didn't answer.

"And if it is not one of those two," Pandora went on. "Well, then, who is it?" She asked it as if she were a lawyer and Gremt were a hostile witness in a courtroom.

"It's far from clear," Gremt said finally. "But I think I know who it is. What I don't know is what it wants and what it means to do in the long run."

"And what is all this to you, precisely?" Pandora demanded.

Arjun was frightened by her tone, and he blinked as if she were a light blinding him with her coldness.

"What does it matter to *you*, in particular," she pressed, "what happens to us, creatures like us?"

Gremt pondered. Sooner or later he must reveal all. Sooner or later he must put forth all he knew. But was this the time for it, and how many times must he confess everything? He'd learned what he needed to learn here from Arjun, and he had comforted Arjun as had been his intention. And he had laid eyes on Pandora to whom he owed an immense debt, but he was not sure he could answer her questions fully.

"You are dear to me," he said to her now in a small but steady voice. "And it gives me a certain pleasure, at last, after all these years, these centuries, to tell you that you are, and that you have always been, a shining star on my path, when you had no way of knowing it."

She was intrigued and mollified, but not satisfied. She waited. Her pale face, though she'd rubbed it with ashes and oil to make it less luminous tonight, looked virginal and biblical on account of her robes and the delicacy of her features. But behind that beautiful face she was calculating: How could she defend herself against a being like Gremt? Could she use her immense strength to harm him?

"No, you cannot," he said, giving her the answer. "It's time for me to leave you both." He rose to his feet. "I urge you to go to New York, to join with Armand and Louis there. . . ."

"Why?" she asked.

"Because you must come together to meet the challenge of the Voice, just as you did long ago to meet the challenge of Akasha! You cannot allow this thing to continue. You must get to the root of the mystery, and that is best done if you come together. If you go there, Marius will follow your lead surely. And so will others, others whose names you do not know and have never known, and surely Lestat will come. And it is to Lestat that people look for leadership."

"Oh why, oh why to that insufferable brat," murmured Arjun. "What has he ever done but make trouble?"

Gremt smiled. Pandora laughed softly under her breath as she glanced at Arjun, but then she fell silent again, thinking, gazing up at Gremt.

She weighed all this calmly. Nothing he'd said shocked or surprised her.

"And you, Gremt . . . why is it that you want the best for us?" asked Arjun. He rose to his feet. "You have been so kind to me. You have comforted me. Why?"

Gremt hesitated. He felt a knot loosened inside him.

"I love you all," he said in a low confidential voice. He wondered if he looked cold to them as he spoke. He was never entirely sure how his emotions registered on this made-up human face, even when he could feel the blood in his veins rushing to his cheeks, feel the tears rising in his eyes. He never knew for sure if all these myriad systems that he so well controlled with his mind were truly working as he wanted them to work. To smile, to laugh, to yawn, to weep—this was nothing. But to truly register what he felt inside his own true invisible heart—well, that was another matter.

"You know me," he said to Pandora. The tears were indeed rising in his eyes. "Oh, how I have loved you."

She sat in the peacock chair like a queen on a throne gazing up at him, the soft black silk hood making a dark frame around her radiant face.

"It was long, long ago," he said, "on the coast of Southern Italy, and a great man, a great scholar of those times, died on that night in a beautiful monastery that he had built called Vivarium. Do you remember these things? Do you remember Vivarium? His name was Cassiodorus, and all the world remembers him, remembers his letters, his books, and most truly what he was, the scholar that he was in those days when darkness was closing over Italy." His voice was rough now with his emotions. He could hear it breaking. But he went on, staring into her placid unwavering gaze.

"And you saw me then, saw me, a bodiless spirit, rise from the beehives in which I'd been slumbering, extended, and rooted through a thousand tentacles in the bees, in their energy, in their collective and mysterious life. You saw me spring loose at that moment and you saw me embrace with all my power the ludicrous figure of a straw man, a scarecrow, a thing of ridicule in a beggar's coat and pants, with an eyeless head and fingerless hands, and you saw me weep in that form, weep and mourn for the great Cassiodorus!"

Red tears had risen in her eyes. She had written of this not long ago, but would she believe now that he was the one she'd seen? Would she remain silent?

"I know you remember the words you spoke to me," he said. "You were so very brave. You didn't flee from something you couldn't understand. You didn't turn away in disgust from something unnatural even to you. You stood your ground and you spoke to me."

She nodded. She repeated the words she'd said to him that night.

"'If you would have fleshly life, human life, hard life which can move through time and space, then fight for it. If you would have human philosophy, then struggle and make yourself wise, so that nothing can hurt you ever. Wisdom is strength. Collect yourself, whatever you are, into something with a purpose.'"

"Yes," Gremt whispered. "And you said more. 'But know this: if you would become an organized being as you see in me, love all mankind and womankind and all their children. Do not take your strength from blood! Do not feed on suffering. Do not rise like a god above crowds chanting in adoration. Do not lie.'"

She nodded. "Yes," she said. A gentle smile broke over her face. She was not failing him in this moment. She was opening to him. He saw the same sensitivity and compassion in her now that he had seen those many years ago. And he had waited so very long for this! He wanted to reach out to her, to embrace her, but he didn't dare.

"I have followed your counsel," he said. Now he knew the tears were streaming from his eyes, though they never had before. "I've followed it always. And I built the Talamasca for you, Pandora, and for all of your kind and for all humankind and I patterned it as best I could on the monks and scholars of that beautiful old monastery, Vivarium, of which not a stone remains. I built it in memoriam to that brave Cassiodorus who studied and dipped his pen to write to the very end, with such strength and devotion, even as the world went dark around him."

She sighed. She was amazed. And her smile brightened. "And so it was from that moment?"

"Yes, that the Talamasca was born," he said. "From that encounter."

Arjun was gazing at him in pure wonder.

She rose from the table.

She moved around it and came towards Gremt. How loving and eager she appeared, how guileless and how fearless. She was no more frightened of him now than she'd been hundreds of years ago.

But he was spent, dangerously spent—more spent than he could ever have imagined by this—and he couldn't bear the sweetness, the joy, of having her in his arms.

"Forgive me," he whispered. He wiped foolishly at the tears on his face.

"Talk with us, stay with us here," she said imploringly. And Arjun uttered the same invitation.

But Gremt did the only thing he could do with his waning strength. He moved away fast, leaving the garden behind him and the lights of the bungalow lost in the forest of bamboo and mango trees.

She could have pursued him. If she did try to pursue, he would have no choice but to vanish, and that he did not want to do. He wanted to remain in this body as long as possible. That was always his choice.

But she didn't pursue him. She accepted his exit. And he knew he'd see her soon again. He'd see them all soon. And he would tell her and all of the others everything.

He followed the road for a long time, gradually regaining his strength, his body hardening once more, his pulse steady, the tears gone and his vision clear.

Headlights now and then picked him out of the darkness as cars swept by, leaving him once more in silence.

So he had told her. He had confided the great secret of the Talamasca to her first of all, before all others, and very soon he would make it known to the entire tribe of blood drinkers.

Never to those mortal Talamasca members who struggled as they always did to continue their studies. No. They would be left in peace to continue with the fables of the Order's origins.

But he would tell it to all of *them*, the great supernatural beings whom the Talamasca had studied from its very beginnings.

And maybe they would understand as she understood, and maybe they would accept as she had accepted. And maybe they would not fail him in those moments of connection he so badly needed with them.

Whatever the case, it was time, was it not, to help them directly, to reach out, to give them what he could as they confronted the greatest challenge in their history. Who better to help them solve the mystery of the Voice than Gremt Stryker Knollys?

12

Lestat

The Jungles of the Amazon

D AVID HAD DRAWN me out. Clever David. He'd called Benji's line in New York, chatting away with Benji on the broadcast about the crisis. He never gave his name. Didn't have to. Benji knew and I knew, and probably a lot of other blood drinkers knew, that cultured British voice.

On and on, David kept warning the young ones to stay out of the cities, to go into the countryside. He warned the old ones who might be hearing some anonymous command to destroy others: Don't listen. Benji kept agreeing. Over and over again, David said, Stay out of cities like Lyon, or Berlin, or Florence, or Avignon, or Milan, or Avignon or Rome or Avignon . . . and so on it went as he named city after city, always throwing in Avignon, and saying that he was certain the great hero, Lestat, was not the one guilty of all this. He'd stake his eternal life on Lestat's honor; Lestat's loyalty to others; Lestat's innate sense of goodness. Why, he, David, wished he had the authority of the pope, so that he could stand in the courtyard of the ruined Popes' Palace at Avignon and declare for all the world that Lestat wasn't guilty of these Burnings!

I burst out laughing.

I was listening in my drawing room in my father's château not four hundred kilometers from the little city of Avignon. There had never been any vampires in Avignon! And no burnings either.

Every night, I'd been listening to Benji. I was sick with worry for those who were dying. It was not all fledglings and the misbegotten. Many of the three- and four-hundred-year-old Children of Darkness were being slaughtered. Perhaps some of those I had known and loved on my long journey had been slaughtered, lost to me and to everyone else forever. When Akasha had gone on her rampage, her great Burning, she'd spared those connected to me, out of favor, but this new Burning seemed infinitely more terrible, more random. And I could not guess, any more than anyone else, who or what lay behind the devastation.

Where was my beloved Gabrielle? And how long would it be before this thing attacked the house of Armand and Louis in New York? I wondered: whoever and whatever it was, did it like listening to Benji's broadcasts, did it like hearing of all the misery it was creating?

"What do you think, Voice?" I asked.

No answer.

The Voice had long ago left me, hadn't it? The Voice was behind this. Everyone knew that now, didn't they? The Voice was rousing engines of murder from long slumber, urging them to use powers perhaps they'd never known they had.

"These old ones are being roused by this Voice," David said. "There's no doubt of this now. Witnesses have seen these old ones at the site of the massacres. So often it's a ragged figure, sometimes a hideous wraith. Surely it is the Voice waking these people. Are not many of us hearing this Voice?"

"Who is the Voice?" Benji demanded over and over again. "Which of you out there has heard the Voice? Call us, talk to us."

David rang off. The surviving fledglings were taking over the airwaves.

Benji had twenty phone lines now to receive those who were calling. Who staffed these lines? I didn't know enough about radio stations, phones, monitors, etcetera to understand how it worked. But no mortal voice had ever been broadcast by Benji, not for any reason, and sometimes one mournful and miserable blood drinker calling in would take an hour to unfold a tale of desperation. Did the other calls pile up?

Whatever the case, I had to get to Avignon. David wanted me to meet him in Avignon, in the old ruined Palace of the Popes, that was plain enough.

Benji was now addressing the Voice. "Call us here, Voice," he was saying in that chipper, confident manner of his. "Tell us what you want. Why are you trying to destroy us?"

I looked around my glorious digs here on the mountain. How I'd worked to reclaim this land of my father, how I'd worked to restore this château completely—and lately with my own hands, I'd dug out secret rooms beneath it. How I loved these old stone-walled chambers where I'd grown up, now transformed with every sweet amenity, and the view from these windows over the mountains and fields where I'd hunted as a boy. Why, why did I have to be drawn away from all this and into a battle I didn't want?

Well, I wasn't going to reveal this place to David or anybody else for that matter. If they didn't have the sense to look for me at Château de Lioncourt in the Auvergne, that was their misfortune! After all, the place had been on all the maps.

I put on my favorite red velvet jacket, slipped on my black boots and my usual sunglasses, and went to Avignon immediately.

Lovely little city, Avignon, with winding cobblestone streets and countless cafés and those old broken-down ruins where once the Roman Catholic pontiffs had reigned in splendor.

And David was waiting for me, sure enough, along with Jesse, haunting the old ruin. Not a single other blood drinker in the city.

I came right down into the dark grassy high-walled courtyard. No mortal eyes to witness this. Just the dark empty broken archways in the stone cloister gazing on like so many black eyes.

"Brat Prince." David rose from his seat on the grass and threw his arms around me. "I see you're in fine form."

"Yeah, yeah, yeah," I mumbled. But it was so good to see him again, to see both of them. Jesse hovered against the old crumbling stone wall, wrapped in a heavy gray muffler.

"Do we have to stand out here in this desolate place, under the shadow of all this history?" I said testily, but I didn't mean it. It was fine with me, this chilly September night with deep winter already in the air. I was embarrassingly glad that they'd forced me to this meeting.

"Of course not, Your Royal Highness," said David. "There's a fine little hotel in Lyon, the Villa Florentine, not far away at all"— he's telling me? I was born here!—"and we have comfortable rooms there." That sounded good enough.

Within fifteen minutes we'd made the little journey, and we

entered the red-carpeted suite by the patio doors and were comfortably settled in the parlor. The hotel was above the town, on a hilltop with a pretty view, and I liked it just fine.

Jesse looked worn and miserably unhappy, dressed in a creased and cracked brown leather jacket and pants, her gray wool sweater high under her chin, muffler covering her mouth, hair the usual shimmering veil of copper waves. David was in his gray worsted wool with a nappy suede vest and flashing silk tie—all bespoke most likely. He was a good deal brighter in tone and expression than Jesse, but I knew the gravity of the situation.

"Benji doesn't guess the half of it," Jesse said, the words just pouring out of her. "And I don't know what I can tell him or anyone else." She sat on the foot of the bed, hands clasped between her knees. "Maharet's banished me and Thorne forever. Forever." She began to cry, but didn't stop talking.

She explained that Thorne had been going and coming since the time Fareed had restored his eyes to him, and he, the great Viking warrior, wanted to stand with Maharet against any force that threatened her.

He'd heard the Voice. He'd heard it in Sweden and Norway, prompting him to clean out the riffraff, speaking of a great purpose. He'd found it easy to shut out.

"And you?" I asked, looking from Jesse to David. "Have either of you heard the Voice?"

Jesse shook her head no, but David nodded. "About a year ago, I started hearing it. About the most interesting words it ever uttered were in fact a question. It asked me whether or not we'd all been weakened by the proliferation of the power."

"Remarkable," I said under my breath. "What was your response?"

"I told it no. I said I was as powerful as I'd ever been, perhaps a little more powerful of late."

"And did it say anything else?"

"It spoke mostly nonsense. Half the time I wasn't even sure it was speaking to me. I mean it could have been addressing anyone. It spoke of an optimum number of blood drinkers, considering the source of the power. It spoke of the power as the Sacred Core. I could hear the capital letters. It raved that the realm of the Undead was sunk now into depravity and madness. But it would go on and on around these ideas, often making little or no logical or sequential sense at all. It would even lapse into other languages and it would, well, it would make mistakes, mistakes in meaning, syntax. It was bizarre."

Jesse was staring at him as if all this was a surprise to her.

"To tell the truth," David explained, "I had no idea it was *the Voice* as people are saying now," said David. "I'm giving you the distilled version. It was mostly incoherent. I thought it was some old one. I mean, this happens, of course. Old ones shoot their messages to others. I found it tiresome. I tuned it out."

"And you, Jesse?" I asked.

"I've never heard it," she whispered. "I think that Thorne is the first to have spoken of it directly to me or Maharet."

"And what did she say?"

"She banished us both. She gave us infusions of her blood. She insisted on this. And then she told us we were not to come back. She'd already banished David." She glanced at him and then went on. "She said pretty much the same things to us she'd said to him. The time was past when she could extend hospitality any longer to others, that she and Mekare and Khayman must now be alone—."

"Khayman wasn't there at the time," David interjected. "Isn't that so?"

She nodded. "He'd been missing for a week at least." She went on with her story. "I begged her to let me remain. Thorne went down on his knees. But she was adamant. She said to leave then, not to wait on anything as cumbersome as regular transportation, but to take to the air and put as much distance between ourselves and her as we could. I went to England immediately to see David. I think Thorne actually went to New York. I think many are going to New York. I think he went to Benji and Armand and Louis, but I'm not sure. Thorne was in a fury. He so loves Maharet. But she warned him not to try to deceive her. She said she'd know if he lingered. She was agitated. More agitated than I'd ever seen her. She pressed on me some routine information about resources, money, but I reminded her she'd seen to that. I knew how to get along out here."

"The infusions of blood," I said, "what did you see in those infusions?"

This was a highly sensitive question to ask a blood drinker, and especially to ask this blood drinker who was the loyal biological descendant of Maharet. But even fledglings see images when they receive the blood of their makers; even they experience a telepathic connection in those moments that is otherwise closed. I stood firm.

Her face softened. She was sad, thoughtful. "Many things," she said, "as always. But this time, they were images of the mountain and the valley where the twins had been born. At least, I think that's what I was seeing, seeing them in their old village and seeing them when they were alive."

"So this is what was on her mind," I said. "Memories of her human past."

"I think so," said Jesse in a small voice. "There were other images, colliding, cascading, you know how it is, but again and again, it was those long-ago times. Sunshine. Sunshine in the valley . . ."

David was giving me one of his subtle little gestures to be gentle, tread lightly.

But we both knew these visions or memories were like unto what mortals think about at the end of their lives, their earliest happiest memories.

"She's in the Amazon, isn't she?" I said. "Deep in the jungles."

"Yes," said Jesse. "She forbade me to tell anyone, and I'm breaking her confidence now. She's in uncharted jungle. The only tribe in the area fled after our arrival there."

"I'm going there," I said. "I want to see for myself what's happening. If we're all to perish because of this Voice, well, I want to hear from her what's going on."

"Lestat, she doesn't know what's going on," said Jesse. "That's what I'm trying to tell you."

"I know—."

"I think all this disgusts her. She wants to be left alone. I think this Voice may be driving her to think about destroying herself and Mekare and, well, all of us."

"I don't think the Voice wants us destroyed," I said.

"But *she* may be thinking of it," said Jesse sharply. "I'm only speculating," she confessed. "I know she's confused, angry, even bitter, and this from Maharet. Maharet of all immortals. Maharet."

"She's human still," David said softly. He stroked Jesse's arm. He kissed her hair. "We're all human no matter how long we go on."

He spoke with the easy authority of an old Talamasca scholar, but I actually agreed with him. "If you ask me," he said softly to Jesse, "finding her sister, being reunited with her sister, has destroyed Maharet."

Jesse wasn't surprised by this or jarred by it.

"She never leaves Mekare alone now," Jesse said. "And Khayman, well, Khayman is hopeless, roaming off for weeks at a time, and stumbling back in with no memory of where he's been."

"Well, surely he's not the source of the Voice," said David.

"No, of course not," I said. "But the Voice is controlling him. Isn't that obvious? The Voice is manipulating him as it has been all along. I suspect the Voice began these massacres with him; and then moved to enlisting others. The Voice is working on a number of fronts, you might say. But Maharet and Khayman are too close for any telepathic bridge. She can't know. And he obviously can't tell her. He hasn't the wits to tell her or anyone."

A dark cold feeling came over me that, no matter how this came to an end, Khayman as an immortal on this Earth was finished. Khayman wouldn't survive. And I dreaded the loss of Khayman. I dreaded the loss of all he'd experienced in his thousands of years of roaming, the loss of the tales he might have told of the early battles of the First Brood, of his later wanderings as Benjamin the Devil. I dreaded the loss of the gentle, sweet-hearted Khayman whom I'd briefly known. This was too painful. Who else wouldn't survive?

Jesse appeared to be reading my thoughts. She nodded. "I'm afraid you're right."

"Well, I think I know what's happening," I said. "I'm going there now. After I see her I'll meet you in Manaus. That's far enough away from her, isn't it?"

David nodded. He said he knew of a fashionable little jungle lodge about thirty miles out of Manaus located on the Acajatuba River. Ah, British gentlemen, they always know how to go forth into the wilderness in style. I smiled. We agreed we'd meet there.

"Are you ready for this journey tonight?" he asked.

"Absolutely. It's westward. We'll gain six hours of darkness. Let's go."

"You do realize there's danger here, don't you?" asked David. "You're going against Maharet's express wish."

"Of course," I said. "But why did you two come to me? Didn't you expect me to do something? Why are you both staring at me?"

"We came to urge you to go with us to New York," Jesse explained timidly, "to urge you to call a meeting of all the powerful ones of the tribe."

"You don't need me to do that," I said. "Go yourselves. Call the meeting."

"But everyone will come if *you* call the meeting," David said.

"And who is everyone? I want to see Maharet."

They were edgy, uncertain.

"Look, you go on ahead of me to the Amazon now, and I'll meet you later this very night. And if I don't—if I don't meet you in two nights at the jungle lodge on the river, well, have a Requiem Mass said for me in Notre Dame de Paris."

I left them then, knowing I'd be traveling much faster and higher than either of them, and also, I went back to my château for my ax.

It was rather silly, my wanting my little ax.

I also stripped off the fancy velvet and lace, and put on a decent heavy leather jacket for the journey. I should have cut my hair for those jungles, but I was too damned vain to do that. Samson never loved his hair as much as I love mine. And then I set out for the Amazon.

Five hours before dawn in that great southerly region, I was descending towards the endless channel of deep darkness that was the Amazon rain forest with the silver streak of river winding through it. I was scanning for pinpoints of light, infinitesimal flickers that no mortal eye could ever see.

And then taking my best shot at it, I went down, crashing through the wet humid canopy, descending through crackling and breaking branches and vines until I landed rather awkwardly in the dense darkness of a grove of ancient trees.

At once I was imprisoned by vines and clattering branches in the understory, but I stood quiet, very quiet, listening, making like a stealthy beast on the silent prowl.

The air was wet and fragrant and filled with the simmering voices of the slithering, twittering, and voracious creatures around me everywhere.

But I could hear *their* voices too. Maharet and Khayman quarreling in the ancient tongue.

If there was a path in the vicinity leading towards those voices, well, I never found it.

I didn't dare try to cut my way through with the ax. That would have made too much noise and dulled the blade. I just made my way slowly, painstakingly, over bulbous roots and through stinging brush, suppressing my respiration, my pulse, as best I could along with my thoughts.

I could hear Maharet's low sobbing voice and hear Khayman weeping.

"Did you do these things!" she was demanding. She was speaking their ancient language. I caught the images. Was he the one who'd burnt the house in Bolivia? Had he done this? What about the carnage in Peru? Was he responsible for the other burnings? Was this his work? All of it? The time had come for him to tell her. The time had come for him to be honorable with her.

I caught flashes from his mind, opened up like a ripe fruit in distress: flames, anguished faces, people screaming. He was in a paroxysm of guilt.

And there came into my mind the badly concealed image of a boiling and smoking volcano. An errant shimmering flash.

No.

He was pleading with her to understand that he didn't know what he'd done. "I never killed Eric," he said. "I couldn't have been the one. I can't remember. He was dead, finished when I found his body."

She didn't believe him.

"Kill me!" he wailed suddenly.

I drew closer and closer.

"You did kill Eric, didn't you? You were the one who did it!"

Eric. Eric had been with Maharet over twenty years ago when Akasha rose. Eric had been at the council table with us when we'd confronted Akasha and opposed her. I had never known Eric, and had never heard of Eric since. Mael, I knew, had perished in New York, though precisely how I wasn't certain. He'd gone into the sun on the steps of Saint Patrick's Cathedral, but surely that had not been enough to destroy him. But Eric? I didn't know.

"It's finished," Khayman cried. "I will not continue. You do what you have to do with me. You do it!" He was wailing like one in mourning. "My journey in this world is finished."

I saw the volcano again.

Pacaya. That was the name of the volcano. The image was coming from her, not from him. He couldn't even know what she was thinking.

I continued moving through the jungles as slowly and silently as I could. But they were so deep into this agonizing discussion, they took no notice.

At last, I came to the black steel mesh of a great enclosure. Dimly through the dense green foliage I could see both of them now in a cavernous lighted room—Maharet with her arms around Khayman,

Khayman with his face in his hands. Maharet was crying with a deep wrenching feminine sound to it, like a young girl crying.

She stood back and wiped her eyes with the back of her hand like a child might do it. Then she looked up.

She'd seen me.

"Leave here, Lestat," she said in a clear voice that carried over the vast enclosure. "Go. It's not safe for you here."

"I wouldn't harm him," Khayman said with a groan. "I would never harm him or anyone of my own will." He was peering through the foliage trying to make me out. I think he was actually addressing me.

"Maharet, I must speak to you," I said. "I don't want to leave here without talking to you."

Silence.

"You know how things are, Maharet. I have to speak to you for myself and for others. Please, let me in."

"I don't want any of you here!" she cried out. "Do you understand? Why do you challenge me?"

Suddenly an invisible forced ripped through the enclosure, uprooting palms, shearing off leaves, and then buckling the steel mesh before it, it drove me backwards, bits and pieces of the mesh flying everywhere in silver needles.

It was the Mind Gift.

I fought it with all my strength but was powerless against it. It hurled me hundreds of yards, slamming me into one crackling tangle of foliage after another until finally I fell against the broad red trunk of an immense tree. I was sprawled on its monstrous roots.

I must have been a mile from where I'd been standing. I couldn't even see the light of the enclosure from here. I could hear nothing.

I tried to stand up but the understory here was too thick for anything but crawling or climbing towards a break in the jungle that surrounded a dim winding pond. A great scummy growth covered much of the surface, but here and there the water reflected the light of the sky like brilliant silvery glass.

It seemed to me that human hands or immortal hands had been at work here, arranging a rim of damp and pitted stones along the banks.

The insects were twittering and whistling in my ears yet staying clear of me. I had a gash in my face but it was of course already healing. They were dive-bombing at the blood and then veering off in natural revulsion.

I sat down on the largest boulder and tried to think what to do.

She wasn't going to permit me to come in, no doubt of that. But what had I just seen? What did it mean?

I closed my eyes and listened, but all I heard were the voices of this rapacious and devouring jungle.

There came a soft living pressure on my back. I went alert instantly. There was a hand on my shoulder. A cloud of the sweetest perfume enveloped me, something of green herbs, flowers, and citrus, very strong. A vague sense of happiness came over me, but this was not originating with me. I knew it was absolutely pointless to struggle against this hand.

Slowly I turned and looked down at the long white fingers, and then up into Mekare's face.

The pale-blue eyes were innocent and wondering, the flesh like alabaster all but glowing in the dark. No expression actually, but a suggestion of drowsiness, of languor and of sweetness. *No harm.*

Just the faintest telepathic shimmer: my image, my image in one of those rock videos I'd made years ago—dancing and singing, and singing about us. Gone.

I searched for a spark of intellect, but this was like the agreeable face of some poor mad mortal in whom most of the brain had long ago been destroyed. It seemed the innocence and curiosity were artifacts of flesh and reflex more than anything else. Her mouth was the perfect pink of a seashell. She wore a long pink gown trimmed in gold. Here and there twinkled diamonds and amethysts sewn exquisitely into the border.

"Beautiful," I whispered. "Such loving work."

I was as near to panic as I'd been in a long time, but then as always happens, always when I'm afraid, when anything is making me afraid, I got angry. I remained very still. She appeared to be studying me in an almost dreamy way, but she wasn't. She might have been blind for all I could tell.

"It is you?" I said. I struggled to say it in the ancient tongue, searching in memory for the smattering of it I knew. "Mekare, is it you?"

There must have been a swelling of great pride in me, ridiculous arrogance to think suddenly with fierce elation that I could reach this creature when all others had failed, that I could touch the surface of her mind and quicken it.

Desperately, I wanted to see that image of me again, from the rock videos. That image or any image, but there was nothing. I sent forth the image. I remembered those songs and canticles of our origins, hoping against hope that this had some meaning for her.

But one wrong word, and think what she might do. She could crush my skull with both hands. She could blast me with obliterating fire. But I couldn't think of this, or imagine it.

"Beautiful," I said again.

No change. I detected a low humming coming from her. We don't need our tongues to hum? It was almost a purr as might come from a cat, and suddenly her eyes were as remote and without consciousness as those of a statue.

"Why are you doing it?" I asked. "Why kill all those young ones, those poor little young ones?"

With no spark of recognition or response, she moved forward and kissed me, kissing the right side of my face with those seashell-pink lips, those cold lips. I brought my hand up slowly and let my fingers move into the soft thickness of her waving red hair. I touched her head ever so gently.

"Mekare, trust in me," I whispered in that old language.

A riot of sounds exploded behind me, again some force tearing through a forest that was almost impenetrable. The air was filled with a rain of tiny falling green leaves. I saw them falling on the viscid surface of the water.

Maharet stood there to my left helping Mekare to her feet, making soft gentle crooning sounds as she did it, her fingers stroking Mekare's face.

I climbed to my feet as well.

"You leave here now, Lestat," said Maharet, "and don't you come back. And don't you urge anyone ever again to come here!"

Her pale face was streaked with blood. There was blood on her pale-green silk robe, blood in her hair, all this from weeping. Blood tears. Blood-red lips.

Mekare stood beside her gazing at me impassively, eyes drifting over the palm fronds, the mesh of branches that shut out the sky, as if she were listening to the birds or the insects and not to anything spoken here.

"Very well," I said. "I came to help. I came to learn what I could."

"Say no more! I know why you came," she said. "You must go. I understand. I would have done the same thing if I were you. But you must tell the others never to look for us again. Never. Do you think I would ever try to hurt you, you or any of the others? My sister would never do this. She would never harm anyone. Go now."

"What about Pacaya, the volcano?" I asked. "You can't do this, Maharet. You can't go into the volcano, you and Mekare. You can't do this to us."

"I know!" she said. It was almost a groan. A terrible deep groan of anguish.

A deep groan came out of Mekare as well, a horrid groan. It was as if her only voice were in her chest and she turned to her sister suddenly lifting her hands but only a little, and letting them drop as if she couldn't manage to really work them at all.

"Let me talk to you," I pleaded.

Khayman was coming towards us, and Mekare turned sharply away and moved towards him and lay against his chest and he enfolded her with his arms. Maharet stared at me. She was shaking her head, moaning as if her fevered thoughts had a little song to them of moans.

Before I could speak again, there came a heated blast of air against my face and chest. It blinded me. I thought it was the Fire Gift, and she was making an immediate mockery of her own words.

Well, Brat Prince, I thought, you gambled, you lost! And you get to die now. Here's your personal Pacaya.

But I was merely flying backwards through the bracken again, smashing against tree trunks, and through clattering crackling branches and wet fronds. I twisted and turned with all my might trying to escape this thing, trying to flee to one side or the other, but it was driving me backwards at such speed that I was helpless.

Finally I was flung down in a grassy place, an open grassy circle of sorts, unable for a moment to move, my body aching all over. My hands and face were badly cut. My eyes were stinging. I was covered with dirt and broken leaves. I climbed to my knees and then to my feet.

The sky above was a deep radiant blue with the jungles rising high all around as if to engulf it. I could see the remains of some huts here, that this had been a village once, but it was now in ruins. It took me a moment to catch my breath and then to wipe my face with my handkerchief, and wipe the blood from the cuts on my hands. My head throbbed.

It was half an hour before I reached the lodge on the banks of the river.

I found David and Jesse in a tasteful tropical suite there, all very civilized and pretty with white curtains and veils of bleached mosquito netting over the white iron bed. Candles burned all through the rooms and the manicured gardens and around a small swimming pool. Such luxury on the edge of chaos.

I stripped everything off and bathed in the fresh, clean swimming pool.

David stood by with a heap of white towels.

When I was myself again, as best as I could be, with these soiled and torn clothes, I went into the cozy little parlor with him.

I related what I'd seen.

"Khayman's in the grip of the Voice, that's clear," I said. "Whether Maharet's heard it or not, I have no idea. But Mekare gave me no hint of menace, no hint of mind or cunning or . . ."

"Or what?" Jesse asked.

"No hint that the Voice was coming from her," I said.

"How could it possibly be coming from her?"

"You're joking, surely," I said.

"No, I'm not," said Jesse.

In a low confidential tone I told them all I knew of the Voice.

I told them how it had been speaking to me for years, how it talked of beauty and love, and how it had nudged me once to burn and destroy the mavericks in Paris. I told them all about the Voice—its games with my reflection in the mirror.

"So you're saying it's some demonic ancient one," said Jesse. "Trying to take possession of blood drinkers, and that it's taken possession of Khayman, and Maharet knows it?" Her eyes were glassy with tears that were slowly thickening into pure blood. She brushed her curling copper hair back from her face. She looked unutterably sad.

"Well, that's one way of putting it," I said. "You really have no clue who the Voice is?"

I lost all taste for this conversation. I had too much thinking to do and I needed to do it quickly. I didn't tell them about the image of Pacaya in Guatemala. Why should I? What could they do about it? She had said she wouldn't harm us.

I went out of the room, motioning for them to let me go, and I stood in this dreamy little tropical garden. I could hear a waterfall somewhere, perhaps more than one, and that throbbing engine of the jungle, that engine of so many voices.

"Who are you, Voice?" I asked aloud. "Why don't you tell me? I think it's time, don't you?"

Laughter.

Low laughter and that same distinctly male timbre. Right inside my head.

"What's the name of the game, Voice?" I asked. "How many are going to have to die before you finish? And what is it you really want?"

No answer. But I felt certain someone was watching me. Someone was off in the jungles beyond the border of this garden, beyond this horseshoe of little thatched-roof luxurious guest suites, staring at me.

"Can you even guess what I suffer?" said the Voice.

"No," I said. "Tell me about it."

Silence. It was gone. I could feel its distinct absence.

I waited a long time. Then I walked back into the little suite. They were sitting together now on the foot of the bed which looked a bit like a shrine with all its draped white mosquito netting. David was holding Jesse. Jesse was drooping like a broken flower.

"Let's do as Maharet asks," I said. "Perhaps she has some plan, some plan she doesn't dare confide in anyone, and we owe it to her and to ourselves to allow her time to work it. I need a plan myself. This isn't the moment for me to act on my suspicions."

"But what are your suspicions?" demanded Jesse. "You can't think Mekare has the cunning to do all this. . . ."

"No, not Mekare. I suspect Mekare is holding the Voice back."

"But how could she do that?" Jesse pressed. "She's only the host of the Core."

I didn't answer. I marveled that she hadn't guessed it. I wondered how many others really hadn't guessed it. Or was everyone out there—Benji and all those calling him—afraid to say the obvious?

"I want you to come with us to New York," said David. "I hope many others are already there."

"What if that is exactly what the Voice wants?" I sighed. "What if it's becoming ever more clever at controlling others like Khayman and enlisting them in its pogroms? We all gather in New York, and the Voice brings a cabal of monsters against us? Seems foolish to make it so easy for the Voice."

But I didn't say this with much conviction.

"Then what is your plan?" asked David.

"I told you. I need time to think on it."

"But who is this Voice?" Jesse pleaded.

"Darling," said David in a low and reverent voice as he embraced her. "The Voice is Amel, the spirit inside Mekare, and he can hear all that we're saying to one another right now."

A look of unspeakable horror swept over her face, and then a sudden collapse into deep quiet. She sat staring in front of her, eyes narrowing and then widening very slowly with her thoughts.

"But the spirit is unconscious," she whispered, pondering it, her soft golden eyebrows knitting. "For millennia it's been unconscious. The spirits said, 'Amel is no more.'"

"And what is six thousand years to a spirit?" I asked. "It's come to consciousness and it's talking and it's lonely and it's vindictive and it's confused and damned incapable, it seems, of really getting whatever it wants. Maybe it doesn't even know what it wants."

I could see David flinching, see his right hand rising just a little, and pleading with me to take the edge off, not to push it.

I stood stock-still looking out into the night, waiting, waiting for the Voice to speak, but the Voice didn't speak.

"Go on to New York," I said. "As long as it can rouse and control others, no place is safe. Maybe Seth and Fareed are headed there. Surely they know what's happening. Get on the radio with Benji and call to Seth. Figure some way to disguise your meaning. You're good at that. Call to any old ones who might help us. If there are old ones out there who can be roused to burn, there are others who can be roused to fight. And we do have some time after all."

"Time? What makes you say that?" asked David.

"I just explained it," I said. "It hasn't figured out yet how to get what it wants. It may not even know yet how to articulate its own ambitions, plans, desires."

I left them there.

It was day now on the European continent, but I didn't want to stay in that wild, primitive, and devouring place. It made me bloody furious that I couldn't get back home.

I went north towards Florida and made it to a fine Miami hotel before dawn. I rented a suite on a high floor with a balcony looking out over warm, sweet Biscayne Bay, and I sat out there, my foot on the ledge, loving the moist tender breeze, and looking at the huge ghostly clouds of the deep Miami sky and thinking about it.

What if I was wrong? What if it wasn't Amel? But then I thought back, back to those first murmurings, "beauty . . . love." It had been trying to tell me something momentous about itself and I had dismissed it. I had had no patience with its ravings, its desperate efforts. *You don't know what I suffer.*

"I was wrong," I said now, watching these huge tumbling clouds shift and drift past me. "I should have paid more attention to what you were trying to say. I should have talked to you. I wish I had. Is it too late?"

Silence.

"You too have your story," I said. "I was cruel not to realize it. I was cruel not to think of your capacity for suffering."

Silence.

I got up and paced the dark thick carpet, then I went back out on the balcony and looked at the lightening sky. Sunrise coming. Relentless implacable sunrise. So comforting to the world of mortal beings and animal things, and the plants breaking through the soil everywhere, and the trees sighing through a billion leaves. And so deadly to us.

"Voice, I am sorry," I said.

I saw Pacaya volcano again, that image that had flashed repeatedly through Maharet's mind, that fiery image. I saw in terror her carrying her sister upwards, like an angel with a child in its arms, until she was above that horrid gaping mouth of fire.

Suddenly I felt the presence of the other.

"No," said the Voice. "It's not too late. We'll talk, you and I. When the time comes."

"Then you do have a plan?" I asked. "You aren't just slaughtering all your own progeny."

"Progeny?" He laughed. "Imagine your every limb hung with chains, your fingers bound with weights, your feet connected by a thousand roots to others. Progeny, be damned."

The sun was indeed rising. It was rising for the Voice too in that jungle. If he was in that jungle.

I closed up the room, pulled the draperies shut, went into the spacious walk-in closet, and lay down to sleep, furious that I wouldn't be able to head for home until the inevitable sunset.

Two nights later, it hit Paris.

The Voice hadn't spoken a word to me in the interim. And then it hit Paris.

By the time I got there it was over.

The little hotel in the Rue Saint-Jacques was burnt to the ground and the firefighters were dousing the blackened ruins with water, the smoke and steam rising between the narrow intact buildings on either side of it.

There were no voices here in the heart of Paris now. Those who had escaped had fled to the countryside and they were still pleading with others to follow their example.

I passed slowly, unnoticed, through the sidewalk spectators—just a flashy young man in violet sunglasses and a worn leather coat with unruly long blond hair, secretly carrying a deadly ax with him.

But I was sure I'd heard one plea, stronger than many of the others, when the Burning had started, when those first howls had drifted over the wind, a woman pleading in Italian for me to come. I was certain I'd heard a sobbing entreaty, "I am Bianca Solderini."

Well, if I'd heard it, it was silent now. It was gone.

I walked along, noting the stains of black grease on the pavements. In one doorway, unmarked as yet, lay a black slimy hulk of burnt bones and shapeless globs of tissue. Could there have been life in that still? How old was that? Was that the beautiful legendary Bianca Solderini?

My soul shriveled. I sauntered closer to it. No one passing me noticed. I touched this mass of steaming blood and guts with my boot. It was melting, the bones losing their shape, the whole little heap melting on the stones. There could be nothing alive there.

"You proud of yourself, Voice?" I asked.

But he wasn't there. Not there at all. I would have known if he was there.

He hadn't spoken to me again since Miami, not in spite of all my pleas, my questions, my long confessions of respect, interest, immense desire to understand.

"Amel, Amel, talk to me," I'd said over and over again. Had it found others to love, others infinitely more malleable and useful?

And more to the point, what was I going to do? What did I have to offer all those who seemed to think, for the most foolish reasons, that I could somehow solve all this?

Meanwhile coven houses and young ones had perished. And now this in Paris.

For hours I searched the Quartier Latin. I searched all of central

Paris, walking the banks of the Seine and homing as I always did to Notre Dame. Nothing. Not a single preternatural voice left in Paris.

All those paparazzi gone.

It was almost like those olden nights when I thought I was the only vampire in the world, and I'd walked these streets alone, longing for the voices of others.

And all the time those other blood drinkers, those evil blood drinkers led by Armand, had been hiding under the cemetery of Les Innocents.

I saw bones in stacks, skulls, rotting bones. But this was no image of the old catacombs of those Children of Satan in the eighteenth century. These were images of the catacombs under Paris today where all the bones of the old cemetery had been moved long after the Children of Satan had been dissolved into ruin.

Catacombs. Images of bones. I heard a female blood drinker crying. Two creatures. And one speaking very rapidly in a low whisper. I knew that timbre. That was the voice I'd heard earlier this night. I left the Île de la Cité, and started for the catacombs.

In a flash I caught a vision of two women together weeping, the elder a white skeletal monster with a hag's hair. Horrid, like something painted by Goya. Then it was gone, and I couldn't home in on it again.

"Bianca!" I said. "Bianca!"

I picked up speed. I knew where those tunnels were, those deep dark ugly tunnels beneath the city whose walls are packed with the disintegrating bones of centuries of dead Parisians. The public was admitted to those underground passages. I knew the public entrance. I was racing towards the Place Denfert-Rochereau, and had almost reached the spot, when a strange sight stopped me.

It was a brilliant flash at the entrance to the tunnel, as if a flame had erupted from the mouth of the charnel house. The dark wooden pedimented building that sheltered the entrance exploded and fell to pieces with a loud clatter.

I saw a female blood drinker with long blond hair, white, immensely powerful, rising from the pavement, and in her arms two other figures, both clinging to her, one with a skeletal white arm and hag hair buried against her bosom, the other, auburn haired and shaking with sobs.

For me, for my eyes, this mysterious being slowed her ascent, and we gazed for one split second at one another.

I will see you again, brave one.

Then she was gone.

I felt a blast of air against my face.

I was sitting on the pavement when I came to my senses.

Sevraine.

That was the name imprinted on my mind. Sevraine. But who was this Sevraine?

I was still sitting there staring at the entrance to the tunnel when I heard fast crisp steps approaching, someone walking steadily, heavily and fast.

"Get up, Lestat."

I turned and looked up into the face of my mother.

There she was after all these years in her old khaki safari jacket and faded jeans, her hair in a braid over her shoulder, her pale face like a porcelain mask.

"Come on, stand up!" she said, those cold blue eyes flashing in the lights of the burning building at the mouth of the tunnel.

And in that moment as love and resentment clashed with humbling fury, I was back at home hundreds of years ago, walking with her in those cold barren fields, with her haranguing me in that impatient voice. "Get up. Move. Come on."

"What are you going to do if I don't?" I snarled. "Slap me?"

And that's what she did. She slapped me. "Get up quickly," she said. "Take me to that glorified shelter you've made for yourself in the old castle. We must talk. Tomorrow night, I'll take you to Sevraine."

13

Marius

Reunion on the Brazilian Shore

I T SEEMED the Voice woke him each evening, telling him to go out and cleanse the country around him of mavericks, that he would be infinitely more content if he did this. The Voice took a gentle tack with him.

"I know you, Marius. I know you well. I know that you love your companion, Daniel. Do as I ask of you and he will never be in danger."

Marius ignored the Voice, as certainly as a priest might ignore the small voice of Satan, calculating all the while: How does this creature get into my brain? How does he manage to speak to me in such a palpable warm way as if we were brothers?

"I am you, Marius, and you are me," said the Voice. "Listen to what I say."

Marius wouldn't let Daniel out of his sight.

The handsome old coven house in Santa Teresa had been burned to the ground. If any of the young survived in Rio de Janeiro they were silent. Even the great country surrounding the city was silent. No sharp, tinny, and piercing cries out there anymore for help.

As they walked along the beach together near midnight, Daniel and Marius, side by side at the end of the waves, Marius listened. He was a beachcomber in khaki, with his sandals tied to his belt. And Daniel was easy in his polo shirt and dungarees, sneakers easily pushing against the hard sand.

Far off in the jungles to the north, Marius heard preternatural voices, faint but filled with rage. Maharet was there now, he knew it. In those Amazonian jungles. He recognized some faint pattern of speech, of telepathic eruption that even the great Maharet could not contain or control.

He and Daniel had to leave Brazil. This was a safe place no longer. Daniel said he understood. "Whither thou goest, I go," he had said. It amazed Marius that Daniel seemed so indifferent to danger, that his zest for all he saw around him remained so strong. Having survived madness, he was now wise beyond his years in the Blood, accepting that another crisis had come, and that he might survive this one as he had survived the Akashan Massacre before. As he himself had put it earlier this evening, "I was Born to Darkness in the midst of a storm."

Marius loved Daniel. He had salvaged Daniel from the aftermath of that storm, and never for one moment regretted it. Marius knew that Daniel had also salvaged him from the same chaos, becoming for Marius someone Marius could care for, someone Marius could personally love. It meant the world to Marius that he was not walking on this beach alone, that Daniel was walking at his side.

The night was magnificent as it so often was over Copacabana Bay, the silvery surf raging on the endless sand, mortals few and far between and keeping to themselves. The great city of Rio was never silent, and the din of traffic and machines, and the teeming mortal voices, blended for Marius with the sweet and incessant symphony of the waves.

All things under Heaven contain some blessing, and so it is with modern noise that it can become the gentle roar of a waterfall in our ears protecting us from disparate and ghastly sounds. Ah, but what is Heaven but a silent and indifferent void through which the shattering noise of explosions echo forever or are heard not at all? And men once spoke of the music of the spheres.

But we are blessed to be tiny beings in this universe. We are blessed to feel momentous because we are larger than these grains of sand.

Something intruded suddenly on his thoughts.

Far ahead in the darkness, he spied a lone figure coming towards them. *Immortal. Powerful. Child of the Millennia.* He drew Daniel close to him, putting his arm around Daniel as if Daniel were his son. Daniel too had sensed the presence perhaps, even heard the subtle heartbeat.

Who are you?

He could pick up no answer. The figure came on steadily, a slim delicate-boned male, in a soft ankle-length white Arabic robe, the robe flapping in the wind. His short white hair was mussed by the wind. The moonlight made an aureole out of it, and the steps came on as the steps of the ancient always do, with measured strength indifferent to the softness of the terrain.

Now is this how it is to happen? Had the Voice roused this rude instrument to smite them with fire?

There was nothing to do but move steadily towards this figure. What good would it do to flee? With one so old, flight might be impossible, for eyes such as these can follow an ascending body everywhere when there is nothing else to distract them.

Again, Marius identified himself silently, but there was no response, not the smallest inkling of a thought, an attitude, an emotion from the other, as he slowly came into full view.

They approached each other in silence, crunch of sand underfoot, sigh of the wind, and then the white-haired one extended his hand. Long almost spidery fingers.

"Marius," he said. "My beloved, my savior of long ago, my friend."

"I know you?" asked Marius politely. Even as he clasped the hand he divined nothing but what the agreeable and open face reflected: friendship. No danger.

But this one was far older than Marius, perhaps as much as a thousand years. His eyes were black and his unblemished skin the color of amber, which made his white hair all the more remarkable, a cloud of white light around his head.

"I'm Teskhamen," said the older one. "And you, you are the one who gave me new life."

"How did I ever do that?" asked Marius. "When and where did we ever meet?"

"Come, let's find a quiet place where we can talk."

"My rooms?" asked Marius.

"If you wish, or the bench up there at the boardwalk. This is a quiet night on the boardwalk. And the sea is like molten silver to my eyes. The breeze is fragrant and comforting. Let's go there."

They climbed the sands together, Daniel hanging slightly behind as if it were the respectful thing to do.

And when Marius and Teskhamen sat down together, Daniel

chose another bench nearby. They were all three facing the distant waves, facing that writhing pearly surf. Beyond the mist the stars climbed forever. Great far-off mountains and rocks were purely dark.

Marius looked at Daniel anxiously. He didn't want a divide from Daniel of even a few feet.

"Don't be concerned for him now," said Teskhamen. "We are more than adequate to protect him, and what stalks the young blood drinkers tonight is on the move in other cities. The young of this place have already been exterminated. It turned them against each other. It played on their distrust of one another and their escalating fear. It was not content merely with the burning of the house; it hunted them down one by one."

"So that is how it is being done."

"That is one way. There are others. It becomes more clever with every passing night."

"I saw it," said Marius. And indeed he had in images, those battles, images he would like very much to forget. "But please, tell who you are and what you want with me." He had said this politely, but he was a little ashamed of himself. After all, obviously this old one was friendly and knowledgeable as to what was happening. This old one wanted to help.

"There must be a gathering," said Teskhamen, "and the place will be New York." He gave a little laugh. "I think Benji Mahmoud has marked the spot there with his enterprising broadcasts, but then two of the authors of the Vampire Chronicles are there already, and they are known to the entire world of the Undead."

"I have nothing against any particular gathering place," said Marius. "And Benji is no stranger to me." Marius had made Benji a vampire, brought him and his companion Sybelle over, and given them to his fledgling Armand, but he saw no reason to confide this to a stranger, a stranger who likely knew it anyway, especially one whose thoughts he couldn't hear. Not even the faintest shimmer came to him.

But he caught suddenly a very strong emanation from Daniel. *He is the one who made you.*

Marius was visibly startled, glancing first at Daniel, who sat staring at him, sideways on the bench with one leg up and his arms casually wrapped around his knee. Daniel was plainly fascinated.

Marius looked back to Teskhamen, this smaller blood drinker who gazed at him with steady black eyes.

"The one who made me is dead," he said aloud, again glancing at Daniel and then back to Teskhamen. "He died the very night I was Born to Darkness. That was two thousand years ago in a forest in northern Europe. Those events are engraved on my soul."

"And on mine," said Teskhamen. "But I did not die that night. And I did make you what you are now. I was the blood god imprisoned in that oak to which the Druids brought you. It was I, that blackened and scarred and ruined thing, that gave you the Blood, and told you to escape the Druids—not to remain imprisoned in the oak as a blood god—but to go down to Egypt, no matter what the cost, and see what had happened to the Mother and the Father, to find out why we had, so many of us, been horribly burned in our very shrines."

"Prisons, you mean, not shrines," Marius whispered. He stared forward at the distant horizon where the dark undulating sea met the silver sky.

Could this be possible?

The horrific sights and sounds of that night came back to him, the deep oaken forest, his own helplessness as, a prisoner of the Druids, he'd been dragged towards the shrine of the god within the tree. And then had come those staggering moments when the burnt and white-haired god had spoken to him and explained the powers of the Blood he would share.

"But I saw them throw your body on the pyre afterwards," said Marius. "I tried to save you, but I didn't know my own strength then in the Blood. I saw you burned." He shook his head, peering earnestly into the being's eyes. "Why would one so old and so seemingly wise lie about these things?"

"I am not lying to you," said Teskhamen gently. "You saw them try to immolate me. But I was a thousand years old then, Marius, per-haps older. I didn't know my own strength either. But when you fled as I'd instructed you to do, when all of them to a man ran after you through that forest, I escaped those burning logs."

Marius stared at Teskhamen, stared at the dark eyes looking at him, at the simple but kindly mouth. Out of the gloom of memory emerged that fragile blackened figure clinging to dark unnatural life through will.

Suddenly Marius *knew*. He knew it now, knew it in countless subtle ways. He knew the being's demeanor, the dark and unwavering gaze. He knew the calm and almost melodious cadence of his speech, and even the contained and almost shrinking posture with which he sat there on the bench.

And he knew why he could hear nothing from this one's mind. This was the maker. The maker had survived.

The older one was smiling at him now as he sat composed with his hands folded in his lap. The soft white *thawb*, or cassock, hung softly about his dignified frame, and he seemed pleased, very pleased, that Marius knew the truth. He was as splendid an immortal now with his smooth tawny skin and full white hair as any Marius had ever seen.

Something quickened in Marius, something he had not felt in a very long time. There was some certainty of goodness, perhaps, that overcame him, some certainty of happiness, of the true possibility of life containing moments of exultation and joy. He'd never really felt that certainty for very long at any one time, and he hadn't expected to feel it now. Yet he was overcome with the purest goodwill, suddenly, that such a thing could be possible, that this one, known to him in a fatal intimacy at the very beginning of his dark journey, could in fact be here with him now.

In the past only young ones and strangers had brought such comfort. Nothing good had ever united him with those first years, nothing to warm the heart.

He wanted to speak but he feared to cheapen his feeling in trying to express it. He sat quiet, wondering if his face expressed the gratitude he felt that this being had come to him here.

"I suffered unbearably," said Teskhamen, "but it was all that you'd revealed to me, Marius, that gave me the strength to crawl away from that pyre and reach for hope. You see, I had never known a being like you, Marius. In that awful northern forest, I had never known anything of your Roman world. I'd known the old Blood religion of Queen Akasha. I'd been her faithful blood god. I knew the worship of the Druids echoing the ancient blood drinker cults of Egypt, and that was all I knew. Not until that night when I took you in my arms to make you the new blood god, and your heart and soul poured into mine."

The smile was gone and Teskhamen's face was reflective, his dark brows knitted, his eyes narrow, as he looked out at the foaming sea. He went on speaking.

"For a thousand years, I'd served the Mother, believed in the old religion. Remain imprisoned until the worshippers bring the evildoers; look into their hearts for right and wrong and truth; and then execute them for the Faithful of the Forest and drink their precious blood. A thousand years. And never had I dreamed of the life you lived, Marius. I'd been born a village child, a farmer's boy, and, oh, what an honor, they told me, that as a young man I had become beautiful enough to offer to the Secret Mother, the Queen Who Reigns Forever, and from whom a poor boy, an ignorant boy, could not conceivably escape."

Marius didn't want to say a word. This was the voice that had lulled him into calm compliance all those centuries ago inside that oak tree. This was the voice that had confessed secrets to him which had given him hope that he might survive that night to live in a new way. He only wanted for Teskhamen to go on.

"And then I saw your life," said Teskhamen, "your life, blazing in the images you yielded to me. I saw your glorious house in Rome, the magnificent temples before which you'd worshipped, with all those pure and lofty columns, and brightly painted marble gods and goddesses so splendidly realized, and those colored rooms in which you'd lived and studied and dreamed and laughed and sang and loved. It wasn't the wealth, surely you understand me. Not the gold. Not the glittering mosaics. I saw your libraries, I saw and heard your quick-witted and curious companions, I saw the full blooming power of your experience, the life of a cultured Roman, the life that had made you what you were. I saw the *beauty* of Italy. I saw the beauty of fleshly love. I saw the beauty of ideas. I saw the beauty of the sea."

A shock passed through Marius but he remained silent.

Teskhamen paused, eyes still fixed on the distant surf. His eyes returned to Marius. He looked past him for a moment and smiled at Daniel, who was listening as if rapt.

"I had never fully understood till that moment," said Teskhamen, "that we are the sum of all we've seen and all we've appreciated and understood. You were the sum of sunshine on marble floors filled with pictures of divine beings who laughed and loved and drank the fruit of the vine as surely as you were the sum of the poets and historians and philosophers you'd read. You were the sum and the fount of what you'd cherished and chosen to abide and all you had loved."

He left off talking.

Nothing had changed in the night.

Behind them the sparse traffic of early morning moved on the Avenida Atlântica. And the voices of the city rose and subsided beneath the hushed voice of the sea.

But Marius was changed. Changed forever.

"Tell me what happened," Marius pressed. The intimacy of that long-ago blood exchange in the oak shimmered in his mind. "Where did you go? How did you survive?"

Teskhamen nodded. He was still looking out to sea. "The woods were thick in those times. You remember them. Moderns have no conception of that old woodland, that savage wilderness of trees ancient and young spreading across Europe—against which each hamlet or village or town must fight for its life. Into that woodland I slithered like a lizard. I fed on the vermin of the forest. I fed on what could not escape me even as I could not walk without pain, even as the sun found me again and again in dank hollows and claimed even more of my skin because I could not dig deep to protect myself from it with these hands."

He looked at his fingers. "In time," he said with a sigh, "I found a woman in a lowly hut, a cunning woman, a healer, such a thing as men call a witch and a hag. Hesketh was her name. She was a prisoner of hideousness as was I.

"But I begged for her patience. She could not destroy me and I fascinated her, and my suffering touched her heart. Oh, this was so remarkable to me. You cannot imagine. What did I know of compassion, of mercy, of love? She had pity on me, and curiosity burned within her. She would not have me suffer. And some bond was forged before language could express it even in the simplest form.

"Even in my weakened state, I worked small miracles for her effortlessly, told her when strangers were approaching, raked their minds for the questions they were coming to ask her, for the curses they wanted her to bring down on their enemies. I warned of anyone who sought to do her harm. An evil lad bent on murdering her, I easily overpowered and from him drank my fill before her unquestioning eyes. I read her thoughts and I found the poetry inside of her, beneath the misfortune of warts and pockmarked skin, of hunched shoulders and deformed limbs. I loved her. Indeed she became, whole and entire, quite beautiful to me—. And she came to love me with her whole heart."

His eyes grew wide as if he were marveling at it all even now. "It was at her hearth I discovered my dormant powers, how with my mind I might kindle the fire when it had gone out, how I might make the water boil. I protected her. She protected me. We had the souls of each other. We loved in some realm where the natural and the preternatural meant nothing. And I brought her into the Blood."

He turned to look at Marius again.

"Now you know what a crime that was against the old religion, to share the Blood with one so malformed. The old religion died for me in that act of defiance and a new religion was born."

Marius nodded.

"I lived with Hesketh for over six hundred years after that, regaining my strength, healing in body and soul. We hunted the villages of the countryside. We fed on the thieves of the roads. But your beautiful Italy, your beautiful Roman world—which has so inspired me— was never to be mine except in the books I read, the manuscripts I stole from monasteries, the poetry I shared for myself with Hesketh by our humble hearth. Nevertheless we were happy, and we were clever. And as our boldness grew, we penetrated the crude castles and fortresses of country lords and even the streets of Paris in our lust to see and to learn. Those were not bad times.

"But you know how it is with the young in the Blood and how foolish they can be. And Hesketh was young and still misshapen, and all the blood in the world could not succor the pain she knew when mortals screamed at the very sight of her."

"What happened?"

"We quarreled. We fought. She struck out on her own. I waited. I felt certain she'd return. But she was caught by mortals, a mob that overwhelmed her, and they burned her alive as the Druids had sought to kill me. I found her remains afterwards. I destroyed the village, down to the last mortal man, woman, and child. But Hesketh was gone from me, or so it seemed."

"You revived her."

"No, that was not possible," he said. "Something infinitely more miraculous happened which was to give my life meaning from that time on. But let me continue: I buried her remains near a vast ruined monastery, deep in the untended forest, a collection of rude buildings made of crudely dressed stones and rough timbers where monks had once studied and worked and lived. There were no longer any fields or vineyards around it, for the woods had reclaimed all. But in the weed-infested cemetery, I found a place for her, thinking, Ah, it is consecrated ground. Maybe her soul will rest. Such superstition. Such nonsense. But the time of mourning is always the perfect time for nonsense. And I stayed nearby in the old scriptorium of the monastery, in a filthy corner, beneath a pile of old rotted furniture which no one, for one reason or another, had ever taken away. Each night on rising, I lit once more the small earthen oil lamp I'd placed on her unmarked grave.

"It was a dark and miserable night when she came to me. I had come to the point where death by any means seemed preferable to going on. All those splendid possibilities I'd seen in your blood, they had come to mean nothing—if Hesketh was not with me, if Hesketh was no more.

"And then Hesketh came, my Hesketh. Hesketh came into the old scriptorium. In the light of broken arched windows I saw Hesketh—solid as I am now. And gone was the warty and pockmarked skin that even the Blood had not been able to smooth, and the twisted and deformed limbs. This was the Hesketh I'd always loved, the pure and beautiful damsel inside the wreckage of malnourished and cruelly formed flesh. This was the Hesketh I'd loved with all my heart."

He paused and studied Marius.

"She was a phantom, this Hesketh, but she was alive! Her hair was flaxen and her body tall and straight. Her pale hands and face were shimmering and soft. And another phantom was with her, as physically visible as was she. This phantom went by the name of Gremt. And it was he who had aided her wandering shade and given it solace and taught her how to appear to eyes such as yours and mine. This was Gremt who had taught her how to hold together the airy physical shape in which she sought to appear. It was he who taught her how to make that shape solid and enduring so that I could reach out and touch her with my hands. I could even kiss her lips. I could even take her in my arms."

Marius said nothing, but he had seen ghosts this powerful himself. Not often, but he had seen them. He'd known of them but not known ever who they were.

He waited but Teskhamen had fallen quiet.

"What happened?" Marius whispered. "Why did this change the course of your life?"

"It changed everything because she remained with me," said Teskhamen, looking at Marius again. "It was no fleeting moment. And with each passing night she grew stronger, and more clever at retaining her physical shape, and Gremt, whose powerful solid shape would have fooled any mortal, shared my hearth in the old monastery as she did, and we spoke of things invisible and visible and of blood drinkers and of the spirit that had come into the ancient Queen."

He paused as if pondering and then went on.

"Of our species and history, Gremt knew all things, things that I did not know, for he'd been watching the course of the spirit Amel inside the Queen for centuries, and he knew of discoveries and battles and defeats of which I'd never heard a word.

"We forged an alliance, Gremt and Hesketh and me. I alone was a true physical being and provided some temporal rhythm for them that I have never fully come to understand. But in that place, that ruined monastery, we signed a pact, and our work together in this world began."

"But what work was this?" Marius asked.

"The work was to learn," said Teskhamen. "To learn why blood drinkers walk the Earth, and how that spirit of Amel makes such wonders possible, to learn why ghosts linger and cannot seek the light that attracts so many souls who ascend without a backward glance. To learn how witches might command spirits, and what those spirits are. We formed a resolve in that old ruined monastery, that as we rebuilt its roofs, its walls, its doorways, and replanted its vineyards and gardens, we would learn. We would be our own sect dedicated to no god or saint but to knowledge, understanding. That we would be the studious and profane scholars of an Order in which only the material was sacred, in which only the respect for the physical and all its mysteries governed all else."

"You are describing the Talamasca to me, aren't you?" said Marius. He was amazed. "This is the birth of the Talamasca that you are explaining."

"Yes. It was the year 748, or so say the calendars of now. I well remember it, because I went to the nearby city early of an evening less than a month after our first meeting—properly dressed and with Gremt's gold—to obtain that old monastery and its overgrown land for us in perpetuity and to safeguard our little refuge from the claims of the mortal world. I led the way. But we all signed the documents.

And I have those parchment pages still. Gremt's name is written on them beneath Hesketh's name and mine. That land is ours to this very time, and that ancient monastery, still existing in the deep forest of France, has always been the true secret Motherhouse of the Talamasca."

Marius couldn't help but smile.

"Gremt was easily strong enough then to travel among humans," said Teskhamen as he continued. "By day or by night, he had been appearing amongst them for some time. And soon Hesketh was moving among humankind with equal confidence, and the Order of the Talamasca was begun. Ah, it is a long story, but that old monastery is our home now."

"I see it," Marius gasped. "Of course. The old mystery is explained. It was you, you who founded it, a blood drinker, a spirit as you call him, and this phantom you loved. But your mortal followers, your members, your scholars, they were never to be told the actual truth?"

Teskhamen nodded. "We were the first Elders," he said. "And we knew from the beginning that the mortal scholars we brought into the Order must never know our secret, our private truth.

"We were joined by other beings over the years. And our mortal members flourished, attracting acolytes from far and wide. As you know, we came to establish libraries and Motherhouses and places where mortal scholars took their vows to study and learn and never judge the mysterious, the invisible, the palpable unseen. We promulgated our secular principles. Soon the Order had its constitution, its rules, its rubric, and its traditions. Soon the Order had its vast wealth. It had a strength and vitality we could never have predicted. We created the myth of 'the anonymous Elders' chosen in each generation from the rank and file, and known only to those who had chosen them, governing from a secret location. But there were no such human Elders. Not until these times, when we have indeed recently anointed such a governing body—and passed to them the reins of the Order as it is now. But we kept always and keep now the secret from our mortal members of who *we* really are."

"In a way, I always knew," said Marius. He couldn't stop himself from asking, "But who is Gremt, this spirit you're describing? From where did he come?"

"Gremt was there when Amel entered the Queen," said Teskhamen. "He was there when the twins, Mekare and Maharet, asked the spirits what had become of Amel. It was he who gave the answer: *Amel has now what he has always wanted. Amel has the flesh. But Amel is no more.* He's of the same ilk as this thing which animates you and you, Daniel, and me. If spirits are brothers and sisters to one another, then he is the brother of Amel. He is Amel's kindred. He was Amel's equal in a realm we cannot see and for the most part cannot hear."

"But why did he come down here to be with you," asked Daniel, "to make this thing, the Talamasca? Why did it attract him, this physical world?"

"Who is to say?" asked Teskhamen. "Why is one human drawn irresistibly to music, another to painting, yet another to the glories of the forest or the field? Why do we weep when we see something beautiful? Why are we weakened by beauty? Why does it break our hearts? He came into the physical for the same reasons Amel hovered over the Queen of Egypt when she lay dying and sought to drink her blood, sought to enter her, sought to be one with her body, sought to know what she saw and heard and felt." He sighed. "And Gremt came because Amel had come. And Gremt came because Gremt couldn't stay away."

There was a long moment of silence.

"You know what the Talamasca is today. It has thousands of dedicated scholars of the supernatural. But it does not know and must not know how it was born. And now its Elders are mortal men, and it is on its own. It is strong, it has its traditions, its sacred trusts, and it no longer needs those of us who brought it into being. Yet those of us who brought it into being can benefit at any moment from its tireless research, can steal into its archives to peruse its treasures, can access its most ancient records or its very latest reports. There is no reason anymore for us to control it. It is now fully on its own."

"It was always your intent to watch us, to watch the progress of Amel," said Daniel.

Teskhamen nodded, but then he shrugged. He made a graceful gesture with his open hands. "Yes, and no. Amel was the torch that led the procession through the ages. But many things have been learned and there are many more to learn, certainly, and the great Order of the Talamasca will continue, and so will we."

He looked from Daniel to Marius.

"Gremt would know more about what he is as well. And Hesketh and all ghosts seek to understand themselves completely too. But we have come now with Amel to a moment we have long dreaded, a moment we knew would come."

"How so?" asked Daniel.

"We are seeing now the moment we have long feared, the moment when Amel, the spirit of the vampiric Blood, comes to consciousness and seeks to direct his destiny for himself."

"The Voice!" Marius whispered. The Voice. The voice that had spoken to him in his thoughts had been Amel. The voice urging him to slay had been Amel. The voice urging one blood drinker to kill another was Amel.

"Yes," said Teskhamen. "After all these long millennia it is aware of itself, and it struggles to feel, and to see, as it did in those first moments when it went into the body and blood of the Queen."

Daniel was dumbstruck. He climbed off the bench and came and seated himself beside Marius, but he wasn't looking at either of the others, but rather into his own thoughts.

"Oh, it was never truly unaware," said Teskhamen. "And the spirits knew it. Gremt knew. Only conscious awareness was *no more*. But that consciousness was always struggling. You might say it has gone through some sort of infancy towards childhood and now seeks to speak as a child, understand as a child, think as a child. And it would be a man. It would put away childish things quickly if it could. And the glass through which it sees is dark indeed."

Marius was quietly marveling. Finally he asked, "And Gremt, its brother spirit, he does see clearly as we see, and speak and understand and think as we think? He knows what Amel does not know?"

"No, not really," said Teskhamen, "as he is not really flesh and blood even as is Amel. He is a spirit still who's learned to take on form amongst us, to sharpen his spirit eyes and his spirit ears through what he grasps of what we see and hear, but he does not feel what we feel or what Amel feels. And his life is to some extent more penitential than ours has ever been."

Marius couldn't contain himself. He stood up and walked slowly back and forth on the paving and then out on the soft warm sand. What do these spirits see when they look at us? He stared down at his own hands, so white, so strong, so flexible, so powerful in every simple human way, and now with preternatural strength. He had always sensed that spirits were attracted to the physical, could not remain indifferent to it, and were creatures of parameters and rules like humans even if they were unseen.

Behind him, Daniel asked, "Well, what will happen now, now that it can speak and plot and connive to destroy the young ones? Why has it done all this?"

Marius turned back and sat down again on the bench. But he could scarcely follow what they were saying. He was thinking of all those intimate whispers of the Voice, all that eerie eloquence, that searching to strike the right pitch.

"The ever-increasing young ones weaken it," said Teskhamen. "Proliferation of the Blood ultimately weakens it. That is my guess, but it is only a guess. I suppose as a scholar I should say that is my working hypothesis. Amel has limits, though what they are no one knows. Gremt and Amel knew each other in the spirit realm in ways that cannot be described.

"Gremt is a powerful spirit now in the body he's made for himself, drawn to himself through some form of etheric magnetism. Oh, after all these centuries the Talamasca knows no more about the science of the supernatural than before. I suspect the blood drinker doctor, Fareed, already has learned infinitely more than we have. We approached the data empirically and historically. He approaches it scientifically."

Marius said nothing. He knew of Fareed and Seth, yes. David Talbot had told him of Fareed and Seth. But he had never laid eyes on either. He had assumed, wrongly, that Maharet would never tolerate their foray into hard science. But in truth, he had not himself been terribly interested. He had had his own reasons for choosing to live away from other blood drinkers with only Daniel for a companion. Daniel had spoken gently a number of times of wanting to approach Fareed and Seth, but Marius had never taken the matter up in a serious way.

"Whatever the case," Teskhamen went on, "these invisible bodies have limits, and Amel has limits. He is not, as the ancient witches supposed, a thing of infinite size. Invisible does not mean infinite. And I think now he resents the drain upon his body. It—he—would limit the population, and how severely no one can know."

"And no one can know that he has always been unconscious," said Marius. He was remembering many things, so many things. "What if two thousand years ago," he asked, "it was Amel who put the wicked elder of Alexandria up to abandoning the Mother and the Father in the sun? He knew, somehow, on some level, that the Mother and Father would survive, but that all the young ones out there would burn, and ones of your age would suffer as you did. What if Amel knew?"

"And when Akasha awakened," asked Daniel, "when she went after Lestat. Was that Amel's doing as well?"

"That we can't know," said Teskhamen. "But I wager he comes to consciousness more often and more strongly when there is no fierce mind in the host body to contest his own churning thoughts."

Churning. That seemed a perfect word for it, Marius agreed. That was a perfect word for his own ruminations. He was seeking to remember so many things, moments over the centuries when he had drunk Akasha's blood, been visited by visions he had thought to come from her. But what if they had not come from her? What if they had come from Amel?

"So that's its goal?" said Daniel. "I mean his goal. Is it to confine us to a small population?"

"Oh, I think he dreams of much-greater accomplishments than that," said Marius. "Can anyone know what his ultimate purpose might be?"

"He rages," said Daniel. "When he's gotten into my head, he's raged."

Marius shuddered. He had so hoped somehow this would all pass without his active acknowledgment, that somehow his time of holding the survival of the tribe in his hands was past. Had he not cared for the Mother and Father for two millennia? But he knew now he could not remain on the sidelines any longer.

"What do you want us to do?" asked Daniel.

"Join Louis and Armand and Benji as soon as you can. Whatever happens, you, the blood drinkers enlivened by this thing and dependent upon it, must come together and be prepared to act. Go to them now. If you go, others will go."

"And you're not one of us?" Marius asked. "You are not coming yourself?"

"I am and I am not. I chose the path of the Talamasca long ago, and that was a path to observe but never to intervene."

"I don't see that that old vow much matters now," said Marius.

"My friend, think on what you're saying," said Teskhamen. "I gave my life into the hands of Gremt, and I have given it since to him and to my fellow Elders of the Talamasca. I'm the only blood drinker among them. How can I walk away from them now?"

"But why should you have to walk away?" Marius insisted. "Why won't you help us? You said yourself that Gremt came into the physical realm to watch this thing, Amel."

"And what if it is Gremt's decision that the body in which Amel resides must be destroyed?" asked Daniel. He spoke calmly, reasonably, as if he had no fear. "I mean last time it was the soul of Akasha that was condemned to perish, but not this thing that animated her. If this thing is condemned, then we all die."

"Ah, but it was not the Talamasca that condemned Akasha's body and soul to death," said Teskhamen. "It was Mekare who slew her, and Mekare and her twin who removed the Sacred Core. We ourselves made no decision."

"Because you didn't have to," said Daniel. "Isn't that so?"

Teskhamen shrugged. He made a little gesture of agreement with his hands.

"And now, you may come to a decision, that's what you're telling us," said Daniel. "You and Gremt and Hesketh and whoever else is with you, if there are other spirit elders with you—you may decide that you think Amel himself should be destroyed."

"I don't know," said Teskhamen softly. "I only know that I stand with Gremt."

"Even if you perish? Or are you certain yourself to return the way Hesketh returned?"

Teskhamen put up his hands again but this time defensively. "Daniel," he said gently. "I honestly do not know."

Marius went silent. He was reaching for courage, true courage to say that if this is what must happen, I will support it, but he did not quite have that courage. His mind wanted possibilities, it wanted some chance of containing or controlling this Voice that did not involve the death of all that he, Marius, was and knew.

"It slays only blood drinkers," he said. "Why should it perish for this? Even now, it's made no real destructive incursion into the world."

Teskhamen's face was unreadable, except for its geniality, its gentleness.

"For now, I can tell you that it's not our intention to remain indifferent," said Teskhamen. "We are with you. That's why I am here.

In time, Gremt will come to you. I'm sure of it. But when that will be, I don't know. Gremt knows so many things. We are your friends. Think back on your own life, of how the Talamasca once supported you, comforted you, helped you to find Pandora. We've never really been your enemy or the enemy of any blood drinker. We've had our battles, when mortal members were brought over, yes."

"Ah, yes, my beloved old friend Raymond Gallant did help me," said Marius. "He gave his whole life to you and he died without ever knowing who founded his Order, he died without ever knowing who or what we were."

"Well, he might have died without that knowledge," said Teskhamen. "But he is with us now. He has been with us since the night he died. I was there when his spirit hovered, remained in the Motherhouse. I saw it when those gathered around his deathbed could not see it. And he is indeed one of us now. He is anchored in the physical now as surely as my Hesketh, and there are other ghosts with us as well."

"I knew it," said Daniel softly. "Of course. You would have gathered other ghosts like Hesketh over the years."

Marius was astonished. He was almost moved to tears.

"Oh, yes, Marius, you will see your beloved Raymond again, I assure you," said Teskhamen. "You will see all of us—and there are indeed many others—and it is not our wish that the blood drinkers of this world be extinguished. It's never been. But allow us our old caution, our old passivity, even now."

"I understand," said Marius. "You want us to come together as a tribe, the very same thing that Benji wants. You want us to do the very best that we can in the face of this challenge—without your intervention."

"You're a splendid being, Marius," said Teskhamen. "Never have you ever bowed the knee to any fancy, fantasy, or superstition. The others need you now. And this Amel, he knows you, and you know him perhaps better than you think. I was made by the Mother. I have that direct and pure primal blood. But you have even more of it than I was ever given. And this Voice, if he is to be understood, controlled, educated, whatever is to happen, you must surely play a role."

Teskhamen started to rise, but Marius still held his hand.

"And where will you go now, Teskhamen?" he asked.

"We must come together ourselves before we meet with you and your kindred," Teskhamen answered. "Believe me, we will eventually come to you. I'm certain of it. Gremt wants to help. I am certain that this is what Gremt wants. I will see you very soon again."

"You give my love to my precious Raymond," Marius said.

"He knows you love him, Marius," said Teskhamen. "Many times he's watched over you, been near you, seen your pain, and wanted to intervene. But he is loyal to us and our slow and wary ways. He is Talamasca as he was when he was living. You know our old motto: 'We watch and we are always here.'"

It was now an hour before sunrise.

Teskhamen embraced them both. And then he was gone. Simply gone. And they stood alone together on the sand as the wind swept in from the endless sparkling surf, and the vast sprawling city behind them slowly came to morning life.

The next night, Marius needed less than an hour to make all arrangements by phone with his mortal agents, and to ship their possessions and clothes, such as they were, to New York. They'd lodge at a small hotel uptown as they'd always done, where a suite of rooms had always been kept in readiness for them. And they would talk then, once they'd reached New York, about when to go to Benji and Armand and Louis and blessed Sybelle.

Daniel was powerfully excited that they were going. Daniel wanted to be with the others, Marius knew this, and he was happy for Daniel, but he himself was full of foreboding.

The encounter with Teskhamen had stimulated him, there was no doubt of that; he was in fact reeling from the shock.

Daniel could not grasp the extent of it. Yes, Daniel had been Born to Darkness in a time of myriad shocks. But, before that, Daniel had been born into a physical world of myriad changes and shocks. He had never known the dreary and weary mind-set of times past. He had never understood the inveterate pessimism and resignation into which most of the world's teeming millions had been born and lived and died.

But Marius had known the millennia, and they had been millennia of suffering as well as joy, of darkness as well as light, in which radical change of any kind too often culminated in disappointment and defeat.

Teskhamen. Marius could scarce believe that he had seen him, spoken to him, that such a momentous thing had taken place—that old god of the grove alive now, articulate and eloquent, and pointing the way to the past and the future in the same breath. A great dark portion of Marius's early history flamed into living color for him, and prompted him to search for a coherent thread to all of his life.

But there was the foreboding.

He could not stop thinking of all those long-ago interludes, when he had lain against the breast of Akasha—her caretaker, her keeper—listening to her heart and trying to fathom her thoughts. *He* had been inside her, this alien creature Amel. And Amel was inside of Marius now.

"Yes, I'm inside of you," said the Voice to him. "I am you and you are me."

There followed silence. Emptiness. And the lingering echo of a threat.

14

Rhoshamandes and Benedict

"B E CALM," he said. "Whatever you saw, whatever almost happened to you, you're safe now. Be calm and talk to me. Tell me precisely what you saw."

"Rhosh, it was unspeakable!" said Benedict.

Benedict sat at the desk with his head down on his folded arms, sobbing.

Rhosh, known to so many others through the ages as Rhoshamandes, sat by the cavernous hearth in the old stone room looking at his fledgling with a mixture of impatience and irresistible sympathy. He had never been able to divorce himself entirely from Benedict's boiling emotions, and maybe he had never really wanted to do that. Of all his companions and fledglings through the centuries, he loved Benedict the most—this child of Merovingian royalty who had been such a dreamy Latin scholar in his time, so eager to understand those years which the world now called the Dark Ages. How he'd cried when brought into the Blood, sure of his ultimate damnation, and only come round to worship Rhoshamandes instead of his Christian god—never believing in a world untainted by fear of perdition. But this great superstitious fear was, however, part of Benedict's eternal charm.

And this hapless child had had a gift for making other blood drinkers better than himself as time passed. Now that was quite a mystery to Rhosh, but it was fact.

It was Benedict who had made the young Notker the Wise of Prüm, who likely survived to this day, a mad genius sustained on music as much as human blood.

Pretty Benedict, always a joy to look at, if not to listen to, whose tears could be as beguiling as his smiles.

Rhoshamandes was dressed in what might have passed for a monk's long hooded robe of heavy gray wool with a thick black leather belt around the waist, and big deep sleeves. But the robe was in fact made from fine cashmere, and the buckle on his belt was pewter and revealed a delicately modeled face of Medusa with writhing snakes for hair and a howling mouth. He wore exquisitely crafted brown leather sandals because he didn't feel the cold here on this craggy green island in the Outer Hebrides.

He had short and very soft golden-brown hair and large blue eyes. He'd been born thousands of years ago on the island of Crete to parents of Indo-European descent, and gone down into Egypt when he was twenty. His skin was the smooth creamy tan of immortals who go into the sun often in order to pass for human, and it made his eyes appear wondrously bright and beautiful.

He and Benedict were speaking English now, the language they'd shared for the last seven hundred years, more or less, the Old French and the Latin having passed from their daily speech but not their libraries. Rhosh knew ancient tongues, tongues never known to Benedict.

"It burnt them all," Benedict sobbed. "It destroyed them completely," he said in his muffled, hopeless voice.

"Sit up and look at me," said Rhoshamandes. "I am talking to you, Benedict. Now look at me and tell me precisely what happened."

Benedict sat back in the chair, his long brown curly hair mussed and falling into his eyes, his boyish mouth quivering. Of course his face was smeared with blood and so were his clothes, his wool sweater and his tweed jacket. Disgusting. Absolutely disgusting. Vampires who spilt blood on their garments either from victims or tears were anathema! Nothing so revolted Rhoshamandes about modern fictive and film vampires as their utter unrealistic sloppiness.

And Benedict looked perfectly like a cheap television vampire with that blood all over him.

He'd be the image of an eighteen-year-old youth forever because that is what he was when he'd been made a blood drinker, just as Rhoshamandes would always look like a man a few years older than that with a fuller chest and heavier arms. But Benedict had always had a childlike personality. No guile, no cunning. He might never have outgrown it in mortal life. Something to do with Christ's command,

"Unless you become as little children, you shall not enter the King-dom of Heaven." Benedict had not only been a monk in his youth, he'd been a mystic.

Who could know?

Rhoshamandes, on the other hand, if it mattered, had been the eldest of ten mortal children and a man at the age of twelve, protect-ing his mother. Palace intrigue. The day she'd been murdered, he'd run away to sea and survived by his wits, amassing a fortune before he journeyed up the Nile to trade with the Egyptians. He had fought many a battle, survived unscarred, but made his wealth by instinct rather than violence—until the Queen's blood drinker slaves cap-tured him and dragged him from his boat.

Rhoshamandes and Benedict were both comely and fine boned, chosen for the Blood on account of their seeming physical perfection. Rhoshamandes had brought over dozens of such beauties as Benedict into the Blood, but none had survived with him, stayed with him, loved him as had Benedict, and when he thought of the times he'd driven Benedict away, he shuddered inwardly and thanked some dark god of the blood-drinking world that he'd always been able to find Benedict and bring him back.

Benedict was sniffling and now and then moaning in his inimi-table charming fashion, trying to regain possession of himself. Bene-dict's mortal soul had been formed in kindness and gentleness and true faith in goodness, and these traits he'd never lost.

"All right, that's better," said Rhoshamandes. "Now recall it all for me."

"Surely you saw it, Rhosh, you saw the images. All those blood drinkers couldn't have perished without your catching images."

"Yes, I did, of course," said the other, "but I want to know just how it got the jump on them when they'd been warned. They had all been warned."

"But that's just it, we didn't know where to go or what to do. And the young ones, they have to hunt. You don't remember what an agony it is for them. I don't know if it was ever an agony for you."

"Oh, stop with all that," said Rhosh. "They were told to get out of London, to get away from that hotel, to move into the country-side. Benji Mahmoud had been warning them for nights on end. You warned them."

"Well, a lot of them did," said Benedict sadly. "Plenty of them did.

But then we got the word. They were being spotted and burned out there—in the Cotswolds and in Bath—and all over!"

"I see."

"Do you? Do you care?" Benedict wiped furiously at his eyes. "I don't think you care. You're exactly as Benji Mahmoud describes. You're an elder of the tribe who doesn't care. You never did."

Rhoshamandes was looking away, out of the arched window, at the darkened land below, and the thick jagged forest that clung to the bluff over the ocean. There was no way in the world he was going to disclose his true thoughts to his beloved Benedict. Elder of the tribe, indeed.

Benedict went on talking.

Old ones had perished the night before. On waking Benedict had discovered the burnt remains of two of them right there in the house. He'd run to alert the others. Get out.

"That's when the walls caught fire," he said. "I wanted to save them, save one of them, anything, anything that I could. But the roof exploded and I saw them in flames all around me. And I saw this thing, this thing standing there, and it looked ragged and grotesque and it was on fire too. Is that possible? I swear it was burning. I went up. I did what I had to do."

He broke into sobs again and buried his face in his crooked arm on the desktop.

"You did right," said Rhoshamandes. "But are you sure this one was making the fire?"

"I don't know," said Benedict. "I think it was. It was a wraith. It was bones and rags, but I think . . . I don't know."

Rhoshamandes was reflecting. Bones and rags on fire. He was in fact nothing as calm inside as he pretended now. He was in fact furious, furious that Benedict had almost been harmed, furious about all aspects of this. But he went on listening in silence.

"The Voice," Benedict stammered. "The Voice, it said such strange things. I heard it myself two nights ago, urging me to do it. I told you. It wanted me and I laughed at it. I told them then it was going to find someone to do its dirty work. I warned everyone. A lot of them left then, but I think they're dead, all those who left. I think it found someone else and that someone else was out there waiting. It's not true about Paris, is it? They were all talking about Paris before this happened—."

"Yes, it's true about Paris," Rhoshamandes replied. "But the massacre was interrupted. Someone or something intervened, stopped it. Blood drinkers did escape. I have a feeling I know what happened there." But he fell silent again. There was no point in disclosing all this to Benedict. There never had been.

Rhoshamandes rose to his feet. He began to pace, his narrow hands together as if in prayer, making a slow leisurely circle in the old stone room, gradually coming up behind Benedict and putting a reassuring hand on his head. He bent and kissed Benedict's head. He stroked his cheek with his thumb.

"There, there now, you are here," he murmured. He drew away and stood before the twin arches of the windows.

Rhoshamandes had built this castle in the French Gothic style when he had first come north to England, and he still loved these narrow pointed arches. The dawn of the truly delicate and ornate Gothic style had thrilled him to his heart. Even now he could be reduced to weeping when he wandered the great cathedrals.

Benedict had no idea how often Rhoshamandes went on his own to walk in the cathedrals of Rheims or Autun or Chartres. Some things could be shared with Benedict and some could not. Benedict never stepped inside a great cathedral without experiencing a crisis of cosmic proportions and weeping in grief for his lost faith.

It occurred to Rhosh idly that the notorious Vampire Lestat would understand, Lestat who worshipped nothing and no one but beauty— but then it was easy to love celebrities like Lestat, wasn't it, to imagine them perfect companions.

Later additions to this castle, Rhosh had designed in the High Gothic style for his own pleasure, and his heart was warmed when those mortals who occasionally stumbled on this place thought it was a triumph.

How he loathed being disturbed here by all this. How much other immortals must loathe it, those who'd made sanctuaries like this so they could have some peace.

He'd never modernized the place. It was as cold and severe as it had been five hundred years ago, a castle appearing to grow out of rocky cliffs on the western coast of a steep, inaccessible, and untamable island.

He'd managed to install generators in the gulch below the cliff some twenty years ago, and tanks for petrol, and to deepen and improve the eastern harbor for his sleek modern boats, but electric power here was reserved entirely for the televisions and the computers, never for lighting or warmth. And those computers had brought him the first word of all this madness, not telepathic voices that he had long ago learned to entirely shut out. No, Benji Mahmoud had told him the times were changing.

How he wanted to keep things as they had always been.

There was no one on this island but the two of them, and down in the gorge the old mortal caretaker and his wife and his poor feeble-minded daughter. The old mortal caretaker saw to the petrol tanks and the generators and the cleaning of these rooms by day, and he was paid well for it. He saw to Rhosh's cabin cruiser in the harbor, that big powerful Wally Stealth Cruiser which Rhosh could effortlessly sail on his own. They were forty miles from the nearest land. That's how Rhoshamandes wanted to keep it.

True, once the great Maharet had come calling. That had been in the nineteenth century and she had appeared on his battlements, a lone figure attired in heavy wool robes waiting courteously for an invitation to enter.

They had played chess, talked. And she had gone her way. First Brood and Queens Blood had no longer meant the slightest thing to either of them. But he'd been left with the impression of insurmountable power and wisdom, yes, wisdom, though he did not like to admit it. And he had admired her in spite of his wariness and the unpleasant realization that her gifts vastly exceeded his own.

Another time the formidable Sevraine had been here too, though he had only caught a glimpse of her in the oak forest that covered the lower southern coast of the little island. Yes, it had been Sevraine, he'd been sure of it.

He'd gone down into the valley and in search of her. But she'd vanished, and to the best of his knowledge she'd never returned. She'd been splendidly attired, in gold-trimmed robes of rich flashing color. And that indeed was how she was always described by those who insisted they'd seen her—the magnificent Sevraine.

Yet another time when he'd been piloting his boat alone through the violent seas off the Irish coast, he'd seen her high on a bluff looking out at him. He'd wanted to drop anchor and go to her. He'd sent her the message. But telepathy was dim or nonexistent among those made in the first thousand years, and it seemed to have become even dimmer now. He had caught no greeting from her. Indeed she'd disappeared. After that he'd searched Ireland for her but never turned up the slightest indication of her presence or a habitation or a coven or a clan. And it was known that the great Sevraine had always about her a number of women, a female clan.

Not a single other blood drinker had ever come here. So this was and always had been the realm of Rhoshamandes. And he envied no one, not the erudite and philosophical Marius, nor the other gentle well bred vampires of the Coven of the Articulate.

Yes, he wanted to know those new poetic vampire writers, yes, he had to admit it, wanted to know Louis and Lestat, yes, but he could live with that longing for centuries. And in a few centuries they might be gone from the Earth.

What was an immortal like Lestat, who had less than three hundred years in the Blood, after all? One could hardly call such a being a true immortal. Too many died at that age and beyond. So yes, he could wait.

And as for Armand, he would despise Armand till the end of his days. He would like very much to destroy him. Again, on that he could wait, but he had been thinking of late the time for vengeance on Armand might be drawing closer. If Rhoshamandes had still been in France when Armand arrived there to lead the Children of Satan, he would have destroyed Armand. But by that time, Rhosh was long gone. Still, he should have done it, should have ravaged that Paris coven. He'd always thought some other ancient one would do it, and he'd been wrong. Lestat had destroyed it and not by force but with new ways.

Ah, but this is my kingdom, he thought now, and how can all this be coming to my shores?

Never had he hunted in Edinburgh or Dublin or London that he hadn't wanted to come home immediately to this zone of quiet and changelessness.

Now this thing, this Voice, was threatening his peace and his independence.

And he'd been talking to the Voice a long time, something which he had no intention of confiding in Benedict. He was furious with the Voice right now, furious that Benedict had been in danger.

"And what's to stop it from coming here?" asked Benedict. "What's to stop it from finding me here the way it's been finding all those others who're trying to escape? It burnt some as old as me."

"Not quite as old as you," said Rhoshamandes, "and not with your blood. There was an old one there, obviously, in thrall to the Voice. It was probably blasting you when the walls went up. If others were burning around you, it had you in its sights. It was in that building and it had you. But it couldn't kill you."

"It said horrid ghastly things to me when it spoke to me," said Benedict. He had recovered himself a little and was sitting back again. "It tried to confuse me, to make me think I was having these thoughts and somehow was its servant, that I wanted to serve it."

"Go, clean all the blood from your face," said Rhoshamandes.

"Rhosh, why do you always worry about such things?" Benedict pleaded. "I'm suffering, I'm in agony here, and all you care about is blood on my face and clothes."

"All right," said Rhoshamandes. He sighed. "So tell me. What is it you want me to know?"

"That thing, that thing when he was talking to me, I mean before the fire . . ."

"Several nights back."

"Yes, then. He told me to burn the others, that he could not come to power until they were wiped out, that he wanted me to kill them for him, and that he expected me to be ready to rush into the flames myself for him."

"Yes," said Rhoshamandes, laughing softly, "he's whispered a lot of that rhapsodic nonsense to me too. He has an exalted idea of himself." He laughed again. "He didn't begin at such a pitch, however. At first it was simply, 'You must kill them. Look at what they're doing to you.'"

Again, he did not let on that he was in a rage, a rage now that the Voice had sought after all their many intimate conversations to enlist his Benedict. Did the Voice see through Rhosh's eyes? Did it hear through his ears? Or could it only pitch its tent inside Rhosh's brain and talk and talk and talk?

"Yes, but then he started all that about his coming into his own. What does he mean?" Benedict brought his fist down on the old oak desk. He'd screwed up his face like an angry cherub. "Who is he?"

"Stop that," said Rhoshamandes. "Be still now and let me think."

He sat down again by the stone hearth. The flames were burning brightly there, fanned by the cool wind that now and then gusted through the glassless windows.

Rhosh had been speaking to the Voice for weeks. But the Voice had been silent now for five nights. Could it be the Voice could not attend to two tasks at one time, that the Voice, if it were to possess some wretched revenant and drive it to burn, could not be speaking politely to Rhosh at the same time or even on the same evening?

Five nights ago the Voice had said, "You of all understand me. You of all understand power, the desire for power, what is at the heart of the desire for power."

"Which is what?" Rhosh had asked the Voice.

"Simple," the Voice had replied. "Those who desire power want to be immune to the power of others."

Then five nights of silence. Mayhem throughout the world. Benji Mahmoud broadcasting all night long from the infamous Trinity Gate house in New York, with recordings of the show looping during his daylight hours so that those in other parts of the globe could hear them.

"Maybe it's time I discovered what's going on here for myself," Rhosh said. "Now listen to me. I want you to go belowstairs and stay there. If some benighted emissary of the thing should crash-land on our wintry little paradise, you'll be safe from it down there. Stay there till I return. This is the same precaution being taken by others the world over. Belowground you are safe. And if this thing talks to you, this Voice, well, try to learn more about it."

He opened the heavy iron-braced oak doors to the bedroom. He had to change his clothes for the journey, another terrific annoyance.

But Benedict came after him.

The fire was low in the bedchamber and glowing beautifully. Heavy red velvet draperies covered the open windows, and the stone floors here were covered with old oak boards and layered with silk and wool Persian carpets.

Rhosh stepped out of his robe and flung it to the side, but then Benedict rushed into his arms and held him fast. He buried his face in Rhosh's wool shirt and Rhosh looked to the ceiling thinking of all this blood smearing onto his own clothes.

But what did it matter?

He embraced Benedict tightly and moved him towards the bed.

It was an old coffered bed from the court of the last Henry. A splendid thing with rich knobby posts, and they loved lying together in it.

He stripped off Benedict's jacket, and then his shirt and his sweater, and brought him down on the dark embroidered covers. He lay beside him, fingers tightening on the pink nipples on Benedict's chest, his lips grazing Benedict's throat, and then he pressed Benedict's head against his own throat and said, "Drink" under his breath.

At once those razor-sharp teeth broke through and he felt the mighty hungry pull on his heart as the blood flowed out of him towards the heart beating against him. A gusher of images opened. He saw the burning house in London, saw that hideous wraithlike thing, saw what Benedict must have seen but never registered, that thing falling to its knees, the rafters coming down on it, an arm cracked loose and flung away in the fire, black fingers curling. He heard the skull pop.

The images dissolved in the pleasure that he was feeling, the deep dark throbbing pleasure he reveled in as the blood was drawn out of him with greater and greater speed. It was as if a hand had ahold of his heart and was squeezing his heart and the pleasure washed out in waves from his heart, passing through all his limbs.

Finally he turned and pulled Benedict off and sank his teeth into his neck. Benedict cried out. Rhosh ground him against the velvet cover, drawing the blood with all his strength, deliberately sending spasm after spasm through Benedict. He caught the images again. He caught the sight of London below as Benedict had taken to the skies. He caught the roar and the scent of the wind. The blood was so thick, so pungent! The fact was every single blood drinker on this Earth had a distinct and unique flavor of blood. And Benedict's was luscious. It took all his determination to let go, to run his tongue over his lips and lie back on the pillow and stare up at the worm-eaten oak ceiling of the bed.

The crackling of the fire seemed hugely loud in the empty chamber. How red was the chamber, from the fire, from the dark red draperies. Such lurid and beautiful and soothing light. My world.

"You go down now to the cellar, as I told you," Rhosh said. He rose up on his elbow and kissed Benedict roughly. "You hear me? You listening to me?"

"Yes, yes, and yes." Benedict moaned. He was obviously weak all over from the pleasure of it, but Rhoshamandes had taken only what he'd given, passing the zinging red ribbon of his own blood through the younger one's veins before whipping it back into himself.

He climbed off the bed and, before the open armoire, pulled on a heavy cashmere sweater and woolen pants, then wool socks and

boots. He chose his long Russian coat for this journey, the black velvet military coat of czarist days with the black fox collar. He pulled a
watch cap down over his hair. And then took from the bottom drawer
of the armoire all the papers and currency he might need, and put
these securely into his inside pockets. Where were his gloves? He put
them on, loving the way his long fingers looked in the sleek black kid
leather.

"But where are you going?" asked Benedict. He sat up, mussed,
rosy cheeked, and pretty. "Tell me."

"Stop being so anxious," said Rhoshamandes. "I'm going west into
the night. I'm going to find the twins and get to the bottom of this. I
know this Voice has to be coming from one of them."

"But Mekare's mindless and Maharet would never do such things.
Everybody knows that. Even Benji says that."

"Yes, Benji, Benji, the great prophet of the blood drinkers."

"But it's true."

"Downstairs, Benedict, before I drag you there myself. I have to
be off now."

It was a fine retreat, that cellar suite of rooms, hardly a dungeon
what with its thick animal skins and abundant oil lamps, and of course
the oak fire laid ready to be lighted. The television and computers
down there were comparable to those up here, and a slender air shaft
actually brought a steady bit of fresh ocean breeze in from a tiny
opening in the rocky cliff.

As Benedict went out, Rhosh went to the eastern wall, lifted the
heavy stag-hunt French tapestry that covered it, and pushed back the
door to his secret office, one of those doors weighted so that no mortal alone could move it.

Familiar smell of beeswax, parchment, old leather, and ink.
Hmmm. He always stopped a moment to savor it.

With the power of his mind, he quickly ignited a bank of candles
on iron candelabra spikes.

The rock-cut chamber was lined with books to the ceiling, and on
one wall hung a huge map of the world painted by Rhosh himself on
canvas to feature the cities that he most loved in correct relationship
to one another.

He stood there gazing at it, remembering all the reports of the
Burnings. They'd started in Tokyo, moved to China, then, Mumbai,
Kolkata, the Middle East. And then broken out madly all over South
America, in Peru, Bolivia, and Honduras.

Then Europe had been stricken. Even Budapest which contained Rhosh's favorite opera house. Maddening.

It seemed there had been a plan at first; but the plan had broken down into utterly random attacks—except for one thing. The Burnings in South America had occurred in an arc that had become a crude circle. Only there did such a pattern appear. And that's where the twins were, he was sure of it, deep within the Amazon. Those who knew for certain were clever indeed, and of course he was far too close to the twins in age to have a telepathic advantage with them. But he knew. They were in the Amazon.

The eccentric Maharet favored jungle locations, and always had since the Sacred Core had been taken into her sister. He had now and then caught some weak flashes of the twins in his dreams, emanating from other minds, conveyed to yet other minds and so forth. Yes, they were in the jungles of the Amazon, the ghastly pair who had stolen the Sacred Blood from Akasha's Egypt.

Rebels, heretics, blasphemers. He'd been nourished on those old tales. In fact they were reputedly the cause of it all, were they not? The twins had brought the evil spirit of Amel into Akasha's kingdom. He didn't really care about that old mythology but he did appreciate irony and patterns in human behavior just as he appreciated these elements in books.

Well, he had scant affection for Akasha, who'd been a raving tyrant by the time he'd been dragged into her presence and forced to drink from the Sacred Fount and pledge his eternal fidelity. Icy merciless goddess. She'd been reigning for a thousand years. Or so they said. How she had inspected him, running her hard thumbs over his head, his face, his shoulders, his chest. How her unctuous fawning priests had examined him in all his parts before he was pronounced perfect to be a blood god.

And what fate had awaited him as a blood god? It was either fight under Prince Nebamun's command with the Queen's defenders or be walled up in a mountain shrine, starving, dreaming, reading minds, passing judgment for peasants who brought him blood sacrifices on holy feasts and beseeched him with endless superstitious prayers.

He'd run away soon enough. He'd planned it early. A wanderer from the isle of Crete, a seagoing wanderer and merchant, he'd never bought the dark tangled beliefs of old Egypt.

But he'd refused to abandon Nebamun in the time of his worst trial, Nebamun who'd always been kind to him. And he was not going

to run when Nebamun stood before the Queen accused of high trea-
son and blasphemy for the frivolous and selfish making of a woman
blood drinker.

Making women into blood drinkers was the decadent and foul
practice of the First Brood rebels, and utterly forbidden to the Queens
Blood. For the blood gods and the dedicated soldiers of the Queens
Blood, there need be only one woman, the Queen. Why would anyone dare to make a blood drinker of a woman? True, it had happened
a few times, but only with the Queen's reluctant blessing. Not even
her own sister had she brought into the Blood. Nor her daughters.

He'd been sure that Nebamun and Sevraine, his bride, were going
to be put to death when Rhosh had delayed his own escape. But it
hadn't happened.

The all-powerful Queen who thought her smallest whim a reflection of the Divine Mind had "loved Sevraine" when she had looked
upon her. And she had let Sevraine drink her powerful blood and
called her handmaiden.

As for Nebamun, for his transgressions and presumptions, his sol-
diering times were over. Shut up in a shrine for all time, he was to
ponder his offenses. Were he to serve obediently for a century he
might be forgiven.

In the early hours of the morning, when the guards of the shrine
slept in a drunken stupor, Rhosh had crept to the brick walls and
begged Nebamun to speak to him.

"Run away, leave this place," said Nebamun. "She has taken my
precious Sevraine and doomed me to this harsh and unbearable existence. The time will come when I'll escape these walls. Leave here
now, my friend. Get as far away as you can. Find the First Brood
rebels if you can, and if you cannot, bring others into the Blood. All
we've defended is lies built upon lies built upon lies. Blood drinkers
of the First Brood tell the truth. She is no goddess. There is a demon
inside her, a thing named Amel. I have seen the work of that demon.
I was there when it possessed her."

For words like that they would have ripped out his tongue. But
no one had heard that night through the brick wall except Rhoshamandes. And Rhoshamandes would forever love Nebamun for those
brave words.

It had been fifty years before Rhoshamandes had returned and
smashed that shrine to dust, freeing Nebamun. As for Sevraine, she'd

long ago betrayed the Queen. She'd had no use for the old religion either. There was a price on her head. She was hated, as were the twins. Cursed for her blond hair and blue eyes, as if these natural gifts alone marked her as a sorceress and a traitor. And she had vanished.

"Well, old friends, wherever you are," said Rhoshamandes out loud in the quiet of his little library. "We may soon have to meet over this present disaster. But for now I'm going forth to find out what I can on my own."

Of course he knew where Nebamun was, he'd known for centuries. Nebamun had become Gregory in the Common Era, and kept a blood drinker family of awe-inspiring stability in the greatest luxury. Just about every year or so, the face of that ancient and powerful Nebamun would flash full bright on a television screen as some mortal commentator spoke of Gregory Duff Collingsworth's vast pharmaceutical empire, his worldly dealings on different continents, even his famous *fin de siècle* tower on the shores of Lake Geneva.

How many catching those televised glimpses recognized that face? Probably no one. Except Sevraine perhaps. But then perhaps Sevraine was with Gregory. And perhaps they too had heard the Voice.

Perhaps the Voice was a consummate flatterer and liar. Perhaps the Voice played blood drinkers against one another.

"You alone, I have loved above all, your face and form and your mind," the Voice had said to Rhoshamandes.

Hmmm. We'll see about that.

He blew out the candles. For some reason his telekinetic powers could never just make them go out. He had to do it with his breath. So that's how he did it.

He went back into his bedchamber and opened another armoire that was indeed a true armoire, holding his weapons, those items he'd collected over the years more for sentiment than any other reason. He took the sharp knife he loved best off the shelf, and tied the scabbard to his leather belt inside his coat. Then he took out another weapon, a small greenish weapon from modern war called simply a hand grenade. He knew what this could do. He'd seen it plenty during the great wars that had laid waste to Europe in the twentieth century. He tucked it into his coat. He knew how to pull the pin and hurl it should the need arise.

Then he went out on the high windswept battlements and stared up at the misty sky and out over the cold, roiling gray sea.

For a moment he was tempted to abandon all this, to return to his library and light those candles again and the oak he'd chopped himself for the little fireplace, to sink down into his velvet chair and pick up one of the many books that he'd been reading of late, and just let the night pass as so many others.

But he knew he couldn't do that.

There was a raw inescapable truth in Benji Mahmoud's chiding words. He and the others like him had to do something. He'd always admired Maharet, and cherished the wee bits of time in the past that he had spent with her. But he knew nothing of her in this era except what others had written. And it was time to go see her himself and get to the bottom of this mystery. He figured he knew exactly who this Voice was, and it was time for Rhosh and the Voice to meet.

He'd never bowed to anyone's authority, but avoiding the wars and quarrels of the Undead had cost him dearly. And he wasn't so sure he was willing to acquiesce or migrate again. The Voice was right about power. We seek power so as not to fall under anyone else's power, yes.

Long years ago, this cold island remote from the British mainland had been perfect for his retreat, even if it did take him one hundred years to build this castle and its dungeons and its fortifications. He'd brought the trees here for the barren gullies and gorges, planting oak, beech, alder, elm, sycamore, and birch. He'd been a benevolent lord to the mortals who constructed this castle, dug out his many secret chambers from the bedrock, and created a refuge eventually which humans could not themselves conquer by any siege.

Even in the last two centuries, this place had been perfect. It had been simple to ferry coal and firewood from the mainland, and to keep a pleasure boat of his own in the little harbor for those times when he wanted to be out on the stormy seas.

But the world was wholly different now.

Coast helicopters regularly patrolled the area, satellite images of the castle could be accessed on any computer, and well-meaning mortals frequently made a nuisance of themselves attempting to confirm the safety and well-being of the inhabitants.

Wasn't it the same now for other immortals, those legendary vampire musicians who lived in the Alps, for instance, Notker the Wise with his fiddlers and composers and immortal boy soprano singers? Those boys were such a treat. (You didn't have to castrate a boy to fix him as a soprano forever. Just give him the Blood.) And wasn't it the same for Maharet and Mekare in their remote jungles, and any other exile from the world who'd counted on the survival of impenetrable wildernesses which were no more?

Only the clever ones like Gregory Duff Collingsworth and Armand Le Russe—who could thrive right in the midst of mortals— were undisturbed by the shrinking of the planet. But what a price they paid.

Where would immortals have to go next to build their citadels? Into the mountain ranges beneath the sea? He'd thought of it of late, he had to admit, a great sprawling palace made of space-age steel and glass in a deep dark ocean ravine, accessible only to those powerful enough to swim to the lower depths. And yes, he had the wealth per- haps to create such a retreat for himself of sorts, but he was angry, angry that he had even to think of giving up this lovely island where he'd been at home for hundreds of years. Besides, he wanted to see trees and grass and stars and the moon from his windows. He liked to chop wood himself for his own hearths. He wanted to feel the wind on his face. He wanted to be part of this Earth.

Now and then he reflected: What if we did come together and use our considerable powers to destroy half the human race? It wouldn't be that hard, would it? Especially when people don't believe you exist. Wholesale destruction and anarchy would make for new wildernesses all over the planet, and blood drinkers could hunt with impunity and have the upper hand once more. But then Rhosh also loved the technological accomplishments of the shrinking planet— great flat-screen televisions, recorded poetry and music, DVDs and the streaming of documentaries and dramatic programs and films to viewers everywhere, magnificent electronic sound systems, satellite broadcasting, telephones, cell phones, electric heat and modern con- struction techniques, synthetic fabrics, high-rise buildings, fiberglass yachts, airplanes, nylon carpet, and modern glass. Saying goodbye to the modern world would be anguishing, no matter how good the hunting became.

Oh, well . . . He had no stomach for destroying half the human race anyway. He had no inveterate aversion to mortals. None at all.

But Benji Mahmoud was right. We ought to have a place here! Why are we, of all the creations, supposed to be damned? What do we do that other creatures do not do, he would like to know. And the fact is, we hide more from each other than from mortals. When had mortals ever troubled Rhosh? When had they ever troubled Notker the Wise if he was still in his alpine musical school for the Undead? Or the clever Sevraine?

He took a deep breath of the fresh sea air.

Not a human soul within forty miles except for the old caretaker's family watching an American television program and laughing in their little cottage down there, their warm parlor with all the blue and white china hanging in the cupboard and their little white dog sleeping on the mat before the stove.

He was prepared to fight for it all, wasn't he? And he was prepared to consider fighting with others for it. But for now, he uttered a prayer to the maker of the universe asking only for his own safety, the safety of Benedict, and his own imminent return.

No sooner had the prayer left his lips, however, than he felt a great doubt. What was it that he meant to do and why? Why challenge the wise Maharet in her own house? And certainly his arriving there unannounced would be seen as a challenge, would it not?

It might be a damn sight better for him to go to New York, and seek out there other immortals who were concerned with the crisis and tell them exactly what he knew of the fickle and treacherous Voice.

There was a sudden sound inside his head as real as a whisper against his ear. Sealed off from the roaring wind, it was loud and distinct.

"Listen to me, Rhoshamandes, I need you." It was the Voice. "And I need you to come to me now."

Ah, was this what he'd been waiting for? Am I the anointed one?

"Why me?" he asked, his words lost in the wind, but not to the Voice. "And why should I believe you?" he demanded. "You betrayed me. You almost struck down my beloved Benedict."

"How was I to know Benedict was in danger?" said the Voice. "If you had gone into London and done my bidding, there would have been no danger for your Benedict! I need you, Rhoshamandes. Come to me now."

"Come to you?"

"Yes, the Amazon jungles, my beloved, precisely as you have surmised. I am in prison. I am in darkness. I wander the pathways of my tentacles and tendrils and my endless withering and coiling and threadlike extremities, searching, searching for those to love, but always—always—I am unanchored and rolled back into this mute and half-blind prison, this miserable sluggish and ruined body that I cannot quicken!—this thing that does not move, does not hear, does not care!"

"You are the spirit Amel, then, aren't you?" said Rhoshamandes. "Or that's what you would have me believe."

"Ah, in this living tomb I came to full self-possession, yes, in this vacuum, in this grim emptiness, and I can't escape it!"

"Amel."

"I cannot possess it!"

"Amel."

"Come to me before someone else does. Rhoshamandes, take me into yourself—into your splendid male body with a tongue and eyes and all its limbs and members—before someone else does this, someone rash and foolish and apt to use me and my ever-increasing power against you!"

Silence.

In shock and wonder he stood there, incapable of a conscious decision. The wind lashed at him, searing his eyes until they teared. *Amel. The Sacred Core.*

Long centuries ago, she'd looked down on him with such lofty contempt. "I am the fount. I possess the Core!"

A storm was gathering to the north. He could see it out there, feel its turbulence, feel the torrent nearing him, but what did that matter?

He went upwards, gathering speed as he ascended into the blasting icy cold, and then he turned southwest feeling wondrously weightless and powerful, heading for the open Atlantic.

15

Lestat

Be It Ever So Humble

WHY EVER did you restore this castle, you who could live anywhere in this wide world? Why ever did you come back here, to this place, and the village? Why did you let that architect of yours rebuild the village? Why have you done all this? Are you mad?"

Beloved Mother, Gabrielle.

She was striding up and down with her hands shoved into the pockets of her jeans, her safari jacket rumpled, her hair loose now in pale-blond ripples down her back from the long braid. Even vampiric hair can retain the rippling waves imposed upon it by a braid.

I didn't bother to answer. I had decided that instead of arguing with her or talking to her, I would enjoy her. I so hopelessly loved her, her defiant demeanor, her unbroken courage, her pale oval face with its immutable stamp of feminine allure that no coldness of heart could alter. Besides, I had too much on my mind already. Yes, it was lovely to be with her again, and yes, it was intense. Woe to the blood drinker who makes a fellow blood drinker of his mortal kin. But I was thinking about the Voice, and I couldn't think of much else.

So I was sitting at my antique gold-and-fruitwood writing desk, my precious bit of genuine Louis XV furniture in this place, with my feet up on it just watching her, my hands folded on my lap. And I was thinking, What can I do with what I know, what I sense?

It was a beautiful sunset, or it had been. And the mountains of my homeland were visible out there with the stars sweeping down to touch them, a clear and perfect night so far from the noise and pollution of the world, with only a few voices coming from that little string of shops and dwellings that made up the village on the mountain road beneath us, and we two here in this room which had once been a bedchamber but which was now a spacious paneled and decorated salon.

My mirrors, my traceries of gold on rosewood, my Flemish tapestries, Kirman carpets, Empire chandeliers.

The château had indeed undergone a magnificent restoration. Its four towers were now complete and a multitude of rooms completely reconstructed and supplied with electric light and heat. As for the village, it was very small, and existed only to sustain the little workforce of carpenters and craftsmen engaged with the restoration. We were too far off the beaten path in this part of the Auvergne even for the tourists, let alone the rest of the world.

What we had here was solitude and quiet—blessed quiet. Quiet such as only the rural world can provide—far from the voices of Clermont-Ferrand or Riom. And blessed beauty all around us in green fields and undisturbed forests in this old part of France where once so many poor and struggling families had suffered so much for every loaf of bread or morsel of meat. Not so now. New highways had opened the mountainous and isolated peaks and valleys of the Auvergne to the rest of the country several decades ago and with them had come the inevitable technological embrace of modern Europe. But it remained the least populated part of France, perhaps of Europe—and this château, surrounded and accessible only through private gated roads, was not even on the current maps.

"It disgusts me to see you going backwards," she declared. She turned her back to me, making a small slender figure against the incandescent light of the window. "Ah, but you have always done what you want to do."

"As opposed to what?" I asked. "Mother, there is no forwards or backwards in this world. My coming here was moving forwards. I was homeless and asked myself, with all the time in the world to ponder it, where I should like to be at home. And voilà! I am here in the castle in which I was born of which a considerable amount remains, though it's buried now beneath plaster and ornament, and I am looking out on those mountains where I used to hunt when I was a boy, and I like this. This is the Auvergne, the Massif Central in which I was born. It is my choice. Now stop the harangue."

Of course she had not been born here. She'd lived perhaps the most miserable decades of her existence here, giving birth to seven sons of which I was the last, and dying slowly in these rooms before she'd come to me in Paris, and been launched onto the Devil's Road as we embraced beside her deathbed.

Of course she didn't love all this. Perhaps there was some special place in this world she loved, loved with the feelings I had for all this, but she was likely never going to tell me.

She laughed. She turned and came towards me in the same marching stride she'd been using all along and took a turn before my desk and walked about staring at the twin marble mantels, the antique clocks, all the things she hated with specific contempt.

I sat back, hands clasped behind my neck, and looked at the murals on the ceiling. My architect had sent to Italy for a painter to do these in the old French style—Dionysus with his band of garlanded worshippers frolicking against a blue sky full of rolling gold-tinged clouds.

Armand and Louis had been right to paint the ceilings of their digs in New York. I hated to admit it, but glimpsing that baroque splendor through their windows had inspired me to give the order for these ceilings here. I resolved never to tell them that. Ah, pang of missing Louis, of wanting so to talk to Louis, pang of gratitude that Louis was with Armand.

"You're yourself again at long last," she said. "I am glad. I am truly glad."

"Why? Our world may shortly end. What does it matter?" But this was dishonest. I didn't think our world was going to end. I wouldn't let it end. I'd fight it ending with every breath in my unwholesome immortal frame.

"Oh, it won't end," she said with a shrug. "Not if we all act together again as we did last time, if we put away our differences as the world is always saying and unite. We can defeat this thing, this raging spirit who thinks his every emotion is unique and momentous as if consciousness itself had just been discovered for his benefit and for his personal use!"

Ah, so she knew all about it. She hadn't been holed up in some North American forest watching the snow fall. She'd been with us all along. And what she'd just said had meaning.

"He does behave that way, doesn't he?" I said. "You put that exactly right."

She leaned against the mantel nearest me, her elbow just able to manage it, and succeeded in looking like a thin graceful boy in that posture, her eyes positively glowing as she smiled at me.

"I love you, you know."

"You could have fooled me on that one," I said. "Hmmm. Well." I shrugged. "Seems lots of people love me, mortal and immortal. Can't help it. I'm just the most dazzling vampire on the planet, though why I'll never know. Weren't you lucky to have me for a son, the wolf killer who stumbled onto the stage in Paris and caught the fancy of a monster." This was dishonest too. Why did I feel I had to keep her at a remove?

"Seriously, you look splendid," she said. "Your hair's whiter. Why is that?"

"Apparently it comes from having been burned. Repeatedly burned. But it's yellow enough still to keep me happy. You look rather splendid yourself. What do you know about all this, what's happening?"

She was silent for a moment. Then she spoke. "Never think they really love you, or love you for yourself," she said.

"Thanks, Mother."

"Seriously. I mean it. Don't ever think . . . Love doesn't really ever function like that. You're the only name *and* face they all know."

I regarded this thoughtfully, then replied, "I know."

"Let's talk of the Voice," she said, leaping right into the subject without preamble. "It can't manipulate the physical. Apparently it can only incite the minds of those it visits. He can't possess the bodies at all. And I suspect it cannot do anything with the host body, but then I have seen the host body less often than you have, and for much less time."

The host body was Mekare. I did not think of Mekare in those terms, but that is what she was.

I was impressed. All this should have been obvious to me before now. I'd regarded every visit from the Voice as some sort of attempt at possession, but the visits had never been that. It could make hallucinations, yes, but it had been working on my brain when it did that. But it had never been able to manipulate me physically into anything. I was mulling over the many things the Voice had said.

"I don't think it can control the host body at all," I said. "The host body has atrophied. Too many centuries with no fresh human blood, no human or vampiric contact, too much darkness for too long."

She nodded. She turned and rested her back against the mantel and folded her arms.

"Its first goal will be to get out of that body," she said. "But then what will it do? It will depend on the new host body and its powers. If we could trick it into a young fledgling body, that might be a very good call."

"Why do you say that?"

"If it's an older body again, a truly old body, it can expose itself to the sun and kill off half the vampires of the world by doing this, just as it happened in ancient times. If it's in a young body, it will destroy itself if it attempts this."

"*Mon Dieu*, I never even thought of that!" I said.

"That's why we have to come together, all of us," she said. "And New York's the place of course. But first we must enlist Sevraine."

"You do realize that the Voice can hear us right now," I said.

"Not unless it's here, in one of us," she said. "The Voice has visited me more than once, and I think it can only be in one place at a time. It hasn't spoken to groups of blood drinkers simultaneously. No. It certainly can't speak to everyone at the same moment. That is not remotely possible for it. No. If it's temporarily anchored in you or in me, yes, it can hear what's being said in this room. But not otherwise. And I don't feel its presence. Do you?"

I was pondering. There was considerable evidence she was right. But I still couldn't figure why. Why didn't the Voice's intelligence permeate all of its immense body, assuming it did have a body as we know the word? But then whose intelligence does permeate its entire body? That of an octopus perhaps? I thought of Mekare and Maharet long ago comparing these spirits to immense sea creatures.

"This Voice moves along its own etheric anatomy," Gabrielle said, "and I use that word simply because I don't know any other to describe it, but I bet your learned friends Fareed and Seth would verify what I'm saying. It moves through its various extremities and cannot be in any two places at once. We must meet with them, Lestat. We must get to New York, and before that we must go to Sevraine. Sevraine should come with us. Sevraine's powerful, perhaps as powerful as the host body."

"How do you know about Seth and Fareed?" I asked.

"From the blood drinkers calling Benji Mahmoud in New York. Don't you listen to them? You with your rock videos and sometime e-mail, I thought you'd be on top of all this technology. I listen to the tramps calling in and talking all about the benign vampire scientist of the West Coast who offers them cash for samples of their blood and tissue. They refer to Seth, his maker, as if he were a god."

"And they're headed to New York?"

She shrugged. "They ought to be."

I had to confess I listened to Benji, but seldom to the others, except in snatches.

"Surely this entire body feels," I said, "as I can feel pain in my hand and in my foot."

"Yes, but you don't have independent consciousness in your head or your foot. Look, what do I know? This Voice comes to me, rattles off some nonsense or other, and then it's gone. It flatters me, exhorts me to destroy others, tells me I am the one and only one that it wants. Others have disappointed it. On and on. I suspect it's saying the very same thing to any number of us, but I'm speculating. It's crude, child-like, then wondrously clever and intimate. But look, I'm speculating, as I said." She shrugged. "It's time to go to Sevraine," she said. "You have to take us there."

"I have to take us?"

"Come on, don't be coy, Brat Prince—."

"You know, I could kill Marius for coining that term."

"No, you couldn't. You love it. And yes, you have to take us there. I don't have the Cloud Gift, Son. I never drank the Mother's blood or Marius's blood."

"But you've drunk from Sevraine, haven't you?" I knew she had. I could see subtle differences in her that were not simply the work of time. But I wasn't certain. "Mother, you have the Cloud Gift and you don't know it."

She didn't answer.

"All of us must come together," she said, "and we don't have time for all this. I want you to take us to Sevraine."

I put my feet on the floor, stood up, and stretched. "Very well," I said, "I rather like the prospect of holding you helpless in my arms as if I might drop you at any point into the sea."

She snickered. Ugly word, but she was still irresistible and pretty when she did it.

"And if I did drop you, you'd realize quick enough you have the Cloud Gift as I said."

"Maybe, maybe not. Why don't we put off that experiment? Agreed?"

"All right. Give me five minutes to tell my architect that I won't be here for a few nights. And where are we going?"

"Oh, that architect, what a nuisance! While you're at it, drain him of every drop of blood in his system. A madman who spends his life restoring a remote château simply because he's paid to do it is a dreary prospect indeed."

"Stay away from him, Mother. He's my trusted servant. And I like him. Now where exactly will we be going, if I may ask?"

"Fifteen hundred miles. To Cappadocia."

16

Fareed

Moment of Decision

FAREED SAT in the darkened study staring at the large glowing monitor before him, and at the great sprawling model he'd made of pixels and light of the supposed body of this entity, the Sacred Core, this Amel, this Voice, which was rousing old ones to destroy vampires everywhere.

On Fareed's desk was a hardcover book, a novel. *The Queen of the Damned*. It was open to pages 366 and 367. Over and over again, Fareed read these pages in which Akasha, the original vampire parent, described the coming of the spirit Amel into her body.

Fareed was trying to envision some theoretical construct of this being, this spirit Amel. But he had come up against questions and mysteries he could not conquer. No instrument on Earth could detect the actual cells of this being, but Fareed had no doubt that it was cellular. And as always he wondered if it were not a remnant of a lost world that had existed on Earth before oxygen entered the atmosphere. Could it have been part of some thriving race eventually shut out of the visible biological world by the rise of those creatures that were not only not poisoned by oxygen but thrived on it? What had life been like for that race? Would they have been visible in some way to the human eye during those millions of years before the rise of oxygen? Did they swim the oxygen-free atmosphere of the world as octopuses swim the ocean? Did they love? *Did they breed?* Had they an organized society of which we know nothing? And what precisely had oxygen done to them? Were they remnants of their former selves—giant etheric bodies of infinitesimal cells which had once possessed a grosser form, struggling with senses so different from ours that we couldn't imagine them?

There was little doubt that at death, the human body set free some sort of etheric "self" that ascended, poetically speaking, to some other realm, and that some of these etheric bodies remained here on Earth—earthbound ghosts. Fareed had seen such ghosts since he'd come into the Blood. They were rare, but he had seen them. Indeed he had glimpsed ghosts who had organized around the etheric body a physical appearance of being human that was made up entirely of particles which they drew to themselves through some sort of magnetism.

What relationship did such ghosts have to these spirits of which Amel was one? Did their "subtle" bodies have something in common?

Fareed would go mad if he didn't find the answers. He and Flannery Gilman, the most brilliant doctor he'd brought over into the Blood—the biological mother of Lestat's son, Viktor—had discussed all this innumerable times searching for the great breakthrough which would bring all the disparate information to order.

Perhaps the ultimate key to Amel would be one of those savvy, clever ghosts who passed for real every day in Los Angeles. Seth had said once when they'd spotted such a ghost walking boldly on the street with palpable footsteps that the ghosts of the world were evolving, that they were growing better and better at entering the physical, at making these biological bodies for themselves. Oh, if only Fareed could speak with one of these ghosts, but every time he'd tried to approach such a specter, the specter had fled. One time it had dissolved right before his eyes leaving behind its clothes. Another ghost had dissolved clothes and all because its garments, obviously, had also been illusory, part of its particle body.

Oh, if there were only time, time to study, to think, to learn. If only the Voice had not precipitated this awful crisis. If only the Voice were not Hell-bent on destruction of the Undead. If only the Voice were not an adversary of its own kind. But there was no evidence the Voice felt that the blood drinkers of the world were its own kind. In fact, there was evidence to the contrary, that it saw itself held hostage in some form which it could not make its own. Did that mean that it wanted to be free again, free to ascend to some atmospheric paradise whence it came? Not likely. No. It had to have a very different ambition, an ambition more compatible with the daring that had driven it down into the body of Akasha in the first place.

Fareed stared at the model he had made of the thing in burning color on the giant monitor.

That it was an invertebrate he was almost certain, that it possessed a discernible brain he was certain; that its nervous system involved numerous tentacles he was certain too. He suspected that in its spirit state it had absorbed some form of nutrients from the atmosphere of the planet. And blood, of course, the capacity to absorb tiny droplets of blood, had been its passage into the visible biological world. Obviously its tentacles involved a huge percentage of its neurons, but apparently did not involve full intelligence or awareness. That was localized in the brain, the Sacred Core, so to speak. And it was now evident, evident from the Voice, that this brain could encode both short-term memories and long-term memories. Its wants were now being expressed in terms of time and memory.

But had it always been so? Had the problem of long-term memory paralyzed this creature for centuries because it had had no way to store or respond to long-term memories in its "spirit" state? Had Amel and other spirits floated in a blessed "now" in their invisible form?

Had it always had personality and consciousness as we know them and only been unable in ages past to communicate? It had certainly communicated in spirit form to the great twin witches. It had loved them, wanted to please them, especially Mekare. It had wanted recognition, approval, even admiration.

But had that consciousness been submerged when the boastful Amel entered the Mother, only coming to the surface now because it found itself lodged in the host body of a woman who had no true thinking brain of her own?

Perhaps history had awakened Amel—the history he'd discovered when the burning rock videos of the Vampire Lestat had been piped into the Shrine of the Mother and the Father, videos that told the tale of how the vampires had come into existence. Had something vital and irreversible been sparked in Amel when he saw those little films on a television screen that Marius had so lovingly provided for the mute Mother and Father?

Fareed sighed. What he wanted more than anything in this world was to be in direct contact with the Voice itself. But the Voice had never spoken to him. The Voice had spoken to Seth. The Voice had undoubtedly spoken to innumerable blood drinkers on the planet, but the Voice shunned Fareed. Why? Why did it do this? And was the Voice from time to time anchoring itself inside Fareed to know his thoughts even if it did not speak to him?

That was conceivable. It was conceivable that Amel was learning from Fareed's analysis more than the Voice cared to admit.

Viktor and Seth came into the room.

They stood in the airy darkness, looking at the monitor, waiting politely for Fareed to disengage and give them his full attention.

It was a very large room, this, with glass walls open to the flat country and the mountains beyond, one of many rooms in this great sprawling three-story medical compound which Fareed and Seth had built in the California desert.

Fareed had found the architecture of this area cold and uninspiring, efficient for work, but sterile for the spirit. So he'd warmed this space and others like it with little touches—marble fireplaces arching over gas grates, his favorite European paintings in gilded frames, and faded antique carpets from his native India. Several immense computers dominated his desk here, monitors aglow and filled with graphs and pictures. But the desk itself was an old Renaissance Portuguese piece of carved walnut found in Goa.

Viktor and Seth had not sat down, though the room was filled with leather easy chairs. They were waiting, and Fareed had to let this go, realize once and for all that he had come to the end of what he could know without confronting the Voice directly.

Finally, Fareed turned in the modern black swivel chair and faced the two who were waiting.

"Everything's been arranged," said Seth. "The plane's ready; luggage loaded. Rose is on the plane, and Viktor will be with her. Rose thinks she is going to New York to see her uncle Lestan."

"Well, we hope that will turn out to be the truth, don't we?" asked Fareed. "And our rooms in New York?"

"Prepared, of course," said Seth.

It had been two years since Fareed or Seth had visited their apartment there or the adjacent small laboratory they maintained on the sixty-third floor of a Midtown building. But this place was always in readiness, and why Fareed was asking foolish questions about this now, he did not know, except that it was a form of stalling.

Seth went on talking as if he were thinking aloud, checking himself on what had to be done. "All the human employees are gone home for indefinite leave with pay; all blood drinkers are in the basement rooms and will remain there until we return. The blood supplies are adequate for a long sequester. The security systems are in operation. This compound's as safe as it ever was. If the Voice launches an attack, well, it won't succeed."

"The basements," Viktor whispered. He shuddered. "How can they stand it, being shut up in a cellar for nights at a time?"

"They're blood drinkers," said Seth quietly. "You're a human being. You forget over and over again."

"Are there no blood drinkers with fears of cellars and crypts?" asked Viktor.

"None that I've ever known," said Seth. "How could there be?"

There was no doubt that the cellars were safe. Yet we are leaving here, leaving this superb and secure installation, to go to New York, thought Fareed, but he knew that they had to do it.

"I don't want to be locked in a cellar, not here or anywhere," said Viktor. "I've had a horror of close dark places ever since I can remember."

Fareed scarcely heard. Seth was assuring Viktor he'd be in an apartment of glass walls in New York high above the streets of Manhattan. No crypts.

Typical of a mortal to obsess about something that was of no importance. Fareed wished he could as easily divert himself from his deeper fears.

Fareed had sat quietly astonished this very morning, over fourteen hours ago, before sunrise, as Seth had connected privately with Benji Mahmoud by phone and told him they were coming. The phone had been on speaker. Seth and Benji had gone back and forth in Arabic for half an hour. And when Seth had revealed the existence of Rose and Viktor, Fareed had been horrified.

But he understood. They were going because they had to go, and they had to trust Benji and Armand and the others in New York with their deepest secrets. Leaving Viktor and Rose behind, leaving them here or anywhere, was simply impossible. Viktor had always been their responsibility, and now Rose was their responsibility as well by decision. And so they would take these two lovely young mortals with them to the command central of the crisis, and lodge nearby.

Fareed had slept the daytime sleep of the dead since that phone call, and awakened at sunset and come to his senses knowing Seth had done what he had to do. He was also certain of Benji Mahmoud's devotion to Lestat, certain of the devotion of all his little family—Armand, Louis, Sybelle, Antoine, and whoever else had joined them. But he knew that the secret of Viktor and Rose would soon leak telepathically. It had to leak.

When this many knew a secret, it was no longer a secret. He looked now at this sturdy and princely young man whom he, Fareed, had brought up from earliest childhood, wondering what really did lie in store for him. Fareed had loved him irresistibly, nourishing him with knowledge, luxury, and above all with a rich experience of the physical wonders and beauty of this Earth through travel and private instruction from his earliest years. The only thing ever denied to Viktor had been childhood, an experience of other children, an experience of being what the modern world calls "normal" with all its attendant risks. That Viktor had never known, and now fate had put him in the path of a young mortal woman whose experience had not been all that different from Viktor's own, and the two had come to love each other. It was no surprise, that. Fareed could not have found a more perfect mate for Viktor than Rose. And vice versa.

Fareed backed off from the full intensity of his own emotions, his deepest fears, his constant obsessive worries about all that had happened, might happen, could happen.

"The blood banks in the rooms belowground . . . ," Viktor said.

"Adequate," said Seth. "Seen to. All of it. Done. I just told you. Dr. Gilman is in charge, and no one will come up out of the cellars until she gives the word. Our beloved savants have their labs down there, their computers, their projects. They are as indifferent to fear as they are to anything pertaining to the world outside their own field. The electrical systems protecting them cannot fail. It would be flat-out ridiculous of the Voice to launch an attack on this location."

"And the Voice is such a paragon of the reasonable and the effective," said Viktor suddenly under his breath. It was as if he couldn't stop himself, and Fareed realized suddenly how very tense and miserable Viktor was, and how excited also.

Viktor wore his usual short-sleeved white polo shirt and jeans, though he was carrying over his arm a soft brown suede jacket for the journey. He was a blond-haired young male in splendid health with a well-developed and muscular frame that was almost that of a man rather than a boy. But in this day and age a man might develop height and musculature until he was thirty. Viktor was six foot one, already one inch taller than his father.

"I'm sorry. Forgive me for interrupting," Viktor said, with his usual courtesy. He'd been deferential to Seth and Fareed and his mother all his life.

"No one expects you to be indifferent to what's happening," Seth said gently. "But we've been through it. This is the way. This is our decision."

Viktor nodded, but his eyes and complexion flashed with a warmth that no preternatural body could ever give forth. Fareed could hear Viktor's accelerated pulse. He caught the faint scent of the sheen of sweat covering Viktor's upper lip and forehead.

In the dim lunar light of the monitors Viktor looked so much like Lestat it was uncanny. He wasn't angry as he looked at Fareed. In fact, it didn't seem that Viktor had ever been angry in his entire short life with anyone. But he did look hurt and young and anxious. His unruly blond hair made him look more boyish than he was. It was long now, almost to his shoulders. And that is how the Vampire Lestat looked most of the time in videos, photos, and even the iPhone snapshots taken of him by vampire paparazzi in Paris.

"I beg you one more time, both of you," Viktor said now in a trembling but rather deep voice, "to bring us over. Rose and me, bring us over! Do it before we make this journey to New York and you plant us, two helpless human beings, in a colony of the Undead."

He had always had a way of being painfully honest and cutting through superfluous language as if every language he had ever learned was a "second tongue." And that voice, that deep male voice, indicated a maturity he really didn't possess yet, as far as Fareed was concerned.

"You won't be in a colony of the Undead," said Fareed reprovingly. "You'll be in our own apartments, and you'll be safe with our guards."

Oh, he was beautifully behaved, never rash, Viktor, and never rebellious, and seldom if ever emotional in a confusing way, but he was a boy of nineteen, one year younger biologically than Rose, almost to the month, by sheer coincidence, and both of them were children.

"Bring us over," Viktor whispered, glancing from Fareed to Seth.

"The answer is no," said Seth. He placed a hand on Viktor's shoulder. The two were about the same height, though Viktor was gaining.

Fareed sighed. He said again what he had said before.

"The Voice slays young blood drinkers," said Fareed. "We will not bring you over and make you vulnerable to his attacks, simply to lose you. As mortals you are infinitely safer. And if this thing ends in ruin for us, you and Rose will survive. You and Rose will walk away. You may never know what happened, and all your life you'll carry the burden of experiences you can't share with others. But you'll walk away. And we want this for you, regardless of what you want."

"That's the love a parent has for its child," said Seth.

Viktor was plainly exasperated. "Oh, what I wouldn't give," he said, "for five minutes with my real father." It wasn't said with malice. It was a simple confession, and Viktor's eyes were wondering as he said it.

"And you will likely get more than that in New York," said Fareed. "That is only one of the reasons we must go there. Because you and Rose must meet with him and he must decide what happens with you."

"Rose is half out of her mind," said Viktor. "This can't end any other way for her but with the Blood. You know this! Do you realize how helpless I feel?"

"Of course," said Fareed. "We feel helpless ourselves. But now we must be going. We'll reach New York before you do. And we'll be there when the plane lands."

Viktor could never know the depth of Fareed's anxiety right now. Fareed had not brought this vital, splendid human being into the world simply to consign him to death, death in any form, yet Fareed knew how desperately and totally this boy wanted the Blood and had to want it. Only Lestat could consign these two to the Blood. Fareed could never do it.

Seth went quiet and still for a moment. But Fareed had heard it too, the thin wirelike voice of Benji emanating from some equipment somewhere in the compound.

"Be assured, the old ones are coming together. Be assured, Children of the Night, you are no longer alone. They are gathering. Meanwhile you must protect yourselves, wherever you are. Now the Voice is seeking to turn you against your fellow blood drinkers. We have reliable reports that that is what it is doing now, entering the minds of the youngest and driving them to fight their makers and their fellow fledglings. You must be on guard against the Voice. *The Voice is a liar.* Tonight young ones have been slain in Guadalajara and in Dallas. The attacks have slowed, but they are still happening."

Slowed. What did this mean?

"Is there any estimate coming from anyone," Viktor asked, "as to how many have been slain?"

"Roughly? Based on the report," said Fareed bringing his fingers together. "I'd say thousands. But then we have no idea how many Children of the Night there were before these massacres started. You ask me, based on all I've read and pondered, well, I would say the population was at the most five thousand the world over before this started, and now it's down below a thousand. As for the elders, the true Children of the Millennia who are impervious to these raids of fire, I calculate there are less than thirty and most descended from Queens Blood and not from First Brood. But no one can know. As for all those in between, the powerful and clever ones like Armand and Louis and Lestat himself, and who knows who else, well, what, maybe one hundred? No one can ever know. I don't think the Voice knows."

It hit him suddenly with dark force that indeed the species could die out without anyone ever documenting fully what had actually happened to it. Its history, its physical characteristics, its spiritual dimensions, its tragedies, the portal it had established between the world of the seen and the unseen—all might very well be swallowed by the same implacable physical death that had swallowed millions of other species on this planet since before recorded time. And all Fareed had sought to know and achieve would be lost, just as his own individual consciousness would be lost, just as *he* would be lost. He found himself breathless. Not even as a dying man in a hospital bed in Mumbai had he confronted his mortality so totally.

He found himself turning slowly in the chair, and reaching for the button that would shut down all his computers simultaneously.

And when the screens went dark, he was peering through the immaculate glass wall at the great sweep of stars that hung over the distant mountains.

Stars over the desert; how bright and magnificent they look.

The ancient Akasha had seen such stars. The young and impulsive vampire Lestat had seen them the night he'd staggered into the Gobi Desert hoping in vain for the rising sun to destroy him.

It seemed horrible to him suddenly that he, Fareed, in any form was on this tiny bit of burnt rock in a system so vast and indifferent to all suffering.

All you can do, he thought, is fight to stay alive, to stay conscious, to remain a witness and hope somehow there is a meaning to it.

And Viktor, Viktor standing behind him had just begun his optimistic and promising journey. How would he and Rose escape whatever was to happen?

He rose to his feet.

"It's time," he said. "Viktor, take leave of your mother."

"I have," said Viktor. "I'm ready."

Fareed took a last look around the room, a last look at his own bookshelves, computers, papers strewn here and there, the tip of the iceberg of twenty years of research, and he realized coldly that he might never see this great research compound again, that he might not survive this crisis precipitated by the Voice, that perhaps he'd come too late with too little into this great realm where he had seen such wonder and promise.

But what was to be done?

He embraced Viktor now, holding him tight and close and listening to that marvelous young heart pounding away with such splendid vigor. He looked into Viktor's clear blue eyes.

"I love you," he said.

"And I love you," Viktor answered without hesitation, holding him tightly with both arms. In his ear he whispered, "Father. *Maker.*"

17

Gregory

*Trinity Gate
Shall We Dance?*

I KNOW," said Armand. "But why would a creature of your age and power want Lestat to exert some kind of leadership?"

He was talking to Gregory Duff Collingsworth as they sat in the long rear salon of Trinity Gate on the Upper East Side—a glass porch that in fact united all three townhouses along the back like the service galleries of old in southern mansions—the glass wall beside them open to a magically illuminated garden of slender oaks and masses of night-blooming flowers. Paradise in New York if ever Gregory had beheld one.

"If I wanted to lead our tribe, as Benji calls it, I would have done something about it long ago," said Gregory. "I would have come forward, identified myself, involved myself. It's never been my inclination. Look, I've been transformed by the last two millennia. I've chronicled for myself that transformation. But in a very real way, I'm still the young man who once slept in Akasha's bed fully expecting to be murdered at any time to satisfy the fears of her king, Enkil. I commanded blood drinkers later, yes, with the Queens Blood, but under her cruel hand. No, life has me at a fever pitch of involvement after all this time, and I cannot back away from the luxury of studying all this and take up the confines of leadership."

"But you think that Lestat will?" asked Armand.

It was unnerving, Gregory thought—this boyish face confronting him, this near-cherubic face, with its warm brown eyes and the soft waving auburn hair, unnerving that all this belonged to an immortal of five hundred years in the Blood who himself had become a leader twice in his existence because of something iron hard and ruthless of which the face reflected nothing.

"I know that Lestat will and that he can," said Gregory. "Lestat is the only blood drinker truly known, in one way or another, to the entire world of the Undead. The only one. If they haven't read his books, they've seen his little films, or heard his songs. They know him, his face, his voice—they feel they know the charismatic being himself. As soon as the crisis of the Voice is past, he will lead. He must lead. Benjamin has been right since the beginning. Why should we continue leaderless and disunited when so much is to be gained by establishing a hierarchy and pooling our resources?"

Armand shook his head.

They sat at a white-marble-top table in two white-painted Chinese Chippendale chairs in this glass garden room with its fragile white lilies and its exquisite wisteria. Gregory was dressed as always in his immaculate three-piece wool suit, hair very short, and Armand, the long-haired angel, wore a severe but beautifully colored dark burgundy jacket with bright gold buttons, and a white shirt that was almost luminous in its silk, with a thick white silk scarf for a tie wrapped around his neck and folded into the open shirt collar.

"These have been good times for you and Louis, haven't they?" Gregory asked, taking a moment to breathe deeply, to sense the moment, to drink in the perfume of the lilies in their painted pots, to look at the shivering wisteria hanging down from the trellis that ran up the wall behind Armand, with its purple blossoms like an abstract painting of a cluster of grapes. That is what wisteria always made Gregory think of, of grapes. . . .

"Yes, they've been good times," said Armand. He looked down at the marble black-and-white chess set between them. His right hand idly cradled the black queen on his side. "And it was a battle for us to achieve what we've achieved here. It's far easier to wander in despair, isn't it, to drift from place to place, never making a commitment. But I forced it. I brought Louis and Benji and Sybelle here. I insisted on it. And Antoine is now a vital part of us. I love Antoine. Benji and Sybelle love him too."

He gestured with his eyes to the open doors. Antoine and Sybelle had been playing together for over an hour, she at the piano as always and Antoine with his violin. It was a waltz from a twentieth-century musical they played now, something "popular" and not highly regarded perhaps in the world of classical music, but surprisingly dark and evocative.

"But there's no point in glorying in all of this just now, is there?" Armand asked. "Not with what we are facing." He sighed. His square face and rounded cheeks added to his childlike appearance. "The time will come when we can talk about all we've witnessed and what we have to offer to one another. But surely this isn't the time, not with the Voice turning blood drinkers against each other all over the American continent. And you know, of course, the young ones are pouring into New York, in spite of our warnings. Benji's told them over and over not to come, to let the elders gather, yet they come. You must hear them even more sharply than I do. They're out there in the park. They think the trees can hide them. They're hungry. And they know that if they trouble the innocent in my domain I'll destroy them. Yet still they're here, and I can smell their hunger."

Gregory didn't respond. There were perhaps fifty at most out there. That was all. Those were the only survivors who had made it this far in their desperation. Even now stragglers and survivors in various cities were turning on each other, battling as the Voice urged them to do, beheading their own former cohorts, cutting out their hearts, smashing their skulls. The cities of the world were filled with black stains upon the pavements where immortal lives had been snuffed out, and remains had been scorched by the sun.

Surely Armand knew that. Gregory did not conceal his own thoughts.

"I'm not sorry they're dying," Armand confessed.

"But the survivors, the survivors are what matter now," said Gregory, "and finding a leader. And if you won't be that leader, you, after all your experience . . ."

"What experience?" asked Armand, his brown eyes brightening angrily. "You know what I was, a pawn, an executioner in the thrall of a cult." He paused, then he uttered the words, "The Children of Satan," with dark smoldering rage. "Well, I'm that no longer. Yes, I've driven them out of this city from time to time, and I once drove them all out of New Orleans when Lestat was suffering there and they were constantly trying to get a glimpse of him. But you'd be surprised if you knew how often I used the Mind Gift to terrify them, force them into retreat. I did that much more than . . . than burn them." His voice trailed away. A blush appeared in his cheeks. "I never took any pleasure in killing any immortal."

"Well, maybe whoever leads today will not have to be a wanton executioner," said Gregory. "Maybe the old crude ways of the Children of Satan have absolutely nothing to do with this. But you don't want to lead. You know you don't. And Marius does not. Marius can hear us now. He's in there listening to the music. He came in half an hour ago. He has no taste to lead. No. Lestat is the logical one to be the anointed leader."

"Anointed?" Armand repeated the word with a slight raise of his eyebrows.

"A figure of speech, Armand," said Gregory. "Nothing more. We've waked from those nightmares of the Queens Blood cult and the later Children of Satan. We are finished with such things. We are in thrall to no belief now except what we can know from the physical world around us. . . ."

"Lestat's 'Savage Garden,'" said Armand.

"Not so savage really," said Gregory. "There is not a single one of us, no matter how old, that does not have a moral heart, an educated heart, a heart that learned to love while human, and a heart that should have learned ever more deeply to love as preternatural."

Armand looked sad suddenly. "Why has it taken me so long?"

"You're so young yet, you know that," said Gregory. "For a thousand years I served that wretched Queen. I suffered under her mythologies. You haven't even been alive that long in any form. That's what you have to grasp, what all the others have to grasp. You are on the threshold of a great journey, and you must begin to think in terms of what you can do as a powerful spiritual and biological being. Stop with the self-loathing. Stop with imagery of 'the damned' this and 'the damned' that! We are not damned. We never were. Who under the sun has the right to damn any living breathing creature?"

Armand smiled. "That's what they all love about Lestat," he said. "He says we're damned and then he behaves as if Hell has no dominion over him."

"It should have no dominion over any of us ever," said Gregory.

"Now we must all talk of these things, all of us, not just you and I, but all of us. And something must be forged here that will transcend the crisis that's brought us together."

A noise from the front of the house suddenly distracted them. They stood and walked swiftly together down the long hallway and towards the open front doors. The music had broken off.

Louis was greeting two blood drinkers who had just arrived, and Gregory saw with relief that these were Fareed and Seth. Louis had taken their heavy coats, coats for the wind and cold altitudes, and was passing them on now to a quiet, obedient mortal servant who slunk away as if he were invisible.

How handsome Louis looked, with his ivory-colored skin and deep green eyes, this somewhat humble and self-effacing being who had given birth to the books of the Coven of the Articulate. Lestat might be the hero of the Vampire Chronicles, but this one, Louis, was the tragic heart. Yet he seemed at long last to have achieved a kind of peace with the ghastly realities of his existence and the existence of all those around him who outranked him in power but not necessarily in insight or wisdom.

Fareed and Seth were robust and vital as ever, mussed, and even flushed from the journey, but obviously glad to be under this roof.

Armand came forward with the deliberate dignity of the receiving master of the house and embraced Fareed and then Seth in the French manner with a kiss on both cheeks. Were they distracted by that angelic face? Probably.

"Welcome to our house," Armand said. "We are so glad you've come."

"Unfortunately the plane's been delayed," said Fareed. He was referring to the plane carrying Rose and Viktor. "I am very unhappy. It won't land before sunrise."

"We have people who can meet the plane," said Armand, "trusted people. They will take care of Rose and Viktor. Now come in and rest awhile."

"Ah, but we have such people too," Fareed said quickly, but not disagreeably. "And please understand, I don't want them under this roof. We'll keep them in our apartments in Midtown for a while."

"This is a secret location?" asked Armand. "We have deep cellars here, inaccessible to mortals and most immortals."

"The boy has a horror of basements and enclosed spaces," said

Fareed. "I've promised he won't be locked in a crypt. He'll feel much safer in our Midtown rooms."

"And the girl. How much does she know?"

"Everything really," said Fareed. "There was no point in tormenting her with lies."

Armand nodded.

"We'll bring them here," said Seth. "We will allow them to meet everyone."

Fareed was obviously shocked. He looked helplessly and a little angrily at Seth.

"If they are to go their own way after this, better they remember us for what we were."

Armand nodded. "We want to make all of you comfortable in any way that we can."

They passed into the parlor. Sybelle's greeting was a quick nod, but Antoine came up with the violin and bow in his left hand to offer his right. Every new encounter with his own kind was treasured by Antoine.

Gregory watched as Marius came forward to embrace the two doctors. Ah, so powerful, this commanding Roman who had kept the Mother and Father safe and secret for two thousand years. If Marius experienced the slightest fear of his elders gathering here he showed not the slightest sign.

His beloved Chrysanthe, in her white-and-silver gown, who had been sitting with Marius—in deep conversation with him as far as Gregory could divine—also came forward and gave her tender, most gracious greeting to the newcomers.

Far off in rooms throughout the three townhouses others were coming to awareness of the latest arrival—Daniel and Arjun and Pandora who'd been talking together somewhere. And Thorne, red-headed Thorne, who had only arrived the night before, and had been in fast conversation with David and Jesse.

Jesse was in no state to be with the entire company. Rather she was someone in deep anxiety, and she had related in a trembling voice to Gregory all that Lestat had told her about the images he had caught from Maharet about the Guatemalan volcano, Pacaya. "But my aunt would never doom the entire tribe to extinction no matter how great her pain," she'd averred. Then she'd given way to tears. Thorne was a friend to her, an old friend, as was David, and they remained closeted away.

"I can show you to your rooms now, if you like," said Louis to Fareed and Seth. "Rooms where you might be alone and rest." He still spoke with a faint French accent, and looked relaxed yet formal in his black wool suit with a flash of green silk at the neck, a shade of green that exactly matched the emerald ring on his left hand.

"In time," said Fareed gratefully with a sigh. "Let us stay here with you, if we might. I heard the music when we were approaching."

"And you shall hear it again," said Sybelle, and with a nod she began again that same vigorous and dark waltz, "The Carousel Waltz." Tall, lanky Antoine had taken his place beside her again, his long black hair loose and unkempt yet not unattractive, certainly not unattractive for a fiddler, and he began to accompany Sybelle, obviously waiting for her to initiate the variations.

Flavius and Davis appeared in the doorway. At once the doctor, Fareed, greeted Flavius and began asking as to the leg, the miracle leg, and they were lost now in conversation. But Seth had taken one of the many small gold music chairs against the wall and was staring at Sybelle and Antoine as they played together. He seemed oblivious to everyone else. Davis too had been distracted and drawn by the music.

Chrysanthe suddenly asked Marius if he cared to dance, and he, quite surprised, immediately accepted.

This startled Gregory. Indeed it shocked him.

"If you don't know how to waltz," Chrysanthe was saying, in her naïve and innocent fashion, "I'll teach you."

But Marius did know how, he confessed with a playful smile, and suddenly they were dancing in wide circles across the hardwood floor in the vast empty room, two stately and charming figures— Chrysanthe with her shimmering bronze hair threaded with pearls and spilling down her back in waves, and Marius staring right into her eyes as he guided her effortlessly in time with the music. He had cut his pale-blond hair short for this evening, and wore the simplest of male attire, a dark dinner jacket and trousers with a white turtle-neck sweater.

He is the most impressive immortal here, Gregory thought, and my Chrysanthe is as beautiful as any, as beautiful as Pandora who is just now coming into the room. I don't like it, their dancing. I don't like it at all.

When had he ever seen blood drinkers dancing? He and Chrysanthe went out into human society frequently and always had, and they had danced, yes, on many a polished dance floor, passing for mortal, but this was wholly different. This was a gathering of immortals, and the dancing of immortals was different.

Suddenly the music was too loud for him, and he felt his pulse in his veins, and he didn't want to watch Marius with his Blood Wife, Chrysanthe. But he didn't want to walk away either.

From far beyond these walls there came voices in the night, the young blood drinkers out there arguing with one another in the park, and suddenly one of them was fleeing from another in terror.

The tempo of the music became ever more rapid. Pandora had begun to dance with Louis, the ancient one with the inevitable living-marble demeanor and the younger, more human Louis beaming down at her as if she were in fact an ingénue in his care. Recent infusions of ancient blood had not entirely altered Louis. He was still perhaps the most human-appearing immortal in the house.

Davis moved out onto the dance floor, alone, his head slightly bowed, left arm raised in an arc, right hand on his waist making his own little private dance to the waltz music with exquisite feline ease. His heavy-lidded eyes were dreamy, and his dark brown skin gorgeous in the light of the chandelier.

Fareed had taken his place beside Seth and appeared to be enraptured now with these goings-on. Vampire musicians were such curiosities and had appeared so seldom in the history of the Undead. What they did with their instruments was always so difficult to analyze. But Gregory was convinced it had to do with the changelessness of the vampiric body and the ever-shifting changes all around them; they did not yield to tempo as did human musicians, but kept rebelling against it, playing with it, threatening to destroy it, yet snapping back into it with surprising suddenness, which gave the music a friable and almost tragic sound.

Armand was suddenly at Gregory's side.

"Rather like fiddling while Rome burns, isn't it?" he asked.

"Oh, I don't know," said Gregory. "But the intensity of this is undeniable. This many of us gathered here in one place. This is . . . I didn't . . ."

"I know, but this time we mustn't scatter like marbles rolling in all directions when it's over."

"No," said Gregory, "it's not possible anymore for us to live isolated from one another and uncooperative with one another. I've known that for a long time."

"Yet it's never worked when I've tried . . ." Armand broke off and turned to the music.

Benji came into the room.

The music stopped.

In his dark gray three-piece suit and matching fedora Benji moved through the crowd with the smiling vigor of a visiting politician, shaking this hand and that, bowing to Pandora, and to Chrysanthe, accepting the kisses of the women graciously and then taking the center of the room, eyes sweeping over all. He was perhaps five feet two inches in height, yet a perfectly proportioned man. His hat was clearly integral to his costume, and no one need bother to tell him that a gentleman takes off his hat indoors, because his hat was not coming off, it was part of him.

"I thank you all for coming," he declared, his boyish voice ringing out clearly and distinctly with a commanding self-confidence. "I've broken off broadcasting to inform you of the following. The Voice has called our phone lines, and spoken to us through the vocal cords of a vampire male. The Voice says it is trying to come to us."

"But how can you be certain this was the Voice?" asked Armand.

"It was the Voice," said Benji with a little deferential bow to Armand. "I spoke to him myself, of course, Armand, and he referenced for me the things he had told me privately." Benji tapped the side of his head beneath the brim of his hat. "He recalled for me the bits of poetry he'd been reciting to me telepathically. It was the Voice. And the Voice says he is struggling with all his might to come to us. Now, ladies and gentlemen of the Night, I must return to the broadcast."

"But wait, please, Benji," said Marius. "I'm at a disadvantage here. What poetry was it exactly that the Voice recited?"

"Yeats, Master," said Benji with a deeper more referential bow. "Yeats, 'The Second Coming': 'And what rough beast, its hour come round at last, / Slouches towards Bethlehem to be born.'"

And he was off without another word for his studio upstairs, tipping his hat as he passed Pandora and Chrysanthe. And the music filled the room again—the throbbing, rushing sound of "The Carousel Waltz."

Gregory moved back, close to the wall, watching the dancers as they resumed. Then he realized that Davis was at his side. He felt the cool touch of Davis's hand on his.

"Dance with me," said Davis. "Come dance at my side."

"How?"

"Oh, you know. You've always known. The way men have always danced. Think back. Long ago, you must have danced with other men." Davis's eyes were moist, searching. Davis was smiling, and he seemed utterly trusting, trusting in Gregory somehow no matter what the future held. How sweet was that trust.

Gregory did think back, yes. Back and back, he went through the memories to those long-ago human nights in ancient Kemet when he had danced, danced with other men, danced at the banquets of the court until he'd fallen down in bliss and exhaustion with the drums still pounding in his ears.

"Very well," he said to Davis. "You lead the way."

How marvelous it was to be drifting into the ancient patterns yet bound up in this new romantic music. How natural it suddenly seemed. And though his eyes were half closed and for a moment all his fear and apprehension was forgotten, he was conscious that other male immortals were dancing too, all around him, each in his own way. Flavius was dancing. Flavius of the miracle limb dancing with that limb. It seemed everyone was dancing; everyone was caught up in this raw and relentless music; everyone had yielded to it, and to this unprecedented and extraordinary moment that stretched on and on.

An hour had passed. Maybe more.

Gregory wandered the house. The music filled it, seemed to reverberate in the very beams.

In an open library, a pretty French library, he saw Pandora talking with Flavius by a gas fire. Flavius was weeping and Pandora was stroking his head, lovingly, tenderly.

"Oh, yes, but we have time now to talk about all of it," she said to him softly. "I have always loved you, loved you from the night I made you, and you have always been in my heart."

"There's so much I want to tell you. There's this longing for a continuity, for you to know."

"To be your witness, yes, I understand."

"Still, after all this time, this unimaginable time, I have these fears."

Fears.

Gregory passed on, silently, not wanting to intrude. Fears. What were his own fears? Was Gregory afraid that in this new coming together, they would lose their little family that had endured for so long?

Oh, yes. He knew that fear. He'd known it as soon as he'd brought his little company through the front door.

But something finer, something greater was possible here, and for that he was willing to take the risk. Even as it chilled him, even as he found himself wandering back towards the music, towards the inevitable spectacle of seeing his beloved Chrysanthe dazzled and entertained by new and magnetic immortals, he knew that he wanted this, this great gathering more than he had ever wanted anything with his entire soul. Were not all of these immortals here his kin? Could they not all become one united and enduring family?

18

Lestat

Sevraine and the Caves of Gold

MILLIONS OF YEARS AGO two great volcanoes poured lava and ash again and again over the land now called Cappadocia, creating a stark and breathtaking landscape of serpentine gorges and valleys and soaring cliffs and countless clustered knifelike towers of stone piercing the sky which have come to be known as fairy chimneys. For thousands of years, mortals have carved deep cave dwellings into the soft volcanic rock, eventually creating virtual cathedrals underground and monasteries and even whole cities remote from all natural light.

Was it any wonder that a great immortal had created a refuge in this strange land where tourists now come to see Byzantine paintings in cave churches, and hotels today offer luxurious accommodations in rock-cut rooms in cliff faces and mountain peaks?

How gorgeous it was under the light of the moon, this magical land in the middle of the Anatolian plain.

But nothing had prepared me for what I beheld as we entered Sevraine's underground domain.

It was just past midnight when we made our way through a narrow winding rocky valley far beyond any human habitation, and how Gabrielle found the entrance in what seemed an impenetrable cliff I wasn't certain.

But climbing the face of this cliff, clinging with preternatural skill to the outcroppings and broken roots that humans might never trust, we made our way into a dark slit of an opening that widened out into an actual low-roofed tunnel.

Even with my vampiric vision, it was difficult for me to make out the shape of Gabrielle moving in front of me, until suddenly after the fourth or fifth turn in the passage, her figure loomed small and dark against the glow of flickering flames.

Two vigorously burning torches marked the entrance into a passage of hammered gold where the air was suddenly cool with currents from the world beyond, and the shimmering metal all around us enclosed us in an eerie light.

On we walked until we reached the first of many broader gold-lined chambers where layer after layer of the precious metal had been hammered over crude stone, perhaps mixed with fresco plaster, I couldn't know, and suddenly the ceilings above us were ablaze with magnificent paintings in the old Byzantine style that had once filled the churches of Constantinople and still filled the churches of Ravenna and San Marco in Venice.

Rows and rows of dark-haired round-faced saints gazed down on us with dark brows and unwavering gravity, clothed in embroidered robes, as we moved deeper and deeper into the underground realm.

At last we emerged on a gallery that wound around the upper part of a vast domed space with the feel of a great plaza. All around us passages opened from this great central place to other parts of the seeming city, while above the dome itself was decorated in brilliant sections of green and blue and gold mosaic swirling with vines and blossoms, bordered in red and gold at the top of the walls.

Grecian columns carved out of the soft rock appeared to hold a structure that was in fact part of the mountain. Everywhere the walls lived and breathed with color and ornament, but there were no Christian saints here. The figures that rose from the floor to gaze at us as we went down the rock-cut stairs were angelic and glorious but devoid of all faith iconography. They might have been celebrated members of our people for all I knew, with their shimmering and perfect faces, and grand robes of crimson or cobalt blue or twinkling silver.

Everywhere I saw mixtures of historical motifs, ribbons of egg-and-dart decoration dividing diamond-shaped panels of multipetaled flowers or dark blue night behind symmetrical stars, or painting so vividly real it seemed a glimpse here and there into a real garden. A great harmony held it all together, and gradually my eyes saw that much that had been done here was ancient and fading, yet other areas were fresh and still smelled of the pigment and plaster recently applied. The whole was a visual wonderland.

The lights. I had not noticed it before but of course all this was seen in a wealth of electric light, streaming from horizontal fixtures tucked everywhere along borders, in corners, and beneath the lower rim of the huge dome. The steady brilliance of electric light came from the many doorways.

We had come to a stop now on the marble tiled floor of this huge piazza-like place. I could feel the fresh air moving around us. It smelled of the night beyond, of water and green things.

From one of the doors came a figure to greet us, a blood drinker who resembled a young woman of perhaps twenty. Oval face, and oval eyes, and a complexion like cream.

"Lestat and Gabrielle," she said as she drew near, her hands extended to include both of us. "I'm Bianca, Marius's Bianca, from Venice."

"Of course, I should have known you immediately," I said. She felt soft and tender to me, remarkably so, in fact, considering she had five hundred years in the Blood and plenty of the blood of the Mother. All those years with Marius during which he protected the shrine of Those Who Must Be Kept, she'd drunk that precious blood. And she'd been made by Marius, and all those made by Marius had been well made, much better made than my fledglings.

I hadn't known to take and give the Blood over and over as Marius had always done.

Bianca wore a simple black robe trimmed in gold, and her long hair was braided with what seemed a leafy vine of gold. And a delicate gold circlet around her head made me think of the painting the mortal painter Botticelli had done of her.

"You come with me, please, both of you," she said.

We followed her down another corridor of splendid gold enameling, bordered in delicately wrought flowering trees with blossoms like jewels, and into another large and splendid chamber.

Behind a long heavy wooden table with carved legs sat Sevraine, who rose now to greet us. It had to be Sevraine. Indeed it was the same powerful and ancient immortal I'd seen rising out of the tunnel in Paris.

She was a strongly built figure with fine high breasts in what seemed a Roman gown of sheer rose fabric crisscrossed with gold ribbons and bound around the waist. With a mane of flowing light blond hair she looked Nordic, and her pale-blue eyes underscored the impression. She was big boned but beautifully shaped all over, down to her tapering fingers, and her lush naked arms.

But before I could fully absorb this miracle, this vision, this creature who was reaching across the table now and inviting us to sit down, I was distracted by two figures who flanked her—one a female blood drinker I knew but couldn't place, a woman taken in her prime with remarkably long dark-ashen hair, hair that was almost a luminous gray, and clever vibrant eyes. *And the other a spirit.*

I knew at once it was a spirit, but it was not like any other spirit I'd seen up close before. It was a spirit clothing himself in actual physical particles, a body of particles that it had made up somehow and drawn to itself, out of dust, air, free-floating bits of matter, and it was so solidly put together, the physical vehicle of this spirit, that it was wearing actual clothes.

This was wholly different from the apparitions of ghosts and spirits I'd known in the past. And I had seen some powerful ghosts and spirits—including the spirit who had called himself Memnoch the Devil—in differing forms. But they had been hallucinations, those ghosts and spirits with their clothes being a part of the illusion, and even the scent of blood and sweat or the sound of a heartbeat had been part of the illusion. When they'd smoked a cigarette or drunk a glass of whiskey or given off the sound of a footstep it had been part of the apparition. The whole vision had been of a different texture than the world around it, the world I inhabited and from which I'd seen it. Oh, so I believed.

Not so at all with this spirit. His body, whatever it was made of, was occupying three-dimensional space, and had weight, and I could hear the sounds of simulated organs inside it, hear the distinct beating of a heart, hear the respiration. I could see the light of the room actually falling on the planes of this spirit's face, see it glittering in his eyes, see the shadow of his arm on the table. No scent, however, except that of incense and perfume which clung to its clothes.

Maybe I had in fact seen such spirits as this—but only fleetingly in the past, and never close enough or long enough to realize that they could be touched, that they were being seen by others.

I felt sure this one had never been a human being. He wasn't a ghost. No, he had to be something originating in some other realm for the simple reason that his body was wholly ideal, like a work of Greek classical art, and there was nothing about it that was particular.

In sum, this was the best spirit body I'd ever beheld. And he was smiling at me, apparently pleased with my quiet but obvious fascination.

He had dark and wavy and perfect hair framing his face in a classical Greek style, and the face could easily have come from a Greek statue. Yet this thing lived and breathed in the body it had assembled for itself. I had no idea how it could have a heartbeat, how the blood could rush to its face now, or appear to do so, as I smelled no actual blood, but it was a splendid spirit.

We had come to the edge of the table. It was perhaps three feet wide, of a wood so old I could smell the generations of oil worked into it. There were playing cards out on the wood, bright pretty glittering playing cards.

"Welcome to you both," said Sevraine. She spoke in a sweet lyrical voice with a girl's enthusiasm. "I'm so happy you've come, Lestat. You don't know how many nights I've heard you out there roaming this land, wandering about the ruins of Göbekli Tepe, and I always dreamed you would find your way here, that you would hear something emanating from these mountains that would prove irresistible to you. But you seemed alone, dedicated to being alone, not eager at all to have your thoughts interrupted. And so I've waited, and waited. And your mother and I have long known each other and she at last has brought you here."

I didn't believe a word she was saying. She coveted her secrecy. She was merely trying to be polite, and I was bound to be polite as well.

"Maybe this is the perfect time, Sevraine," I said. "I'm happy to be here."

The mysterious woman had risen at Sevraine's right and so had this male spirit on her left.

"Ah, young one," said the woman and immediately I knew this voice from the charnel house under Paris. "You have ridden the Devil's Road with greater zeal than any I've ever known. You don't know how many nights from my grave I followed you, catching one image of you after another from the minds that doted on you. I dreamed of waking merely to talk to you. You burnt like a flame in the blackness in which I suffered, beckoning me to rise."

A chill came over me. I took both her hands.

"The old one," I said in a whisper, "from Les Innocents! The one who was with Armand and the Children of Satan!" I was astonished. "You're the one I called the old Queen."

"Yes, beloved one. I'm Allesandra," she said. "That's my name. Allesandra, daughter of Dagobert, last king of the Merovingians and brought into the Blood by Rhoshamandes. Oh, what a splendid pleasure it is to behold you here in this safe and warm place!"

These names powerfully excited me. The history of the Merovingians I knew, but who was this blood drinker Rhoshamandes? Something told me I'd soon find out, not here perhaps but somewhere and in short order as the old ones, like Sevraine, continued to let down their guard.

I wanted to embrace this woman. The table stood between us. I had half a mind to crawl over it. Instead I squeezed her hands ever more tightly. My heart was pounding. This moment was too precious.

"You were like a Cassandra in that doomed old coven," I said. My words came in a rush. "Oh, you don't know the sadness I felt when they told me you were dead. They said you'd gone into the flames. I tell you it was anguish I felt! I had so wanted to take you out of those catacombs and into the light. I had so wanted—."

"Yes, young one. I remember. I remember all." She sighed and lifted my fingers to her lips, kissing them as she went on. "If I was Cassandra in those nights, I was unheeded and unloved even by myself."

"Oh, but I loved you!" I confessed. "And why did they say you'd gone into the fire?"

"Because I did, Lestat," she said. "But the fire would not have me, did not kill me, and I tumbled down, and down amid smoking timbers and old bones as I wept, too weak to rise, and was finally entombed with the remains of the cemetery beneath Paris. I didn't know my own age then, beloved. I didn't know my gifts or my strength. It was the way then of the very ancient, to pass in and out of history, and in and out of lunacy, and I think there are others still in those tunnels beneath the city. Ah, what an agony that slumber amid whispers and howls. Your voice was the only voice that ever actually pierced my uneasy dreams."

How lovely she was, the flower of the twisted old stem she'd been then.

I muttered something about how I'd longed even back then to see what she could have been. I stopped myself. It was so presumptuous and selfish. She was restored after all. She was here, vital, vibrant, part of this new and astonishing age. But she didn't correct me. She didn't shrink from me. She only smiled.

Sevraine was pleased with all this. And this woman who hardly seemed old at all now, nothing like the wretched hag she'd been in those eighteenth-century nights, was flushed with pleasure.

Finally I put my knee on the table and leaned forward and clasped Allesandra's face in my hands and kissed her.

In those earlier times, she'd been doomed, a dead thing in medieval garb, even to a filthy and ragged veil and wimple. Now her healthy silvery ashen hair was free and came down in dark waves over her shoulders. The robe she wore was fresh and soft like that of Sevraine, only it was a pale green, a green like the grass of the world of the day, that bright and beautiful. Around her neck was a single bright ruby on a chain. *Allesandra, daughter of Dagobert.* Her lips were dark and red like that ruby.

What a monster she'd appeared back in those nights, a face deformed by madness like the face of my maker, Magnus. But she was free now, freed by time, freed by survival to be something else, something entirely different and wondrous and sweet and vital.

"Yes, young one. Yes, and thanks to you, your voice, your videos and songs, your desperate revelations, I have slowly come back to myself. But I've been a pawn of this Voice. I have been the dupe of this Voice!" Her face darkened, and for a moment it seemed to crumple into that of the medieval horror she'd been before. "Only now I am in the helping hands of others."

"Put that aside," said Bianca. She was still beside me on my right, with Gabrielle on my left. "It is over," said Bianca. "The Voice will not triumph." But she was trembling with some sort of inner conflict, some battle between anguish and optimism.

Sevraine turned slowly to the spirit. He had stood quite still all this time regarding me with his bright but quiet blue eyes as if he could actually see through them, process through them all that lay before him. He wore a fancy, glittering decorative Indian garment called a sherwani, a kind of robe that went down to his ankles, I supposed, though I couldn't see below the top of the table, and his skin was amazingly realistic, nothing as synthetic looking as our skin always looks, but natural-looking skin made up of tiny changing pores and the soft down that covers humans.

"Gremt Stryker Knollys," he said, extending his hand. "But Gremt is my simple and true name. Gremt is my name for you and for all those I love."

"And you love me? Why?" I asked. But it was thrilling to be talking to this spirit.

He laughed softly and politely, unshaken by my sharp question. "Doesn't everyone love you?" he asked sincerely. It was as human a voice as I'd ever heard, tenor in pitch, even. "Isn't everyone hoping for you to somehow lead the tribe when this present war has been brought to the finish?"

I looked at Sevraine. "Do you love me?" I asked. "Are you hoping for me to lead this tribe?"

"Yes," she said with a radiant smile. "I am hoping and praying you will lead it. Surely you cannot expect me to lead it."

I sighed.

I looked at my mother.

"We do not have to talk about this right now," my mother said, but there was something about her remote half-lidded regard of me that chilled me. "Don't worry," she crooned with a cold ironic smile. "No one can crown you Prince of the Vampires against your will, can they?"

"Prince of the Vampires!" I scoffed. "I don't know," I said.

I looked back at the others. I wished I had a full night to take in all of these revelations, these new and startling encounters, just to try to fathom the limits of this splendid Sevraine, or why the tender Bianca was suffering so, because she couldn't conceal the pain.

"But I'll tell you that, why I am suffering," Bianca said, drawing near but talking in a normal and not a confidential voice, her arm slipping around me. "I lost one I loved in the attack in Paris, a young one, one I'd made and lived with for decades. But this was the Voice at work, not the one he'd brought out of the earth to do his bidding."

"And that was I," said Allesandra, "roused by the Voice. And given the unholy strength by the Voice to climb out of that tomb of bones and filth. That sin lies on me."

I saw it now in horrific flickering images, a wraith of a woman, a macabre skeleton of a creature with hag hair, sending a fatal jet of heat at the house in the Rue Saint-Jacques. And revenants rushing to their very doom as they fled the doors and windows right into the path of the murderous power. I saw Bianca down on her knees on the pavement wailing, hands pressed to the side of her head, face upturned. I saw the wraith approach and reach out for her, as if the very personification of Death had paused in its rounds to show compassion to one lone soul.

"Many have been duped by the Voice," said Gabrielle. "And not so many have survived it and turned away with such immediate disgust. That counts for much as far as I'm concerned."

"It counts for everything," said Bianca gravely.

Allesandra's face was sad. She appeared to be dreaming, to have slipped away from the present time and back into a great limitless gulf of darkness. I wanted to reach out and take her hand, but it was Sevraine who did this.

All the while the spirit, Gremt Stryker Knollys, gazed on without a word. He was seated now as he had been before.

Others were coming into this large room.

For a moment I didn't believe my eyes. There was a ghost there, surely it was a ghost, in the person of an elderly man with dark gray hair and skin that suggested mother-of-pearl to me. He was in a body as solid as the body of the spirit Gremt. And he too wore real clothes. Breathtaking.

And two exquisitely groomed and exquisitely dressed female blood drinkers were with him.

When I saw who they were, who they actually were, these two with their coiffed hair and soft silken robes, I started crying. They came at once to me, and both embraced me.

"Eleni and Eugénie," I said. "Safe after all this time." I could hardly speak.

Somewhere in a chest locked away, a chest that had survived neglect and fire, I still had in my possession all the letters once written to me from Paris by Eleni, the letters that had told me of the Théâtre des Vampires in the Boulevard du Temple that I had left behind in my wanderings, the letters that told me of its prosperity with the Paris audiences, of Armand's governance, and of the death of my Nicolas, my second fledgling, my only mortal friend, and my greatest failure.

This was Eleni, and her companion Eugénie, fresh and perfumed and quietly resplendent in their simple silk garments. They were dark-eyed with soft almond-colored skin and dark hair loose over their shoulders. And I had thought them long gone from the Earth, gone in this or that catastrophe—a mere memory of the century of white-powdered wigs consumed by time and violence.

"Come, let's all sit down together," said Sevraine.

I looked around a bit dazed, a bit uncertain. I wanted somehow to sink into some shadowy corner and think about what was happening, absorb what was happening, but there was no time or place for this. I was shaken and at a loss. Indeed, I was overwhelmed when I contemplated how many other reunions and shocks awaited me, but how could I shrink from this? How could I resist it? Yet if this was what we all wanted, if this is what we dreamed of, in our grief and our loneliness—being reunited with those we'd lost—then why was I finding it so very hard?

The ghost, the puzzling ghost of the elderly man with the dark gray hair, had taken a seat beside Gremt, and he sent me a quick sharp telepathic introduction. *Raymond Gallant.* Did I know that name?

Eleni and Eugénie went around the table and sat beside Allesandra.

I saw a hearth now to the far left, well stacked with burning logs, though the light of the fire was lost in the great electric illumination of this golden room with its twinkling and flickering walls and ceiling. I saw a multitude of things—sconces, bronze sculptures, heavy carved chests. But nothing registered for the moment except that I was suffering a kind of paralysis. I worked against it. I had to look at the faces that surrounded me.

I took the empty high-backed chair opposite Sevraine. That's what she wanted. Gabrielle sat beside me. And it was quite impossible to ignore that I was the center of attention, that all these beings were connected by earlier encounters, or even long history, and that I had much to learn.

I found myself looking at this ghost, and then the name hit me. Raymond Gallant. Talamasca. A friend to Marius in the Renaissance years, before and after Marius had been attacked by the Children of Satan and his Venetian palazzo destroyed. A friend who had actually helped him, through the Talamasca, find his beloved Pandora, who'd been traveling Europe in those nights with an Indian blood drinker named Arjun. Raymond Gallant had died in very old age in an English castle belonging to the Talamasca, or so Marius had always believed.

The ghost was looking at me now with the most genial eyes, smiling eyes, friendly eyes. His clothes were the only decidedly Western garb in the room besides mine—a simple dark suit and tie, and yes, absolutely, they were real, these garments, not part of his complex and marvelously realized artificial body.

"Are you ready to join the others in New York?" asked Sevraine. She had a simplicity and directness that reminded me of my mother. And I could hear that powerful heart of hers beating, that ancient heart.

"And what good would that do?" I asked. "How can I affect what's happening?"

"Plenty," she said. "We must all go there. We must all come together. The Voice has contacted them. The Voice wants to join them."

I was shocked and skeptical. "How is that possible?"

"I don't know," she said. "And they don't know either. But the Voice has endorsed Trinity Gate in New York as the place for us to meet. We must go there."

"What about Maharet?" I asked. "And what about Khayman? How can the Voice . . . ?"

"I know what you're saying," said Sevraine, "and again I am saying that we must gather under Armand's roof. No one of us can stand against Maharet and Khayman. I've been to their encampment. I've tried to talk with Maharet. She would not admit me. She would not listen to me. And with Khayman beside her, I can't prevail against her. Not alone. Only with others. And the others are meeting in New York."

I bowed my head. I was shaken by what she was saying. Surely it wasn't coming to that, a battle of the ancients, a battle involving force, but then what other kind of battle would it be?

"Well, then let the great Children of the Millennia gather," I said. "But I'm no Child of the Millennia!"

"Oh, come now, Lestat," she answered. "You've drunk the Mother's blood in staggering amounts and you know it. You have an indomitable will that counts for a supernatural gift in itself."

"I was Akasha's dupe," I said. I sighed. "So much for will. I have indomitable emotions. That's not the same as having indomitable will."

"Now I know why they call you the Brat Prince," said Sevraine patiently. "You're going to New York and you know you are."

I didn't know what to say. What could it conceivably mean that the Voice meant to join a New York meeting if the Voice was emanating from Mekare? Would the Voice somehow through Khayman force the twins to travel to New York? I couldn't figure it. And what of Maharet envisioning that volcano and their fiery finish? Did the others know about that? I didn't dare to think of it in this company of minds that could rake mine with total ease.

"Believe me," said Sevraine. "I offered my presence, my sympathy, and my strength to Maharet only nights ago and I was rebuffed. I have told her in plain words who the Voice is and she has refused to believe it. She insists the Voice cannot be what we know it is. Maharet is a bruised and broken soul now. Maharet cannot stop this thing. She can't fathom that the Voice is coming from her own sister. Maharet is ruined."

"I can't give up on her that easily," I said. "I understand what you're saying. It's true. I went there and tried to talk with her and she forced me to leave. She used her power to physically push me away. Quite literally. But I can't give up on her as broken and bruised. That can't be right. The last time, when we all faced annihilation, she and Mekare saved us! We would all have died if . . . Look, we ought to go to her now. You, me, Marius, whoever else we can find . . ."

"Say this to them when we meet, all of us, under Armand's roof," Sevraine said.

But I was horror-struck at the thought of what might be happening in that jungle compound now. What if the Voice through Khayman found some way to do away with Maharet? It was unthinkable to me, and equally unthinkable that I might stand by and let this happen.

"I know this," said Sevraine. She was responding to my thoughts. "I am fully aware of it. But as I told you, this creature's destiny has been fulfilled. Maharet's found her twin, and in her twin she's confronted the nothingness, the emptiness—the sheer meaninglessness of life—that all of us face sooner or later, and maybe more than once, and maybe even many times. Maharet has not survived this final encounter. She has divorced herself from her mortal family. She has nothing now to sustain her. The tragedy of her mindless sister, Mekare, has devoured her. She's finished."

"You go join the others," I said. "I'll go back to the Amazon now and I'll take my stand with her. I can reach there before sunrise in that hemisphere."

"No, you mustn't do this." It was the voice of the spirit, Gremt. He was still sitting quite calmly to Sevraine's left as before. "You're needed at the conclave, and that's where you must go. If you return to Maharet's sanctuary now, she'll only drive you away again. And she may do worse."

"Forgive me," I said, straining to be courteous, "but what has this to do with you?"

"I knew this spirit, Amel," he answered, "for thousands of years before he came into the physical. If he had not come, not fused with Akasha, I might never have come, never have sought to take on a body and walk on the Earth in the guise of a human. I've been prompted in all I've done by him, by his descent into flesh and blood and my own love of flesh and blood. I followed him here."

"Well, that's a staggering revelation," I said. "And how many others like you are roaming around this Earth, may I ask, watching this pageant for pleasure?"

"I'm not watching the pageant for pleasure," he replied. "And if there are others from our realm who've concerned themselves with these events, they haven't made their presence known to me."

"Stop, please," Sevraine implored me. "It will all make more sense to you if you realize this being founded the Talamasca. Now, you know the Talamasca. You know their principles. You know their high-minded goals. You know their dedication. You loved and trusted David Talbot when he was still the Superior General of the Talamasca, a mortal scholar who did all in his power to be your friend. Well, Gremt Stryker Knollys founded the Talamasca, and that should answer all your questions as to his character. I don't know what other word to use but 'character.' You need not doubt Gremt."

I was speechless.

Of course I'd always known that some supernatural secret burned at the heart of the Talamasca, but what it was I'd never been able to fathom. And to the best of my knowledge, David did not know. And neither did Jesse who had also been a child of the Order long before her aunt Maharet had brought her into the Blood.

"Trust in me," said Gremt. "I am on your side now. I fear Amel. I have always feared him. I have always dreaded the day he would come into his own."

I listened patiently but said nothing.

"Tomorrow at sunset, we should all leave here together," said

Sevraine. "And there I'll find those as old as I am, as powerful. I'm convinced of it. This conclave will draw them there and under moral constraints which I welcome and respect. Perhaps some have already arrived. And then we'll be in a position to determine what to do."

"And meanwhile," I said softly, "Maharet grapples with this on her own." I sought to banish all images of that volcano, Pacaya, in Guatemala, where our collective destiny might just end.

Sevraine's eyes locked on mine. Had she seen it?

Of course I know your fears, but why frighten the others? We do what we must do.

"Maharet will accept no one's help," said Gremt. "I too went to her. It was no use. I knew her when she was a mortal woman. I spoke to her when she was a mortal woman. I was among the spirits who listened to her voice." His voice remained even but he was becoming emotional, emotional as any genuine human being. "And now after all this time, she does not trust me, or listen to me. She cannot. In her mind she lost the voices of the spirits when she entered the Blood. And any spirit who seeks to incarnate as I've done she can't trust. She can only regard me with abhorrence and fear." He stopped, as if he couldn't continue. "I've always somehow known that she would turn her back on me when I stood before her, when I confessed to her that it was I, I who'd . . ." And now he could not say anything more.

His eyes were glazed with tears. He sat back and appeared to take a deep breath, seeking to silently collect himself, and he pressed the fingers of his right hand hard against his own lips.

Why was this so seductive to me, so fascinating? Our emotions came from our minds, did they not, yet softened or hardened our physical bodies. And so his powerful spirit agitated this artfully made physical form in which he resided, with which he had become one. I felt drawn to him. I felt that he was no alien thing at all, but something very like us, a mystery whole unto himself, of course, but very like us.

"I have to go to Maharet," I said. I started to rise. "I have to stand with her now. You go to the conclave of course, but I'm going to her."

"Sit down," said Gabrielle.

I hesitated and then very reluctantly obeyed. I did want to reach the Amazon with hours to spare.

"There are other reasons why you should come with us," said Gabrielle, in the same firm voice.

"Oh, I know, don't tell me!" I said angrily. "They want me there. The young ones are clamoring for me to go. They attach some special importance to me. Armand and Louis want me to come. Benji wants me to come. I've heard it over and over."

"Well, all that is true," said Gabrielle. "And we are a quarrelsome and independent species and we do need any charismatic leader who is willing to take the helm. But there are other reasons."

She looked at Sevraine.

Sevraine nodded. And Gabrielle went on.

"You have a mortal son there, Lestat, a young man of less than twenty years. His name is Viktor. He knows you are his father. He was born of a mortal woman in Fareed's laboratory, a woman named Flannery Gilman who is now in the Blood. But your son is not in the Blood."

Silence.

Not only did I not speak, I couldn't think. I couldn't reason. I must have looked like someone who has lost his senses. I stared at Gabrielle and then at Sevraine.

I had no words for what I was feeling. I had no way to comprehend the scope of what was going on not in my mind but in my heart. I could feel the eyes of all present on me, but it didn't much matter. I looked at them but I didn't really see them or care about them— Allesandra sitting there staring at me quietly with Bianca beside her, a picture of sympathy and sadness. And Eleni watching me fearfully, with Eugénie all but hiding behind her. And the spirit and the ghost with such emotional expressions. A son. A mortal son. A living breathing son of my flesh. Oh, Fareed, he must have planned it from the start with that enticing bedroom and the warm, sweet-faced Dr. Flannery Gilman so ready with her tender mortal mouth and her hot naked limbs. I'd impregnated her! The possibility had never occurred to me. Not for one second had I thought such a thing possible.

From Sevraine's mind there came a fully realized image of this boy.

He was looking directly at me in this image, a young man with my square face and somewhat short nose, and my unruly blond hair. Those blue eyes seemed my eyes and yet they weren't my eyes. They were his own. That was my mouth, all right, sensuous, and a little large for the face, but it had nothing of the cruelty of my mouth. Just a beautiful young boy, in spite of looking like me, a beautiful young man. The face vanished. And I saw a flash of images now of this young man perhaps as Sevraine had once seen him, striding along an American street, dressed in regular clothes, jeans, a sweater, sneakers, a healthy, glowing young man.

Pain. Unspeakable pain.

It didn't matter who in this world or any other was staring at me, watching me, seeking to share this moment or merely shuddering as I experienced it. Just didn't matter. Because in pain like this one is always alone.

"I have another shock for you," said Sevraine.

I didn't reply.

"There is a young woman with Viktor whom you also love," said Sevraine. "Her name is Rose."

"Rose?" I whispered. "Not my Rose!" This pain was rolling suddenly towards fury. "How in God's name did they get their hands on my Rose?"

"Let me tell you," said Sevraine. "Let me explain." Then slowly in a low voice she told me what had befallen Rose. She told me how my attorneys were trying to reach me, but then I'd been ignoring all "worldly messages of late," and she recounted the details of an assault on Rose, her blindness, the scarring of her face and throat, and how she had cried out for me over and over in her agony, and how Seth had heard that cry, how Fareed had heard it, and how, on my behalf, they had intervened.

Oh, Death, you are so determined to have my beloved Rose. Death, you cannot stop seeking to take my precious Rose.

"The girl was given just enough of the Blood to cure her blindness," said Sevraine. "But never enough to take root in her. Just enough of the Blood to heal her esophagus, heal her skin. But never enough to begin the transformation. She's still fully human and she loves your son, and he loves her."

I think I murmured something like "This is all Fareed's doing," but my heart wasn't in it. I didn't care. I absolutely didn't care. The rage was gone. Only the pain remained. I kept seeing the image of the boy and I needed no one to give me an image of my beloved Rose, my sweet brave Rose, who'd been so happy when I last saw her, my tender, loving Rose whom I'd given up for her sake, knowing that she was now too old to be near me anymore, too old to be confused by what I was. My Rose. And Viktor.

"These things are now commonly known," said Sevraine, "because this boy and this girl have been brought by Fareed and Seth to join the others. And you must go there too. Leave Maharet to her own resources. The meeting is what matters. Whatever happens to Maharet, the Voice will still be the challenge. And tomorrow at sunrise, we must go."

I sat still staring at the surface of the table, thinking of what all this might mean.

A long moment passed and then Eleni said tenderly, "Please, do come with us to join the others. It's past time for us to be there."

I glanced at her, at her eager face and that of Eugénie beside her. And my eyes passed over the strangely expressive faces of Raymond Gallant and then Gremt. How infinitely more human they seemed than the rest of us.

"Listen to me," said Gabrielle impatiently. "You can't conceivably respond to all these revelations now. No one can. But be assured that this girl, Rose, is on the verge of madness as always happens with those who know too much of us. Viktor on the other hand has always known you were his father, and he grew up with his mother's love and knows what she is too. So let's be on our way tomorrow night to resolve this, if nothing else, and then the matter of the Voice."

I nodded, trying not to show a bitter smile. What a hand they had played! Had it been deliberate? Calculating? Didn't much matter in the scheme of things. It was what it was.

"You think these matters are more important than the Voice?" I asked. "You think these matters cannot wait a little longer? I don't know what I think. I can't think. My mind's not made up."

"I think if you return to Maharet," said Gabrielle, "you'll be very disappointed at what you find out. And she may very well destroy you."

"Tell me what you know now!" I said. I was suddenly furious. "Tell me now."

"What matters is what *all of us* know when we gather," said Gabrielle. She was as angry as I was. "Not what I suspect, or what fragmentary images I've caught or someone else has caught. Don't you understand? We're facing a worse crisis than we did last time, can't you see that? But we have Sevraine, and this ancient one Seth, who's even older than she is, and who knows who else? We should go to them, not to Maharet."

"And you knew I had a son and you never told me," I said suddenly, impulsively, "and you knew what had happened to my Rose."

"Stop, Lestat, please," said Sevraine. "You're hurting my ears. Your mother only found these things out from me and went to fetch you immediately and bring you here as I asked. You have been living in your own well-fortified and solitary world. You gave no hint that any of this concerned you. Now come with us to join the others as we ask."

"I want to find David and Jesse . . . ," I said.

"David and Jesse have joined the others," said Gremt.

"And what do *you* know of Maharet right now!" I demanded. I hit the table with my fist.

"I'm not omniscient," said Gremt quietly. "I could leave this body and I could travel there—invisible, silent—easily enough. But I've forsworn that power. I've trained myself to walk and talk and see and hear as a human being. And besides, whatever is happening with Maharet, none of us can change."

I pushed back the chair and rose to my feet. "I have to be alone now," I said. "This is all simply too much. I have to wander out there, be alone. . . . I don't know what I'll do. We have several hours more to talk about it. I want to be alone. You should go on to New York, that's certain. All of you should go. And you should fight this Voice with all your power. As for me, I don't know."

Sevraine rose and came around the table and took me by the arm.

"All right then," she said. "You go wandering if you must. But I have something that might help you with your meditations, something I arranged especially for you."

She led me out of the room and down a long passage that was covered in soft glittering gold like so much of what I'd already seen. But soon another cruder and unadorned passage led us away from this one and down a long steep rock-cut stairs.

It seemed we were in a labyrinth. And I caught the scent of human beings.

We came finally to a long ramp that led into a small room illuminated only by a couple of thick candles on ledges, and there beyond a wall of iron bars stood a golden-skinned human being staring at me out of the shadows with bitter furious black eyes.

The scent was overpowering, delicious, almost irresistible.

The man began to shake the bars with all his strength and rail at Sevraine in the most vulgar and coarse French I'd ever heard. He hurled one threat after another at her of confederates who would come to rip her limb from limb and visit every erotic abomination on her that he could conceive.

He swore his "brothers" would never let anyone live who had done harm to him, that she didn't know what she had done to herself, and so forth and so on, round now in circles, damning her under the worst words ever created in any language to denounce a female being.

I was fascinated. It had been a long time since I'd encountered anyone so totally given over to evil, and so blatant in his fury. The smell of the sea came off his filthy dungarees and his sweat-soaked denim shirt, and I saw scars cut into his face and into his right arm that had hardened into seams of pure white flesh.

Behind me a heavy door was closed.

The creature and I were alone. I saw the key to his cell on a hook to the right of the gate that held him back, and I took it down while he went on raving and cursing, and I turned it slowly in the lock.

He flung the gate back immediately and lunged at me, his hands moving to my throat.

I let him do this, let him hurl his full force at a body that did not yield even by a quarter of an inch. And there he was, trying to press his fingers into my neck and utterly impotent to make the slightest indentation in my skin and staring into my eyes.

He backed up, calculating, and took another tack. Did I want money? He had plenty of money. All right, he was dealing here with something he hadn't encountered before. Yes, we weren't human. He saw that. But he wasn't stupid. He wasn't a fool. What did we want?

"Tell me," he roared at me in French. His eyes moved feverishly over the ceiling, the floor, the walls. The doors.

"I want you," I said in French. I opened my mouth and ran my tongue under my fangs.

He didn't believe what he saw, of course he didn't believe, that was preposterous that such creatures as that were real. "Stop trying to frighten me!" he roared again.

He fell into a crouch, shoulders hunched, arms at the ready, fingers balled into fists.

"You're enough to take my mind off anything," I said.

I moved closer, sliding my arms around him, sliding them right against that delicious salty sweat, and drove my teeth swiftly into his neck. That's the least painful way to do it, go right for the artery and just let that first pull on his heart quiet his fear.

His soul broke open like a rotten carcass, and all of the filth of his life spent in smuggling and thievery and random murder, always murder, murder after murder, poured out like black viscid crude oil in his blood.

We were on the floor of the cell. He was still alive. I was drinking the last dregs slowly, letting the blood drain from his brain and his internal organs and pulling it towards me with the steady slow cooperation of his powerful heart.

He was a little boy now, a trusting little boy filled with curiosity and dreams and roaming some countryside very like my own fields and slopes in the Auvergne, and there was so much he wanted to know, so much he wanted to fathom, so many things that he would do. He would grow up and discover the answers. He would know. The snow fell suddenly on the place where he was playing, running, jumping, and spinning in circles with his arms out. And he threw his little head back to swallow the falling snow.

The heart stopped.

I lay there for a long moment, still feeling the warmth of his chest against me, the side of his face under me, feeling some last quiver of life pass through his arms.

Then the Voice spoke.

The Voice was there, low, confidential, right there. And the Voice said:

"You see I want to know all those things too. You see, I wanted to know, wanted to know with my whole heart, what is snow? And what is beautiful and what is love? I still want to know! I want to see with your eyes, Lestat, and hear with your ears, and speak with your voice. But you have denied me. You have left me in blindness and misery and you will pay for that."

I climbed to my feet.

"Where are you, Voice?" I asked. "What have you done to Mekare?"

He wept bitterly. "How can you ask me such a question? You, of all the blood drinkers spawned by me and sustained by me. You know how helpless I am inside of her! And for me you have no pity, and only hate."

He was gone.

I tried to anatomize how I knew, what it was I felt, when he left me, what were the tiny indications of his sudden abandonment, but I couldn't really even remember all the tiny little aspects of it. I just knew he was gone.

"I don't despise you, Voice," I said aloud. My voice sounded unnatural in the empty stone chamber. "I have never really despised you. I was guilty of only one thing, not knowing who you really are. You might have told me, Voice. You might have trusted me."

But he was gone, gone to some other part of the great Savage Garden to do mischief, no doubt.

I left the dead man, since there seemed no proper place to dump his bloodless carcass, and I started back through the maze to find the others.

Somewhere along the way, when stone passages had once more given way to brightly painted passages and golden passages, I heard singing.

It was the softest most ethereal singing, words spun out by high clear soprano voices in Latin, one thread of melody interweaving with another, and under this the sounds of what had to be a lyre.

The sounds of running water came to me with the exquisite music, singing—running water, splashing water, and the laughter of blood drinkers. Sevraine laughing. My mother laughing. I smelled the water. I smelled sunlight, green grass in the water. Somehow the freshness and sweetness of the water mingled in my mind with the richly satisfying blood that had just flooded my mouth and my brain. And I could all but see the music in golden ribbons winding through the air.

I came to a large, cavernous, and brightly lighted bath.

Glittering mosaics covered the uneven ceiling and walls, tiny bits of gold and silver and crimson marble, malachite and lapis lazuli and shining obsidian and flakes of glinting glass. Candles burned on their bronze stands.

Two gentle dancing waterfalls fed the large rock-cut basin in which they bathed.

They were all standing in the water—the women—together under the soft sparkling downpour, some naked, some clothed in sheer gowns that had turned transparent with the water, faces glistening, hair slicked into long serpentine streaks of darkness over their shoulders. And in the far-left corner were the singers—three white-robed blood drinkers obviously made in boyhood, singing in high sweet soprano voices, castrati made by the Blood.

I found myself transfixed by the vision of this. The women beckoned me to come into the bath.

The musicians sang on as if blind to all those present, though they were not, each strumming the strings of a small ancient Greek-style lyre.

The room was warm and moist and the light itself was golden from the candles.

I moved forward, stripping off my clothes and joining them in the fresh sweet-smelling pool. They poured the water over me from pink-throated seashells. And I splashed it again and again against my face.

Allesandra, naked, danced with her arms up, singing with the boy sopranos, though in words of Old French, some poetry of her own, and Sevraine, her body frighteningly pale and hard, the water glancing off it as if it were marble, kissed me on the lips.

The sharp yet exquisitely controlled singing pierced me, paralyzed me, as I stood in the cool flowing water. I closed my eyes, and thought, Always remember this. *Always remember though agony and fear crouch at the door.* This. The throb of the lyre strings, and these voices weaving like vines together, climbing to heights undreamt of by the logical fearful mind and descending slowly to blend in harmony again.

Through the flashing waterfall I looked at them, these boys, with their round faces and their short curling blond hair; very slightly they swayed with the music and it was the music that they saw, not us, not this place, not this now.

What does it mean to be a singer in the Blood, a musician, to have that purpose, that love affair to carry you through the ages—and to be as happy as all of these creatures seemed to be?

Later on, dressed in fresh garments provided by the mistress of the palace, I passed a long shadowy chamber in which Gremt sat with Raymond Gallant. There was a blood drinker with them, as ancient perhaps as was Sevraine. And other ghosts there as beautifully realized in material bodies as were Gremt and Raymond Gallant.

I was immediately fascinated, but I was also very tired. Almost deliciously tired.

One of these ghosts rose to greet me and beckoned for me to wait as I stood in the door.

I backed up into the passage as this phantom moved out of the room and towards me, not out of fear so much as overwhelming reluctance. I knew where I stood with any human on the planet; I knew what I faced with any blood drinker. But I did not begin to know what I faced with a self-possessed ghost in a solid body.

He stood before me, smiling, the light from the shadowy conference room illuminating his rather remarkable face. Smooth forehead, Grecian features, and long ashen-blond hair.

He was dressed in a long simple black silk soutane. And it was a real garment, made of raw silk. This skin was not real, no, and the organs within were simulated well but not real, and who knew what soul lay behind these cheerful, friendly eyes?

Once again, I felt keenly that these spirits or ghosts clothed in bodies of their own making were exactly like us. They were incarnated souls as we were incarnated souls.

"I've waited a long time to beg your forgiveness for what I did to you," he said in French. "I have hoped and prayed always that you were glad of it finally, glad to be living and breathing now, hard as it's been for you on the Devil's Road."

I said nothing. I was trying to figure what this could possibly mean. That a ghost could speak so distinctly in a deep human voice amazed me. It truly seemed to be coming from his vocal cords. The illusion was perfect.

He stood eye to eye with me. He smiled. He reached for my hands and took them in his. "If only there were time for a long meeting," he said, "a time for me to answer your inevitable questions, time for me to let your anger rise."

Soft dusty fingers. They gave off warmth like human fingers.

"What anger?" I asked.

"I'm Magnus, the one who made you and abandoned you. And I will always bear the guilt for that."

I heard but I didn't believe. I didn't believe in the possibility of it. My human soul refused. And yet I knew this creature wasn't lying to me. This wasn't the season for lies. This was the season for revelations. And this creature or being or entity or whatever it was, this thing was telling me the truth.

I don't know how many minutes passed as we stood there.

"Don't judge me by what you see here," he said. "For a ghost can perfect a body himself which nature never gave him, and that's what I've done. The ghosts of this world have learned much over the centuries, especially the last few hundred years. My body resembles yours now, fine and strong and well proportioned, the body for which you died, and I have given myself your eyes, your shining blue eyes. But I do beg your forgiveness, for bringing you into this realm we now share."

A cool draft moved through the passage.

I felt a tingling on the surface of my skin. I was trembling. I heard my heart in my ears.

"Well, as you said, if only there were time," I responded. "But there isn't time now, is there? It's almost dawn." I struggled to form each word. "I can't stay with you now." I was so grateful for this, so grateful that I had to leave him, and move sluggishly, almost drunkenly, away. Shock and shock and greater shock.

I glanced back at him. How sad he looked standing there, how forlorn and burdened with grief and sorrow.

"You burn bright, Prince Lestat," he said. And tears rose to his eyes.

I hurried away. I had to. I had to find some graceful and secret place to lie down in solitude. There was no traveling for me tonight. It was too late. There was only the hope of sleep now. And up ahead, Sevraine was waiting for me and gesturing for me to hurry.

Give me this little rock-cut tomb of sorts, this shelf on which to lie. Give me these satin pillows, so cool, and these soft woolen covers. Give me this and let me weep alone here. And let me forget all but darkness as you shut the door.

And to think—on rising we would go into the Kingdom of Greater Shocks.

And all I'd been before this night was gone, absolutely gone. The world I'd only inhabited a short time ago seemed bleak and empty and over now.

All my struggles, my triumphs, my losses, were being eclipsed by what was being revealed now. Had ever ennui and despair been banished by such revelations, such precious gifts of truth?

19

Rhoshamandes

Murder Most Foul

FOR TWO NIGHTS, Rhosh had been holed up in a luxury hotel in Manaus, waking up to look out on the small Amazonian city and the jungles beyond stretching into infinity. He was furious. He had sent for Benedict, and Benedict had come, as always frayed and exhausted from the lonely journey through miles of uncharted sky, and was now equally agitated by sleeping in this multistoried mortal hostel with only a hiding place in a closet to keep him safe from the sun and from prying mortal eyes.

There was good hunting for a blood drinker in this city and in its surrounding areas, but that was about all that could be said for it in Rhosh's estimation, and he was desperate to penetrate the compound of Maharet, Khayman, and Mekare, but he could not.

Each night the Voice urged him to be strong, to attack the defenses of the twins, to force his way in. But Rhosh was wary. He could not overcome the combined strength of Khayman and Maharet. He knew this. And he did not trust the Voice when it said they would never attack him, that he would take them by surprise and find them surprisingly vulnerable to his gifts and his will.

"I need you to free me from this creature," the Voice continued to insist. "I need you to free me from this Unholy Trinity which keeps me captive here, blind and immobile and unable to fulfill my destiny. And I do indeed have a destiny and have always had a destiny. Do you know what I have endured to learn how to express myself as I am talking to you now? You are my hope, Rhoshamandes, you have five thousand years in the Blood, do you not? You are stronger than they are because you know how to use your gifts and they are reluctant."

Rhosh had given up arguing honestly with the Voice. The Voice was a conniver and a child.

Rhosh feared Maharet. He always had. Who in the Blood was more powerful than Maharet? She had a thousand years on him, but she had something else. She'd been one of the first ever made, and her spiritual resources were a legend.

If the earliest children of First Brood and Queens Blood hadn't been deaf to each other telepathically, this drama would have come to a close well before now. If Maharet could hear the Voice speaking to Rhoshamandes, it would be finished for Rhosh, he was sure. Even now he wondered if this miserable humid and tropical place was not to be the end of his long journey on this Earth.

But just when his thoughts sank into discouragement, the Voice would come, whispering, cajoling, wheedling. "I will make you the monarch of the tribe. Don't you see what I am offering you? Don't you grasp why I need *you*? Once inside your body, I can walk into the sun of my own free will because your body is strong enough for this, and all over the world young ones will burn. But you and I inside of you will only be kissed by that golden light. Oh, I remember now, yes, I remember, the blessed peace and strength that came to me when Akasha and Enkil were put into the sun. Golden brown they became, and no more than that, but all over the world children burned. My strong blood was restored to me. I was myself in flashes of waking wonder! We will do that, don't you see, when I am in you and you can brave the sunlight. And you love me! Who else loves me?"

"I love you all right," said Rhosh grimly. "But not enough to be destroyed trying to take you into me. And if I did have you inside me, would you feel what I feel?"

"Yes, don't you see? I am entombed in one who feels nothing and desires nothing, and never drinks, never drinks of the life-giving human blood!"

"When I expose myself to the sun, I know pain as I'm falling into unconsciousness and pain for months after I wake. I do it only because I must to pass for human. Are you willing to know that pain?"

"That is nothing to the pain I know now!" he said. "You'll wake to golden skin as you know, and so many others will have died, mercifully died, died! And we will be stronger than ever! Don't you see? Yes, I will feel what you feel. But once you have the Sacred Core in you, *you will feel what I feel too.*"

The Voice rambled on.

"Did I ever promise the Queen of Egypt that I could support a legion of blood drinkers? Was she mad? Were the First Brood not mad? They knew what I was and who I was and yet they stretched my body and my power beyond all reasonable limits, greedy and wanton, passing the Blood to anyone who would revolt against Akasha, and she made this Queens Blood as if the size of her guard was all that mattered—until I was as a human bleeding from all limbs and all orifices, unable to think, to dream, to know. . . ."

Rhosh was listening but not much. *You will feel what I feel, too.*

The possibilities were blazing in his mind as he stood at the window looking out over the nighttime city of Manaus.

"What else would you want of me, other than that I sleep under the sun to burn off the riffraff?" The riffraff? More than the riffraff would burn. All the many younger ones would burn—Lestat, his precious Louis, Armand that vicious and notorious tyrant, and of course the little genius Benjamin Mahmoud.

And all of their generations would burn. Vampires would burn who had a thousand years in the Blood, or even two thousand. It had happened before. And Rhoshamandes knew this. It wasn't legend. He had been burned a shining mahogany brown and suffered agony for months after the King and Queen had been dragged into the Egyptian desert by the wicked elder. Had the elder had the strength to leave the Divine Parents in the sun for three days, Rhoshamandes might have died. And the elder would have died. And who would have come to the rescue of Akasha or Enkil? It would have been the finish there and then. Somewhere in the world Sevraine and Nebamun and countless others must have suffered a similar fate. For those who survived and grew stronger, many perished driven to further immolation by the pain of their existence. He remembered all that. Yes, he remembered.

But no one knew how many years in the Blood were needed to survive such a holocaust. Oh, well, maybe the great doctors Fareed and Seth knew. Maybe they had made studies, calculations, based on interviews with blood drinkers, analysis of accounts in the Vampire Chronicles. Maybe they had made projections. Maybe they could transfuse blood from the ancients to the young ones with glistening plastic sacks and shining plastic tubes. Maybe they had a store of ancient blood in their vaults, drawn out of the veins of the great Seth.

"Oh, yes, they are very clever," said the Voice, ignoring Rhosh's earlier question and addressing his rambling thoughts. "But they have no love for me. They are treacherous. They speak of 'the tribe' as does Benji Mahmoud as if I were not the tribe!" He roared in anguish. "As if I, I, Amel, were not the tribe!"

"So you don't want to fall into their hands," said Rhosh.

"No, never! Never!" The Voice sounded frantic. "Think what they might do to me! Can you imagine?"

"And what could they possibly do?" asked Rhosh.

"Put me in a tank of the Blood, my Blood, Blood I made, put me in a tank of it where I would be blind and deaf and mute and trapped in even deeper darkness than I am in now."

"Nonsense. Somebody would have to feed and sustain such a tank. They'd never do such a dangerous thing. And you are not a separate element now. Even I know that. You are wed to the brain of Mekare, wed to her heart to pump blood to her brain. If they were to simulate such an arrangement, as I said, someone and indeed more than one would have to maintain it and sustain it. That will never happen to you."

The Voice was clearly mollified.

He dropped his voice to a whisper. "I must be quiet now but you must come to me. She comes. She's hunted and she is full of despair. She dreams of plunging herself and Mekare and me into a lake of fire! She mourns her lost fledglings. She has driven away those who love her."

Rhoshamandes shook his head. Under his breath he murmured a desperate negation.

"Listen to me!" pleaded the Voice. "She needs but one word of encouragement from some despairing soul like herself, I tell you, and she will take Mekare in her arms and go at once to this volcano called Pacaya. Do you know where that is?"

"Pacaya," whispered Rhosh. "Yes, I know where it is."

"Well, it is where our story will end in fire if you do not come! It could happen this very night, I tell you!"

"You can't read her mind, can you? You're entombed in her maker. You can't . . ."

"I do not read her mind from Mekare's mind, you fool," said the Voice. "I go stealthily into her mind as I go into yours! She cannot lock me out! But oh, if I were to seek to speak to her how I would terrify her, how I would drive her over the edge!"

Pacaya, an active volcano in Guatemala. Rhosh was gasping for breath. He was trembling.

"You must come now," said the Voice. "Khayman is lost somewhere in the north where I sent him to destroy. He is a ruin of himself, I tell you. He was never crafted for eternity as you were. The mere sight of him goads her to despair. He is a broken instrument. Come to me now. Do you know what a machete is? There are machetes all over in this place. Machetes. You know how to use a machete? Free me from this body! And if you do not, I will sing my songs to someone else!"

It was gone. He could feel that it was gone.

Where had it gone? Off to turn some desperate fearful blood drinker somewhere against another? Or to tempt Nebamun wherever he might be, or even Sevraine?

And what precisely would happen if the Sacred Core was transferred to such a being? What if the very worst happened and somehow that impulsive Lestat de Lioncourt got control of it in his young body? Perish the thought.

And Pacaya, what if she took her twin with her, rose into the air, and sought out that inferno? Oh, what agony would descend on each and every member of the tribe throughout the world as unquenchable heat and flame sought to burn the host of the Sacred Core?

Benedict had fallen asleep on the bed. Barefoot in freshly laundered jeans and a white dress shirt open at collar and cuffs, he lay there dreaming.

There was something about the sight of him sleeping so trustingly that touched Rhoshamandes. Of all the blood drinkers Rhosh had ever made or known, this one's body and face were a true reflection of his soul no matter how much time passed. This one knew how to love.

No wonder it had been Benedict who brought the memoirs of the Vampire Chronicles to Rhosh and insisted he read them. No wonder Benedict had so cherished Louis de Pointe du Lac's suffering and Lestat's wild rebellion. "They understand," he'd told Rhosh. "We cannot live without love. Doesn't matter how old, how strong, we are, what we possess. We cannot exist without love. It's absolutely impossible. And they know it, young as they are, they know."

Rhosh sat down gently beside him, and touched his back. The cotton shirt was soft, clean against his smooth skin. His neck and his soft curly brown hair were silky. Rhosh bent to kiss his cheek.

"Wake up now, Ganymede," he said. "Your maker needs you." He ran his hand over the boy's hips, and his slender powerful thighs, feeling the iron muscles under the starched denim. Had there ever been a more nearly perfect body in the Blood? Well, perhaps, in Allesandra, before she'd become a crone of her own making, twisted, leering, mad, a ragged monster of the Children of Satan. But this was surely the next-best body, wasn't it?

Benedict woke with a start staring blindly forward.

"The Voice," he murmured against the pillow. "The Voice is saying come, isn't it?"

"And we will, but you are to stay some twenty feet behind me. You come when I call to you."

"Twenty feet against monsters like this."

Rhosh stood and pulled Benedict to his feet.

"Well, fifty feet then. Stay out of sight, but near enough to hear my slightest command and come instantly."

How many times had Rhosh instructed Benedict in how to use the Fire Gift, how to muster it and send it against any blood drinker who ever tried to use it against him, how to fight off the power of another older killer, how to slam back with full force against gifts that seemed on the surface to be overwhelming? How many times had he demonstrated how he might do things with his mind which he'd thought impossible, opening doors, shattering them, blowing them off their hinges?

"No one knows the full measure of anyone else's powers," he'd said countless times over the centuries. "You survive the attacks of others when you fight! Fight and flee. Do you hear me?"

But Benedict was no natural warrior. In that short span of his mortal life on Earth, he'd been a prayerful scholar, only tempted by the sensuality of the natural world all around him to abandon his Christian god. He'd been a being made for monastery libraries and royal courts, a lover of gorgeously illustrated manuscripts and books, of flutes and drums and lutes playing, of blended voices in song, of the love of men and women in silken beds, and in perfumed gardens. Not a warrior, no, never. He'd only sinned against his Christian god because he couldn't see the harm in loving passion. And the satisfaction of his rampant desires had always been easy, harmonious, pleasant.

A deep chill passed through Rhosh. Perhaps he had done the very wrong thing bringing Benedict here, but was he not infinitely more vulnerable miles away, even in the crypt, to some trickery on the part of the Voice?

Well, there was no time to go over a plan now, not when Maharet was returning to her fortress and when she might, with those preternatural ears, hear what she could not hear telepathically.

"Put on your shoes, we're going now."

Finally, they stood like dark shadows in the open window. Not a single mortal eye saw them ascend.

And only moments passed before they came down silently into the jungles surrounding Maharet's compound.

"Ah, you are here and not a moment too soon," said the Voice, fearlessly inside Rhosh's head. "And she is here. She comes and she leaves the gates open behind her. Hurry before she presses all her magical electric buttons and closes me off in this prison!"

He stepped inside the great wire-mesh enclosure, and walked quietly towards the lighted archway.

"The machetes. Do you see them?" said the Voice. "They are against the wall. They are sharp."

Rhosh was tempted to say, If you don't shut up, you're going to drive me mad, but he didn't. He clenched his teeth, lifted his chin slightly.

And yes, he did see the long wooden-handled machete lying on the wooden bench among the pots of orchids. He did see the blade glinting in the light from the arch, though it was caked with mud.

"She dreams of Pacaya," said the Voice. "She sees its boiling crater. She sees white steam rising to the dark sky. She sees lava flowing down the mountain in fiery fingers of light. She thinks nothing can live in that inferno, not her, not her sister—."

Oh, if he could only shut out the Voice.

"And I dare not seek to deter her for I am what she fears above all things!"

There was a dark shape to his left. He saw it just as he picked up the machete and watched the caked mud fall off the blade.

Slowly he raised his eyes to see the figure of one of the twins star-ing at him—one, but which one?

He was petrified, holding the machete in his hand. Those blue eyes were fixed on him in a kind of dreamy indifference, the light from the doorway slicing out the edge of the smooth expressionless face. The eyes moved on away from him indifferently.

"That is Mekare," the Voice whispered. "That is my prison. Move on! Move on as if you know where you are going! Do you know where you are going?"

A soft brokenhearted crying reached his ears. It was coming from the lighted room beyond the archway.

He made his way forward on the soft earthen path, clutching the machete in his right hand, fingers massaging the rough wooden handle. Strong, heavy handle. Monstrous blade. Two feet in length perhaps. A powerful cleaver. He could smell the steel blade, smell the dried mud, and smell the moist earth all around him.

He reached the doorway.

Maharet sat in a dark brown rattan chair with her face in her hands, her body clothed in a long robe of dark rose cotton. Long sleeves covered her arms, and her fingers as white as her face were dripping with the delicate blood of her tears, her long copper hair tossed behind her, covering her bent back. She was barefoot.

She cried softly.

"Khayman," she said softly in an agonized voice. And slowly she sat back turning to face him wearily.

With a start she saw him there in the doorway.

She didn't know who he was. She couldn't pick his name suddenly from all the years, all the many years.

"Kill her," said the Voice. "Get rid of her now."

"Benedict!" he said loudly, distinctly, most certainly loud enough for his companion to hear, and at once he heard the boy coming through the garden.

"What is it you want of me?" asked the woman facing him. The blood made two fine strokes down her cheeks like the painted tears of a French clown with a china face. Her eyes were rimmed in red, her eyebrows gleaming golden.

"Ah, so it's brought you here, has it?" she said. She rose to her feet in one swift movement, the chair thrown back and over behind her.

Some five feet stood between them.

Behind him, Benedict stood, waiting. He could hear Benedict's breath.

"Don't speak to her!" cried the Voice inside his head. "Don't believe what she says to you."

"What right have you to be here?" she demanded. It was the ancient tongue now.

He kept his face a mask. He gave not the slightest indication that he understood her.

Her face changed, her features knotting, her mouth twisting, and he felt the blast hit him full force.

Back he hurled it against her. She staggered and fell over the chair.

Again, she hit him with it full force to drive him back and away.

"Benedict!" he cried.

And this time he sent the Fire Gift at her with all his power, lunging for her as he did so, the machete raised.

She screamed. She screamed like a helpless village woman in a war, a powerless and frantic being, but as she reached for her chest with both hands, she sent the Fire Gift against him and he felt the intolerable heat just as she was feeling it, felt his body burning in unspeakable pain.

He denied the pain. He refused to be defeated, refused to freeze in panic.

He heard Benedict shouting as he sought to drive her back, Benedict's left hand on his back. It was an ugly battle cry, and he heard the same coming from his own lips.

Again, he mustered his power and aimed it at her heart, as he brought down the machete with all his physical strength sinking the blade deep into her neck.

A dreadful roar rose from her. Blood shot up out of her mouth in a horrid fountain.

"Khayman!" she roared, the blood bubbling from her lips. "Mekare!" Suddenly a whole litany of names broke from her, names of all she'd known and loved, and the great choking wail, "I am dying. I am murdered!"

Her head was falling back, her neck twisting desperately, her hands reaching up to steady her own head, the blood splashing all over her cotton robe, all over her hands, splashing on him.

He grabbed the machete with both hands and slammed it into her neck again with all his force, and this time, the head came off and flew through the air and landed on the moist earthen floor of the room.

Her headless body sank down to the ground, its hands reaching up desperately, and as it fell forward on its breasts, the hands clawed at the earth, clawed like talons.

The head lay there staring to one side, the blood flowing slowly out of it. Who knew what prayers, what pleas, what desperate entreaties, still came from her?

"Look at it, the body!" Benedict wailed. He beat on Rhosh's back with his fists. "She's crawling to it."

Rhosh charged forward, his boot crunching into the headless torso, crushing it down into the mud, and switching the machete to his left hand, he grabbed up the bleeding head by the copper hair.

Her eyes shifted and fixed him firmly as the mouth gaped, and a low whisper came from the quivering lips.

He dropped the machete. And backing up, shoving Benedict out of his path, nearly stumbling over the flailing body, he swung the head against the wall again and again, but he could not break the skull.

Suddenly he dropped the thing, dropped it into the dirt, and he was down on his hands and knees, and Benedict's boot came down right in front of him, and he saw the machete come flashing down and slice into the shining copper hair, slice through it, slice into the skull, and the blood bubbled up crimson and glittering.

The head was on fire. Benedict was blasting it. The head was in flames. He knelt there a mute witness—helpless, utterly helpless—watching the head blacken and burn, watching the hair go up in sizzling smoke and sparks.

Yes, the Fire Gift. Finally he rallied. He sent it with full fury. And the head was curling up, black, like that of a plastic doll on a burning trash heap, and the eyes gleamed white for one second before they turned black, and the head was as a lump of coal with no face, no lips. Dead and ruined.

He scrambled to his feet.

The headless body lay still. But Benedict was now blasting this too, blasting the blood that was flowing out of it, and the whole prone figure there went up in flames, the cotton robe consumed.

In a panic, Rhosh turned right and left. He stumbled backwards. *Where was the other one?*

Nothing stirred. No sound came from the garden enclosure.

The fire crackled and snapped and smoked. And Benedict was catching his breath in anxious musical sobs. His hand was on Rhosh's shoulder.

Rhosh stared at the darkened mass that had been her head, the head of the witch who had come to Egypt long ago with the spirit Amel, who had gone into the Mother, the head of the witch who had endured for six thousand years without ever going down into the earth to sleep, this great witch and blood drinker who had never made war on anyone except the Queen who'd torn her eyes from her and condemned her to die.

She was gone now. And he, Rhosh, had done this! He and Benedict, at his instigation.

He felt a sorrow so immense he thought he would die from the weight of it. He felt it like his very breath gathering in his chest, in his throat, threatening to suffocate him.

He ran his fingers back through his hair, tearing at his hair, pulling it suddenly in two hanks, pulling it till it hurt, and the pain sliced into his brain.

He staggered into the doorway.

There, only ten feet away, stood the other—unchanged—a lone robed figure in the night, looking around her with a drifting gaze, a glinting drifting gaze at leaves, at trees, at creatures moving in the high branches, at the moon far above the compound.

"Now, you must do it!" roared the Voice. "Do to her what you have done to her sister, and take the brain from her and into yourself. Do it!" The Voice was screaming.

Benedict stood beside him, clinging to him.

Rhosh saw the bloody machete in Benedict's right hand. But he didn't reach for it. The sorrow was knotted inside him, twisted, like a rope pulled tight around his heart. He couldn't speak. Couldn't think.

I have done wrong. I have done unspeakable wrong.

"I'm telling you, do it now," said the Voice in a tone of perfect desperation. "Take me into your body! You know how to do this! You know how it was done to Akasha. Do it now. Do it as you did to that one! Do it. I must be freed from this prison. Are you mad? Do it!"

"No," said Rhosh.

"You betray me now? You dare? Do as I tell you."

"I can't do it alone," Rhosh said. For the first time he realized he was trembling violently all over, and a blood sweat had broken out on his face and on his hands. He could feel his heart knocking in his throat.

The Voice had given way to cursing, babbling, screaming.

The mute woman stood there unchanged. Then the distant cry of a bird seemed to waken her, and she bowed her head just a little to the left, towards Rhosh, as though she were looking upwards for that bird, that bird outside the wire mesh of the garden.

Slowly she turned and walked slowly away from Rhosh through the gentle crowd of fern and palm, her feet making a soft unhurried trudging sound in the soil. A kind of humming came from her. On she moved, away from him.

The Voice was crying. The Voice was weeping.

"I tell you I cannot do it without help," Rhosh said. "I need help. The help of that vampire doctor if I'm to do it, don't you see? What if I start to die when she does, what if I can't do what Mekare did when she killed Akasha! I can't do it."

The Voice whimpered, and sobbed. It sobbed like a broken and defeated thing. "You are a coward," the Voice whispered. "You are a miserable coward."

Rhosh made his way to a chair. He sat down, leaning forward, his bloody arms clutching his chest. *And I have done unspeakable evil. How can I live now after what I've done?*

"What do we do?" asked Benedict frantically.

Rhosh scarcely heard him.

Evil. Without question. Evil by all I've ever held to be right or just or good.

"Rhosh," Benedict pleaded.

Rhosh looked up at him, struggling to focus, to think.

"I don't know," Rhosh said.

"Khayman is coming," said the Voice miserably. "Will you let him murder you without a fight?"

It was an hour before Khayman appeared.

They had buried Maharet's remains. They lay in wait, the two on either side of the door, both armed now with the machetes from the garden.

Khayman returned weary and listless, windblown and sad, and came into the room like a laborer so tired from his work that he couldn't even seek a chair to rest. For a long moment, he stood there breathing slowly and evenly with his hands at his sides.

Then he saw the dark greasy bloodstains all over the mud floor. He saw the soot, the ashes.

He saw the earth churned up where she had been hastily buried.

He looked up and then he spun around, but he had no chance.

With the two machetes, they hacked at his powerful neck from both sides, almost instantly decapitating him.

No words came from him, and when his head fell, his black eyes were wide with astonishment.

Rhosh picked up the head and drank from the neck.

He held it with both hands as he drank, and though his vision misted and his heart beat in his eyes and in his ears, he could see the headless body dying as he pulled the blood from the brain—this powerful, thick blood, this viscid delicious ancient blood.

Never could he have drunk a drop from Maharet. Never. The mere thought of it revolted him. And indeed he did not think of it. But now he thought only, This is a warrior as I was a warrior, this is the leader of the First Brood who fought Queens Blood, and he is in my hands now, Khayman, the defeated leader—and Rhosh drank and drank the blood, and the images poured forth into him, the portal between First Brood and Queens Blood opened, images of this being when he had been young, vital, and human. No. Rhosh dropped the head. He didn't want those images. He didn't want to know Khayman. He didn't want those images inside his brain.

He burnt the body and the head.

There was a fountain in the garden outside, a Grecian fountain. When it was all finished and the body was buried, he went there and washed his hands, and his face, and rinsed out his mouth and spit the water down on the earth.

Benedict did the same.

"And what will you do now?" asked the Voice. "This thing in which I am entombed will seek shelter from the sun soon, for that is absolutely all that she knows, the sum total of all her discernment and all her millennia."

The Voice laughed. He laughed and laughed like a mortal on the verge of madness. He laughed a high-pitched and genuine laugh as if he simply couldn't help himself.

The jungle around them was waking. The morning air had

come, that air that all blood drinkers know when the hour of dawn is approaching, when the morning birds sing, when the sun is nearing the horizon.

Mekare moved slowly as a great reptile across the garden and into the room and across the mud floor and through a doorway to an inner chamber.

Rhosh would not remain in this place, no. He wanted to be gone now. He felt sick remaining in this room.

"And so we shall seek shelter at the hotel tonight," said Rhosh. "And then we will think what to do, how to get that Fareed to assist us."

"Well, I can give you a little assistance, my timid charge," said the Voice bitterly. He had finally exhausted himself with his laughing. He had an anguished tone Rhosh had never heard before. "I will tell you precisely how to enlist the cooperation of Fareed. I would have told you long before now if I'd known you were such a miserable coward, such a bumbler! Remember these names: Rose and Viktor. For Rose alone, Fareed may not do your bidding. For Viktor, he will do anything, and so will the elite of the tribe, the entire blessed elite of the tribe now gathering under the roof of this house in New York called Trinity Gate."

He began to laugh again, wildly, uncontrollably, a laugh more filled with pain than any Rhosh had ever imagined. "And Lestat will do your bidding too, I'm certain of it. Oh, yes. You coward. You can make them cooperate, for the love of Viktor!"

He went on laughing.

"This Viktor is Lestat's son, the son of his body and blood, the son of his genes, his human offspring. You get hold of this son and you will be the victor, and so shall I. Get that boy in your hands, in your power, do you hear me? And we will triumph together. And once I am inside you, they will not dare to anger you. You and I shall rule them together."

Part III

RAGNARÖK
IN THE
CAPITAL OF THE
WORLD

20

Rose

In the Topless Towers of Midtown

H E WAS IRRESISTIBLE. Rose had been listening to him
for hours. She could have listened forever to his faintly
sonorous voice. Viktor too had been listening, standing
quietly by the open kitchen door. Viktor in his jeans and white polo
shirt with that loving smile playing on his lips distracted her by his
sheer presence. She wanted to be in his arms again, alone, soon, in the
bedroom down the hall.

But right now she was listening to Louis.

Louis shied away from bright electric lights, a soul of the nineteenth century, he confessed, preferring these old-fashioned candles
and especially here in this high glass apartment with the brightness
of Midtown all around them providing all the nighttime illumination
that they might ever need.

Indeed, the sky was never black above the great sharp gleaming
silver point of the art deco Chrysler Building, and the countless towers crowding it, in this safe weald of myriad lighted windows that
seemed to hold them here more securely in space than the steel gird-
ers of this skyscraper whose elevators had brought them to this car-
peted haven on the sixty-third floor.

Guards in the next-door apartment. Guards in the marble lobby
downstairs, guards out on the narrow pavements of Fifty-Seventh
Street. Guards in the apartment above and in the apartment below.

And Thorne here, the red-haired blood drinker, the Viking

blood drinker, in a gray wool coat, standing like a sentinel beside the entrance to the hallway, his arms folded, staring out at the night. If he heard what they were saying to one another, he gave no sign of it. He'd been motionless since he'd arrived.

They sat across from one another—Louis and Rose—at a small round glass table with modern black-enameled Queen Anne chairs. He wore a long sweater of black wool that curled at the neck. His hair was as black as the sweater but it was glossy, and his eyes were shining like the emerald ring he wore on his hand.

His face was so bright, it made her think of something D. H. Lawrence had written, a line from *Sons and Lovers*, about a man's face in his youth having been "the flower of his body." For the first time Rose sensed she knew now what Lawrence had meant.

Louis was saying in his patient tender voice,

"You think you know, but you can't know. Who wouldn't be blinded by the offer of eternal life?" He'd been there for hours, patiently answering Rose's questions, explaining things about his own point of view. "We don't have eternal life firmly within our grasp. We have to work at it to remain 'immortal.' All around us we see other blood drinkers perish—because they don't have the spiritual stamina for this, because they never transcend the first few years of shocks and revelations, or because they're killed by others, ripped right out of life by violence. We're only immortal in the sense that we don't age, that illness can't take us down, in that we have the potential to live forever, but most of us live very short lives indeed."

She nodded. "What you're trying to tell me is that it's a completely final decision," she said. "But I don't know if you can possibly understand how total my obsession with it has become."

He sighed. There was a sadness about him even in his brightest moments when he'd been talking of Lestat and Lestat's ebullience and refusal to accept defeat. He'd smiled then and it had been rare sunshine, that smile. But his charm was obviously wrapped up in melancholy and unshakable gloom.

Viktor came forward and for the first time in an hour took a chair between them. Faint scent of that Acqua di Giò that was now all over her pillow and her sheets, and all over her dreams.

"What Louis is saying," he said to Rose, "is that once we do pass that barrier we'll know things that we'll never be able to change or forget. Sure, we are obsessed now. We want it. How can we not want it? From our point of view, it's not discussable. But he's trying to warn us: once we cross we'll be obsessed by something totally different and that obsessive awareness—that we're not alive anymore, not human— that's never going to be undone. That's never going to go away. You follow me? What we're obsessed with now, that may go away."

"I understand," said Rose. "Believe me, I do."

Louis shook his head. He drew up his shoulders and then slowly relaxed again laying his right hand idly on the table. He was looking at the table but he was looking at his thoughts.

"When Lestat comes, it will be his decision, of course."

"I'm not so sure why that should be," said Viktor. "I'm not sure at all why I can't make the decision with the agreement of Fareed or Seth. Fareed brought me into this world, really. Not Lestat."

"But nobody's going to make the decision except Uncle Lestan," said Rose. "That's clear enough. No one is willing to make it. And frankly, well, this evening we've had a chance to speak our hearts about this, and I'm grateful. We've had a chance to say out loud what *we* want."

Viktor looked at Louis. "You say wait. You say 'take your time.' But what if we die while we're waiting? What then? What would you think? Would you regret our having waited? I don't know the point anymore of waiting."

"You die to become this," said Louis. "You can't grasp it. You die. You can't become what we are unless you die. I suppose finally I'm saying this. You think you are making what the world calls an informed decision, but you're not. You can't. You can't know what this is like, to be both alive and dead."

Viktor didn't answer. He didn't even seem overly concerned. He was so excited that they were here, so excited that they'd come this far. He was full of anticipation.

Rose looked away and then back at the pensive face of Louis, at his dark green eyes, and the set of his mouth. A handsome man of twenty-four maybe when he'd been brought over, and what a scathing portrait he'd given the world of Uncle Lestan, his maker, Lestat. But that didn't matter now, did it? No, not at all.

She thought of the others whom she'd glimpsed last night, coming into the rooftop ballroom of the huge house called Trinity Gate. She had become used to the preternatural glow of Fareed, even of the powerful Seth, who always stood away from the bright electric lamps when he'd come to her, who spoke from the shadows in a low secretive voice as if he were afraid of its volume, its vibrato. But nothing had prepared her for seeing them all in that huge ballroom at the top of the long flight of marble stairs.

Fareed had been uneasy with her being brought there. She knew it. Could feel it. It was Seth who'd made the decision for her and for Viktor, Seth who had said, "Why keep them locked away?"

As far as Rose could see, Seth's mind was made up.

Gilded tables and chairs had been scattered on the periphery all along both sides of the dance floor, against walls of French doors paneled in mirrored glass. Drowsy green palms and blue and pink and red flowers in bronze pots were placed every few feet in tasteful groupings.

And at the end stood the grand piano and the cluster of musicians and singers, blood drinkers all, who'd enchanted her with their physical beauty as well as the sounds they made—violinists, harpists, singers making a symphony of sorts that filled the immense glass-ceilinged room.

There had been bright unnatural faces everywhere under the three crystal chandeliers in the dreamy gloom. The names had passed her in a steady numbing current as she was introduced—Pandora, Arjun, Gregory, Zenobia, Davis, Avicus, Everard. . . . She couldn't remember them all, couldn't recall at will all the remarkable visages, the particularities that had enthralled her as she was brought from table to table across the dark polished floor.

And then the striking otherworldly musicians, the tall, bald-headed, and smiling Notker who bowed to her, and his violinists from the mountains and the young boys and women who'd been singing with such brilliant and throbbing soprano voices, and then Antoine, Antoine who looked like the impersonation of Paganini with his violin, and Sybelle, Sybelle in long black chiffon, her neck positively wrapped in diamonds, rising from the piano bench to take her hand.

Out of the pages she'd read, out of the fictions that had permeated her dreams, they'd come alive around her, along with a multitude of strangers, and she had found herself seeking desperately to engrave every moment on her quivering heart.

Viktor had been so very much more prepared for it, a human child brought up amongst blood drinkers, easily clasping hands and nodding and answering questions, though he had stayed right at Rose's side. He'd picked the long white silk dress for her out of her closet, and worn a black velvet jacket with a boiled shirt for the occasion, beaming down at her again and again as if he were proud to have her hand on his arm.

She'd felt certain the blood drinkers were all concealing their curiosity and amazement at seeing them, which was so funny because she was so very shocked at seeing all of them.

Marius had embraced her, the only one to do it, and whispered poetry to her: "'Oh, she doth teach the torches to burn bright! / It seems she hangs upon the cheek of night / Like a rich jewel . . .'"

He'd kissed Viktor also. "Such a gift you are for your father," he had said. And Viktor had smiled.

She had known Viktor was on the edge of tears that Lestat had not come yet. But Lestat was on his way. That was now certain. He'd gone south on an errand to the Amazon that could not wait. But he was coming, most definitely coming. Seth assured them of this himself. He claimed to have heard it from an unimpeachable source, Lestat's own mother.

And Rose had been on the edge of breaking down at that news. But all this had made the suspense not only endurable but engulfing. Surely, Seth wouldn't have revealed the full depth of their world to her if Uncle Lestan—if Lestat was not to give both of them the Dark Gift.

"The Dark Gift." She liked to whisper those words.

There had come a moment last night when it seemed the entire company was on the dance floor, and some of the blood drinkers were singing softly with the musicians and the entire ballroom was wrapped in a cloud of golden light.

She had been dancing with Viktor, and he had bent and kissed her lips.

"I love you, Rose," he had said. And she'd dug deep down into her soul at that moment and asked herself could they turn away from this, actually turn away from it, and go to some other place, some safe place where their natural love for each other would be enough to dim the memories of this? She and Viktor had known surely the most tantalizing intimacy, the sweetest affection, the purest lovemaking she had ever imagined. It had erased for her all the ugliness and horror of what had happened with Gardner, all the shame and the crushing disappointment. By day when blood drinkers slept and their mysteries were gone along with them, she'd held Viktor against her heart and he'd held her, and that had been its own miracle, its own sacrament, its own gift.

She shuddered.

She realized now that Louis was looking at her and so was Viktor. Louis very likely had been reading her thoughts. Had he seen those images of her with Viktor, together? She blushed.

"I think Seth has made the decision," said Louis, speaking to her very thoughts. "Otherwise he would have never brought you to Trinity Gate last night. No. He's only waiting for Lestat to ratify it. He's made up his mind."

Rose smiled, but felt the sting of tears in her eyes.

"He'll come tonight, I know he will," said Louis.

"Fareed places a high value on human life, human experience," said Viktor. "Maybe my father does too. I think that Seth cares nothing for human experience much at all."

Rose knew that Viktor was right. She remembered too vividly the first time she'd ever laid eyes on Seth. It had been in the small hours, and she'd been in pain. Needles, tape, monitors all around her. Viktor wasn't coming back until morning, and Dr. Gilman could not be found.

Seth had come to her, a dark-eyed man in the ubiquitous white scrubs of the hospital, who stood at a remove from her bed, talking to her in a low voice.

He'd told her the pain would vanish if she would listen to him, just follow his words, and sure enough as he talked to her about the pain, as he asked her to describe it in colors, and to picture it, and to say what and where she felt it, the pain had melted away.

She'd cried. She'd told him about Uncle Lestan and how he'd wanted her to be a happy healthy young woman and how she'd ruined it again and again. Maybe she'd never been good enough, she'd said, for life.

A soft cold laugh had come from Seth. He'd explained with great authority that she had ruined nothing, that life was in charge of life, that pain was everywhere, that it was as much a part of the process of life as birth and death. "But joy, the joy you've known, the love you've known, that is what matters, and we, the conscious ones, the ones who can grieve, only we can know joy."

It had been a strange meeting. And she hadn't seen him again till she was much better, and she'd been certain then that he was no more human than Uncle Lestan was human, and she'd known by then too that Fareed wasn't human and Dr. Gilman wasn't human either, and that Viktor knew all this with a far greater understanding than she could possibly have. She'd been wrestling with it, pacing the floor of her room in the desert hospital, interrogating her own senses, her own sense of normality, and Seth had appeared and said: "Don't let us drive you mad." He'd moved out of the shadows and taken her hands in his. "I am just what you think and what you fear," he'd told her. "Why shouldn't you know? Why shouldn't you understand?"

The effect of those nighttime conversations had been incalculable, and the first time that she and Viktor had been intimate, she'd said in his ear, "Don't be afraid for me. I do know what they are. I know all about it. I understand."

"Thank Heaven," Viktor had replied. They had snuggled together spoon fashion and he had kissed her hair. "Because I can't lie about it anymore. I can keep secrets. But I can't tell lies."

She looked at him now, looked at the manner in which he sat there in the chair, looking at the far glass wall and the vibrant cityscape beyond it. And she felt such love for him, such love and trust.

She looked at Louis, Louis who was watching her again as if reading her thoughts.

"You've been more than kind," she said, "but if we're cast out of all this, if that's what ultimately happens, I don't know what future there can be for us."

She looked at Viktor. His expression told her nothing, except that he loved her, and that he had a patience with this that she didn't have.

She tried to imagine it, them together, married, with children, their very own rosy-cheeked children, little children, drifting through the world on the magic carpet of the wealth bequeathed to them by beings of a secret and unknown realm. She couldn't imagine it, couldn't.

But surely somehow it would never come to that. This would not all be consigned to miraculous memory meant to fade with every passing year.

She looked at Louis.

And he gave her one of those rare bright smiles. He seemed warm and human suddenly and too grand to be mortal all at the same time.

"It really is a gift, isn't it?" asked Rose.

A shadow fell over his expression, but then he smiled again and he took her hand. "If Lestat can make it right, well, then, it will be made right," he said. "For both of you. But there are other things happening just now, other things and no one is going to bring you into our world until those challenges have been met."

"I know," she said. "I know."

She wanted to say more, that it was so kind of Louis to stay with them, to wait with them, when obviously it must have been difficult to leave the ever-growing crowds at Trinity Gate, but she'd said this over and over. And she knew that her thanks to anyone and everyone were becoming a kind of burden, and she left it where it was.

She got up and went to the great wall of glass to look out at the city, to let her eyes move through this glamorous wildwood in which life itself was teeming everywhere around her as surely as it did in faraway streets below, and only yards away it seemed there were darkened windows revealing smoky and ghostly offices and crowded bedrooms and living rooms, and rooftops lying before her with gleaming blue swimming pools and some with green gardens, perfect gardens like toy gardens, with toylike trees she felt she could reach out and pick up with her fingers, and all this stretching on towards the great distant shadow of Central Park.

I want to remember these nights always, she thought. I want to fix them forever in my memory. I want to lose nothing. When it's done, when it's decided and it's over, I will write a memoir seeking to capture everything forever. When it's happening it is too beautiful, too overwhelming, and you can feel it's being lost with every breath you take.

Quite suddenly a deep dark mass appeared above her, something like a cloud forming and descending right before her eyes. In a split second it thickened and rose up in front of her virtually blinding her as she fell back away from the transparent wall.

A great boom sounded, a great terrible crashing roar and a clatter, and she felt herself falling and all around her came down a rain of broken glittering glass. Her head hit the hardwood floor. There were deafening noises, furniture being smashed, pictures and mirrors falling, and the loud cold wind was rushing through the room. Doors slammed. More glass was breaking. She rolled over on her side, her hair whipped against her face by the wind, her hands grasping for something, anything firm, to steady her when she saw the treacherous glass splinters all around her, and she began to scream.

She saw Thorne fly at a brown-haired figure clothed all in black who stood before the overturned and broken table. But the figure slammed Thorne away with such force he appeared to fly across the length of the room. Louis lay sprawled on the floor in a pool of blood.

Viktor came rushing towards Rose.

The brown-haired figure snatched up Viktor in one arm though Viktor was fighting against him with all his strength, and as Thorne rushed at the figure again, he grabbed Thorne's hair with one hand and hurled him away once more.

For a moment this tall creature who held Viktor effortlessly in the grip of his left arm looked down at Rose and came towards her, but Louis rose up behind him like a great shadow and the stranger veered, spinning backwards and smashing Louis with his right fist.

Again and again, Rose screamed.

The figure rose off the floor, wrapping both arms around Viktor, and it went out through the great jagged hole in the glass wall. It went out and upwards and vanished into the sky. And she knew where that brown-haired one had taken Viktor, she knew—up and up, faster than the wind and towards the stars. Powerful as Uncle Lestan, unstoppable as Uncle Lestan, who'd rescued her from that little island in the Mediterranean so very long ago.

Viktor was gone!

Rose couldn't stop screaming. She crawled on her knees through the broken glass. Thorne lay to the far right, his face and head covered in blood. Louis crawled towards Rose.

Suddenly Louis was on his feet. He lifted her in his arms and carried her out of the room, out of the cold lashing wind. Thorne was staggering right behind him, hitting the walls on both sides like a drunken man, blood pouring down into his eyes.

Louis rushed with her down the long hallway. She clung to him crying, as he carried her into the bedroom that was hers in this place and put her down gently, gently as if she'd break on the white bed.

Thorne clung to the sides of the doorway as if he might fall.

There were voices in the hallway, feet pounding, shouts.

"Tell them all to get out," said Louis. "Call the house. We're going there now."

She tried to stop crying. She was choking. She couldn't breathe.

"But who was it, who took him, who did it?" she sobbed. Again, she began to scream.

"I don't know," Louis said.

Louis wrapped her up in the white cover of the bed, cradling her, rocking her, kissing her until she went quiet.

Then he carried her out of the apartment and held her tight against him in the elevator as they went down to the underground garage.

Finally, when they were in the car moving uptown sluggishly on Madison Avenue, with Thorne in the front seat beside the driver, she'd been able to stop crying altogether as she leaned against Louis's chest.

"But why did he take Viktor, why, where has he taken him?" She couldn't stop asking, couldn't stop.

She could hear Thorne in a low voice talking to Louis.

She felt Louis's right hand around her forehead, turning her face towards him, and his left hand lightly touching her waist. He bent his head and pressed his ear against her neck. His skin was silky, just like Uncle Lestan's skin had always been, cold, but like silk.

"Rose, Lestat's come. He's at the house. He's waiting for you. You're safe. You're all right."

She stopped sobbing only when she saw him.

He stood in the front hallway with his arms out, her uncle Lestan, her beloved uncle Lestan, an angel to her, timeless, unchanged, forever beautiful.

"My Rose," he whispered. "My darling Rose."

"They took Viktor, Uncle Lestan," she sobbed. "Someone took him!" The tears ran down her face as she looked up at him. "Uncle Lestan, he's gone."

"I know, my darling. And we will get him back. Now come to me," he said, his powerful arms closing around her. "You are my daughter."

21

Rhoshamandes

The Devil's Gambit

H E WAS in a rage. But then he'd been in a rage since he'd struck down Maharet, since he'd doubled over with the machete in his hands, confronted with what he'd done, and the ghastly realization that he could not possibly undo it.

And now that he had Viktor in his hands, which the Voice had so furiously urged him to achieve, he was more than ever boiling with rage, against the Voice, against himself, against the wide world in which he'd survived for so long and in which he now found himself trapped and certain of nothing except that he had not wanted this! He personally had never wanted it.

He stood on the broad wooden deck of this house in Montauk on the shore of Long Island—staring out over the cold glassy Atlantic. What in the name of Hell was he to do now? How could he possibly achieve what the Voice insisted he must achieve?

The word had gone out over the airwaves immediately that Viktor had been kidnapped. Benji Mahmoud had been cagey and brilliant: an ancient immortal had committed a dastardly deed (yes, the vile little vampiric Edward R. Murrow had used that term) in kidnapping "one cherished by all the elders of the tribe" and he had called to the Children of the Night throughout the world to listen for the malignant heart and mind of this ancient one, to discover this one's evil designs and to call the numbers at Trinity Gate in New York as soon as the monster and his helpless victim were discovered!

Benedict sat in the spacious barren all-too-modern "living room" of this glorified peasants' hut on this expensive coast only hours by car from New York staring at the screen of the laptop as he listened to Benji's reports.

"Lestat de Lioncourt has arrived! There are now innumerable elders amongst us. But again, I caution you, Children of the Night, lay low where you are. Do not seek to come here. Let the elders meet. Give the elders a chance to stop the destruction. And search, search for this evil outlaw among us who has kidnapped one of our own from us. Search but take care. An ancient one can conceal his thoughts, but he cannot conceal the powerful beating of his heart, nor can he entirely conceal a low humming sound emanating from his very person.

"Call us with all reports. And please, I beg the rest of you, stay off the phone lines until the kidnap victim is found or until you have further reports from me."

Benedict shut down the volume. He got up from the low-slung synthetic couch that smelled vaguely of petrol chemicals.

"But that's just it," said Benedict. "There are no young blood drinkers around here, none, they were all driven out of the New York hunting ground a long time ago. We've scanned this entire area. There's nobody out here but us, and even if they do find us, what does it matter, as long as I'm standing right beside him when you make your case to Fareed?"

It struck Rhoshamandes again as it had in the jungles of the Amazon that Benedict had been displaying an amazing gift for battle and intrigue ever since this nasty business had started in earnest.

Who would have expected the mild-mannered and genuinely loving Benedict to drive his machete into Maharet's skull at the moment when Rhosh was frozen with panic?

Who would have expected him to so handily carry the violent but helpless young Viktor to the bedroom upstairs and lock him securely in the large windowless bathroom, remarking so coolly, "Best place for a mortal, obviously, with all that plumbing."

Who would have expected Benedict to have been so handy with hardware-store chains and padlocks to secure that bathroom prison with such simple and clever gestures, piling a store of wood and nails and a hammer nearby if further security measures were needed?

And who but Benedict would have outfitted the bathroom before-

hand with every conceivable amenity—scented candles, toilet arti-
cles, even popular magazines, a "microwave oven" for the cooking
of the stacks of canned foods he'd bought, and heaps of plastic forks
and knives and spoons as well as paper bowls and dishes. He'd even
included a little refrigerator in the bath full of carbonated sodas and a
bottle of the finest Russian vodka, and had thrown in several soft new
blankets for the boy and a pillow so he could sleep "comfortably" on
the tiled floor when exhaustion eventually got the best of him.

"We don't want him to panic," Benedict had said. "We want him
to remain calm and cooperative so this thing can be finished."

By day the boards and nails would make his escape impossible,
and for now, when he became panicky, he could press the intercom to
speak to his captors.

That he had not done yet. Perhaps he was simply too angry to
utter coherent words. That would not have been surprising.

One thing was certain. Someone very powerful had taught this
human how to completely lock off his mind from all telepathic intrusion. He was as skilled at that as any scholarly member of the Talamasca. And as far as Rhosh knew, no mortal or immortal could open
a telepathic line to others without opening himself to intrusion. So
that meant the boy wasn't frantically attempting to send messages to
others. And maybe he didn't know how. The vampires who brought
him up might have taught him many things, but not how to be a
human psychic.

Rhoshamandes didn't much believe in human telepathy anyway.
But he had to stop thinking about this! He had to stop thinking
about all the different ways this spectacular gambit might fail, and
it strongly occurred to him that he ought to call Trinity Gate now
and return the boy and throw himself on the mercy of the gathering
blood drinkers!

"Are you insane," said the Voice to him. "Are you simply out of
your mind? You do that and they'll destroy you. What in the world
would prompt them to have the slightest mercy? Since when do blood
drinkers have honor?"

"Well, they had better have some or this plan simply isn't going to
work," said Rhosh.

Benedict knew Rhosh was talking aloud to the Voice. But he
remained attentive, desperate to know what was happening.

"I'll tell you this much on my honor," said Rhosh aloud for the benefit of Benedict as well as the Voice. "The very first thing I will do when I have the power is destroy that little Bedouin! I'm going to take that noisy, impudent little monster in my hands and squeeze the life and the blood and brains out of him. I'm going to drain him dry, and tear his remains into shreds. And I'll do that in the presence of his blessed Sybelle and his blessed Armand and his blessed maker, Marius."

"And just how," asked Benedict gently, "are you going to seize and maintain power?"

"It's pointless bothering with that question," said the Voice. "I've explained myself to your starry-eyed acolyte over and over. When you have me inside you, no one can harm you! You will be as untouchable as Mekare is now."

Mekare.

Without Benedict, would Rhosh have ever dared to attempt moving her? Again Benedict had taken the lead.

The night after the killing of Maharet, as Rhosh called his mortal agents to arrange for a domicile in North America, Benedict had gone off into the jungle to find Mekare a tender young female victim from one of the naked tribes. Benedict had put this frightened and utterly malleable woman into Mekare's arms, the whole while whispering softly to Mekare that she should drink, that she needed the strength, that they had a journey to take, and he'd sat there patiently waiting till the silent monster had slowly wakened to the smell of the blood, slowly lifted her left hand as though it were an unbearable weight and laid it on the breast of the prone victim.

With lightning speed, she'd closed her teeth on the sweet little girl's neck, drinking slowly until the heart was stopped, and could pump no more blood into her. Even after that she drank, her powerful heart drawing the blood until the victim was pale and shriveling. Then she'd sat back, eyes empty as always, her pink tongue licking her pretty lips slowly and efficiently. There wasn't the tiniest spark of reason in her.

And it was Benedict who suggested that they wrap her, that they find the finest coverings or garments that they could and that they wrap her as if she were a mummy in those garments and then they might carry her north safely to accomplish their purpose. "Remember, Marius wrapped the King and Queen," he'd said, "before he moved them from Egypt." Yes, well, if Marius had been telling the truth in that old story.

It had worked. Her fine green robe of interwoven silk and cotton with its trimming of gold and jewels had been spotless, no need to change it. Only wrap her gently in fresh-washed sheets and blankets, slowly, slowly, binding her gently, whispering to her the whole while. It seemed she'd welcomed the soft silk scarf blindfold. Or she hadn't cared. She hadn't cared anymore about anything. She was way past caring. Way past sensing that anything around her was amiss. Oh, that we become such monsters, it was unthinkable. It made Rhosh shudder.

Only once had there been a bad moment, an alarming moment. Benedict after binding her head securely in silk had backed off suddenly, almost stumbling in his haste to get away from her. He stood staring at her.

"What is it!" Rhosh had demanded. The panic was contagious. "Tell me."

"I saw something," Benedict whispered. "I saw something I think that she is seeing."

"You're imagining it," said Rhosh. "She sees nothing. Go on, finish."

What had that been, that thing that Benedict had seen?

Rhosh didn't want to know, didn't dare to want to know. But he couldn't stop wondering.

When they'd had her securely bound like a dead one in a shroud, it had been possible then to leave that horrid place, that awful place that had been Maharet's hearth and sanctum. Rhosh had had enough of looking through the storerooms, of looking at books and parchments and ancient keepsakes, enough, the desks, the computers, all of it. It was tainted with death. He would have taken the jewels perhaps and the gold, but he didn't need these things, and he couldn't bear to touch them. It was sacrilege somehow, stealing the personal treasures of the dead. He'd been unable to reason himself out of it.

When they were at the edge of the garden enclosure, he'd turned back, pulled the pin from the grenade he'd brought with him, and hurled it into the lighted doorway. The explosion was immediate. The flames raged through the buildings.

Then they had brought the silent burden to these shores, to a planned location obtained through the mortal attorneys with the least amount of delay, and put her to rest in a cool darkened cellar with its small windows soon boarded up by the ever-resourceful Benedict. Only the heartbeat of that bundled body gave evidence of life.

Benedict stood beside him at the railing of the deck. The wind off the Atlantic was deliciously cold, not as fierce as the winds of the northern seas, but bracing, clean and good.

"Well, I understand, you'll be untouchable, but how can you maintain power over them, enough, say, to kill Benji Mahmoud before their very eyes?"

"What are they going to do about it?" asked Rhosh. "And suppose I threaten them that I'll lie in the sun at dawn, as does happen to be my custom, by the way, and can be no more—unless I and they want the younger ones to be devoured by fire when my body, the Source Body, suffers that insult?"

"Would I die," asked Benedict, "if you did that? I mean once you have the Sacred Core?"

"Yes, but I'd never do it!" Rhosh whispered. "Don't you see?"

"Then what good is the threat? If they know you love me—?"

"But they don't know," said the Voice. "That's the thing. They don't know. They know almost nothing about you!" The Voice was fuming again. "And you can strengthen your friend with your blood, strengthen him to where he suffers from such a burning but not fatally! Why have you not given him more of your blood over the centuries? And then of course your blood will be the Source Blood and the strongest that there is, and you will feel the engines of power grinding in you with a new efficiency and fury—."

"Leave this in my hands," said Rhosh to Benedict. "And no, you might not at all die, were I to make good on my threat. Burn yes, but die no. And I will give you my blood." He felt like a fool suddenly obeying the Voice's orders.

"But you could never make another blood drinker," said Benedict, "because if you did you wouldn't be able to make the threat . . ."

"Stop talking," said Rhosh. "I have no choice now, do I, but to follow this through! I must get Fareed to put the Sacred Core into me. Never mind all the rest. Just remember the instructions I've given you. Be ready at any moment for my phone call."

"I am," said Benedict.

"And don't, whatever you do, don't call me. Keep the phone ready. And when I call and instruct you to begin torturing the boy—that is, if I have to do that—then you must do it and they must be able to hear his screams through the phone."

"Very well!" said Benedict disgustedly. "But you do realize I've never tortured a human being before."

"Oh, come on, it won't be that difficult! Look at what you've done already. You've taken to this, you know you have. You'll figure a way to make him scream. Look, it's simple. Break his fingers, one by one. There are ten of them."

Benedict sighed.

"They will not harm me as long as the boy is in our hands, don't you see? And when I return here with Fareed, we'll deal with the goddess in the cellar, you understand?"

"All right," said Benedict with the same tone of bitter resignation.

"And then I will be the One! And you will be my beloved, as you have always been."

"Very well."

Truly, with his whole soul, he wished he had not killed Maharet and Khayman. With his whole heart he wished there were some escape now from this. *Blood guilt.* That had been the name for what he was feeling now. Thousands of years ago as a boy on Crete he'd known what blood guilt was when you killed those who were your own, and Maharet and Khayman had not been enemies.

"Oh, junk poetry, junk philosophy," sang the Voice. "She was going to plunge with her sister into the volcano. I told you. You did what you had to do, as moderns so simply put it. Forget the ways of ancient cultures. You are a blood drinker of immense physical and spiritual power. I will tell you what is sin and what is guilt. Now go to them and make your demand and leave your acolyte here to slice off the head of that boy upstairs if they do not give in to you."

"When they find out—."

"They know," said the Voice. "Turn up your computer volume, Benjamin Mahmoud is telling them everything."

And it was true.

He sat down on the couch beside the laptop with its glowing screen. The website of Benji Mahmoud now showed of all things Benji's very own likeness, not in a still photograph but in a video. There he was with his black fedora and his sharp penetrating black eyes, his round face fiercely animated with the tale he told:

"Lestat is with us. Lestat has been to the jungles of the Amazon seeking the Divine Twins, the keepers of the Sacred Core, and Lestat has come back to tell the tale: the great Maharet has been murdered. Her companion Khayman has been murdered. Their remains were left in a shameful shallow grave, their house desecrated. And the silent one, the passive one, the brave and enduring one, Mekare, is missing. Who has done these things we know not, but we do know this. We stand united against this wicked one."

Rhosh sighed and sat back on the white couch.

"What are you waiting for?" asked Benedict.

Their house desecrated!

"Let them come together," said the Voice. "Let them weigh their losses. Let them weigh what they stand to lose. Let them learn obedience. The hour of midnight has not yet struck. And by that time they will have come to realize their helplessness."

Rhosh didn't bother to answer.

Benedict started to question him again.

"Go see to the prisoners," he said to Benedict and went back out to look over the sea and seriously consider drowning himself, though he knew it wasn't possible and he had no choice now but to play this game to the finish.

22

Gregory

Trinity Gate
Inheriting the Wind

G REGORY HAD to admire this enigmatic Lestat. Never mind
that Gregory was in love with him. Who could not admire
a creature with such perfect poise, such perfect pitch for
what to say to each and every blood drinker who approached him, a
creature who could lapse into the greatest tenderness with his mortal
ward, Rose, in his arms, and then turn with such fury on Seth, the
powerful Seth, demanding to know how and why he'd exposed "these
mortal children" to such disasters?

And then how easily he'd wept when greeting Louis and Armand
and his lost fledgling, Antoine, whom he'd long ago consigned to history, alive here and thriving with Benji and Sybelle. How consider-
ately he'd held Antoine's hand as the other stammered and trembled
and tried to express his love, and how patiently he'd kissed Antoine
and assured him that they would have many nights together, all of
them, and they would come to know each other and love each other
as never before.

"We must all come to the table and talk of what's happening,"
Lestat had said, so easily assuming command. "Armand, I say let's
do this in the attic ballroom. I'll be there as soon as I've taken Rose
safely down to the cellar and talked with her. And Benji, you must be
there. You must shut down broadcasting long enough to be there, do
you understand? No one can absent himself or herself. The crisis is

too great. Maharet, Khayman, murdered, their house burned, Mek- are gone. The Voice is inheriting the wind, and we have to hold this tent together against it!"

Gregory was tempted to applaud. It was fireworks in the front hallway.

Armand had agreed at once as though it were the most natural thing in the world to do what Lestat wanted.

But wasn't it what they all wanted?

And what a dashing and beautiful figure Lestat was. The James Bond of the Vampires indeed. How had he managed under such pres- sure to show up at Trinity Gate in a fresh and show-stopping ensemble of Ralph Lauren wool plaids and pastel linen and silk, with brown- and-white wing-tip shoes, and his full shining mane of blond hair— just possibly the most fabled head of hair in the vampire world—tied at the back of his neck in black silk beneath a diamond brooch that might have ransomed a king but likely not his son, Viktor?

The plaid coat was a long hacking jacket, exquisitely like a frock coat of an earlier time when fashion had been more daring and con- sciously romantic, and it fairly well concealed some sort of weapon, a large weapon that he carried—scent of wood and steel—without losing its beautiful shape and cut.

Oh, this was the blood drinker of *now*, the vampire of *now*, for cer- tain. Who else could better grasp that *now* was the Golden Time for all the Undead, transcending all ages past, and who else better to take the helm at this perfect moment? So what if it had taken this crisis to bring him to himself?

Beside Gregory, Zenobia, Avicus, and Flavius evinced the same complete admiration and fascination, Flavius laughing softly under his breath.

"He is all that anyone ever said he was," he whispered to Gregory.

And Gregory felt that giddy ridiculous feeling so many mortals have described over the millennia—of utter devotion to another so well expressed in the old phrase "I'll follow him anywhere!"

And Gregory did feel that. Yes, I would follow him in whatever he decides to do and put all my strength, all my gifts, at his disposal. But didn't all the others feel precisely the same thing? Hadn't all the arguments and uneasy conversations stopped? The whole house had assembled in the drawing room, the hallway, on the stairs. Weren't all united? Didn't even Gregory's beloved Sevraine and the inscrutable and ever-diffident Notker the Wise stare at Lestat with the same complete submission? Even Lestat's mother, slouching against the front door in her dusty khaki, was eyeing her son with a certain iron satisfaction, as if to say, Well now, maybe something will indeed happen.

Rose, poor Rose, poor mortal Rose, poor tender terrified Rose with her huge searching blue eyes and her thick blue-black curling hair. The sooner she was brought over the better. A mortal mind could be damaged beyond repair by what this girl had witnessed.

She was clinging to Lestat, like a shivering bride in her white silk dress, trying so desperately and selflessly to keep her weeping silent, and he, like a mighty bridegroom, held her in his arms, reassuring her once again as he gave her over to Louis. "Give me one precious moment, my dearest," he said to her, "and I will be with you. You are safe now."

Gregory stared astonished as Lestat gestured for his mother to step aside, and opened the front door. He went out onto the little portico and stared right at the young fledglings gathered three deep on the pavement in the deep shadows of the giant trees that crowded the narrow street, whose electric lamps had been mysteriously disengaged several nights ago.

A roar went up such as Gregory had never heard from assembled blood drinkers in all his life. Not even the old armies of the Queens Blood had ever roared in such support for a leader.

All this while, these young ones had defied Benji's warnings, gathering hour by hour to watch the house, and struggling to glimpse the faces that appeared at the windows, scrutinizing each passing car for new arrivals, though in fact arrivals seldom if ever came by car, and those that did, managed to slide into the underground garage beneath the third townhouse of the assemblage.

Not a single immortal within the house had dared to acknowledge the existence of these desperate creatures, not for an instant, except Benji through the radio broadcast only and always urging them gently not to gather, and to please go away.

Yet they had come, and now they remained, irresistibly drawn to the only place around which they had hope.

And this bold bright gentleman vampire, Lestat, went right down the steps now to the pavement to greet them.

Reaching out, he drew them to himself in a huge tight circle, telling them all in his commanding voice to be wise, to be careful, and above all to be patient!

All around Gregory, blood drinkers within the house moved to the windows to watch this absolutely unprecedented spectacle—the peacock prince with his dark creamy skin and impeccable clothes, taking the time to talk to his subjects, and they were indeed his subjects, the rambling, scrambling baby vampires all trying to assure him of their love, their devotion, their innocence, their desire for a "chance," their pledge to feed on the evildoer only, to have no more quarrels, no fights, to do what he wanted, what he said, to have his love and his protection as a ruler.

And all the while, the iPhones were flashing, even cameras were flashing, and the taller stronger males were struggling to appear gentlemanly as they sought the front ranks, sought to grip his hand, the females throwing him kisses, and those in the back jumping up and down to wave to him.

Beside Gregory, Benji Mahmoud was overcome with joy.

"Do you see this?" he shouted and jumped in the air now as if he were still the twelve-year-old boy he'd been when the Dark Blood took him.

"I am so sorry," Lestat said to the crowd in the most genuine and persuasive voice, "that I have taken so long to come to my senses, to know your needs, to know your desperation. Forgive me that I let you down in the past, that I ran from you, that I hid myself from those whose love I'd sought and then disappointed. I'm here now and I tell you we will survive this, do you hear me, and Benji Mahmoud is right. Out of the mouths of babes! He's right. 'Hell shall have no dominion!' "

Again, the roar went up from them as if a tempest had hit the narrow street. What in the world did the mortals in those buildings across the way think of such things? What about the few cars that tried to make their way towards Lexington or Madison Avenue?

What did it matter? This was Manhattan where a crowd this size might loosely assemble outside a nightclub or for a gallery opening, or for a wedding, and were they not quick to get out of the way of the mortal world if they had to? Oh, the daring of it all, to go right out there and speak to them, to trust that such a thing was possible.

Sixty centuries of superstition, secrecy, and elitism were being overturned in one precious moment.

Lestat backed up the marble steps towards the portico, pausing with upraised hands, letting all those iPhones and cameras snap, even beaming at a mortal couple, young, curious, tourists in the big city, who passed wondering what manner of celebrity was this and then hurried on, slipping through the shifting blood drinkers as if they were mere Goth kids who would never harm anyone.

"Now you must let us do our work!" declared Lestat. "I ask you to listen to all that Benji has to say especially on this night of all nights, and be patient with us. I'll come back to you myself in person when I have something important, truly important, to tell you."

A young female dashed forward and kissed his hand; the males were giving off raucous cries of support. Indeed deep guttural sounds were breaking out in the crowd such as bloodthirsty mortal soldiers used to make but which were now the stuff of sports audiences in packed arenas. Woot, woot!

"Where shall we search for Viktor?" a male cried out from the middle of the empty street. "Benji's told us to search, but where do we begin?"

Gregory could see that this shocked Lestat. He hadn't been prepared for this. Apparently, he hadn't known that Benji had sent out the word as soon as Viktor was kidnapped. But Lestat rose to the moment.

"He that brings Viktor back safe to these front steps," he called out, "shall have his fill of my powerful blood in my grateful embrace, I swear to you."

Again the whole shifting and glittering assembly roared in unison.

"But be careful as you search, as you listen, as you use your gifts, to cast a net for his voice, for images of him and where he's held captive. For this thing that has Viktor is merciless, an outcast and a slayer of the greatest of his own kind, and therefore desperate. Come to us, here, or call Benji with any intelligence. Now be safe, and be wise, and be good! Be good!"

The crowd was screaming.

With a great wave of his right hand, Lestat backed through the open door and then he closed it.

He stood there as if catching his breath, his back to the dark-paneled wood, and then he looked up, his large blue-violet eyes flashing over the surrounding faces like lights.

"Where has Louis taken Rose?" he asked.

"Downstairs, the cellar," said Gregory. "We will see you in the attic."

The whole congregation moved upwards, to the giant ballroom where the meeting would take place.

By the time Gregory reached the top floor and walked into the vast dimly lighted space, a conference table had been arranged by bringing lots of smaller square tables, each covered in gold leaf, to form one great glittering rectangle with chairs up one side and down the other.

This was directly beneath the central chandelier and illuminated by the chandeliers before and after it.

All the residents and guests of the house were streaming into the room.

"Is there to be an order as to where we take our places," asked Arjun in a polite voice as he approached Gregory.

Gregory smiled. "I don't think it matters as long as there's a vacant chair at that far end, at the head of the table."

Suddenly he realized that Sevraine was standing beside him, his ancient and precious Blood Wife, Sevraine. But there was no time for taking her in his arms, for telling her what a joy it had been earlier to see her come through the back garden and into this house with all her company.

She couldn't possibly read his thoughts, but she knew what they were nevertheless.

"We have the future now," she whispered. "Does it matter that we've wasted so many opportunities to meet in the past?"

And he said with a soft sigh, "I honestly do believe that is true. We have the future." But he was reassuring himself now as well as he was reassuring her.

23

Lestat

In the Multitude of Counselors

THERE MUST HAVE BEEN forty or forty-five members of the Undead in the ballroom when I entered it with Louis. I was carrying Rose. We had had the briefest of reunions in the quiet of a cellar room, but I had been unable to quiet her fears, or my own for that matter as to leaving her, and so I'd vowed not to let her out of my sight.

"Be still, my darling," I whispered to her. "You're with us now, and everything is made new."

She snuggled against me, helpless and trusting, her heart beating dangerously fast against my chest.

I stared at the assemblage. There were sixteen or seventeen blood drinkers flanking the broad table, made up as it was of two rows of small square tables, and most of these blood drinkers were speaking quietly to one another in little informal groups, Antoine with Sybelle and Bianca with Allesandra, and some alone, such as Marius or Armand, or my mother, merely watching and waiting without a word. Daniel was next to Marius. Eleni and Eugénie were beside Sevraine. On the far sides of the vast room were other small groups, though why they were out of the way like that I had no idea. One or two were obviously ancient. And the others were far older than I was.

The long broad rectangular table had no chairs at this end facing the door.

And at the other hand the lone chair was empty. Benji Mahmoud was standing by that chair. I sucked in my breath when I saw that empty chair. If they thought I was going to take that chair, they were crazy. Or mad, to put it with more gravitas and grace. I wasn't going to do it. The two chairs nearest the head of the table were empty too.

Louis brought the bundle of silk pillows and we walked down the length of the ballroom as the others fell silent unevenly. By the time Louis laid out the cushions to make a small square bed with bolsters for Rose in the corner, no one was speaking.

Her arms felt hot around my neck, and her heart was pounding.

I put her down on the pillows and brought the blankets up over her. "Now you be quiet, and don't try to follow what's happening. Just rest. Sleep. Be confident that Viktor will be recovered. Be confident, you're in our care."

She nodded. Her cheek burned against mine as I kissed her.

I stepped back. She looked like a dewy pink mortal princess deposited there in the shadows, curled up now, with the blankets covering her, bright eyes peering ahead of her at the great grouping around the table.

Benji beckoned for me to come to the head of the table. He gestured to Louis that he take the chair opposite Benji's own. At Benji's side, Sybelle stared at me with rapt fascination, and, to her left, my tender fledgling musician Antoine could not have looked more worshipful.

"No," I said. I did walk up to the head of the table, yes, but I didn't take the chair. "Who places me at the head of this assembly?" I demanded.

No one responded.

I looked down the two rows of faces. So many I knew and so many I didn't know, and so many ancient and obviously supremely powerful. And none of the ghosts here or the spirits.

Why not? Why had the great Sevraine brought three ancient female blood drinkers who were off to the side against the wall of French doors, just watching us, but not the spirits and the ghosts of the Talamasca?

And why were they all looking at me, this august company?

"Now, listen to me," I said. "I don't have three hundred years in the Blood as you say it now. Why am I standing here? Marius, what do you expect of me? Sevraine, why aren't you in this place? Or you?" I turned to one of the smoothest blood drinkers of the group. *Gregory*. "Yes, all right, Gregory," I said. "Is there anyone who knows our world and their world out there better than you do, Gregory?"

He looked to me to be as old as Maharet or Khayman, and his demeanor was so human as to have convinced anyone. Polish and capability, and fathomless strength, that's what I saw in him, clothed as he was in some of the fanciest duds the modern world has to offer, with a handmade shirt and a gold watch on his wrist that was worth as much as diamonds.

No one moved or spoke. Marius was regarding me with a faint smile. He wore a black suit, simple, with shirt and tie. Beside him, Daniel was similarly dressed, fully restored, this child who'd been so mad and lost after the last great debacle. And who were these others?

Suddenly the names were coming at me telepathically in a chorus of salutation: *Davis, Avicus, Flavius, Arjun, Thorne, Notker, Everard*—.

"Very well, stop, please," I said, putting up my hand. "Look, I went outside and spoke to the crowd because somebody had to do it. But I can't be the leader here."

My mother, halfway down the table away from me on the left, started laughing. It was soft laughing but it made me positively furious.

David, who sat beside her, as always the British Oxford Don in his Harris tweed Norfolk jacket, suddenly rose to his feet.

"We want you to lead," he said. "It's that simple."

"And you must lead," said Marius who sat opposite him and had turned to me without rising, "because no one else feels he or she can effectively do it."

"That's absurd," I said, but nobody heard it because I was drowned out by a chorus of exhortations and encouragements.

"Lestat, we don't have time for this," said Sevraine.

Another very commanding female blood drinker, who sat beside Gregory, echoed the same words. She told me in a quick telepathic burst that her name was Chrysanthe.

She stood now and said in a soft voice, "If anyone here had been willing to lead, well, it would have happened a long time ago. You've brought something entirely new to our history. I beg you now. Follow through."

Others were nodding and whispering in agreement.

I had a multitude of objections. What had I ever done but write books, tell stories, take to the rock music stage, and how could they romanticize this out of all proportion?

"I'm the Brat Prince, remember?" I said.

Marius waved that away with a bit of a laugh and told me to "get to it!"

"Yes, please," said a dark-skinned blood drinker who introduced himself as Avicus. The one beside him, *Flavius*, blond and blue-eyed, only smiled at me, gazing at me with a trusting admiration that I saw on other faces here too.

"Nothing effective will be done," said Allesandra, "if you do not take the helm. Lestat, I saw your destiny in you centuries ago in Paris when you came striding fearlessly through the mortal crowd."

"I'm in agreement," said Armand in a low voice as if talking to me alone. "Who but the Brat Prince to take charge? Beware of anyone else here who might try."

Laughter all around.

Allesandra, Sevraine, Chrysanthe, and Eleni and Eugénie looked like queens of ages past in their simple jeweled gowns, with hair as spectacular as the gold trimming on their sleeves, and the rings on their fingers.

Even Bianca, the fragile grieving Bianca, had a majestic poise that commanded respect. And the petite Zenobia, her dark hair trimmed like that of a boy, in her exquisite blue velvet suit, appeared a cherubic page boy from a medieval court.

We each bring to this realm of ours a certain charm, I thought to myself, and obviously I can't see myself as they see me. I, the bumbler, the blunderer, the impulsive one. And where the Hell was my son!

Deep in my mind a thought did flash for a moment that one who commands must of necessity be wildly imperfect, boldly pragmatic, capable of compromises impossible for the truly wise and the truly good.

"Yes!" said Benji in a whisper, having caught this from my mind.

I looked at him, at his small radiant face, and then back at the assembly.

"Yes, you have it there exactly," said Marius. "Wildly imperfect, boldly pragmatic. My thoughts as well."

David had taken his seat again but this time the smooth one rose, the one named Gregory. This was surely one of the most impressive blood drinkers I'd ever beheld. He had a self-possession to rival that of our lost Maharet.

"Lead for now, Lestat," Gregory said with decorous courtesy, "and we shall see what happens. But for now, you must lead us. Viktor's been taken. The Voice has turned its fury against those of us who've been deaf to it and is now seeking to shift itself out of the body of Mekare, wherever that body is, and into the body of another, one chosen to do the will of the Voice. Now surely all of us will collaborate in what we do here. But you be the leader. Please." With a bow, he sat down and folded his hands on the gold table.

"All right, what are we to do then?" I said. Out of sheer impatience, I decided to be the chairman if that's what they wanted. But I did not take the chair. I stood there beside it. "Who is this one who took my son?" I asked. "Does anyone have the slightest clue?"

"I do," said Thorne. He sat directly under the central chandelier and it made a blaze of his long red hair. His clothes were simple, a working man's clothes, but he had the casual look of a soldier of fortune. "I know him, this one—brown hair and blue eyes, yes—I know him, but not by name." He went on. "He hunted the lands of the Franks in my time, and he goes back to the early times, and he made these women here—." He pointed to Eleni and Allesandra.

"Rhoshamandes," said Gregory. "How is it possible?"

"Rhoshamandes," said Allesandra in wonder, glancing at Eleni and at Sevraine.

"Yes, that's who he is," said Thorne. "I didn't have a chance against him."

"He's a blood drinker who has never battled with others," said Sevraine. "How did he fall under the spell of the Voice? I can't imagine it, or what drove him to murder Maharet and Khayman on his own. It's madness. He used to avoid quarrels. His domain is an island in the North Sea. He's always kept entirely to himself. I can't fathom this."

"But it was Rhoshamandes," said Louis quietly. "I see his image in your minds and this is the blood drinker who broke the glass wall and took Viktor. And I'll tell you something more. This being is not so very skilled at what he's set out to do. He wanted to take Rose, but he simply couldn't manage it, and he never harmed me or Thorne, when he might easily have destroyed me, and possibly Thorne too for all I know."

"He has five thousand years in the Blood," said Sevraine, "the same as I." She looked at Gregory with the most tender expression and he nodded.

"He was my friend and more than that," said Gregory, "but when

I rose in the Common Era, I never knew him. What was between us was in those dark nights near the beginning, at the end of the first millennium in our time, and he did great things for me, out of nothing but personal devotion." Obviously some painful recollection was restraining him. He let the matter drop.

Benji raised his hand but spoke out before anyone had a chance to respond.

"Who's heard from the Voice? Who's heard him tonight here?" He looked around expectantly.

No one responded.

Antoine, my beloved fledgling from New Orleans, said softly that he'd never heard the Voice. Sybelle said the same. So did Bianca.

Then Notker spoke up, this bald but handsome blood drinker with the saddest eyes, big puppy eyes, beautiful and swimmingly deep but pulled down at the ends to make him look tragic even if he was smiling.

"He last spoke to me three nights ago," said Notker. "He told me he had found his instrument, that he'd be imprisoned no longer. He told me to remain in my home—my home is in the French Alps as many of you know—and to keep my people there, that what was to happen with him had no bearing on me. He said he would come into his own, and only the young and the weak would die, and my children were too old, and too strong to be affected."

He paused, and then went on.

"There are many here in this room whom this Voice would call young and weak." He looked directly at Armand who sat a few chairs away from me on the left and opposite him. He looked at Louis. He didn't bother to look at Sybelle or Benji or Antoine, or even Fareed.

"And I will tell you something else," said Notker. "This Voice can drive a person mad. There is no stopping it now. Months ago, yes, before the killing began, one could block it. But not now. It's too strong."

This amazed me. I hadn't reflected on this. But it made perfect sense. The more the Voice killed off the vampires of the world, the stronger the Voice became.

"That's true," Benji declared. "That's what the young ones are reporting from all over. There's no shutting him out now. The killings have made him strong."

Fareed rose to his feet. He'd been sitting quietly beside Seth. They both wore what I would call cassocks of black velvet, with high neatly fitted collars and long rows of jet buttons. He stood facing me.

"The Voice wants to be transferred from the body of Mekare into the body of this chosen one, this anointed," he said. "And he wants me to affect this. He has told me. He told me the night we arrived here. He wants the cooperation of me and of Seth. I've never answered the Voice. And true the Voice is becoming remarkably strong. I can still shut out the Voice but it's difficult. The Voice must be seen as a force which can harry and drive to madness any mind it possesses. This is now part of the picture. I will not do what the Voice wants. I will not bring an end to the innocent Mekare. At least not, not as things now stand."

He took his seat and Seth rose. Of all the vampires gathered, Gregory and Seth were perhaps the most powerful. And there was clearly no enmity between them. Gregory was looking eagerly to Seth, and Seth was collecting his thoughts slowly, his eyes moving from one to the other of all those assembled—except those behind him against the wall.

"We must remind ourselves," said Seth, "that the Voice knows what we are saying to one another. It can obviously, at will, visit any of us, and see through our eyes and hear through our ears, but it cannot visit more than one, or so it seems. But since there is no way to take the Voice by surprise by any decision we make here, then I will say this outright. The Voice must not pass into this one, Rhoshamandes. This one is not spiritually strong. Strong he is in the Blood, yes, but he is not spiritually strong. How do I know this? I know this by what he has already done—the brutal slaughter of Maharet and Khayman who were hacked to death as if by common marauders. And if the Voice takes over such a mind, the Voice will rule it."

All around the table others nodded, murmured their agreement. All were horrified by what had befallen the great Maharet and the helpless Khayman. I was horrified. I never wanted to relive my last visit to the burnt-out compound, my discovery of those hasty graves. A deep rage was gathered in me against this murderous Rhoshamandes. But we did have to speak more of this now.

"That mustn't happen," I agreed. "The Voice cannot go into Rhoshamandes. Absolutely must not happen."

I'd told them when I arrived what I'd found in the jungle compound. The bodies mutilated and hastily buried, the place burnt. I'd

told them of the wreckage, ancient books destroyed, chests of venerable jewelry and treasured objects torn open and scattered and blackened with soot. But I referred to it briefly again for any here that had
not heard or understood.

"Common marauders indeed," I said with disgust.

Jesse bowed her head. I saw the blood tears coming to her eyes. I
saw David embrace her.

Pandora, who sat with her head bowed and her arm around her
companion, Arjun, wiped the blood tears from her eyes.

Armand spoke up now, not bothering to stand or raise his own
voice, but merely addressing the group in a way that forced them to
focus more attentively on him. Excellent trick of those who whisper
so you must move forward to hear them.

"What is the character of the Voice?" he asked. "It's never spoken
to me. What is the soul behind the Voice?"

"Well, you know damned good and well," said Benji, "that it's
Amel, the spirit familiar of Mekare that went into Akasha and lost
its mind for all this time, these aeons of time, these epochs, these
millennia."

"Yes, but what's the character of the Voice?" asked Armand.

"Without morality of any kind," said one of the younger ones who
hadn't uttered a word until now. This was a fashionable black-haired
vampire in a rather snappy three-piece leather suit and a high-collared
shirt with a raging red tie. He turned in his chair to face me. He said
his name aloud for all, "Everard," and then proceeded.

"It wants to destroy the young ones, it turns them against each
other. It rouses the old. But all these things you know, all of you
know this. It has no morality. No character. No love of its own tribe,
as Benji says. It is a tribeless monster. It's promised to destroy me."

"And me as well," said Davis, a stunning silky black blood drinker
of staggering beauty. "And it could drive anyone out of his head, just
out of his head."

Arjun, the black-haired companion of Pandora, nodded. "Madness," he whispered. "He is the breath of it in the brain."

Allesandra rose to her feet. "It came into me," she said. "It drew
me out of the earth. It has great powers of persuasion." Allesandra's
voluminous hair made a frame for her long oval face, her narrow
almond-shaped eyes. What a beauty she was now, even more powerful than she'd been two nights ago, with absolutely nothing left of

that mad queen of old under Les Innocents. But she still had that regal bearing, and that stentorian voice. "It convinced me that I could free myself from a grave in which I'd lain for over two hundred years; it brought my mind back to me and then set me against the others of Paris. It spoke intimately to me. It knew my suffering, and told me of its own. It must not get into Rhoshamandes." She paused now looking to Eleni and Eugénie and to Bianca. "Rhoshamandes has no true moral strength of his own," she said. "He never did. When we his fledglings were captured by the old Children of Satan, he never rescued us. He shrank from war with those monsters. He left us to our doom."

There were many nods and affirmation around the table, though obviously Eleni was uncertain on this, but didn't care to speak.

"No, he's peace loving by nature, but not weak," said Gregory. "You're not seeing him in the proper light. He's never cared to be a warrior. The life never satisfied him but that does not mean he is weak."

"But the point she makes," said Sevraine, raising her voice, "is that he is too weak to battle the will of the Voice."

"And he's old enough," said Seth coldly, "to take the Voice into him, burn himself in the sun, and kill scores of younger blood drinkers, and that's precisely what the Voice wants. I tell you again, he is not spiritually strong."

"But why?" asked Louis. "What so offends the Voice about the young ones?"

"They weaken him," said Seth. "They have to. That's why his telepathic power is increasing now. The uncontrolled proliferation of young ones drains him. His physical body—this unimaginable vehicle by which we're all kept animated—is not infinite in size." He glanced at Fareed, who nodded. "And when the fledglings proliferate, he wants them burnt off. Now how precisely he is strengthened remains a mystery. Does he taste blood in the Core Body more exquisitely? Does he see through the eyes of the Core Body with greater acuity? Can he hear sounds more sharply? We don't know. We do know his actual telepathic voice is stronger now as the result of the killings. That we do know. But I wager you this. It was he, the Voice, that drove the elder in those long-ago nights at the dawn of the Common Era to leave Akasha and Enkil in the sun to cause the first Great Burning. And it was he in some guise in the mind of Akasha who drove her to exterminate so many of the tribe before she wooed Lestat for her even-darker purposes."

"You can't be sure of any of that," said Pandora. It was her first time to speak and she was plainly reluctant, almost shy. She wiped at the blood in her eyes again. There was a shrinking quality to Pandora, a passivity, a diffidence that made her less visible than the other females here, though she was just as gifted in every way. She was dressed in a Western gown of soft Indian fabric and embroidery, almost the equal of Arjun's long jeweled sherwani. "All those centuries," she said, "that I communed with her, I never saw anything stirring in her, ever, that might have been Amel."

"I'm not so sure you're right," said Marius with a little flash of annoyance. He would never ever be patient with Pandora.

"I'm not so certain either," I said. "I was with Akasha very briefly. But I saw things—moments when she appeared to lock up, to stop as if something invisible had taken control of her. There wasn't time to know."

No one challenged me.

"But I must say this now," I continued. "I don't think the Voice is necessarily unredeemable. That is, not if we're not unredeemable. I think the Voice has in the last twenty years taken a major step on a wholly new journey."

I could see this shocked some of those who were looking at me. But it hadn't shocked Marius or David. As for Seth, it was impossible to tell.

"Does it matter now?" I asked. "I'm not sure it does. I want to get Viktor back. I've never laid eyes on my son. I want him here safe, and the Voice knows this. But as to the Voice himself, as to Amel himself, he is far from a conscienceless and insensitive monster."

"Why ever do you say this?" asked Benji. "Lestat, this is unbelievably vexing. How can you say this? This thing is murdering us."

Sybelle gestured for him to be quiet.

"The Voice has been speaking to me for a long time," I said. "I first heard the Voice only a few years after Akasha was destroyed. I think the damaged mind of Mekare let the Voice come to consciousness. And I know my video films, my songs, whatever I did there in broadcasting our history, all those images, might well have stirred the Voice inside Akasha just as they stirred Akasha's conscious mind."

They all knew the old story of how a giant video screen in the shrine of Akasha and Enkil had brought my rock music experiments right to the King and Queen. No need to dwell on that now.

"The Voice came to me early on. And maybe to me on account of those videos. I don't know. But sadly, I didn't know who or what the Voice was. And I didn't respond as I should have."

"You're saying things would be different now," asked David, "if you had known and had responded in some other way?"

I shook my head. "Don't know. But I can tell you this. The Voice is an entity with his own distinct story. The Voice suffers. He's a being that has imagination. One has to have imagination and empathy in order to know love and beauty."

"Whatever makes you think that?" asked Marius in a gentle reproving voice. "Ruthless amoral beings can appreciate beauty. And they can love."

"But I think it's true, what Lestat is saying," said young Daniel. He made no apology for contradicting Marius now. They had been together for a long time. "And I'm not surprised to hear this. Every single one of you that I've ever known has had this capacity, to appreciate beauty and to love."

"Well, you're proving my point exactly," said Marius.

"Enough of this," said Seth. "I want Viktor back. He is our son as much as yours."

"I know that," I answered.

"But if the Voice has empathy," Benji cried, sitting forward, his fedora dipping down over his face. "If the Voice has imagination and knows how to love, well, then the Voice can be reasoned with. That's what you're driving at, right?"

"Yes," I replied. "Of course. Which puts our friend Rhoshamandes in a very dangerous situation. The Voice switches loyalties easily. The Voice is desperate to learn as well as to achieve his ends."

Everard laughed. "That's the Voice all right. Fickle. That's this demon that can slide into your mind or mine or yours or yours like a spider sliding down the slippery shining thread of its web and try to make you do things that you would never do."

All this while neither Bianca nor Jesse had spoken. They were in fact sitting side by side, Jesse weary and worn and broken by the news of Maharet's death, and Bianca still in a private Hell on account of her lost companion, but suddenly it was as if neither of them could stand it anymore, and after some silent agreement, Bianca rose and demanded in a shrill tone, "What is the point of all this? We're helpless in the face of this Voice and what it wants! Why do we sit here talking, trying to reason this out? This Voice, look what it has done to us! Look! Is no one here going to weep for Maharet? Is no one here going to ask for a moment of silence in her memory? Is no one going to speak for those who might have lived forever and are now dead and gone in the earth as easily dispatched as if they were mortals?"

She was trembling. Her eyes fixed on Armand who sat nearer to me on the opposite side of the table from her. Armand's face was the picture of shock and pain as he gazed on her. In fact it was so darkened and so vulnerable that it didn't seem to be Armand's face. And then she turned and glared at Marius as if making some silent demand. He too looked at her with the deepest sympathy. Then she sank down in her chair and put her face in her hands, and wept silently.

Jesse barely stirred. Jesse the young one, made by Maharet with the ancient blood in her, white-faced, shivering with the most human emotions, yet sustained by such powerful blood. Fareed concealed the same formula infinitely better than she did.

"My beloved aunt was indeed thinking of destroying the tribe," Jesse said. "She promised me she would not do it. But she thought about it continuously."

"This is true," David said. He was right beside her.

"I understand why Rhoshamandes did the bidding of the Voice," said Jesse. "And I know that if my aunt had wanted to live, she could have stopped Rhoshamandes. She could have stopped any one of us, even you, Gregory, or you, Seth. Or you, Sevraine. She was no stranger to defending herself. Her power was beyond our imagining. So was her experience. She was dying inside. And she let Rhoshamandes take her life."

She sat back in the small gilded chair. David kissed her cheek.

I threw up my hands. "It's true," I said. "Maharet was thinking of destroying herself and Mekare. Of carrying Mekare with her into a core of an active volcano. I saw the images of this coming from her. Pacaya in Guatemala is that volcano. I hate to say it. I hate to admit it, because she should not have died as she did at the hands of this unspeakable Rhoshamandes! But it's true."

Everyone waited, but it was clear I would not go on and neither would Jesse, and finally Marius rose to his feet with his usual commanding air and waited for all eyes to fix on him.

"Look, it's plain we can't surprise the being, and we can't deceive the being," he said. "And we can't live without him. So let's resolve where our strongest defense lies. We will agree to nothing unless Viktor is returned unharmed. And then we will listen to the Voice, to what the Voice has to say about what it wants."

"It cannot claim Rhoshamandes!" said Allesandra heatedly.

"No, it cannot," said Notker. "And I can plainly tell you that his most devoted confederate, the one who must be his ally in this, is as peace loving and unprepared for a battle like this as is his master."

"And who is that ally?" demanded Allesandra.

"It must be Benedict," said Notker. "It can be no other."

"Aye, Benedict," said Sevraine. "Of course. It's with Benedict that he lives on this island in the northern seas. It's with Benedict that he's lived for centuries."

"Benedict," whispered Allesandra, "not the poor benighted saintly boy he brought over from the monks!"

"Benedict?" asked Eleni. "Benedict was the one from whom Magnus—your maker, Lestat—stole the Blood. Why he's barely twice my age in the Blood. He's never been strong, never. Why, his entire charm is that he's as fragile as a wisteria blossom, as an orchid. But how do we know that this is Rhoshamandes's only ally?"

"I wager it is," said Notker, "because I know of no other. And by the way, this 'poor benighted saintly boy' brought me into the Blood and he did a fine job of it."

There was a soft ripple of laugher in the room, but it died almost immediately.

"But what a mystery we have here," said Notker. "We have the gentle Rhoshamandes that fed off beauty and poetry and music, and brought over those who pleased him, and never had the strength to fight for any of them against others, and now Benedict, saintly Benedict. And you, Lestat, you say the Voice loves. You say it loves and it has imagination and a soul. Well, we have a puzzle here in that it has picked two remarkable blood drinkers."

"Perhaps they were the only two," said Seth coldly, "who would tolerate the Voice's schemes, who fell prey to his ridiculous fantasies."

"Why ridiculous?" asked Marius. "What do you mean?"

It was Fareed who answered for Seth. "Lestat's right. The Voice is just beginning its journey as a conscious entity. It might have wielded some dark brutal influence on the Core Body in ages past, but it is a child now in the realm of purpose. And we don't know its full intent. I suspect that switching bodies, being removed from the mute and near-blind Mekare into the vigorous body of Rhoshamandes, a personable male of undoubted gifts, is just the first step for the Voice."

"Well, that's why we have to stop it," said Marius.

"Can't it be taken out of a vampiric body in some way?" asked Benji. "Dr. Fareed, can't you put it in some sort of machine in which it's fed the Blood constantly yet unable to see and hear or travel through its own invisible web?"

"It's not a web, Benji," said Fareed patiently. "It's a body, a great invisible but palpable body." He sighed. "And no, I cannot devise a machine to sustain it. I wouldn't know where to begin. Or whether such a scheme would work, and when this thing is removed from the Core Body we begin to die, all of us, don't we? This is what you've told us happened before."

"It is what happened," said Seth.

"But the Core Body was dying," said Marius, "when last it was removed. What happens if you remove it while the Core Body lives, heart and brain connected?"

"Nonsense," said Seth. "The thing lives in the brain, and when you remove the brain, the Core Body begins to die."

"Not necessarily. . . ." said Fareed.

"Of course," sighed Marius. He shrugged and made a helpless gesture. "This is beyond my grasp. Utterly beyond my grasp. I simply can't—." He stopped.

I sympathized. I knew almost nothing about the mechanics of what we'd all witnessed when Akasha had been killed. All I knew was that Mekare had devoured her brain and that had been sufficient for Amel to take root inside her.

"The point is that clever as we may be," said Seth, "we are not able to make a machine to sustain Amel, and we are not at all able to imagine an infinitely secure means of sustaining such a machine even if we could build one. We would still be harnessed to the Voice in such a scenario, of course. And the Voice might be constantly on the prowl, so to speak, to find an ally to free it."

"It would be," I said. "And who could blame him? You've been talking about this idea of a machine as if this being weren't sentient, and capable of excruciating pain. Well, he does feel such things. I'm telling you there must be a solution to all this which doesn't involve the hopeless imprisonment of Amel. His imprisonment in Mekare is what led to this! Yes, her injured mind gave him a vacuum in which to come into his own. And I confess I stimulated him when I stimulated Akasha. No doubt of that! But Amel feels and Amel wants and Amel loves."

"I wouldn't call him Amel," said Marius. "That is far too personal. So far he is the Voice."

"I called him the Voice when I didn't know who he was," I objected. "And others who described him as the Voice didn't know who he was."

"We still don't really know who he is," said Marius.

"So what are you saying, Lestat?" asked Armand in that subtle tone of his. "You are saying this spirit, Amel, is good? Lestat, all we ever learned of it from the twins was that it was evil."

"Not so," I said. "That is not really what the twins told us at all. Besides why would it be inherently either good or evil? And what the twins described was a playful, boasting spirit that loved Mekare and sought to punish Akasha for ever harming her, and somehow this spirit went into Akasha's body and became one with her, one with the one he hated. And now six thousand years later, he finds himself restored to the body of the one he loved, and she's dead to him, dead to everything."

"Ah, that is a beautiful story," said Pandora under her breath.

"But that doesn't make him good!" said Armand.

"And that doesn't make him evil either," I said. "When Maharet told us these old tales she made it clear: good spirits were those who did the bidding of witches; bad ones did mischief. That's a very primitive and near-useless definition of evil or good."

I was suddenly aware of Benji gesturing to Armand, asking him to be quiet, and Louis also. And I saw that Marius was making a similar gesture with his hands low to the table, as if to say, Be quiet. And no sooner had I picked up on this than Armand picked up on it.

I thought for a moment, pressing my fingers together right under my eyes. Then I said, "Look, I'm not speaking for the Voice's benefit. I'm not trying to trick him by praising his sensibilities or his growth or his capacity to love others. I'm saying this because I believe it. The Voice can tell us things no other entity in this world can, and that includes perhaps other spirits who are among us—." I glanced knowingly at Sevraine. I was speaking now of Gremt. "Entities that aren't really confiding in us! Or helping us. Such spirits may be so angry at Amel, so against him, so inveterately his enemy from the time before time that they can't be counted on right now to help us."

"We don't know that," said Sevraine. "We only know they will not help. You're speaking of powerful spirits who may in time help us but for now are waiting, waiting to see what we aim to do."

"No, I would not count out those spirits," said Pandora suddenly. "They may help us yet."

"Precisely," said Sevraine.

At once everyone was in a bit of an uproar. But it was plain many at the table knew what we were talking about and many did not. Benji did not. Neither did Louis or Armand, but Marius knew and so did Pandora. And even the flashy and dapper Everard knew.

"The Talamasca will not help us yet," said Marius. "But they are with us in this."

"The Talamasca's made up of spirits?" demanded Benji. "Since when did that come to be known!"

Quickly, Marius told him to be quiet, that it would all be explored.

And then I held up my hands for silence. I fully expected to be ignored, but the exact opposite happened.

"My point is simply that this Amel is a spirit of immense knowledge and secrets and he happens to be *our* spirit!" I waited. "Don't you see? We cannot keep talking about him as if he were a cheap villain who's broken into our existence simply to inconvenience us and frighten us and bully us and demand things from us. He's the fount of our very life." I leaned forward and rested my hands on the table. "So he kills," I said. "We kill. So he slaughters mercilessly. Who here of my age or older has not done the same? This entity, this being, is at the root of what we are. Whether he has any plan or not, beyond taking possession of Rhoshamandes, he has a destiny! We all do! That's what this crisis has taught me. That's what Benji's incessant urgings have taught me! We are a tribe with a destiny and it's a destiny worth fighting for. And Amel feels what we feel, that he is a being condemned to suffer for reasons he cannot know, a being who wants to love and wants to learn, who wants to see and feel, and he, like us, has a destiny worth fighting for."

Utter silence.

There was almost no movement, except that they were all glancing to one another. Then in a low voice Seth spoke.

"I think," he said, "that Prince Lestat has made an excellent point."

Marius nodded.

"So what you're saying," said Benji, "is that the Voice is a member of the tribe."

I laughed. "Well, yes!"

"And he's evil and we are evil," whispered Armand.

"That's not so!" said Benji. "We are not evil. You will never understand that. Never."

A change came over Seth. It was sudden. He rose to his feet and so did Sevraine and also Gregory.

"What is it?" I asked.

"Rhoshamandes. He's coming," said Seth. "He's drawing near."

"He's overhead, directly," said Gregory.

Marius rose to his feet with them.

I stood there with my arms folded, listening. I glanced over my shoulder at Rose, who lay in uneasy sleep under her blanket. I looked at Louis who was watching me intently.

But anyone could hear it now, hear its footsteps, and plainly they all did except for Rose, who slept.

He, this being with his mind closed shut like a vault, was walking with intentionally audible steps down an iron staircase somewhere, likely from a portal on the roof, and into the hallway beyond the entrance to the ballroom.

Slowly he came into a view, a startlingly good-looking young man in face and form but a blood drinker of five thousand years most certainly. He had dark brown hair and mild, very open grayish-blue eyes, and he was dressed in an impressive military jacket, black velvet, forest-green trim, very flattering to his tall well-made frame, and he walked right up to the foot of the table.

"Rhoshamandes," he said. There was a flicker of hesitation in his face. Then he bowed to the assembly. And with nods, he gave his greetings, "Sevraine, my dearest. And Gregory, Nebamun, my old friend, and my darlings, Allesandra, Eleni, Eugénie. And Notker, my beloved Notker. And Everard, my dearest Everard. And to all of you, my salutations. And to you, Prince Lestat, I am at your service, so to speak, as long as we can come to an agreement. Your son is as yet unharmed."

A vampire, a male who was part of Notker's group, rose now and fetched a chair from against the wall and brought it to the table.

But this stately and impressive creature walked around to one side and made his way to Jesse, standing behind her, over her, and bending to speak to her intimately.

"It was never my wish to harm Maharet," he said. "And I wish with all my heart and soul I'd found some way to avoid it. I did it because she meant to exterminate us all. I swear to you this is true. And I killed Khayman because I thought when he came to grasp what I'd done, he'd seek to punish me for it."

She stared straight forward, her eyes dull and red, and gazing off as if she hadn't heard. She didn't move. David did not look up at Rhoshamandes either.

Rhoshamandes sighed. And when he did that a rather casual and cavalier expression passed over his handsome features, a rather dismissive expression. It was only there for a second, but I caught it and was startled by it, startled by the hardness of it in contrast to these elegant and sensitive words.

He turned and went back to the foot of the table, so to speak, and sat down in the chair that had been provided for him.

"You know what I want," he said. He addressed me. "You know what Amel wants. You know you, Lestat, you know that your son is with Benedict." He reached into his pocket and held up a shining iPhone for all to see and then placed it before him on the table. "I press the button here and Benedict kills Viktor." He paused, his eyes sweeping the table up and down and then settling on me. "But that does not have to happen, does it? And of course I have Mekare in a safe place, as you no doubt have surmised."

I said nothing. With the power of his mind, he might send a blast from that phone, I figured. But did he know that? I certainly didn't know it for certain. I hated him. I loathed the very sight of him.

"Need I remind you that if anything happens to me," he went on, "the Voice will incite Benedict to immediately kill your son, and you may never find out the location of Mekare."

The others stared at him in cold silence.

24

Lestat

He Who Cuts the Knot

I TRIED TO PENETRATE the creature's mind, trying to pick up the faintest image from it that might indicate precisely where Viktor was, and where Mekare was. And I knew surely that every other blood drinker at the table was doing this. Nothing. And whether the Voice was inside this being right now, looking through his eyes at me and at all of us, I couldn't know.

"I can explain to you simply enough," said Rhoshamandes, "what I want. The Voice wishes to come into me. I am loath to attempt this on my own. I feel I need the assistance of others here, most particularly Fareed, this vampire doctor. I need his help."

Fareed said nothing.

"If we agree to proceed, I'll take Fareed with me now, and when the deed is done, when Mekare is mercifully freed from this Earth, and the Voice is in me, I will return Fareed and Viktor unharmed. I will then possess the Sacred Core. And I will become the leader, so to speak, of this tribe." He smiled coldly as he looked at Benji. "I assure you, I'm neither despotic nor obsessively interested in the conduct of blood drinkers. Like many a being who rises to power, I rise not because I want power, but because I don't intend to be governed by anyone else."

He was about to go on when Seth gestured for his attention. "Have you no hesitation," he said, "about living with this Voice inside you night after night for the rest of your immortal journey in this world?"

Rhoshamandes didn't immediately answer. Indeed his face went blank and became a bit rigid, a bit grim. He stared at the shiny little mobile phone in front of him and then he looked again at me and then at Seth.

"I am committed now to doing what the Voice wants," he said. "The Voice wants to be freed from Mekare. The Voice can only temporarily possess any one of us at any given time, and the Voice does not see clearly or hear clearly through us when it possesses us. And in Mekare it is trapped in an instrument so damaged and blunted, so destroyed through isolation and privation, that it cannot hear or see at all."

"Yes," said Fareed quietly. "We all know this. We're well aware of what the Voice is experiencing now. But Seth's question was for you. How are you going to survive with the Voice inside you, night after—?"

"Yes, well, I will!" came the answer, emphatically and impatiently. Rhoshamandes flushed. "Do you think I have a choice?" he said. Then he drew back gesturing for silence. The Voice was talking to him, no doubt.

I was trying to conceal my thoughts completely, which meant leaving them in an inchoate state as best as I could, but clearly this creature was miserable, I could see it, miserable and conflicted, and his pale eyes, fixing on me again, couldn't express anything but a deep frustration that bordered on pain.

"This must be followed to the finish," he said now. "Fareed, I must ask you to come with me."

"And what happens," asked Sevraine suddenly, "when the Voice tires of being in your body, Rhoshamandes, and decides it wants to be transferred to another?"

"Well, very likely that is never going to happen!" Rhoshamandes flashed furiously, "because the Voice has things to learn in my body, a world to see as he's never seen it before. This thing, this, this Voice . . ." He was stammering now in frustration. "This Voice has only just come to consciousness."

"Yes, and it wants a better host body," said Seth in a strong cold tone. "And it's chosen you, a splendid male specimen, but once you take it into yourself you do realize it might just drive you stark raving mad."

"We're wasting time," said Rhoshamandes. "Don't you understand?"

"What? That you're a pawn or a slave of this thing?" Seth was facing him and I couldn't see his face except in semiprofile, but his tone was withering as before.

Rhoshamandes sat back in the chair and put up his hands. He stared at the phone again.

Suddenly Benji slid out of his place at my right and silently hurried down the length of the table until he stood at Rhoshamandes's left and then he stared down at the phone.

"You touch it, and the boy dies!" said Rhoshamandes. He was now full of rage. His eyes were blazing as he glared at Benji, and his mouth was contorted, his lips pressed together and then released in a vicious sneer. "As I said, one errant signal from that phone and Benedict kills Viktor—."

"And when that happens," said Sevraine, "we destroy you, don't we, in the most painful way because you no longer have any bargaining power whatsoever. What makes you think you can get what you want here?"

"I warn you!" He put up his right hand. Right, I was noticing. He'd taken out the phone with his right hand. Right-handed. "This will happen as the Voice has decreed."

Marius cleared his throat and sat forward, hands clasped on the table. "The Voice is young to govern this tribe. And I think if you have the Sacred Core within you, you will expose yourself to the sun—and more of the younger generations of us will perish, because that's what the Voice wants."

"What of it!" demanded Rhoshamandes.

"What of it?" asked Marius. "All of us here have younger fledglings whom we love! You think I want to sit idly by while you destroy Armand, or Bianca?" He was allowing his own rage to rise. "You think I want to see Benji and Sybelle die?"

"Doesn't matter what you want," said Rhosh. "Do you realize that if you don't respond to this offer within the next few minutes, if I fail to contact Benedict, he'll kill the boy as directed, and I'll withdraw from you—and make no mistake, I will do that so swiftly you'll never catch me, and we will simply have to go over all this again, and again, and again, until the Voice achieves his purpose?"

"That sounds rather cynical to me," said Marius.

"And to me also," said Gregory. This was the first time he'd spoken.

"Don't you realize what you're dealing with!" Rhoshamandes glared at Gregory. "Nebamun," he said, appealing to him by his ancient name. "The Voice hears every word we're saying here. The Voice is here with us. The Voice can direct Benedict to kill the boy—."

"Ah, but will Benedict do this for the Voice," asked Gregory, "without a word from you?"

"I think not," said Allesandra. "I think your gentle Benedict is a poor choice of ally in this."

"Don't be such a fool!" said Rhoshamandes. He was desperate. "You don't know where Mekare is."

"Small matter, that," said Marius, "since she's safe wherever she is for the moment since you cannot take the Sacred Core from her without help."

"Oh, yes, I can and I will." He stood up. "I can leave here and kill that mortal boy and work the transfer just as it was worked before. Why, I might very well compel Viktor to assist me."

I started to laugh. I couldn't stop myself. I laughed. I just broke down laughing and then bending forward, my left hand on my waist as I laughed, I shot the Mind Gift at the iPhone and brought it right to me at my end of the table.

"Don't you dare touch it!" Rhoshamandes roared. I knew the volume of his voice was hurting Rose, had to be hurting her, and could be heard out there on the street by any of the young who might be lingering about.

I laughed harder. I just couldn't stop it. I really didn't want to be laughing like this, but I couldn't stop.

I snatched up the phone and shoved it in my pocket, and using the seat of the chair beside me as a step, I mounted the table, and laughing uncontrollably I started to walk down the length of it towards him.

"Oh, Voice," I said through fits of laughter. "You are such a precocious child! However did you think this stupid plan would work!"

The Voice came into my head in a fury. "I'll destroy your son!" he cried. "You will not block me in this."

"Yes, yes," I said, laughing, taking one stride after another on the gilded blocks of the table. "I know. I have heard your threats before, haven't I? Don't you realize that I am the only one here who actually loves you?"

I had reached the end and suddenly sat down on the edge of the table to one side of Rhoshamandes, who was glaring at me now in fury.

I snatched my ax from inside my coat with my right hand, as with my left I grabbed Rhoshamandes's left forearm, and I brought the ax down with a loud crash on his left wrist. In a tenth of a second it was done. The crescent blade flashed beautifully in the light.

The severed hand flew across the table. Rhoshamandes screamed in terror. Others around the table were gasping audibly, and shifting in their chairs.

Rhoshamandes stared at the hand, the blood pouring from his wrist, and tried to jerk himself free from me.

But just as I'd hoped, he couldn't do this. He couldn't move.

Marius and Seth and Sevraine and Gregory had all risen and were staring at him, pinning him there obviously with the Mind Gift as I knew they would.

The blood continued spurting out of his left arm, gushing on the table.

He tried to stifle another scream but he couldn't.

"Is there any place," I asked, "where we might burn that hand? I mean I can incinerate it here easily enough but I don't want to scorch the table."

"No!" he bellowed. He went mad trying to free himself from me, squirming, struggling against my hand and the invisible force that held him. I could see the preternatural flesh healing the breach at his wrist.

"You call that stupid little sorcerer's apprentice of yours now," I said, "and you tell him to free my son, or I'll hack you up piece by piece. And I'll burn each piece in front of you." I leaned down and looked into his eyes. "Don't think about trying to loose that fatal fire on me," I said. "Or they'll burn you black and dead at once."

He was frozen in rage and panic. Unfortunate for him.

I yanked his arm out and swung the ax again right below his shoulder, slicing the arm free.

The screams that erupted from him shook the chandeliers. He stared down at the stump.

I flung the arm down the length of the table to the middle. At once several of the others pushed away from it, with the scrape of their chairs on the boards, and shrank back.

He stared at his arm, unable to stop the screams ripping from him until he clamped his right hand over his mouth. A long ghastly moan came from him.

More of the others had risen and were backing away from the table, a reaction that didn't surprise me.

Seeing someone dismembered is difficult even for vampires of supreme detachment and self-control—even when they know that the limbs can be reattached and thrive again. And of course, speaking of burning the limbs, well . . . that would take care of any future reattachment, wouldn't it?

"We need a brazier with coals," I said. "Or should we simply incinerate these fragments with the Fire Gift?" I glanced at the others, then back at Rhoshamandes "I'd tell the Voice to go to Hell, if I were you, and I'd call Benedict now and tell him to release my son."

I drew the phone out of my pocket.

"Benji, put the little thing on speaker, will you?" I slapped it down on the table.

Benji did as I had asked.

"I see your arm is already healing, friend," I said. "Maybe I should chop off both your legs at the same time."

With the greatest restraint, Rhoshamandes held back his sobs. I saw pure agony in his eyes as he looked at me, and then back at the severed arm and hand.

"I will command Benedict to kill the boy," said the Voice, filled with panic and rage as surely as Rhoshamandes was. "I will tell him now."

"No, you won't, Voice," I said under my breath. I looked down as I spoke to make it clear to everyone present that I was talking to the enemy himself. "Because if Benedict were like to do it, it would be done. He won't do any such thing until he knows his maker's safe. I'll wager his loyalty to his maker is a Hell of a lot stronger than his loyalty to you."

I turned to Rhoshamandes. "Now make us hear your fledgling Benedict talking through that phone now, clearly and distinctly, or I will chop off both your legs and split your breastbone with this ax."

Rhoshamandes put his right hand to his mouth now as if he were about to be sick. His face was blanched, and covered in a thin film of blood sweat. He was trembling violently. He reached for the phone and lifted it and struggled apparently to make his trembling fingers and thumb obey him.

He dropped the phone back onto the table, or it slipped out of his blood-tinged sweating hand.

All waited.

A voice came out of the phone, the voice of a blood drinker.

"Rhosh? Rhosh, I need you. Rhosh, everything has gone wrong!"

The Voice cursed me in French. Then in English. I was an abomination to it. Did I know that? I was anathema. I was all things foul and worthy of damnation.

"Benedict," I said coolly, "if you don't release my son unharmed, I'm going to chop your maker into pieces, do you understand? I've already chopped off his right hand and his arm. I'm going for his nose next, then his ears. And I'll burn these parts before I go for his legs. Do you want me to send you pictures of this?"

Indeed Benji was already snapping pictures with his own phone. The number from which Benedict was talking was plainly readable on Rhoshamandes's phone.

Benedict began weeping.

"But I can't," he said. "Please don't hurt him. I can't. I mean I . . . I mean Viktor's free. He's free. Rhosh, let me speak to Rhosh, Rhosh, I need your help, Rhosh help me. She's come alive. She's woken up. She's broken out of her bonds. Rhosh, she's going to destroy me. Viktor's free. Viktor has run away. Rhosh, everything went wrong."

Rhosh sat back in the chair and looked at the dark glass ceiling. A long shudder passed through his body. The stump below his shoulder had sealed itself off and he was no longer bleeding.

"Oh, Benedict," he said with a long groan.

"Tell us exactly where you are!" said Benji. "Tell us now. You force me to trace this phone of yours, and I swear to you, Lestat will split this creature's tongue."

I laughed. I couldn't help it. The Voice had fallen into a nest of sighs, gasps, malicious whispers, and growls.

"You've got to come!" said Benedict. "She's after me. She's walking along the beach."

"Take to the air," said Rhoshamandes in a low groaning voice. "She doesn't know she has that gift."

"But I did," Benedict stammered. "I'm up here safe on this bluff, but Rhosh, if I leave here and if she wanders off, if I lose sight of her, if we lose her, Rhosh, help me. If she falls down somewhere in the sun, if the sun strikes her, if we lose her . . ."

"You'll die," I said. "Where are you? Tell us now!"

"Montauk, the Atlantic coast, the tip of Long Island. Old Montauk Road. For God's sake, come."

At once Fareed and Seth made for the door.

"I want to come with you!" I shouted.

"No, stay here, please, and keep him here!" said Seth, with a nod to Sevraine and to Gregory. "Trust us to bring them back." He looked down at the phone. "Benedict, you harm that boy and we will kill you when we find you. And your maker will die here. You'll never see him again."

"I won't hurt him," Benedict said. "He's fine. I never wanted to hurt him. He's unharmed. He's walking inland towards the road. I didn't hurt him at all."

"I want to go with you," said Jesse, rising from her chair. David was right with her. "If anyone can calm Mekare, I can. Otherwise you might not be able to take her to safety. Let me come."

"Let us both come," said David.

"Of course, go," I said. "All of you, go."

Seth nodded, and they all left together.

The Voice was cursing me in some ancient language, promising to destroy me, promising me the most terrible reckoning, and I sat there at the end of the table, one knee up, the other leg dangling over the edge, the ax still in my right hand, and contemplated whether or not I wanted to go on chopping up this creature—well, just a little so that Benedict might hear him scream. I couldn't quite make up my mind.

And I could not stop thinking, This is the monster who murdered Maharet, the great Maharet who had never done him a particle of harm. This is the monster who attacked her as brutally as I am attacking him now.

I could hear Sybelle crying. I could hear a female voice, I think Bianca's voice, trying to quiet her. But she couldn't stop crying.

All the fight had gone out of Rhoshamandes. Sevraine was staring at him, fixedly, and so was Gregory—both clearly holding him there through their power. But I wondered if it was even necessary now.

He was defeated, staring dully at the table before him, but he was no longer trembling, no longer sweating, and then that expression came over him again, that same look of cavalier dismissal, almost a facial shrug, and he seemed to collapse mentally into himself.

"This is not the finish," the Voice snarled at me. "This is only the beginning. I will drive you out of your mind before this is finished. You will beg me to leave you alone, on your knees. You think this is finished? Never."

I turned him off. Just like that. Turned him off. But it didn't last.

He blasted through within a split second. It was as they had said. He was stronger. "I will make your existence miserable from now on and forever until I accomplish my purpose and then I will do to you all that you have done to him, and to me."

Allesandra walked slowly towards us and round in back of Rhoshamandes. She stood behind Rhoshamandes's chair and put her hands very lightly on his shoulders.

"Don't hurt him anymore, please," she said, appealing to me. "You have cut the Gordian knot, Lestat. Splendid. It is all splendid. But the Voice tricked him. The Voice duped him, as it duped me."

The Voice said, "You think you can shut me out! You think it's so easy? You think it's easy now that I'm stronger? You think you can do it now that I've recovered so much strength?"

"Voice," I said with a sigh. "Maybe we both have much to learn."

He began to weep. It was as loud and clear in my head as if he was in the very room. Again, I tried to shut him out. Again, I could not.

I opened my coat, wiped the blood off my ax on the lining of it, such pretty brown silk lining, and then I hooked the handle back in there under my arm.

"Give me back my arm and my hand, please," said Rhoshamandes.

"I will when my son is restored to me," I said.

To my astonishment, the sound of weeping came from the phone.

The Voice was quiet, but I could hear a low hiss that told me he was still here.

"Rhosh, are you there?" Benedict asked in a ragged aching tone.

"Yes, Benedict, I am. Are you watching her?"

"She's just walking along the sand. She sees me. She knows where I am. She's moving slowly towards me. Rhosh, this is horrible. Rhosh, talk to me."

"I'm listening, Benedict," said Rhosh wearily.

"She knows I'm the one who struck the fatal blow," Benedict cried. "Rhosh, it's all my fault. I kept thinking about it. I couldn't stop thinking about it, because I got this flash from her when I was binding her up. This flash, that she was with her sister, and her sister Maharet was alive and sitting beside her there and staring at me, and that's what I saw from her mind. And after you left, Rhosh, there was another one of those flashes from her, of the two of them together, and I knew she was awake down there, and I didn't know what to do, and then Viktor, Viktor set the house on fire."

We sat listening to this, all of us, without a word. Even the Voice was listening, I was sure of it. In the far corner, my beloved Rose was sitting against the wall, her knees drawn up, her fingers splayed in front of her eyes.

"He lit a fire in there, Rhosh. There were all these scented candles, matches, I didn't think, I never thought. He set a bundle of towels on fire in the shower stall. He set a towel on fire under the door, the wooden door. . . ."

"I understand Benedict," Rhosh said with a long sigh. His eyes were wearily fastened on his severed arm and hand.

"I went up there to put the fire out, and to try to make him stop it, to make him be patient. I told him no one was really going to hurt him! And then I heard sounds from the cellar. She was coming. I knew it. She was coming after me. I was talking to Viktor and she was there, Rhosh, in the door. I was terrified, Rhosh. Terrified and I couldn't get that image out of my head of bringing that blade down to kill Maharet. She knew. She saw it. She knew. And I thought, She's going to destroy me now, crush me with those white hands. But she just moved right past me and she went up to Viktor. She went to Viktor and, Rhosh, she started stroking his face and kissing him. And I ran."

He broke down in sobs.

Rhosh raised his eyebrows in the most bitter ironical expression, and perhaps this was far more indicative of his true heart than that cavalier dismissive expression that kept competing with it as he continued to look at his severed parts.

"I have to go now," said Benedict miserably. "They're down there on the beach with her. They have Viktor. But where should I go?"

"Come here," I said, "and collect your maker because as soon as my son is safe in my arms, I'll give him back what I've taken from him." I promised nothing else.

I stood up and turned and faced the others. I wondered how many of them wanted me to be their leader now. Well, I had given them a gruesome taste of what I was capable of, acts that were far more difficult to perform for anyone with a drop of humanity in him than simply blasting others away with invisible force or exterminating heat. I'd given them a really good taste of what sort of ruler I might be.

I expected a certain amount of contempt with an equal measure, I hoped, of grudging sympathy, but I saw nothing but simple expressions, eyes fixed on me as agreeably and even generously as ever. True, Sybelle was crying and Bianca was trying to comfort her, but I sensed no hostility from any of them.

Flavius was actually smiling at me. And Zenobia and Avicus were entirely calm. Pandora seemed lost in her own thoughts, and Arjun merely gazed at me with obvious admiration.

Gregory had a subtle smile on his face. And Armand's expression was very nearly the same. There was even the faintest smile on Louis's face, and that amazed me, though there was some other element in it, which I couldn't define. Notker was gazing at me with an open, affable expression, and Sevraine was looking coldly at Rhoshamandes without the slightest apparent emotion, while Eleni was looking up with frank admiration and Eugénie merely watched without obvious concern.

Armand stood up, his eyes as innocent and submissive as they always appeared.

"They'll be coming into the back garden," he said. "Let me show you the way."

"I think you should destroy this one," said Benji with a serious frown as he looked at Rhoshamandes. "He cares nothing about any of us. He cares only for his Benedict and himself."

Rhoshamandes showed no sign that this surprised him or even that he'd heard.

"Lestat," said Benji. "You are our prince now. Destroy him."

"He was tricked," said Allesandra again softly.

"They killed the great Maharet," said Notker under his breath. He gave a little shrug, one eyebrow raised eloquently. "They killed her. They took counsel from no one. They should have come to you, to the others here, to us."

"Except the Voice bewitched them," said Allesandra, "and the Voice lies and the Voice is treacherous."

I could hear the Voice snickering and murmuring and then he cried out, startling me, positively screaming in my head, exploding all rational thought, but I quickly regained my poise. "Destroy him," said the Voice. "He bungled everything."

I almost laughed out loud, but pressed my lips together in a bitter smile.

But Rhoshamandes knew what the Voice had just said to me. Rhoshamandes had picked it up from my mind.

He looked at me, but nothing changed in his calm face, and then slowly he looked away.

"I gave my word," I said to Benji. "When Viktor comes, we'll give him back these fragments. I can't break my word."

I went round the table and towards Rose.

She lay pale and shuddering against the satin pillows. I collected her in my arms and carried her out of the ballroom behind Armand.

25

Lestat

The Garden of Love

I**T WAS** a vast space, walled in brick, and lined with young oak trees rising some three stories with bright green leaves. There were banks of flowers, and pathways winding through patches of flowers, and all of this artfully lighted with electric bulbs concealed at the roots of the trees and the shrubbery, and little Japanese stone lanterns here and there on patches of grass with flickering flames.

The dull soothing roar of Manhattan seemed to enfold it as surely as the dim hulking outline of tall buildings behind it and on either side. Three townhouse gardens had been joined, obviously, to make this little paradise, this lovingly tended place that seemed as verdant and vital as an old New Orleans courtyard, safe from the throbbing world around it, and existing only for those who knew its secret or had the keys to its formidable gates.

Rose and I sat on the bench together. She was dazed, silent. I said nothing. What was there to say? She was a nymph beside me in her white silk dress, and I could feel her heart beating rapidly, hear the anguished thoughts struggling to achieve some coherence in her feverish mind.

I held her firmly with my right arm.

We were gazing on this little wilderness of thick pink hydrangea and luminous calla lilies, of creeping moonflowers on tree trunks and glistening white gardenias that gave off the most intoxicating scent. High above, the sky shone with reflected light.

They appeared as if out of nowhere. Fareed, with this radiant mortal boy in his arms. One moment we were alone, and then we saw them standing against the back wall, before the stately promenade of trees, and the boy—the young man—came towards us ahead of the dark hesitating figure of Fareed.

Rose ran to him. She rushed towards him and he took her at once in his arms.

Had I met him anywhere in this world, I would have been staggered by his resemblance to me, the bright golden hair, the way my hair had once been before the Dark Blood had lightened it and the repeated burnings had lightened it so that it shone almost white. That was how it had once looked, full and natural, like that, and this was a face I knew that looked at me now, a face that so resembled the boy I myself had once been.

I could see my brothers in him, my long-forgotten brothers who'd died unmourned in the mountains of the Auvergne, bodies left to rot by a mob of peasants in those awful days of revolution and destruction and competing visions for a brand-new world. A raft of sensations caught me off guard—smell of sunshine on the haystacks, and the straw bed in the sunlit room of the inn, taste of wine, sour and acidic, and the dreamy drunken vision from the inn window of that ruined château rising out of the very rocks, it seemed, a monstrous yet natural excrescence, in which I'd been born.

Rose released him tenderly as he walked towards me and I took him in my arms.

He was already passing me in height, and sturdier and more robust than I'd ever been, a human child of modern times of plenty, and out of his heart there came a palpable generosity of spirit, a great respecting curiosity and willingness to know, to love, to be overwhelmed. He was totally without fear.

I kissed him over and over. I couldn't help it. This was such fragrant and flawless human skin, this, and these eyes that looked into mine hadn't a particle of evil in them, and no conception of me or us as evil, and much as I couldn't understand this, I warmed to it almost to the point of tears.

"Father," he whispered.

I nodded, at a loss for words, and then murmured, "So it seems, and so it is. And the world's never given me such a treasure." But how weak these words seemed.

"You're not angry?" he asked.

"Angry! How could I be?" I responded. "How could I possibly be angry?" I embraced him again, held him as tight as I dared.

I couldn't conceive of his life, it was impossible, and the images flashing before me were fragmentary and did not achieve a story that I could follow at all.

Suddenly the Voice overpowered me.

"Enjoy your moment!" said the Voice, seething with anger. "Enjoy it, because you're not long to have many like it." And it began to sing loudly an ugly Latin hymn of gruesome metaphors that I'd heard many a time before.

I couldn't hear what Viktor was saying to me. The Voice was unstoppable. I tried to cut it off but it was rumbling on and on with the hymn. Rose was standing behind Viktor, and he turned and put his arm around her. She was obviously afraid.

I saw Mekare standing near. And Rose had seen her too. She was with Jesse and David and appeared bewildered but subdued—as white as calcite, her tangled red hair shimmering in the garden lights. Her gown was wrinkled and torn. Her feet were bare.

David and Jesse led her towards the back steps of the townhouse, but she stared at Viktor when she saw him, and though she still followed their lead, she slowed her pace. She looked at me and then at him. She stopped.

There came that flash from her, that flash that Benedict had described, Benedict who was here in the garden now with Seth. That flash of Maharet and Mekare together, seated in some quiet and restful spot. I saw it. The Voice was jabbering. It was a green spot in sunshine, and the twins were clear eyed and young. Just for a second they both appeared to look at me, long-dead daughters of another spring, and then this was gone.

"Can you see all this, Voice?" I asked. "Did you see that place?"

"See it, yes, I see it, I see it as you see it, because you see it, yes, I see it, and I knew it and I was a spirit there! So what!"

The Voice went on, roaring its curses, a lot of figurative ancient language that had little or no real meaning anymore. "A tomb!" he groaned. "A tomb."

And on she went into the house, the tomb, and then the miserable and weeping Benedict followed, not even glancing in our direction. Such a submissive and defeated figure, this Benedict, pretty like his maker, with sad reddened eyes, and walking with a modern demeanor, casually, without that sense of presence so effortlessly reflected by the older ones. You would have thought: Just a kid, just a student somewhere, just a boy.

Seth stopped.

"What do you want to do with him?" he asked me. "With them both?"

"You're asking me?" I said a little angrily. "Maybe we should decide that as a council." I could barely hear my own voice over the Voice. "I swore only to give Rhoshamandes back his severed limbs, but after that?"

"Kill them both," said the Voice. "They failed me. Kill them cruelly."

"The others will accept your decision, obviously," said Seth. "You're our leader now. Why wait for a council? Give the word."

"Well, I haven't really been anointed ruler yet, have I?" I said. "And if I have, well, I will call for a council before they're sentenced to death. Keep them here alive."

The Voice railed.

Viktor stood there staring at me as I spoke to Seth as if every little expression or nuance in my tone was of interest to him, absorbed him, transfixed him.

"As you wish," said Seth. "But I doubt anyone will question you if you terminate them both."

Terminate. Such a word. "That's unfortunate, if that's the case," I answered. "And it will not happen that way."

So this was his concept of monarchy, was it? Absolute tyranny. Good to know.

If he'd read my thoughts, he gave no sign. He nodded.

And he and Benedict moved on.

26

Lestat

Hostages to Fortune

WE TALKED in the library for hours. At first, I thought the Voice would render it impossible with all his ranting and screaming. But I was wrong.

It was a fine library, one of several in the three-part compound, and nothing innovative, only the same tried-and-true European decor that always warmed my heart. Walls of books to the plastered ceiling, books with fabulous titles including great novels and plays and classical histories and modern geniuses of prose—and the ceiling a work of art with its ornate running cornices and central medallion, and a chandelier of modest size and fine crystal casting a warm light over all. The murals were Italian, and slightly faded as if years of soot or smoke had overlaid them, but I found it better in some ways than the garish brightness of new work.

There was the usual French desk in the corner, the computers and flat screens, and the inevitable oversized leather chairs gathered around an antique mantelpiece of gray marble, with two bowed Grecian figures, heavily muscled and all but nude, supporting the overhanging shelf. And the mirror, the inevitable mirror rising from the mantel shelf to the ceiling, very broad and high, framed in gold with a mass of carved roses at the very top. Very similar all this to the rooms and fireplaces I designed for myself.

The fire was gas but it was beautiful. I'd never seen more artfully made porcelain logs.

And we talked there, Viktor and I together for hours, and then Rose came because she couldn't stay away, and no one had asked her to, but she'd wanted to give us this time.

At first I did strain to hear him in spite of the antics of the Voice. But within minutes, the Voice grew bored or had simply run out of invective and begun to mumble almost sleepily and was easy to ignore. Or maybe the Voice began to listen, because the Voice did indeed remain.

Viktor told me all about his life, but I still couldn't absorb it, this child reared by blood drinkers, knowing from the earliest age that I was his father, looking at rock videos of me revealing our history in images and song. Viktor knew all those songs I'd written. When he was ten years old, his mother had gone into the Blood. This had been agony for him, to see her transformed, but he'd tried to hide it from her and from Seth and Fareed but there was no hiding things from parents who could read your mind. And they were his parents, the three of them, and now he had a fourth parent. He said he was blessed. He'd always known his destiny was the Blood, that with every passing year he came ever closer to being with his mother and with Seth and Fareed.

I nodded to all this. I wanted more than anything to listen. He had a simple straightforward manner, but he sounded like a much older man than he was. He'd had very little time as a small child, really, with human beings, being educated directly by his mother and by Fareed. Sometime around the age of twelve, he'd started to have lessons on history and art from Seth, who tended to speak of the entire sweep of time in these matters, and often confessed what he himself was seeking to understand. Then had come painful years in England at Oxford where he'd gone as a prodigy and tried to mingle with other mortals, tried to love them and understand what they were and to learn.

"I was never frightened by any blood drinker ever in any way," he explained, "until this Rhoshamandes came, until he crashed through that wall. I knew he wasn't going to kill me, not immediately, that was obvious, and as for Benedict, Benedict was as kind as Seth or Fareed."

The Voice remained silent. I felt keenly that the Voice was hanging on Viktor's every word.

"When I burned the towels in the shower and under the door, I drew Benedict out immediately," said Viktor. "It was the simplest trick. He was in a panic. He's not what anybody would call clever. I've understood since early childhood that immortals aren't necessarily brilliant or cunning, or profoundly talented. They develop over centuries. Well, he's gullible. He's no nonpareil like Fareed or my mother. And that also makes him dangerous, very dangerous. He lives for Rhosh's commands. The whole time he was locking me up in that bathroom, he kept assuring me I'd be comfortable, well treated, Rhosh assured it. Rhosh wasn't cruel. Rhosh would free me soon enough. Rhosh and Rhosh and Rhosh."

He shook his head, and shrugged.

"Putting out the burning towels was easy. The house wasn't in the slightest danger. In fact I'm the one that sprayed the fires out with the handheld shower nozzle. He just stood there wringing his hands. He started apologizing to me, begging me to bear with all this, saying Rhoshamandes was only using me for leverage, that everything was going to work out and I'd be with you before dawn."

"Well, he was right about that much," I said with a short laugh. "What about Mekare? What happened exactly when she came up the steps?"

"I thought Benedict would die on the spot," said Viktor. "If immortals could seize up and die of heart failure, well, he would have been dead. The door was open and she came down a kind of landing towards us and she was looking directly at him, moving towards him with a kind of sluggish gait. I mean it was horrible actually, the way she was moving. But then she saw me, and her eyes tightened on me. She went right past him into the bathroom. He had to jump aside for her. And she came towards me. Again, I've never been frightened of blood drinkers, never, and she was just a little older than Seth. The sheer whiteness of her skin, that was the most startling aspect of her. Of course I knew all about her, I knew who she was."

He was wondering at it again, shaking his head. I try to anatomize his expression. It wasn't humility that he displayed, but rather a purity of heart that took things as they came without an obsession with self. I'd never been half as virtuous as he was when I'd been a young man.

"I greeted her respectfully," he explained. "I would have done that at any time. And then she touched me in the gentlest way. Her hands were freezing cold. But she was gentle. She kissed me. And that's when he bolted. This didn't register with her right away. I think she thought I was you. I think she thought I was you and she didn't question how that could be. She looked at me like she knew me, but when she did look back and see that he was gone, she turned and moved away from me.

"I waited till she was gone. I waited till she was all the way down the stairs and moving out the door. Then I went in search of a phone. I was going to call Fareed or Seth. Rhoshamandes had taken my phone. I figured it was somewhere. But I couldn't find it. And the house had no landline. I could have used Benedict's computer, probably, to reach Benji, but I didn't think things through. I wanted to get away. I was afraid Benedict would be back at any moment, or she would come back. I didn't know what to do.

"I took off on the road. I was still walking towards the front gates of the property when Seth appeared."

I nodded. It was as I'd imagined. Benedict had been the worst choice of an accomplice for all this, as the others had said. But neither of those two, Rhoshamandes or Benedict, was inherently vicious. And it is a great fact of history that the most mediocre and well-meaning imbeciles can strike down the mighty with surprising effectiveness when there is such a huge disparity of souls.

Did this make me more forgiving towards them? No. Maharet had died a shameful death, and I was in a rage over it, and had been since I saw the burnt-out rooms in the Amazon and the burnt remains. The great Maharet. I had to suppress this rage for the time being.

There was an interval of silence and the Voice railed at me that I'd better enjoy this little cozy tête-à-tête with my son because it might well be my last. But he was dispirited. This was all halfhearted.

Viktor had questions for me then about what happened, and when he started to talk again, the Voice went quiet.

I was rather reluctant to tell him what I'd done, but Rose had witnessed it so I did. "We're all human and preternatural," I said. "No matter how long we live. And few humans can bear seeing a hand or an arm chopped off. It was the best way to paralyze him, to shift the power in the room with one or two strokes. And frankly I suspect most blood drinkers aren't able to do that sort of chopping unless it's in the heat of battle when we're all butchers and fighting for our lives. I knew it would be a stalemate. It was a gamble, of course, but one I had to take. If Rhosh had fled . . ."

"I understand," said Viktor.

He was in complete agreement. He had not wanted to play any role in the Voice's game.

The Voice was listening quite attentively. I knew this. How I knew, I wasn't certain, but I could feel the intensity of his engagement.

Viktor and I talked on a long time after that. He told me about his studies at Oxford and later in Italy and how he had fallen in love with Rose.

They were well matched when it came to gifts, Viktor and Rose. Rose had bloomed into a graceful and striking young woman. Her black hair and her blue eyes were not the sum of it. She had a delicacy of form and feature that I found irresistible, and her face was stamped with a mysterious expression that elevated her from the merely beautiful to a different and very seductive realm. But Rose had a vulnerability to her that shocked Viktor. Rose had been wounded and defeated in ways Viktor scarcely understood. This had apparently sharpened his attraction to Rose, his desperate need to be with her and protect her and make her part of himself.

It struck me how very strange it all was that she should come to be the mortal in this world that Viktor, given his origins, should love. I'd sought to protect her from myself, and my secrets. But this never really works. And I should have known that it would not. In the last two years, I'd kept away from her with the best of intentions, certain she must meet her challenges without me, and disaster had nearly destroyed her, yet she'd found herself in the arms of my son. I knew how it had happened, beat by beat, yet it still amazed me.

I knew what he wanted. I knew what she wanted. This Romeo and Juliet, so bright and filled with human promise, were dreaming of Death, certain that in Death they would be reborn.

Rose was cuddled up beside Viktor in the big leather wing chair by that time, and he was holding her with obvious affection and her face was white with exhaustion. She seemed about to faint. I knew she had to rest.

But I had more to say. And why should it be delayed?

I stood up, stretched, feeling something like a silent nudge from the Voice, but no annoying nonsense, and I went to the mantel and placed my hands on it, and looked down in the dancing gas fire.

It was almost dawn.

I tried to think, for decency's sake, of what life might be for these two if we denied them the Dark Gift. But this was pointless. Really pointless. I didn't know that I could live with such a decision, and I was certain that they could not mentally or spiritually survive such a denial.

Yet I felt compelled to ponder. And ponder I did. I knew what Rose was suffering now, blaming herself for all her many misfortunes, none of which had ever been her doing. And I knew how much she loved Viktor and how much he loved her. Such a bond would strengthen both of them through the centuries, and I had to think now in terms of our tribe, our species, being something not accursed, no, never accursed—a tribe that must no longer be left to sink or swim in a sea of self-loathing and haphazard depravity and aimless struggle. I had to think of us as these two young ones saw us—as living an exalted existence that they wanted to share.

In sum, my change of heart towards my own nature, and the nature I shared with all the Undead, had to begin in earnest right now.

I turned to face them.

Rose was quite awake now, and they looked at me not with desperation but with a quiet trusting resignation.

"Very well then," I said. "If you would accept the Dark Blood, so be it. I don't oppose it. No. I do ask that the one who gives it to you be skilled at the giving. And Marius would be my choice for this, if he is willing, as he knows how to do it, passing the blood back and forth over and over, creating the most nearly perfect effects."

An immense change came over them silently, as they appeared to realize the import of my words. I could see that Viktor had a multitude of questions to ask me, but Rose had a quiet dignified expression on her face that I hadn't seen in her since I'd arrived. This was the old Rose, the Rose who knew how to be happy, not the quivering battered one making her way through the events of the last months with fragile and desperate faith.

"I say Marius as well for other reasons," I explained. "He has two thousand years and he is very strong. True there are others here who are infinitely stronger, but with their blood will come almost a monstrous power that is better understood when it is accrued over time. Believe me, I know, because I've drunk the Mother's Blood and I have far too much power for my own good." I paused. "Let it be Marius," I said. "And those who are older can share their blood with you and you will share some of their strength and that will be a great gift as well."

Viktor seemed deeply impressed with these thoughts, and I could see it was with difficulty that he questioned me.

"But, Father," he said. "All my life I've loved Fareed, and Fareed was made by Akasha's son."

"Yes, Viktor," I said. "This is true, but Fareed was a man of forty-five when he received Seth's blood. You're a boy and Rose is a girl. Take my advice in this, but I'm not unshakable on this point. Tomorrow we can make this decision, if you like, and it can be done at any time."

Viktor rose to his feet and Rose stood straight and confidently beside him.

"Thank you, Father," said Viktor.

"Now, it's almost dawn. I want you safely in the cellars."

"But why? Why must we be in the cellars now?" Viktor asked. He obviously didn't like the idea of being in a cellar.

"Because it's safest. You can't know what the Voice has done."

"That's very true," the Voice said in me with a laugh, a positive cackle.

"It might well have incited other blood drinkers to incite mortals against us," I said. "I want you in the cellar until sunset. This compound has a great staff of mortal guards, and that is good but I must take every precaution. Please do as I say. I'll be in this room for the time being. That's already been arranged. And I will see you both very soon indeed."

I held them both to me for a long moment before they left.

The door had the usual ornate little brass keys and a big brass bolt. I locked it up.

I fully expected the Voice to start ranting. But there was only silence and a dim little sound, almost a comforting sound, from the play of the gas flames on the porcelain logs. They had a rhythm all their own, these gas flames, a dance of their own. When I turned out the lights the room was pleasingly shadowy and dim.

I was steeling myself for the Voice.

Then the inevitable paralysis started to come over me. The sun rising over Manhattan. I kicked off my shoes and lay down on the long damask couch with a plump little needlepoint pillow for my head and closed my eyes.

There came a flash of the twins again. It was just as if I was there with them in that grassy place in the warm sunshine. I could hear the insects swarming in the fields nearby, swarming in the green shade beneath the nearby trees. And the twins were smiling and talking to me, and it felt we'd been talking forever, and then came the sound of the Voice weeping, and I said, "But what do you want me to call you! What is your true name?"

And in a tearful tone, he said, "It's what she always called me. She knew. My name is Amel."

27

Lestat

Mirror, Mirror on the Wall

AFTER SUNSET, I went on the air immediately with Benji. The Voice had whispered hateful words in my ear when I awakened, but it was completely quiet now.

We were in the fourth-floor studio with its microphones, phone banks, and computers, and Antoine and Sybelle were with us, Antoine to man the phones.

I was very proud of my handsome Antoine, proud of his composing, his piano playing, his violin playing, proud of his expertise with all this modern equipment, but there was not time now for any real reunion with him. That would have to wait. That I'd keep him close after this was a foregone conclusion. He was my fledgling and I would assume full responsibility for him.

But the broadcast was on my mind now. Benji reminded me that vampires all over the world were listening, that even the fledglings crowding the street below could hear the broadcast through their cell phones, and that my remarks would be recorded, and replayed all through the next day. When Benji gave me the signal, I started to speak in a low voice well below the frequency that mortal ears could hear.

I explained that Viktor, the unfortunate victim of a blood drinker kidnapping, had been returned safely and order in our world was being restored. I told the young vampires of the world who the Voice was and explained various ways of defending oneself against the

Voice. I explained this was Amel, the spirit that animated all of us and had only just come to consciousness. I explained I was in direct communication with the Voice and would do my best to quiet him and discourage him from attempting any more mischief. I assured them finally that I felt the Burnings were over for the most part—we had had no word of the Burnings in two nights, according to Benji—and that the Voice was now occupied in other ways. Then I made them a promise. Within a few nights, I would come to speak to them at some place where we might gather unseen. I did not know yet where that was to be. But I would give them the location when I did know and I would give them time to assemble.

When I said those words, I heard them roaring with approval in the street below, a ghost of a sound rolling up the walls and penetrating this studio. Benji smiled triumphantly, gazing at me as if I were a god.

"For now, you must do as I say," I said into the microphone. "You know what I am going to explain to you. But you must hear it again. No quarreling whatsoever amongst yourselves. No one, but no one, must strike out at another blood drinker. This is forbidden! And you must hunt the evildoer, never the innocent. There are to be no exceptions. And you are to have honor! You must have honor. If you do not know what honor is, then look it up in your online dictionaries and memorize the definition. Because if we do not have honor, we are lost."

I sat there in silence for a moment. Again, they were roaring and cheering in the street below. I was gazing off and into my thoughts. I knew the lights were flashing as calls were coming in from all over the world. Through Antoine's earphones I could hear him greeting each caller, and stabbing the lighted button to put each caller on hold.

The Voice had not said a word. And I wanted to say more as to the Voice, and so I did.

I was brief on this. But I said it.

"Understand, Children of the Night, that the Voice may have knowledge to share with us. The Voice may have gifts to give to us! The Voice may well become a precious gift to us in himself. The Voice is after all the fount of all we are; and the Voice has only just begun to express himself, to tell us what he wants us to know. No, we must not allow ourselves to be duped by the Voice into destroying one another. Never. But we must have patience with the Voice. We must have respect, and I mean this, we must have *respect* for who and what the Voice is."

I hesitated. I wanted to say more.

"The Voice is a mystery," I said, "and this mystery must not be treated by us with hasty and foolish contempt."

Inside me there was a silent convulsing as if Amel were responding and wanted me to know he was responding, but he didn't speak.

I went on talking again. I spoke of many things. I spoke softly into the microphone and spoke into a great silence—I spoke of the Little Drink and the art of it, to feed without taking life, I spoke of the elegance of compassion, to feed without cruelty. "Even mortals follow such rules when they hunt game," I said. "Are we not better than they are?" I spoke of territories where the evildoers still congregated, places of violence and want where humans were driven to cruelty and murder. I spoke of great communities devoid of such desperate villains, which could not become the hunting grounds of the Undead.

"This is the beginning," I said. "We will survive; we will define ourselves."

A deep conviction of all this had rooted itself in me. Or rather I was finding it within me, because perhaps it had always been there. "We will not behave as things to be despised simply because we are despised!" I said. "We must emerge from this crisis with a new will to prosper." I paused. Then I repeated the word "prosper." And I said again, because I couldn't stop myself. "Hell shall have no dominion over us. Hell shall have no dominion."

There came again that low rumbling explosion of applause and cheering from the streets around us, like a great sigh as it expanded and then began to die away.

I pushed the microphone back and in a silent passion left the studio as Benji began to answer the calls.

When I came down into the drawing room on the first floor, I saw that Rhoshamandes and Benedict were there surrounded by Sevraine, Gregory, Seth, and Fareed and others, and they were all in fast conversation with one another. Nobody, not even Rhoshamandes or Benedict themselves, asked if they might now be released.

There was so much more to be done, to be decided, so much more that the blood drinkers around the world could not fully understand. But for now, all was well under this roof. I sensed this. I felt it.

Rhoshamandes, dressed in fresh clothes, his arm and hand restored to him, was actually telling Eleni and Eugénie and Allesandra about his life after he'd left France centuries ago, and Gregory was asking him small rather interesting questions, and this proceeded, all of this, as if we'd never been at war the night before, and I'd never acted like the monster I was. And it was certainly proceeding as if he'd never murdered the great Maharet.

When he saw me in the door, Rhoshamandes only nodded at me and, after a respectful second or two, went back to what he'd been saying, about this place he'd built for himself, this castle in the northern seas. He appeared indifferent to me. But I secretly loathed the sight of him. And I could not stop myself from imagining what it had been like when he slaughtered Maharet. I could not forgive him for having done this. I was offended by this entire civilized gathering. I was deeply offended. But what did that matter? I had to think now not merely for myself but on behalf of everyone else.

There would come a time perhaps to reckon with him, I figured. And very likely he harbored a hatred for me on account of what I'd done that would bring about a time of reckoning for both of us much sooner than I desired.

On the other hand, perhaps the secret of his brutality was a shallowness, a resilience born out of cosmic indifference to what he'd done.

There was another blood drinker staring at him coldly from a distance, and that was Everard, the spiffy black-haired fledgling of Rhoshamandes now making his home in Italy, who sat silently in one of the corners of the room. His eyes were fixed on Rhoshamandes with cold contempt, but I caught glimpses of a mind there that was seething and making no effort to conceal its torment. Ancient fires, rituals, eerie singing in Latin, all this drifted through his consciousness as he stared at Rhoshamandes, quite aware of my presence and yet allowing me to glimpse these thoughts.

And so this fledgling hates his maker and why? Was it on behalf of Maharet?

Slowly, without turning his head Everard looked up at me and his mind went quiet and I caught from him the distinct response that he did indeed hate Rhoshamandes but for more reasons than he could say.

How in the world could any prince keep order amongst these powerful beings, I thought. Indeed the sheer impossibility of it rather crushed me.

I turned and left them all that way.

Way upstairs, Sybelle was playing her music. This must have been in the studio. Possibly Benji was breaking up the broadcast with it. It was comforting, the melody. I listened with all my being, and I heard only gentle voices all through the various chambers that made up this great and glorious house.

I was tired all over, dreadfully tired. I wanted to see Rose and Viktor, but not before I'd spoken to Marius.

I found him now in a library very much different from the one I'd come to love, a more dusty and crowded affair in the middle townhouse of the Trinity Gate complex, a room full of maps and world globes, and stacks of periodicals and newspapers as well as books climbing the walls, where he was at a battered old oak table spotted with ink, poring over a huge book on the history of India and Sanskrit.

He'd put on one of those cassocks that Seth and Fareed obviously favored, but his choice had been for a deep red-velvet fabric, and where he'd gotten it I had no idea, but it was Marius through and through. His long full hair was loose on his shoulders. No disguises or subtle accommodation of the modern world required under this roof.

"Yes, they have the right idea, surely," he said to me, "when it comes to clothing. Why I have ever bothered with barbarian garb, I'll never know."

He was talking like a Roman. By barbarian garb he meant trousers.

"Listen to me," I said. "Viktor and Rose must be given the Blood. I am hoping that you will do this. I have my reasons, but where do you stand with being the one?"

"I've already spoken to them," he said. "I'm honored and willing. I told them as much."

I was relieved.

I sat down in a chair opposite his, a big Renaissance Revival chair of carved wood that Henry VIII might have loved. It was creaky but comfortable. Slowly I saw the whole room was more or less Tudor in style. This room had no windows. But Armand had given it the effect of windows by heavy gold-framed mirrors set in every wall, and the hearth was Tudor, with black carvings, and heavy andirons. The coffered ceiling was scored by dark beams. Armand was a genius at these things.

"Then it is just a matter of when," I said with a sigh.

"Surely you don't want to bring them over until some decision has been made about the Voice," said Marius. "We need to meet again, all of us, don't we, as soon as you're willing?"

"Well, you would think in terms of the Roman Senate," I said.

"Why isn't he in my head or yours?" Marius asked. "Why is he so quiet? I would have thought he'd be punishing Rhoshamandes and Benedict but he isn't."

"He's in my head now, Marius," I said. "I can feel him. I've always known when he was absent or leaving. But now I know when he's simply there. It's rather like having a finger pressed against one's scalp or cheek or the lobe of one's ear. He's here."

Marius looked exasperated, and then plainly furious.

"He's stopped his relentless meddling out there," I said, "that's what matters." I gestured to the front of the house, towards the street where the young ones were milling, towards the wide world which lay to the east, and the west, and the south and the north.

"I suppose it would be pointless for me to scrawl a message to you on paper here," said Marius, "because he can read it through your eyes. But why bring over these two until we're certain that this thing is not yet going to destroy the entire tribe?"

"He's never wanted to do that," I said. "And there is no ultimate solution so long as he exists. Even in the most agreeable host, he can still plot and then travel, and then foment. I don't see any end to that except for one."

"Which is what?"

"That he might have some larger vision, some infinitely larger challenge, with which to occupy his mind."

"Does he want that?" Marius asked. "Or is that not something you've dreamed up, Lestat? You are such a romantic at heart. Oh, I know you fancy yourself hard-boiled and practical by nature. But you're a romantic. You always have been. What he wants perhaps is a sacrificial lamb, a perfect blood drinker, old and powerful, whose functioning brain he can take over and control relentlessly as he gradually obliterates its personality. Rhoshamandes was his prototype. Only Rhoshamandes wasn't vicious enough or foolish enough—."

"Yes, that does make sense," I said. "I'm exhausted. I want to go back to that little retreat I've found in the other building."

"What Armand calls the French library."

"Yes, exactly," I said. "He couldn't have designed a more perfect spot for me. I need to rest. To think. But you may do this with Viktor and Rose whenever you wish, and I say the sooner the better—don't wait, don't wait for any resolution that may never come. You do it, go on and do it, and you'll make them strong and telepathic and resourceful, and you'll give them the best instructions, and so I leave it to you."

"And if I do it with a bit of ceremony?" he asked.

"Why not?" I remembered the description of the making of Armand, how he'd taken the young Armand into a painted room in his Venetian palace and there amid blazing multicolored murals he had made him, offering the blood as sacrament with the most appropriate words. So different from my own making, that ruthless Magnus who was now a wise ghost, but had been then a warped and vile blood drinker, tormenting me as he brought me over.

I had to stop thinking of all this. I was bone tired, as mortals say. I rose to go. But then I stopped.

"If we are to be one tribe now," I said. "If we are to be a true sodality, then we can and should perhaps have our own ceremonies, rites, trappings, some way of surrounding with solemn enthusiasm the birth of others into our ranks. So do it as you wish and make a precedent, perhaps, that will endure."

He smiled.

"Allow me one innovation at the start," he said, "that I perform the rites with Pandora, who is nearly my same age, and very skilled at making others, obviously. We will share the making of each between us so that my gifts will go into both Rose and Viktor, and her gifts will go into both as well. Because you see, I cannot really bring both of them over perfectly at the same time on my own."

"Of course, as you wish," I said. "I leave this in your hands."

"And then it can be done with grace and solemnity for both at the same time."

I nodded. "And if they emerge from this telepathically deaf to one another, and deaf to both of you?"

"So be it. There's a wisdom in it. Let them have their silence in which to learn. When has telepathy really done us any great measure of good?"

I gave my assent.

I was at the door when he spoke again.

"Lestat, be careful with this Voice!" he said.

I turned around and looked at him.

"Don't be your usual impulsive self in lending this thing a sympathetic ear."

He stood and left the table, appealing to me with his arms out.

"Lestat, no one is insensible to what this thing endures in the body of one with dimmed eyes and stopped ears, a thing that can't move, can't write, can't think, can't speak. We know."

"Do you?"

"Give Seth and Fareed time, as long as the thing is quiet, to ponder this."

"What? The making of a ghastly machine?"

"No, but possibly some vehicle can yet be found—some fledgling brought over for the very purpose, with senses and faculties intact, but with little intellect or sanity at stake, and with a physicality—as a fledgling—that can be controlled."

"And this fledgling would be kept a prisoner, of course."

"Inevitably," he said. His arms dropped to his sides.

Inside me the Voice gave a long low agonized sigh.

"Lestat, if it's in your mind, it's going to go for your mind. And you must call us, all of us, to your aid if this thing begins to push you to the brink."

"I know that, Marius," I said. "I've never known myself, but I know when I'm not myself. That is certain."

He gave a soft despairing smile and shook his head.

I went out.

I went back to the French library.

Someone had been in here, one of those quiet, strange mortal servants of Armand's who went about the house like obedient somnambulists—and this one had dusted and polished, and laid out a soft green silk cover for me, over the back of the darker green damask couch.

The two small lamps burned on the desk.

I turned on the computer long enough to confirm at clear volume what I already knew. Benji was broadcasting vigorously. No Burnings anywhere on the planet. No word of the Voice from far and wide. No calls coming in from desperate victims.

I shut off the machine.

I knew *he* was with me. That subtle touch, that embrace of invisible fingers on the back of my neck.

I sat down in the largest of the leather wing chairs, the one in which Viktor and Rose had cuddled together last night, and I looked up at the great mirror over the mantel. I was pondering the hallucinations the Voice had once created for me in mirrors—those reflections of myself which he had so playfully ignited in my brain.

Those were hallucinations, surely, and I wondered just how far he might take such a power. After all, telepathy can do infinitely more than invade a mind with a logical string of words.

A quarter of an hour passed during which I considered all these things in an unguarded way. I looked dreamily at the giant mirror. Was I longing for him to show himself as my double, as he'd done before? Longing to see that clever impish face that wasn't my face and had to be some semblance of his intellect or soul?

The mirror reflected only the shelves of books behind me, the polished wood, the many differing volumes of varying thickness and height.

I became drowsy.

Something appeared in the mirror. I blinked, thinking that perhaps I was mistaken, but I saw it more clearly. It was a tiny amorphous reddish cloud.

It was swirling, growing bigger, and then shrinking and then expanding again, indistinct in shape, swelling, fading, growing ever more red, thickening again.

It began to grow larger, giving the illusion that it was coming closer to me, traveling steadily towards me from some point very far away, deep in the world of the mirror, where its diminutive size was an illusion.

Steadily towards me, it moved, and now it appeared to be swimming, propelling itself by the writhing work of myriad red-tinted tentacles, gossamer and transparent tentacles, moving as if through water, as if it were a sea creature of innumerable translucent arms.

I couldn't take my eyes off it. It seemed the mirror was just a piece of glass. It was traveling towards me from a vast dark and cloudy world in which it was purely at home.

Suddenly it resembled nothing so much as a reddish Medusa's head but with a tiny dark visage, tiny, and with writhing red serpentine arms beyond count. They had no serpent heads, these arms. And the entire image retained its ruby-red-tinged transparency. The face—and it was a face—grew larger and larger as I stared at it amazed.

It became the size of an old silver half dollar as I watched, and the countless translucent tentacles seemed to elongate and become ever more delicate, dancing as they did so, dancing, reaching outward beyond the frame of the mirror on either side.

I stood up.

I moved towards the fireplace. I looked directly into the mirror.

The face grew larger and larger and I could now make out tiny glittering eyes in it, and what seemed a mouth, a round mouth of elastic shifting shape, a mouth seeking to be a mouth. The great mass of crimson tinted tentacles now filled the mirror to the very frame.

The face grew bigger, and it seemed the mouth which was only a dark cypher stretched into a smile. The eyes flashed black and filled with life.

Bigger and bigger grew the face as though the being were indeed still moving towards me, moving towards the barrier of this glass that divided us, and the face slowly grew to be the size perhaps of my own.

The dark eyes expanded, took on the human accoutrements of eyelashes and eyebrows; a semblance of a nose appeared, and the mouth had lips. The whole mirror now was filled with the deep pellucid red of this image, a soft elusive red, the color of blood suffusing the tubular tentacles and the face, the slowly darkening face.

"Amel!" I cried out. I gasped for breath.

The dark eyes grew pupils as they looked at me, and lips smiled as the opening had smiled before. An expression bloomed on the surface of the face, an expression of unutterable love.

Pain fused with the love, undeniable pain. The expression of pain and love so fused in the face that I could hardly bear to look at it, aware suddenly of a huge pain inside me, inside my heart, pain blooming in me as if it were unstoppable, out of all control, and would soon be more than I could bear.

"I love you!" I said. "I love you!" And then without words I reached out towards it. I reached out and I told it that I would embrace it, I would know it, I would take into myself its love, its pain. *I will take into myself what you are.*

I heard the sound of weeping only it had no sound. I heard it rising all around me the way the sound of falling rain can rise as it strikes more and more surfaces around one, pattering on streets and roofs and leaves and boughs.

"I know what's driven you to these things!" I said aloud. I was crying. My eyes were filling with blood.

"I would never have hurt that boy," whispered the Voice inside me, only it was coming from this face, this tragic face, these lips, this one looking into my eyes.

"I believe you," I said.

"I will never hurt you."

"I will give you all that I know," I said, "if only you'll do the same with me! If only we can love one another! Always, completely! I will not suffer you to go into any other but me!"

"Yes," he said. "You have always been my beloved. Always. Dancer, singer, oracle, high priest, prince."

I reached out for the mirror, slapping my hands on the glass. The eyes were huge, and the mouth was long and serene with curving lips, expressive lips.

"In one body," said the Voice. "In one brain. In one soul." A sigh came from it. A long agonizing sigh. "Don't fear me. Don't fear my suffering, my cries, my frantic power. Help me. Help me, I beg you. You are my redeemer. Call me forth from the tomb."

I reached out with every fiber of my being, my hands pressing the glass, shuddering against it, my whole soul wanting to pass into the mirror, into the bloody-red image, into the face, into the Voice.

And then the image was gone.

I found myself on the carpet, sitting there, as if I'd been pushed or fallen backwards, staring up at the bright empty mirror reflecting again the contents of the room.

There was a knocking at the door.

Somewhere a clock was striking the hour. So many chimes. Was it possible?

I rose to my feet and went to the door.

It was midnight. The last chime had just echoed through the hallway.

Gregory and Seth and Sevraine were there. Fareed was with them and David and Jesse and Marius. Others were nearby.

What had drawn them here now, just now? I was dazed. What could I say to them?

"There is so much we want to talk about," said Gregory. "We're not hearing the Voice. None of us are. The world's quiet, or so it tells Benji upstairs. But surely this is only an intermezzo. We must plan."

I stood there quietly for a long moment, hands clasped just under my chin. I lifted my right hand, one finger raised.

"Am I your leader?" I asked. It was so hard for me to speak, to form the simplest words. "Will you accept my decision as to the disposition of the Voice?"

No one answered for a moment. I couldn't shake off the languor I felt. I couldn't rally. I wanted them all to leave me now.

Then Gregory said softly, "But what possible disposition for the Voice can there be? The Voice is in the body of Mekare. Mekare is quiet now. The Voice is quiet. But the Voice will begin to scheme again. The Voice will plot."

"This creature, Mekare," said Sevraine, "she is a living thing. She knows, in some brutal and simple way, she knows her tragedies. I tell you she knows."

Seems Fareed said something about reasoning with the Voice, but I scarcely heard him.

Seth asked me if I was hearing the Voice. "You are communing with it, aren't you? But you've sealed yourself off from us. You're battling the Voice alone."

"So this is the decision you want from me?" I asked. "That the Voice remain with Mekare?"

"What other decision can there be for now?" asked Sevraine. "And whoever else takes this Voice into himself risks being driven mad by it. And how can anyone seize Amel from Mekare without ending her life? We have no recourse but to reason with it as it lives inside of her."

I drew myself up. I had to appear alert, even if I was not, in control of my faculties, even if I was not. I was by no means irrational. It's simply that I had to return to a state of examining these things on my own which I could not share.

Gregory was trying to read my thoughts. They all were. But I knew too well how to lock them out. And in the dark little sanctum of my heart I saw that blood-red face, that suffering face. I beheld it in pure wonder.

"Put aside your fears," I said. My tongue was thick, and I didn't sound like myself to me. I looked directly at Gregory, then at Seth, then at each of the others in so far as I could see them. Even at Marius who reached out to grasp my arm.

"I want to be alone now." I removed Marius's hand from me. The Latin words came to me. "*Nolite timere*," I said. I gestured for patience as I started to close the door.

Slowly they withdrew.

Marius bent forward to kiss me and he told me that they would all be in the house till morning. No one was leaving. Everyone was here, and that when we were ready to talk with them further, they'd come together at once.

"Tomorrow night," said Marius, "at the hour of nine, Viktor and Rose will be brought over by Pandora and me."

"Ah, yes," I answered. "That's good." I smiled.

At last, the door was shut once again, and I moved back into the room. I sat down again, on the leather ottoman of one of the chairs, near to the fire.

Moments passed. Perhaps half an hour. Now and then I drew to myself the random sounds of the house, and the great metropolis beyond, and then banished those sounds as if I were a magnet at the center of a consciousness greater than myself.

It seemed the hallway clock struck the hour. Chimes and chimes and chimes. And then after the longest time, the clock chimed yet again. The house was quiet. Only Benji's voice went on way up there in his studio, talking gently and patiently to the young ones, those isolated on far continents and in far cities, still desperate for the comfort of his words.

Easy to close myself off from that. And the clock chiming again as if it were an instrument being played by my hand. I did like clocks. I had to admit it.

There came that vision of sunshine and green fields. The soft musical sound of the insects humming and the soft rustle of trees. The twins sat together and Maharet said something to me in the soft ancient tongue that I thought very amusing and very comforting, but the words were gone as fast as they'd come, if there had ever been words before.

There was a slow trudging step in the hall beyond the door, a heavy step that made the old boards creak and the deep sound of a powerful beating heart.

The door opened slowly, and Mekare appeared.

She'd been lovingly restored since last night, and wore a black wool robe trimmed in silver. Her long hair was brushed and clean and lustrous. And someone had also fastened a fine collar of diamonds and silver around her neck. The sleeves of the gown were long and full, and the robe draped exquisitely on her, on the girlish body that was now a thing of stone.

Her face was fiercely white in the light of the fire.

Her pale-blue eyes were fixed on me but the flesh around them was softened as it had always been. The fire glinted on her golden eyelashes, on her golden eyebrows, and on her white hands and face.

She came towards me with those slow steps as if the effort cost her body pain, pain that she did not acknowledge, but pain which slowed her every movement. She took her place in front of me, the fire just to her right.

"You want to go to your sister, don't you?" I asked.

Very slowly, her pink lips, so very like the pink insides of a seashell, spread into a smile. The masklike face fired with subtle perception.

I rose to my feet. My heart was pounding.

She lifted her two hands, palms turned inwards, and gradually brought her fingers to her eyes.

With her left hand poised, she reached with her right hand for her right eye.

I gasped, but it was done before I could stop her, and the blood was pouring down her cheek, the eye gone, plucked out and fallen to the floor, and only the empty bleeding socket was there and then her fingers—the first two fingers—once more jabbed, jabbed into the blood and broke the tender bones, the tender occipital bones, at the back of the eye socket. I heard the little cone of bones snap and shatter.

I understood.

She reached out to me, imploring me, and out of her there came a low desperate sigh.

I took her head in my hands and closed my lips on the bleeding eye socket. I felt her powerful hands caressing my head. I sucked with all my strength, drawing as strongly as ever I'd drawn blood in my life, and I felt the brain coming into my mouth, flowing viscous and sweet as the blood, flowing out of her and coming into me. I felt it fill my mouth, a great gusher of tissue against all the tender flesh inside my mouth, and then filling my throat as it passed down into me.

The world went dark. Black.

And then it exploded with light. All I could see was this light. Galaxies exploded in this light, whole sweeping pathways of innumerable stars pulsed and disintegrated as the light grew brighter and brighter. I heard my own distant cry.

Her body had gone limp in my arms, but I wouldn't let it go. I held fast, drawing on the blood, drawing on the gusher of tissue, drawing and drawing and hearing the beat of her heart swell to deafening volume and then stop. I swallowed again and again until nothing but blood was in my mouth. My own heart exploded.

I felt her body fall to the floor but I saw nothing. Blackness again. Blackness. Disaster. And then the light, the blinding light.

I lay on the floor my arms and legs outstretched, and a great searing current was moving through my limbs, through my organs, through the chambers of my heart. It pervaded every cell of my skin, all over my body, my arms, my legs, my face, my head. Like electricity it burned through every circuit of my being. The light flashed and brightened. My arms and legs were flopping and I couldn't control them but the sensations were orgasmic and they had become my body, all heavy tissue and bone suddenly gathered up into this weightless yet glorious thing that I was.

My body had become this light, this throbbing, pulsing, shivering light, this simmering light. And I felt as if it were pouring out of me through my fingers and my toes, through my cock, through my skull. I could feel it generated and regenerated inside me, inside my pounding heart and pouring out so that I seemed immense, immense beyond all imagining, expanding in a void of light, light that was blinding, light that was beautiful, light that was perfect.

I cried out again. I heard it but never meant to do it. I heard it.

Then the light flashed as if to blind me forever, and I saw the ceiling above me, and I saw the circle of the chandelier—the flashing prismatic colors of that chandelier. The room came down around me as if descending from Heaven and I was not on the floor at all. I was standing on my feet.

Never in all my existence had I felt so powerful. Not even ascending with the Cloud Gift had I ever known such fearlessness, such buoyancy, such limitless and utterly sublime strength. I was climbing to the stars yet I had not left the room.

I stared down at Mekare. She was dead. She had sunk to her knees and then fallen on her right side, her blighted eye socket hidden, her left profile perfect as she lay there staring forward with one half-lidded blue eye as if she were asleep. How beautiful she looked, how complete, how like a flower fallen there on the gravel path of a garden, how destined for this fragile moment.

The sound of wind filled my ears, wind and singing as if I'd passed into realms of angels, and then voices assailed me, voices from everywhere, rising and falling in waves, relentless voices, voices in splashes, as if someone were splashing the very walls of my entire universe with great splashes of molten gold paint.

"Are you with me?" I whispered.

"I am with you," he said clearly, distinctly in my brain.

"Do you see what I see?"

"It's magnificent."

"Do you hear what I hear?"

"It's magnificent."

"I see as never before," I said.

"As do I."

We were wrapped in a cloud of sound together, immense, unending, and symphonic sound.

I looked down at my hands. They were throbbing as was all my body, as was the whole brilliant world. Never had they seemed such a miracle of texture and perfection.

"Are these your hands?" I asked.

"They are mine," he said calmly.

I turned to the mirror.

"Are these your eyes?" I asked, staring into my own.

"They are mine."

I gave a long low sigh.

"We are beautiful, you and I," he said.

Behind me in the glass, behind my still awestruck face, I saw them all. They had all come into the room.

I turned to face them. Every single one of them was gathered here now from right to left. They were astonished. They looked at me, not a single one speaking, not a single one looking with surprise or horror at the body of Mekare on the floor.

They had seen it! They had seen it in their minds. They'd seen it, and they knew. I had not shed her precious blood. I had not done her violence. I had accepted her invitation. All of them knew what had happened. They'd felt it, inescapably, just as I'd felt it on that long-ago day when Mekare took the Core from Akasha.

Never had they or any gathering of persons looked so very distinct to me, each individual there radiant with a subtle power, each stamped with a signature of distinct and defining energy, each marked with a unique gift.

I couldn't stop looking at them, marveling at the details of their faces, at their delicate flashing expressions playing over eyes and lips.

"Well, Prince Lestat," cried Benji. "It is done."

"You are our prince," said Seth.

"You are anointed now," said Sevraine.

"You were chosen," said Gregory, "by him and by her, by him who animates all of us, and by the one who was our Queen of the Damned."

Amel laughed softly inside me. "You are my beloved," he whispered.

I stood silent, feeling a slow subtle movement inside of my body, as if some fine tangle of tendrils were moving purposefully out of my brain and down the length of my spine and then out again through my limbs. I could see this as I felt it, see its subtle golden electric pulse.

Out of the depths of my soul, my soul that was the sad and struggling sum of all I'd ever known, I felt my own voice yearning to say, *And I will never be alone again.*

"No, you will never," said the Voice, "you will never be alone again."

I looked at the others once more, all gathered there so expectantly and in awe. I could see the muted wonder in Marius, and the quiet sad trust in Louis, and the childlike amazement in Armand. I saw their doubts, their suspicions, their questions all so uneasily subsumed in the moment by wonder. I knew.

And how could I ever explain how I had reached this moment, I who had been Born to Darkness of rape, and sought for redemption in a borrowed mortal body, and followed spirits yet unexplained to realms of inexplicable Heaven and nightmarish Hell, only to fall back again to the brutal Earth, broken, and battered, and defeated? How to explain why this, this alone, was the bold and terrifying alliance that would give me the passion to travel the road of the centuries, of the millennia, of the aeons of uncharted and unimagined time?

"I will not be the Prince of the Damned," I said. "I give no power to that old poetry! No. Never. We claim now the Devil's Road as our road, and we will rename it for ourselves and our tribe and our journey. We are reborn!"

"Prince Lestat," said Benji again, and then Sybelle echoed it, and then Antoine and Louis and Armand and Marius and Gregory, Seth, Fareed, Rhoshamandes, Everard, Benedict, Sevraine, Bianca, Notker, all of them echoed it, and on the words kept coming from those for whom as yet I had no names.

Viktor stood in the shadows with Rose, and Viktor said it and so did Rose, and Benji shouted it again, throwing up his hands and balling his fists.

"They are beautiful," said Amel. "These children of me, these parts of me, this tribe of me."

"Yes, beloved, they have always been that," I answered. "That has always been true."

"So beautiful," he said again. "How can we not love them?"

"Oh, but we do," I said. "We certainly do."

Part IV

THE PRINCIPALITY
OF
DARKNESS

28

Lestat

The Prince's Speech

M Y FIRST TRUE DECISION as monarch was that I wanted
to go home to France. This monarch was going to rule
from his ancestral Château de Lioncourt on one of the
most isolated mountain plateaus of the Massif Central where he had
been born. And it was also decided that Armand's luxurious house
in Saint-Germaine-de-Prés would hence forward be the Paris headquarters of the court.

Trinity Gate would be the royal residence in New York, and we
would have the ceremony for Rose and Viktor tomorrow night at
Trinity Gate as planned.

An hour after the transformation—when I was at last ready for
it—we took the remains of Mekare from the library, and buried
them in the rear garden in a spot surrounded by flowers and open to
the sun in the day. We were all to a one gathered for this, including
Rhoshamandes and Benedict.

Mekare's body had turned to something resembling clear plastic,
though I detest the crudeness of that word. What blood she'd retained
had pooled as she lay on the floor and her remains were largely completely translucent by the time we carried her to her grave. Even her
hair was becoming colorless, and breaking apart into myriad silver
needlelike fragments. So Sevraine and my mother and the other
women laid her out on a bier for the burial, placing the missing eye
back into its socket, and covered her over with black velvet.

We stood silent at the site as she was laid to rest in what was a shallow but completely adequate grave. Flower petals were gathered by some of us from throughout the garden and these were sprinkled over the bier. Then others gathered more flowers. I turned back the velvet one last time and bent down to kiss Mekare's forehead. Rhoshamandes and Benedict did nothing, because they obviously feared the censure of all if they tried to make any gesture. And Everard de Landen, the French-Italian fledgling of Rhoshamandes, was the last to place several roses on the corpse.

Finally, we began to fill the grave with earth, and soon all sight of Mekare's form was lost.

It was agreed that two of those vampire physicians working for Seth and Fareed would go to the Amazon compound and exhume whatever remained of Khayman and Maharet and bring those relics here to be laid to rest with Mekare sometime in the coming month. And of course I knew full well that Fareed and Seth would harvest samples from those remains. Possibly they had done it with Mekare, but then again perhaps not, as this was a solemn occasion.

David and Jesse would also go there to retrieve whatever had survived of Maharet's library and archives, of her keepsakes and belongings, and any legal papers that were worth preserving for her mortal family or for Jesse herself.

I found all this unrelievedly grim, but I noticed that the others, to a one, seemed comforted by these arrangements. It took me back to the night long ago when Akasha had died at the hand of Mekare. I realized with shame I had not the slightest idea what had become of her corpse.

Not to care, not to question, not to bother—all this had been part of the old way for me, one of shame and melancholy, an existence in which I assumed completely that we were cursed and the victims of the Blood as surely as mortals thought themselves to be the guilty victims of Original Sin. I had not seen us as worthy of ceremonies. I had not believed in the small coven that Armand had sought to rescue from those ghastly nights when he created the old Night Island for us to gather in the Florida climes.

Well, I saw the sense of all this now. I saw its immense value, for the old and the young.

I had been tired before the momentous change had been worked and, elated as I was—and the word does little justice to what I felt—I was still tired and needing to be alone now, alone with Amel.

But before I retired for the night, back to the French library, I felt we had to meet in the attic ballroom once more around the long rectangular gilded table that was still in place as it had been for our first assembly.

For one thing, every single immortal inhabitant of the household was watching me, trying to figure how Amel was infecting and affecting me, and I knew this, and so I had no hesitation about spending more time with them now.

So we returned to the long golden table and chairs. I stood at the head as before. Rose and Viktor kept to the wall with those retiring blood drinkers brought to Trinity Gate by Notker and Sevraine, whom I was determined to come to know before I left this place.

Whatever it might have been like for Akasha or Mekare to hold the Core, I couldn't know. But for me, having Amel inside of me multiplied and expanded my senses and my energy beyond measure. I still saw each of them and all of them when I looked at the assembly in a new and remarkably vivid way.

"I think this ballroom should be the place for Rose and Viktor to receive the Dark Gift," I said. "The table should be broken up and its parts put back on the periphery. I think the place should be filled with all the flowers from the shops of Manhattan that it can hold. Armand's local mortal agents can surely see to this during the daylight hours." He at once agreed. "And I suggest that all be present under the roof, but not in this room, leaving this room alone to Rose and to Viktor and Pandora and Marius for the giving of the Gift."

No one objected.

"Then at such a time as the ceremony is complete, others may be invited up, one by one, to give their ancient blood. Gregory, Sevraine, Seth. Perhaps you will agree to this. Marius, and Pandora, you will approve. Rose and Viktor, you will be willing. And I will give you a measure of my blood then too."

Agreement all around.

"Marius and Pandora can then take the fledglings down to the garden," I said, "for the physical death and its pain. And when that's past, they can be clothed in new garments and come into the house reborn. After that, Marius and Pandora can take our young ones out to experience the hunt for the first time."

Again there was obvious and enthusiastic agreement.

Rhoshamandes asked for permission to speak.

I gave it.

His arm and his hand had been working perfectly since their reattachment with no problem whatsoever as I knew they'd be, and he was handsomely clothed in a tailored gray leather jacket and a sweater of lighter gray wool.

He looked cool and collected and charming as if he'd never hacked anyone to death or kidnapped anyone, or threatened to kill my son if he didn't get his way.

"I can well understand if no one wants me to do more than be a quiet prisoner here," he said. "But I will give my blood to the young couple if they will accept it. And maybe this can go towards my forgiveness by this group."

Viktor and Rose waited on me for my response. And I, after looking intently at Rhoshamandes and Benedict for a long moment, noting the dazzling equanimity of the former and the obvious abject misery of the latter, said yes to this if Marius and Pandora approved, and if Viktor and Rose gave their consent.

Understand, I could hardly believe myself that I was doing this, but the Prince was in charge now and the Brat Prince was no more.

The motion carried, so to speak.

"I am sorry from my heart," said Rhoshamandes, with amazing calmness. "I have truly in my long life among the Undead never sought conflict even when others thought I should. I am sorry. I lost my own fledglings to the Children of Satan rather than make war. I ask the tribe to forgive me, and to accept me as one of its own."

Benji was staring at him with fierce narrow black eyes, and Armand was looking up at me from his chair with slightly raised eyebrows, and Jesse merely looked at him coldly, her arms folded. David had no discernible expression, but I felt I knew what he was thinking even though I couldn't read his thoughts.

What precisely are we to do with this one if we don't accept him back into the tribe? And what danger is he to anyone if we do?

Well, as I saw it, he was no danger. If he was not accepted, well then, he might become a danger, especially if others took this to mean that he had been "proscribed" like the ancient enemies of the dictator Sulla, who were then free game to be murdered by their Roman brethren. I was no Sulla.

I listened quietly for the voice of Amel, conscious that I wanted very much to know what he had to say. All had changed between us so totally that he was no longer even the specter in my mind of the old Voice. But if I had underestimated the complexity of all this, I did want a hint of that now.

In the silence, I heard his faint whisper. "I used him. Can we not be thankful that he failed?"

"Very well," I said. I turned to Rhoshamandes. "I say your apology is accepted. You are a member of this tribe. I can see no threat from you now to anyone here. Who disagrees with me on this? Speak up or forever be quiet."

No one spoke up.

But there were tears in the eyes of the regal, ashen-haired Allesandra when I said this and Rhoshamandes nodded and took his seat. I'm not sure anyone but I caught Everard's sharp personal glance to me and the confidential negative shake of his head.

Benedict looked confused, and so I directed my remarks to him.

"You are now once more in good standing," I said. "Whatever you did, and why ever you did it—all this is now closed."

But I knew this was small comfort to him. He'd live for years with the horror of what he'd done.

It was by that time almost 4:00 a.m., and sunrise would occur in slightly over two hours.

I stood silent at the head of the table. I could feel all these eyes on me as fixed and probing as ever, but I felt most keenly the scrutiny of Seth and Fareed, though why I wasn't sure.

"We have much to do," I said, "all of us, to establish what it means for us and for all those blood drinkers out there the world over that we are now one proud tribe, one proud People of Darkness, one proud race that seeks to prosper on this Earth. And as it has fallen to me to rule, by invitation and by unique selection, I want to rule from my home in the Auvergne.

"I live now in my father's castle there, almost fully restored, a great stone edifice including as many comfortable chambers as this amazing house in which we're gathered now. And I will be your prince."

I paused to let the point be absorbed, then I went on.

"Prince Lestat I will be," I said. "That is the term that's been offered to me over and over in one form or another, it seems. And my court shall be in my castle, and I invite all of you to come there and help forge the constitution and the rules by which we'll live. I will need your help in deciding a multitude of questions. And I will delegate to those of you who are receptive various tasks to help us move to a new and glorious existence which I hope that all the blood drinkers of the world will come to share."

Benji was now close to tears. "Oh, if only this were being recorded!" he declared. Sybelle told him to be quiet, and Armand was laughing silently at him but also motioning for him to restrain himself.

"You may report my words in full whenever you wish," I said. "You have my express permission."

With a subtle gesture he opened his spiffy little jacket to reveal an iPhone peeping out of his inner pocket.

"Marius," I said, turning to him. "I ask that you write for us all the rules by which you've lived and prospered for centuries, as I've never found anyone more ethical in these matters than you are."

"I'll do my best with this," said Marius.

"And Gregory," I said. "Gregory, you who have survived with such astonishing success in the mortal world, I ask that you help to establish a code by which blood drinkers can effectively interact with mortals to preserve their material wealth as well as their secrecy. Please give us the benefit of all you've learned. I have much to share on this and so does Armand, but you are the past master."

"I'm more than willing," said Gregory.

"We must assist the most befuddled fledgling out there in obtaining whatever papers and documents are required to move from place to place in the physical world. We must do our best to halt the creation of a class of desperate vampiric tramps and marauders."

Benji was beside himself with excitement at all these proceedings. But he was shocked when I turned now to him.

"And you, Benjamin, obviously you must be our Minister of Communications from now on; and wherever in the world I am I will be in communication with you here at your headquarters every night. We must talk, you and I, about the radio program and the website, and what more we can do together through the internet to gather the lost sheep in the Blood."

"Yes!" he said with obvious joy. He lifted his fedora in salute to me and it was the first time that I'd seen his adorable little round face and cap of curly black hair for what they were.

"Notker," I said. "You've brought your musicians here, your singers, your violinists, and they've joined with Sybelle and with Antoine, and given us the extraordinary pleasure that only blood drinker musicians and artists can give. Will you come with me to my court in the Auvergne and help to create my court orchestra and my court choir? I want this with my whole heart."

"Oh, my prince, I'm at your service," said Notker. "And my own humble fiefdom is only minutes away from you in the Alps."

"Seth and Fareed," I said. "You are our physicians, our scientists, our bold explorers. What can I do? What can all of us do to support you in your ongoing work?"

"Well, I think you know," said Seth. "There's much we can learn from you and from . . . Amel." Understatement. Burning eyes.

"You'll have my complete cooperation always," I said. "And you'll have your rooms at my court and whatever else you need or desire. And I will be open to you, and offer you whatever knowledge or experience that I can."

Fareed was smiling, obviously pleased, and Seth was satisfied for the moment but not without grave suspicions of what might lie ahead.

"We will never again, any of us here, be isolated from one another, in exile, and unreachable." I stopped, taking the time to meet the eyes of each and every one present. "We must all promise. We must maintain our lines of communication, and we must seek to see how we may benefit from one another as a united people. For that is what we are now, not so much the Children of Darkness, but the People of the Savage Garden, because we have come of age as such."

I stopped. People of the Savage Garden. I didn't know if it was the right or ultimate term for us. I had to think on that, the matter of an ultimate term—consult, listen to the inevitable poetry that would rise to create a term from all the tribe. For now I had done the best that I could do. There was so much more to be done. But I was tired, raggedly tired.

I motioned that I needed a moment to collect my thoughts. And I was startled to hear a soft applause break out in the room that soon included everyone, it seemed, and then died away quietly.

So much more to say.

I thought again of Magnus, that ghost, Magnus who'd come to me in the golden caves of Sevraine's little city in Cappadocia. I thought of Gremt, the grand spirit who had been there too.

"And we must take up one more matter now," I said. "It's the matter of the Talamasca. It's the matter of what they've made known to me and Sevraine about their members."

"And to me as well," said Pandora. "I've met Gremt as I know you have, the spirit who in fact brought the Talamasca into being."

"And I too have been contacted by them," said Marius. "And a meeting with them soon might be to the benefit of us all."

Again, I listened for Amel, but there was only silence, and the warm subtle embrace under my skin that let me know he was there. I was looking down. I waited.

"Learning, Prince Lestat," he said in the lowest whisper. "Learning as I have never dreamed it was possible to learn."

I looked up. "Yes, and we will indeed meet with them, meet with those who've revealed themselves to us, and we will determine among other things how to treat the old ongoing mortal Order of the Talamasca whom these spectral founding fathers have apparently cut loose to pursue its own destiny."

Seth was marveling, obviously wanting to know so much more on this.

"Now, if there's nothing more," I said, "I'd like to retire. I've made that French library my lair and it's waiting for me and I need to rest perhaps more now than ever before in my life."

"One thing more," said Seth. "You hold the Core now. You are the Source. You are the Primal Fount."

"Yes?" I responded calmly, patiently, waiting.

"Your fate is our fate," he said.

"Yes?"

"You must vow never to slip away from us, never to seek to hide from us, never to be careless with your own person, any more than any earthly monarch on whom the peace of a realm depends."

"I'm aware of that," I said. I suppressed a little flash of anger. "I am yours now," I said, as difficult as it was to say this. A chill ran through me, an awful foreboding. "I belong to the realm. I know."

Suddenly Everard spoke up, the young blood drinker from Italy.

"But is this thing quiet inside you now?" he asked. "Is he quiet!"

A ripple of alarm ran through the gathering, though why I'm not sure. This question was on the mind of nearly everyone here. It had to be.

"Yes, Amel is quiet," I said. "Amel is satisfied. Amel is at peace."

"Or maybe he's somewhere else at this very moment, perhaps," said my mother.

"Yes," said Everard, "off making some more horrible trouble."

"No," I replied.

"But why?" asked Rhoshamandes. "Why is he content?" It was said with total sincerity, and for the first time in his face I saw a glimmer of actual pain.

I reflected for a moment before responding. Then:

"Because he can see and he can hear more clearly than ever," I said. "And this is what he's longed for. That's what he has always wanted. To see and hear and know in this world, the physical world, our world. And he is watching, and learning, as never before."

"But surely," said Zenobia, the diminutive friend of Gregory, "he saw and heard when he was in Akasha all that time, before Mekare ever came."

"No," I said. "He didn't. Because in those times, he didn't know how."

Pause.

The various amazing minds of the room pondered.

Inside me, Amel gave the softest most eloquent laugh with nothing of humor in it and everything of wonder that I could hope to hear.

I raised my hands for patience.

I had to sleep. And the morning was creeping up on the young ones with its sly burning fingers, and it would soon be creeping up even on me.

"Rose and Viktor," I said. "This day will be your last on Earth when the sun is visible to you and when the sun is your friend." I felt a sudden throb in my heart. I swallowed, trying to keep my voice steady. "Spend this day however you wish, but be wise and stay safe and come home to us at sunset . . . to reaffirm your decision."

I saw my son beaming at me, and beside him Rose looking on in quiet wonder. I smiled. I put my fingers gently to my lips and let the silent kiss go.

I left the room quickly. There would be time to embrace them, and to weep, yes, to weep as I held their warm, tender mortal bodies in my arms, only some thirteen hours from now when the night threw its inevitable mantle once again across the great Savage Garden that was our world.

As I lay down to sleep in the French library, I spoke softly to Amel.

"You're quiet," I said, "strangely quiet but I know you are there."

"Yes, I'm here," he said. "And it's as you told them. Do you doubt your own explanation?" There was a pause but I knew he was going to say something more. "Years ago," he said, "when you were a mortal boy in your village in France you had a friend, a friend you loved."

"Nicolas," I said.

"And you and he would talk."

"Yes."

"By the hour, by the day, by the night, by the week and the month . . ."

"Yes, always in those days when we were boys together, we would talk."

"Do you remember what you called it, your long flowing exchange?"

"Our conversation," I said. I marveled that he knew. Did he know because I knew? Could he search through my memory when I wasn't remembering? I was drowsy and my eyes were closing. "Our conversation," I said again. "And it went on and on. . . ."

"Well, we are having '*our* conversation,' aren't we?" he asked. "And *our* conversation will go on forever. There is no need for haste."

A great warmth came over me as if I'd been wrapped in a blanket of love.

"Yes," I whispered. "Yes."

29

Lestat

Pomp and Circumstance

AT SUNSET, the word went out that I would come before all in the park, at a deserted location well hidden from the mortal world. And as I set out to go, dressed in a new red-velvet coat and black pants and nice spiffy midcalf boots generously provided by Armand along with some old-fashioned lace at my throat, I discovered that Seth and Gregory were coming with me, that under no circumstances would they allow the Prince to walk amongst his people unguarded. Thorne and Flavius also accompanied us without a word.

I accepted it.

There were perhaps seventy-five fledglings in the gathering at eight o'clock and I had little difficulty greeting each with a clasp of hands and a promise that we would all work together to prosper. All had been young mortals when made, most dressed in black, some elegantly in old romantic nineteenth-century jackets or dresses, and others in the most exquisite black fashions of the present time, and still others were ragged, unkempt with matted hair—but all surrounded me with open hearts, with touching willingness to follow me and what I might demand. And one or two older ones were there, too, blood drinkers as old as Louis or myself. But there was no one older.

Taking a position in the middle of a circle, I explained that I was now their prince and I wouldn't fail them. I did not tell them yet that I contained the Sacred Core. I saw no reason for that to be announced in vulgar fashion in such a place, or for it to be announced by me personally at all. But I did assure them that the rampage of the Voice had been ended.

The darkness was soothing here, and there was a certain quiet, with the distant buildings of Manhattan flanking the park on either side, and the overhanging trees partially concealing us. But I knew I had to be quick. There were curious mortals about. And I wanted no disruption.

I told them all now that they were to be assured of my guidance.

"I'll soon set up my court to which you can come at any time, with rooms there for wayfarers, and *all* wayfarers. And the voice of Benji Mahmoud will never cease to offer you invaluable counsel. But if we are to cease from all battles and gang wars, and to live in secrecy and harmony with one another, then there must be rules, the very things I fought all my life, rules, and there must be a willingness on your part, for your own sake, to obey them."

Again came that soft but mighty roar I'd heard from them on the sidewalk before the townhouse only a night ago.

"You must leave this city," I said. "You must not congregate any more before Trinity Gate. Please, I ask that you agree to this."

There were nods, cries of affirmation, of "yes" from all sides.

"This city," I said, "great as it is, cannot sustain so many hunters, and you must find hunting grounds where you can feed on the evil-doer and leave the innocent unmolested. Understand. This you have to do, and there is no escaping it."

Again came their chorus of praise and agreement. So eager, so innocent, they seemed, so charged with collective conviction.

"There is no reason under the moon and stars," I said, "why we cannot prosper. And prosper we will."

A louder roar, and the innermost circle pressing in even as Gregory and Seth gestured for them to hold where they were.

"Now, give me time," I said. "Give me opportunity. Wait to hear from me and I promise your patience will be rewarded. And spread the word far and wide that I am your leader now and you can trust in me and what we will all achieve together."

I then took my leave, once again clasping hands on both sides as Gregory, Seth, Flavius, and Thorne escorted me out of the park. We ignored a deluge of irrepressible questions I could not answer now.

When I entered the townhouse, I saw in the drawing room the unmistakable figures of Gremt Stryker Knollys and Magnus, along with an impressive white-haired ancient blood drinker, and other ghosts—striking ghosts as solid and real seeming as Magnus. The shining and cheerful ghost of Raymond Gallant was among them. Had he met with Marius? I certainly hoped so. But Marius wasn't there.

Armand was with them and so were Louis and Sevraine and they all stared silently at me as I came into the room. I was alarmed at the sight of this ancient blood drinker simply because he hadn't come to us before. But I could see at once by the manner of everyone present that this was some sort of decorous or amicable meeting. And Seth and Gregory didn't follow me but remained in the hallway, with Flavius and Thorne, but they did not seem concerned.

Gremt and Magnus were robed as before, but this ancient blood drinker who gave me his name telepathically as "Teskhamen" wore a handsome modern suit of clothes. The other ghosts were all attired in the same way, except for the one woman ghost, who wore a fashionable long dress and a slim black coat. The group was very simply astonishing.

Did Louis and Armand know these were ghosts? Did they know this Gremt was a spirit? And who was this Teskhamen, a blood drinker who knew these ghosts obviously, but hadn't made himself known to us until now?

After a moment's hesitation, Louis left the company and Armand stepped back into the shadows. Sevraine gave a warm embrace to the blood drinker, and then took her leave as well.

The clock was chiming the half hour. I had only thirty minutes to be with Rose and Viktor.

I approached Gremt. I realized that the first time I'd encountered this spirit I'd found him intimidating. I hadn't admitted it to myself. But I knew it now because I was not in any way afraid of him. And a certain definite liking of him arose in me, a certain warming to him because I had seen emotions in him that I understood. He wasn't without emotion now.

"You know what's happened," I said. He was staring at me intently, staring, and perhaps staring through me, and through my eyes at Amel. I couldn't know. But Amel was quiet. Amel was there as he always would be, but not a sound came from him.

And not a sound came from Gremt either. That this being was in fact a spirit and not some species of biological immortal was almost impossible to grasp as I looked at him. He appeared so very vital, and so complex and obviously filled with feeling. He was not at ease.

"Soon," I said, "I want to talk to you, to sit down with you, if you will, and talk—with you and Magnus here and all of your little company. I'm going home as soon as I can to my father's house in France, in the country where I was born. Will you come to us there?"

Again, no response and then Gremt seemed to pull himself up, to force himself to be alert, and he gave a little shiver, and then spoke.

"Yes," said Gremt. "Yes, thank you, most definitely. We want very much to do that. Forgive us for interrupting you without warning. I realize that you're expected elsewhere. It's only that we could not stay away."

The blood drinker, Teskhamen, a spare white-haired being of considerable elegance, stepped forward. He introduced himself again with a soft agreeable voice. "Yes, you will forgive us, I hope, for coming to you so unexpectedly. But you see we are so eager for a meeting, and simply could not, after what has happened, remain away."

What did they know of what had happened? But then of course they knew. How could they not? Ghosts, spirits, what limits were there to what they could know? For all I knew they'd been in the house, present invisibly when I had taken Amel into me.

But it did seem this Teskhamen wanted to put me at ease.

"Lestat," he said warmly. "We are the ancient Elders of the Talamasca. You've been told this. We are the founders of the Order. In a sense, we are the real Talamasca and the enduring Talamasca—no longer in need of the mortal Order that survives—and we want to talk with you very much."

Armand standing silently against the wall said and did nothing.

"Well, I couldn't be more eager to talk to you myself," I said. "And I understand why you came. And I suspect I understand why you've cut loose your mortal scholars. I think I do, at any rate. But I need time to prepare my home in France, before I see you. And I ask that you come to me there, and soon."

"My name is Hesketh," said the woman, "and we are so longing for this meeting. We can't tell you how very much we want it." She had her smooth blond hair swept back from her face in rather beautiful waves, held in place by bits of pearl and platinum and then flowing over her shoulders in a timeless fashion.

She extended to me a gloved hand, a hand covered in soft gray kid leather, and of course it felt as vital as a human hand. I could feel the deceptive pulse in it. Why did they make themselves so perfectly physical? Her eyes were arresting, not only because they were such a dark shade of gray but because they were a little wider apart than most people's eyes, and that gave her face a certain mystery. All the details of her, eyelashes, eyebrows, succulent lips—were exquisitely convincing and fetching. I had to wonder precisely what accounted for this and the other gorgeous illusions I was seeing here. Was it skill, magnetism, aesthetic depth, genius? *Was it the soul?*

The other ghosts hung back. And one of them, a very personable young male, rather husky, with dark olive skin and curling black hair, appeared to have been weeping. I couldn't help notice that Armand was almost directly behind him and rather close to him. But there was no time for me to be noticing all these things, or puzzling over them.

"What makes us the physical beings we are? It is all of those things," said Gremt responding directly to my thoughts and of course reminding me that he could do this. "Oh, we have so much to tell you, so much to . . . And we will come to you in France as soon as you tell us to come. We have a house there not very far at all from yours, a very old house that goes back to our earliest times together." He was cheerful suddenly and almost excited. "This has been our wish for so long." He stopped as if he'd said too much but his expression never really changed.

The ghost of Magnus, as solid as before, hung back, but there came from his face a look of love, of doting love.

This caught me off guard.

"Listen, my friends," I said. "There are important things happening under this roof tonight and I cannot invite you to remain and to sit down with us just now. You must trust me, and trust in my goodwill. But soon, under my roof in France, it's agreed, we will indeed come together." We were repeating ourselves, weren't we? This was like a dance.

"Yes," said Gremt, but his eyes were almost glazed, as though his physicality was as much at the mercy of his emotions and obsessions as that of a human.

Yet he didn't move to take his leave. None of them did. And suddenly I caught on. They were deliberately biding their time, drawing out the essentially formal and meaningless conversation because they

were studying me at close hand. They were likely monitoring countless aspects of my physicality of which I was totally unaware.

They knew Amel was inside me. They knew that Amel and I
were one. They knew that Amel was studying them, too, just as I was
studying them, and as they were studying me.

I think something dark and slightly ominous must have appeared
in my expression or my demeanor because all at once they seemed to
react, to gather themselves up, to exchange infinitesimal signals and
to look to Teskhamen for a decisive gesture or word.

"You will excuse me now, won't you?" I said, striving to be gracious, as gracious as I could. "There are others waiting for me. I'm
leaving for home in a matter of nights to prepare a place for a wholly
new—." I stopped. A wholly new what?

"A wholly new reign," said Magnus gently. There was the same
loving smile on his lips.

"A wholly new era will suffice," I said. "I'm not sure I want it to be
called a reign."

He smiled at this as though he found it not only impressive but
somehow endearing. I didn't know whether I was feeling love or
hatred for him. Well, it certainly couldn't be hatred. I was too completely happy to be alive.

I had the sense again that they were studying me in ways I couldn't
fathom, searching my face and form for signs of what was within.
Yet Amel was silent. Amel was not helping me with them. Amel was
there, yes, but utterly quiet.

Teskhamen caught my hand. His was far colder than mine. It had
the hard icy texture of the Children of the Millennia. But his face was
very warm and he said, "Forgive us for troubling you on this night,
and so soon. But we were eager to see you with our own eyes. And we
will go now, yes. I give you my apologies for our conduct. I think we
are more impetuous and perhaps more excited than you can know."

"I understand," I said. "Thank you, my friends." But I couldn't
repress my suspicions as they took their leave now, moving in a small
loose body past me out of the drawing room into the hall and through
the front door.

Armand went with them, his arm around the dark-haired ghost,
the ghost who had been weeping, and the door was closed.

I realized that I was alone with Louis in the empty hallway. The
others had gone.

"You know who they are?" I whispered.

"I know what they told me," he said, walking along with me. "And I know what they told you. And the others obviously know who they are and they're not afraid of them. Yet all wait for you to take command, you to come, you to greet them and invite them to your home in France. You are the leader, Lestat, no doubt about it. All know it. And these ghosts and spirits or whoever they are—they know it too."

I stopped. I put my arm around him. I held him close to me.

"I'm Lestat," I said in a low voice. "Your Lestat. I'm the same Lestat you've always known, and no matter how I'm changed, I'm still that same being."

"I know," he said warmly.

I kissed him. I pressed my lips to his and I held this kiss for a long silent moment. And then I gave in to a silent wave of feeling, and I took him in my arms. I held him tight against me. I felt his unmistakable silken skin, his soft shining black hair. I heard the blood throbbing in him, and time dissolved, and it seemed I was in some old and secret place, some warm tropical grotto we'd once shared, ours alone in some way, with the scent of sweet olive blossoms and the whisper of moist breeze. "I love you," I whispered.

In a low intimate voice, he answered: "My heart is yours."

I wanted to weep.

But there was no time.

At that moment, Gregory and Seth reappeared with Sevraine, and Sevraine told me that they had seen to the ballroom and all was in readiness. Marius and Pandora were prepared. The candles had been lighted.

"I'm sorry about our unexpected guests," said Sevraine. "It seems a true prince is much in demand. But you go now to those waiting for you."

Viktor and Rose were in the French library.

They had chosen a kind of muted finery for the ceremony. Rose wore a long-sleeved dress of soft clinging black silk that left her throat bare, and hung beautifully to her feet. And Viktor wore a simple *thawb*, of black wool. The severity of these garments made their shining complexions all the more vivid, their lips all the more naturally pink, and their eager eyes all the more heartbreakingly innocent as well as vibrant.

I wanted to be with them, but I felt immediately that I was going to weep, that I couldn't prevent it, and I almost fled. But this really was not a choice available to me. I had to do what was right for them.

I took them in my arms and asked if they were still resolved to come to us.

Of course they were.

"I know there's no turning back for either of you," I said. "And I know you both believe that you're prepared for the road you're taking. I know this. But you must know how much I grieve right now for what you might have been in the course of time, and what now you will never be."

"But why, Father?" asked Viktor. "Yes, we're young, we know this. We don't challenge it. But we're already dying as are all young things. Why can't you be completely happy for us?"

"Dying?" I asked. "Well, yes, that's true. I don't say it's not true. But can I be blamed for wondering what you might have been in ten more years of mortal life, or twenty or thirty? Is that dying, for a young man to grow into a man in his prime, for a beautiful young bud of a woman to become the full blossom?"

"We want to be forever as we are now," said Rose. Her voice was so sweet, so tender. She didn't want this to be painful for me. She was comforting me. "Surely, you of all people understand," she pressed.

How could I? What was the point of reminding them that I'd never chosen the Blood. I'd never had such a chance. And what was the point of sentimentalizing the fact that had I lived out my life as a mortal man, even my bones would be gone now, perished in the earth, if I'd died in my bed at the age of ninety?

I was about to speak to them when I heard Amel inside me. He spoke in the softest whisper.

"Keep to your vow," he said. "They are not dying. They are coming to you as a prince and princess to be part of your court. We are not Death. No. We have never been, have we? We are immortal."

His voice was so resonant, so subtle in tone, that it shocked me, but this was in fact the same tone he'd used since he'd come into me. And yet it was the Voice that I'd been hearing for decades.

"Give them courage," he whispered. "But I leave you these moments. They are yours more truly than they are mine."

Inwardly I thanked him.

I looked at them, Viktor to my left, at eye level with me, and Rose gazing up, her face a perfect oval framed by her shining black hair.

"I know," I said. "I do know. We can't ask you to wait. We shouldn't. We can't live either with the simple fact that some gruesome accident might take you away from us at any random moment. Once the Blood's been offered, there is no waiting, no preparing, not really."

Rose kissed me on the cheek. Viktor stood patiently beside me, merely smiling.

"All right, my babies," I said. "This is a grand moment."

I couldn't prevent the tears. The clock would soon strike nine.

High above in the ballroom, Marius and Pandora waited, and it would have been purely selfish of me to delay this further.

The whole great house of Trinity Gate was scented with flowers.

"It *is* the finest gift," I whispered, the tears tinting my vision. "It is the gift that *we* can give, which means life everlasting."

They clung to me tightly.

"Go now," I said. "They're waiting for you. Before the sun rises, you'll be Born to Darkness, but you will see all light then as you've never before imagined it. As Marius once said, *'an endless illumination in which to understand all things.'* And when I set eyes on you again, I'll give you my blood as my blessing. And you will really be my children."

30

Cyril

The Silence Heard Round the World

H E WAS HUNGRY AGAIN, and disappointed to be bothered by it so soon. He listened and the great emptiness amazed him. He lay in his cave, in blessed solitude and darkness, and he thought, They are all gone.

Quiet the cities around him. Quiet the land. Only the cries and rumbling and human voices.

Except for that radio voice, that blood drinker from America speaking through a computer or a cellphone somewhere out there in the wilderness of Tokyo.

"The Voice is now one of us. The Voice is the root of our tribe."

What could that possibly mean?

He slipped out into the warm night.

Seems it was another one now speaking through the radio and not one of those desperate young ones weeping to Benji Mahmoud for solace or help. No. It was a calm voice simply talking, talking about the quiet that had descended over "our world."

Before midnight, Cyril had visited the silence of Beijing and the silence of Hong Kong.

Was it thirst that had awakened him, or was it curiosity? Something had happened, as remarkable as the waking of the Queen years ago, something as remarkable as the coming of the Voice.

They were gone, the others!

On he moved to Mumbai, and then to Kolkata and on towards the cities of the two rivers and the mighty Nile.

Gone, all of them, everywhere, those miserable little monsters struggling for their rung on the ladder to eternal life.

At last he stood in the ancient city of Alexandria, in the small hours, near dawn—this modern metropolis he so loathed on account of the stones and blood buried beneath it, the old catacombs in which the wicked Queen had been worshipped by the priesthood that had taken him out of life so long ago.

Even here the voice of Benji Mahmoud continued but it was recorded now. "It is a new era. It is a new time. We are the People of Darkness, we are the People of Everlasting Life. The Prince has spoken. The Prince rules."

The Prince? He couldn't fathom it. Who was the Prince?

He walked through a narrow street, listening for that recorded broadcast, until he came upon a small dark tavern filled with drunk lazy mortals on whom he might easily feed. Skins of all nations here. That pulsing twanging music he hated. And in the corner on a filthy little table against a wall covered with a beaded curtain stood the computer through which Benji Mahmoud addressed the world.

A pretty mortal girl, puffing on a long pink cigarette, listened to Benji Mahmoud and laughed under her breath. She saw Cyril. *Come here, big boy, just let me make you happy, come on, closer, closer. Daggers in the back room.* Her skin was thick with tinted powder, her eyes rimmed in kohl. She had the red smile of a child witch.

He sat down beside her in the shadows. The stench of the place was vile, but he wouldn't be here very long. And the smell of her blood was pure. All lies die in the blood. All evil is purged in the blood.

"You know," she said to him in English, "he could make you want to be a real vampire." And she laughed again, a rich cynical ugly laugh, lifting her yellow drink and spilling it down the front of her dark dress.

"Never mind that," he said as he kissed her.

She pushed at him helplessly as he sank his teeth. *Sold into it at twelve years old. Honey, tell me all about it!* And the blood sang and sang its ancient and unchanging song.

He walked away from the city.

He walked away from the damp hazy air of the Mediterranean, inland to the everlasting sands. He would sleep here in the land of Egypt, maybe for years, he would sleep in the land of his birth. Why not?

Finally, he stood alone under the great dark sky, away from all human sounds and scents, with the cold desert wind washing him, cleansing away the filth that clung to him of foreign lands.

Then the Voice sighed inside his head.

"Oh, spare me!" Cyril cried. "Get away from me! Don't torment me here."

But the Voice spoke to him now with an inflection he'd never heard before, and with a deep resonance that was wholly new. It was beautiful. And yet it was the Voice, and the Voice said,

"Cyril, come home. Come home to the tribe. At last we are one."

31

Rose

The People of the Moon and Stars

THE VOICE OF PANDORA called to her from far away: "Rose, drink!"

And she could hear Marius calling to her and Viktor, Viktor's desperate plea.

"Rose, drink."

The burning droplets hit her lips, trickled into her mouth. Poison. She couldn't move.

Gardner had ahold of her and was whispering in her ear, "Would you disappoint me yet again, Rose! Rose, how dare you do this to me!" *To me, to me, to me.* The echo faded into the roaring voice of the minister's wife, Mrs. Hayes, "And if you cannot convict yourself of sin, deeply convict yourself and admit your sin, and all the dreadful things you've done, and you know what you have done, you can never be saved!" Her grandmother was talking to them. She was in the little lawyer's office in Athens, Texas, but she was right there with Gardner. *Don't want the child, really, don't know who the father was.*

Gardner clung to her, his breath hot in her face, his fingers closing on her throat. How could that be true when her body was gone? She floated in this darkness, sinking ever deeper and deeper. The dark clouds rolled upwards, thick and swelling and blinding.

Viktor cried out, and Pandora and Marius called to her, but they were fading.

Oh, she'd seen such wondrous things when Pandora held her. She'd seen the Heavens, and she'd heard the music of the spheres. Never had anything been more grand.

Gardner's fingers bit into her neck. Her heart jumped and then slowed. It was so slow, the beat of her heart, and she was so weak, so dreadfully impossibly weak. Dying. Surely she was dying.

"Do you realize what this means, Rose, if you do this to me?" Gardner demanded. "You made a fool of me, Rose. You destroyed my life, my career, all my dreams, all my plans, ruined by you, Rose."

"If we knew who the child's father was," said the old woman in her slow Texas voice, "but you see, we had no contact with our daughter and, really, we just . . ."

Don't want me and why should you? And whoever did, that wasn't paid to want me, paid to educate me, paid to take care of me, paid to love me. Why isn't it over? Why am I sinking farther and farther down?

Uncle Lestan came towards her. Uncle Lestan, shining, and striding towards her, in his red-velvet jacket and his black boots, coming on, unstoppable, fearless with his hands out.

"Rose!" he cried.

She screamed his name!

"Uncle Lestan, take me, please, don't let them . . . ! Help me."

Gardner choked the voice out of her.

But Uncle Lestan loomed over her, his face shimmering in the light of the candles, all those candles, candles and candles. "Help me!" she cried, and he bent to kiss her, and she felt those needles, those dreadful sharp needles in her neck.

"Not enough blood!" cried Marius.

"Just enough," said Uncle Lestan, "to let me in."

The blackness had weight and mass and thickened around them. They were all talking at once, Gardner, Mrs. Hayes, and her grandmother. "She's dying," said someone, and it was one of those girls at the school, the horrible school, but the other girls laughed and jeered. "She's faking, she's a liar, she's a slut!" Laughter, laughter rolling up into the blackness with Gardner chanting, "You're mine, Rose, I forgive you for what you did to me, you're mine."

Uncle Lestan grabbed Gardner by the throat and dragged him away from her. Gardner snarled and screamed and fought. He bit into Uncle Lestan's hand but Uncle Lestan tore Gardner's head from him, stretching his neck like a long wrinkled elastic stocking—she gasped, she screamed—and Gardner's head melted, mouth turning downwards, eyes bleeding downwards, black and fluid and ghastly, and his head flopped down at the end of the broken wrinkled neck, and the body dropped into a sea of blood. Beautiful blood.

"Rose, drink from me!" said Uncle Lestan. "I am the Blood. I am the life."

"Don't you do that, child!" screamed Mrs. Hayes.

She reached for Uncle Lestan's golden hair, reached for him, for his shining face.

Your blood.

It filled her mouth! A great moan broke from her. She became the moan. She swallowed over and over again. The blood of Heaven.

Gardner's body floated in a stream of blood, dark ruby-red and blackish blood, and the face of Mrs. Hayes expanded, grew immense, a gleaming white mask of wrath. Uncle Lestan snatched at it, tore it loose like a fragile veil, and her voice died as her face died, like a flag burning, and he sent it down into the dark blackish blood current. Her grandmother, the old Texas woman, was sliding downwards with her hands out, paling, disappearing into the river of blood too.

Like Dante's river of blood, flowing on, bubbling, crimson, black, beautiful.

"And Hell shall have no dominion," said Uncle Lestan.

"No, no dominion," she whispered, and they were rising upwards, rising the way they had from the Greek island that was breaking into pieces below them, pieces falling into the foaming blue sea.

"Blood child, blood flower, blood Rose," said Uncle Lestan.

She was safe in his arms. Her lips were open on his neck and his blood was pumping through her body, pumping into her skin, her tingling, prickling skin. She saw his heart, his blood-red heart, throbbing and brightening and the long lovely tendrils of his blood surrounding her heart and enclosing it and it seemed a great fire burned in his heart and her heart, too, and when he spoke, another immense voice echoed his words.

"Finest flower of the Savage Garden," he said. "Life everlasting."

She looked down. The rolling smoking darkness was evaporating and disappearing. The dark river of blood was gone. The world sparkled beneath the mist with thousands and thousands of tiny lights, and above them was the firmament—all around them was the firmament and the galaxies of song and story and the music, the music of the spheres.

"My beloved Rose, you are with us now," said Uncle Lestan. *With her now, with us,* said the other voice, the echoing voice.

The words flowed into her on the blood that throbbed in her arms and legs, burned in her skin. Marius whispered into her ear that she was theirs now, and Pandora's lips touched her forehead, and Viktor, Viktor held her even as Uncle Lestan held her, *My bride.*

"You've always been mine," Lestat said. "For this you were born. My brave Rose. And you are with us and one of us, and we are the people of the moon and the stars."

32

Louis

"Its Hour Come at Last"

Trinity gate was quiet tonight, except for Sybelle and Antoine playing a duet in the drawing room and Benji upstairs talking confidentially to his best friend who just happened to be the whole world.

Rhoshamandes and Benedict had gone to the opera with Allesandra. Armand and Daniel Malloy were out hunting alone in the gentle warm rain.

Flavius, Avicus, Zenobia, and Davis had gone home to Geneva, along with an eager, desperate blood drinker named Killer who had shown up at the door, in Old West garb of dungarees and a shaggy-sleeved buckskin jacket begging to be allowed in. Friend of Davis, the beloved of Gregory. They'd welcomed him at once.

Jesse and David were in the Amazon at Maharet's old sanctuary with Seth and Fareed.

Sevraine and her family had also gone home, and so had Notker and the musicians and singers from the Alps.

Marius remained, working in the Tudor library, on the rules he would present to Lestat in time. Everard de Landen remained with him, poring over an old book of Elizabethan poetry, interrupting Marius softly now and then to ask the meaning of a phrase or a word.

And Lestat was gone, gone with Gabrielle and with Rose and Viktor, and with Pandora and Arjun, and Bianca Solderini, and Flavius, and with Gregory and Chrysanthe—to his castle in the mountains of the Massif Central to prepare for the first great reception of the new court to which they would all come. How fine and perfect Viktor and Rose were. And how they loved each other still, and how they'd welcomed their new vision, their new powers, their new hopes. Ah, just brave fledglings.

Only a little rain fell on this garden bench behind the townhouse, tucked as it was beneath the largest of the oaks, the raindrops singing in the leaves overhead.

Louis sat there, back to the trunk of the tree, a copy of his memoir, *Interview with the Vampire,* the memoir that had sparked the Vampire Chronicles, open on his lap. He wore his favorite old dark coat, a little threadbare but so comfortable, and his favorite old flannel trousers and a fine white shirt Armand had forced upon him with buttons of pearl and outrageous lace. But Louis had never really minded lace.

Unseasonably warm for September. But he liked it. Liked the dampness in the air, liked the music of the rain, and loved the seamless and never-ending roar of the city, as much a part of it as the great river was a part of New Orleans, the innumerable population around him holding him safe in this tiny walled place that was their garden, where the lilies opened their white throats and powdery yellow tongues to the rain.

On the page, Louis read the words he'd spoken years ago to Daniel Malloy when Daniel had been an eager and enchanted human, listening to Louis so desperately, and his tape recorder had seemed such an exotic novelty, the two together in that bare dusty room on Divisadero Street in San Francisco, unnoticed by the Undead world.

" 'I wanted love and goodness in this which is living death. It was impossible from the beginning, because you cannot have love and goodness when you do what you know to be evil, what you know to be wrong.' "

With his whole being Louis had believed those words; and they had shaped the blood drinker that he was then, and the blood drinker he remained after for many a year.

And was that dark conviction not still inside him, under the veneer of the resigned and contented creature he appeared to be now?

He didn't honestly know. He remembered completely how he had spoken then of chasing "phantom goodness" in its human form. He looked down at the page.

" 'No one could in any guise convince me of what I myself knew to be true, that I was damned in my own mind and soul.' "

What had really changed? He'd learned once more somehow, after Lestat had shattered the Undead realm with his antics and his pronouncements, to live from night to night in a semblance of happiness, and to seek for grace once more in the music of operas, symphonies, and choruses, and in the splendor of paintings old and new, and in the simple miracle of human vitality all around him—with Armand and Benji and Sybelle at his side. He had learned his old theology was useless to him and perhaps always had been, an incurable canker inside him rather than a spark to kindle any kind of hope or faith.

But now a new vision had taken hold of him, a new witness to something he could no longer deny. His mind was no longer stubborn and locked against its vagrant possibilities and wild, escalating light.

What if the old sensibilities that had forged him had not been the sacrosanct revelation that he had once assumed? What if it were possible to invest every cell of his being with a gratitude and acceptance of self that could bring not mere contentment but certain joy?

It seemed impossible.

Yet undeniably, he felt it happening. He felt some overall quickening that was so surprisingly new for him that no one save himself could or would understand. But no other understanding was needed. He knew this.

For what he'd been, the being he'd been, required no confessions to those he knew and loved, but only that he love them and affirm their purpose with his transformed soul. And if he had once been the soul of an age as Armand had long ago told him he was, well, so be it, because he saw that dark and lustrous age with its decayed beliefs and doomed rebellions as only a beginning—a vast and fertile kindergarten in which the terms of his struggle had not been without value but were now most certainly the phantoms of a past from which he had, in spite of himself, exorably emerged.

He had not perished. That might be his only significant accomplishment. He had survived. Yes, he'd been defeated, more than once. But fortune had refused to release him. And he was here now, whole, and quietly accepting of the fact though he honestly did not know why.

But what loomed ahead of him now were challenges more wondrous and splendid than he'd ever foreseen. And he wanted this, this future, this time in which "Hell would have no dominion" and in which the Devil's Road had become the Road of the People of Darkness, who were essentially children no more.

This was beyond happiness and beyond contentment. This was nothing other than peace.

From the depths of the townhouse came the music of Antoine and Sybelle with a new melody, a furious Tchaikovsky waltz, ah, the waltz of "The Sleeping Beauty," and on and on the music surged in Antoine's magnificent glissandos, and Sybelle's pounding chords.

Oh, how differently he heard this triumphal music now than he had once heard it, and how he opened himself to it, acknowledging its magnificent claims.

He closed his eyes. Was he making lyrics for this swirling melody, was he forming some affirmation for his soul? "Yes, and I do want this, yes, I do take it, yes, I hold it in my heart, the will to know this beauty forever, the will to let it be the light on my path. . . ."

On they went, faster and faster, the piano and the violin singing of gaiety and glory as if they had always been one.

A random noise pierced his thoughts. Something wrong. Be *en garde*. The music had stopped.

Over the top of the brick wall to his left, he saw a human crouched in the darkness, incapable of seeing him there as he saw the human. He heard the soft stealthy sounds of Sybelle and Antoine drawing near to the glass porch that ran along the back of the three townhouses. He heard the mortal intruder's labored breath.

The intruder, dressed in black garments and black skull cap, dropped down into the wet grass. With deft feline movements he darted out from the shrubbery and into the dim yellow light from the house.

Scent of fear, scent of rage, scent of blood.

He saw Louis now, the lone figure on the bench beneath the tree, and he stiffened. Out of his slick black Windbreaker jacket he raised a knife that shone like silver in the semidarkness.

Slowly he came towards Louis. Ah, the old menacing dance.

Louis closed the book but he didn't put it aside. The scent of the blood made him faintly delirious. He watched this emaciated yet powerful young man come closer. He saw the malignant face infinitely more clearly than the man, hardened with purpose, could see his.

The man was sweating and breathing raggedly, crazed with drugs and seeking for anything he might snatch to find the anodyne for his twisting gut. Such beautiful eyes. Such black eyes. Why these walls and not some other garden meant nothing in the scheme of things to this one, and before Louis could utter a word to him, the man had resolved to sink the knife into Louis's heart.

"Death," Louis said now loudly enough to stop the man, though he was only a few feet away. "Are you ready for this? Is this what you truly want?"

A sinister laugh came from the intruder. He stepped forward crunching the lilies, the stout white calla lilies, underfoot.

"Yeah, death, my friend!" the man said. "You're in the wrong place at the wrong time."

"Ah, but for your sake"—Louis sighed—"would that were true. But it has never been less true than it is now."

He had the man in his grip.

The knife was gone, lost in the wet leaves. Sybelle and Antoine waited in the shadows behind the wall of glass.

The man fought and kicked in a small useless fury. Oh, how Louis had always cherished the struggle, young muscles straining against him and the inevitable strangled curses like so much unwitting applause.

He drove his fangs right into the arterial stream. How ever translate for a mortal world the heat and purity of this simple feast? Salt and blood, and dark shiny brittle fantasies of victories, all flowing into him and out of the victim with the last protest of his dying heart.

It was finished. The man lay dead among the lilies. Louis stood wondrously satisfied and reanimated, the night opening up above him through luminous clouds. And the music inside the house began again.

Flushed with blood, flushed with the old deceptive but seductive sense of illimitable power, he thought of Lestat across the sea. What charms would his great castle hold, and what manner of court would convene there in chambers of stone that Louis so longed to see? He had to smile when he thought of the easy swagger with which Lestat had fulfilled the tribe's collective dreams.

The road ahead could not be smooth, and simplicity could never be the goal. The burden of conscience was part of Louis's human heart and the heart of every blood drinker he had ever known, even

Armand. And the struggle for goodness, actual goodness, would and must obsess them all. That was the miracle which now united the tribe.

How wondrous it seemed suddenly that such a struggle could now lay waste with such undeniable power the old dead dualities which had enslaved him for so long.

But he looked down at the man who lay dead at his feet, and a terrible sorrow took hold of him.

Death is the mother of beauty.

It was a line from a poem by Wallace Stevens, and it came to him now with a painful irony. Beauty for me perhaps but not beauty for this one whom I have destroyed.

He knew terror for a moment, terror that might never really leave him no matter how much he came to understand, or to learn. Terror. Terror that this tender young mortal might have lost his soul to utter meaninglessness and annihilation, and that all of them, his blood drinker brothers and sisters, no matter how powerful, how old, how grand, might someday fall victim to the same brutal end.

After all, what ghost or spirit, no matter how eloquent or skilled, could claim that anything of sentience lay beyond the thick mysterious air surrounding this planet? Again he thought of Stevens's poem.

> *Shall our blood fail? Or shall it come to be*
> *The blood of paradise? And shall the earth*
> *Seem all of paradise that we shall know?*

His heart was breaking for the young man who lay there dead, eyes closed in the final sleep. The remains were already slowly perishing in the warm rain. His heart broke for all the victims everywhere of blood lust, and war, and accident, and old age, and illness, and unendurable pain.

But his heart broke a little for once for himself too.

And that perhaps was the real change in him, the change that he welcomed—that he could see himself as part now of all this great and glistening world. He was not part of some mindless force that sought to destroy it. No, he was part of *it*. He was part of this, this night with its sweet mild rain, and this whispering garden with its fragrant flowers and its trees, and the breezes that moved their branches. And he was part of the roar of the city rising around him, and part of the sharp shining music that came from within the house. He was part of the grass beneath his feet, and the tiny relentless hordes of winged things that sought to devour the human waiting there helplessly for a proper grave.

He thought of Lestat again, confident, smiling, wearing the mantle of power as easily as he had always worn his finery, old and new.

He said under his breath:

"Beloved maker, beloved Prince, I will be with you soon."

Tuesday
November 26, 2013
Palm Desert

Appendix 1

Characters and Their Chronology

Amel—A spirit manifesting to humans six thousand years ago or in 4000 B.C.

Akasha—The first vampire, made by a fusion with the spirit Amel six thousand years ago, or in 4000 B.C. Thereafter known as the Mother, or the Sacred Fount, or the Queen.

Enkil—The husband of Akasha and the first vampire made almost immediately by her.

Khayman—The second vampire made by Akasha within the first years after the fusion.

Maharet and Mekare—Twin witches born six thousand years ago. Mekare was made a vampire by Khayman. Maharet was made by Mekare. Khayman, Maharet, and Mekare became the First Brood rebelling against Akasha and making other blood drinkers when and where they chose.

Nebamun, later Gregory Duff Collingsworth—Made by Akasha in the first few years to lead her Queens Blood troops against the First Brood.

Seth—The human son of Akasha, brought into the Blood perhaps fifteen to twenty years after the fusion.

Sevraine—A Nordic woman brought into the Blood illegally by Nebamun (Gregory) about five thousand years ago, or one thousand years after the Blood Genesis. The maker of several vampires yet unnamed.

Rhoshamandes—A male from Crete, brought into the Blood at the same time as Sevraine, to serve in the Queens Blood. Made directly by Akasha.

Avicus, Cyril, Teskhamen—Egyptian blood drinkers made by the priests of Akasha's cult well before the Common Era, drinking the Mother's blood but not made by her.

Marius—A Roman patrician, kidnapped by the Druids, and brought into the Blood shortly after the birth of Christ, or at the dawn of the Common Era. Made by Teskhamen, who was shortly thereafter presumed dead.

Pandora—A Roman patrician woman named Lydia, brought into the Blood by Marius in the first century.

Flavius—A Greek slave brought into the Blood by Pandora during the first century.

Mael—A Druid priest, the kidnapper of Marius, brought into the Blood by Avicus, and presumed dead.

Hesketh—A Germanic cunning woman, brought into the Blood by Teskhamen in the first century. Murdered in the eighth century.

Chrysanthe—A merchant's wife from the Christian city of Hira. Brought into the Blood by Nebamun, newly risen and named Gregory, in the fourth century.

Zenobia—A Byzantine woman, brought into the Blood by Eudoxia (now dead), who was made by Cyril around the sixth or seventh century.

Allesandra—A Merovingian princess, daughter of King Dagobert I, brought into the Blood in the seventh century by Rhoshamandes.

Gremt Stryker Knollys—A spirit who enters the narrative in the eighth century (748).

Benedict—A Christian monk of the eighth century, brought into the Blood by Rhoshamandes around the year A.D. 800.

Thorne—A Viking, brought into the Blood by Maharet around the ninth century of the Common Era.

Notker the Wise—A monk and a musician and a composer brought into the Blood by Benedict around A.D. 880, maker of many musician vampires as yet unnamed.

Eleni and Eugénie de Landen—Fledglings of Rhoshamandes made in the early Middle Ages.

Everard de Landen—A fledgling of Rhoshamandes made in the Middle Ages.

Arjun—A prince of the Chola dynasty in India, brought into the Blood by Pandora around 1300.

Santino—Italian vampire made during the time of the Black Death. Longtime Roman coven master of the Children of Satan. Presumed dead.

Magnus—An elderly alchemist who stole the Blood from Benedict during the 1400s. The maker of Lestat in 1780.

Armand—A Russian icon painter kidnapped in the vicinity of Kiev and brought to Venice as a slave, and made into a vampire by Marius around 1498.

Bianca Solderini—A Venetian courtesan made in the Blood by Marius around 1498.

Raymond Gallant—A faithful mortal scholar of the Talamasca, presumed dead in the sixteenth century.

Lestat de Lioncourt—Seventh son of a French marquis, made a vampire in the year 1780 by Magnus. Author of the second book in the Vampire Chronicles, *The Vampire Lestat.*

Gabrielle de Lioncourt—Lestat's mother, made by him in the Blood in 1780.

Nicolas de Lenfent—Close friend of Lestat, made into a vampire by Lestat in 1780 and long dead.

Louis de Pointe du Lac—A Louisiana French colonial plantation owner, brought into the Blood by Lestat in 1791. Louis began the books known as the Vampire Chronicles with *Interview with the Vampire* in 1976.

Claudia—An orphan, brought into the Blood around 1794. Long dead.

Antoine—A French musician, exiled to Louisiana and brought into the Blood by Lestat around 1860.

Daniel Malloy—An American male of about twenty who enters the narrative when he "interviews" Louis de Pointe du Lac about his life as a vampire, resulting in the publication of *Interview with the Vampire* in 1976. He is brought into the Blood by Armand in 1985, some nine years later.

Jesse Reeves—Mortal descendant of Maharet, brought into the Blood by Maharet in 1985.

David Talbot—Superior General of the Talamasca, brought into the Blood in 1992 by Lestat. David, the victim of a body switch, lost his original biological body, that of an elderly man, before being made into a vampire in the body of a much younger man.

Killer—An American male vampire of unknown origin, founder of the Fang Gang, who entered the narrative about 1985.

Davis—A black dancer from New York, a member of the Fang Gang, brought into the Blood by Killer sometime before 1985.

Fareed Bhansali—A brilliant Anglo-Indian doctor and surgeon, brought into the Blood by Seth around 1986 in Mumbai.

Benjamin (Benji) Mahmoud—A twelve-year-old Palestinian Bedouin boy, brought into the Blood by Marius in 1997.

Sybelle—A young American pianist, about twenty, brought into the Blood by Marius in 1997.

Rose—An American girl of around twenty rescued as a small child by Lestat from an earthquake in the Mediterranean around 1995. His ward.

Dr. Flannery Gilman—An American doctor and discredited vampire researcher, brought into the Blood by Fareed in the early twenty-first century.

Viktor—A human experiment conducted under the auspices of Fareed Bhansali and his maker, Seth, along with Dr. Flannery Gilman before her induction into the Blood.

Assorted unnamed fledglings, ghosts, and spirits.

Appendix 2

An Informal Guide to the Vampire Chronicles

1. *Interview with the Vampire* (1976)—In this, the first published memoir of a vampire within his tribe, Louis de Pointe du Lac tells his life story to a reporter he encounters in San Francisco—Daniel Malloy. Born in the eighteenth century in Louisiana, Louis, a rich plantation owner, encounters the mysterious Lestat de Lioncourt, who offers him immortality through the Blood and Louis accepts—beginning a long spiritual search for the meaning of who and what he has become. The child vampire Claudia and the mysterious Armand of the Théâtre des Vampires are central to the story.

2. *The Vampire Lestat* (1985)—Here, Lestat de Lioncourt offers his full autobiography—recounting his life in eighteenth-century France as a penniless provincial aristocrat, a Parisian stage actor, and finally as a vampire in conflict with other members of the Undead, including the coven of the Children of Satan. After a long physical and spiritual journey, Lestat reveals ancient secrets about the vampire tribe that he has kept for more than a century, emerging as a rock star and rock video maker, eager to start a war with humankind that might bring the Undead together and end in vampiric annihilation.

3. *The Queen of the Damned* (1988)—Though written by Lestat, this story includes multiple points of view from mortals and immortals all over the planet, responding to Lestat's revealing rock music and videos, which awaken the six-thousand-year-old Queen of the Vampires, Akasha, from her long slumber. The first book to deal with the entire tribe of the Undead around the world. This novel contains the first inclusion of the mysterious secret order of mortal scholars known as the Talamasca, who study the paranormal.

4. *The Tale of the Body Thief* (1992)—Lestat's memoir in which he recounts his disastrous encounter with a clever and sinister mortal named Raglan James, a sorcerer experienced in switching bodies—a battle which forces Lestat into closer involvement with his friend, David Talbot, Superior General of the Talamasca, whose scholarly members are dedicated to the study of the paranormal.

5. *Memnoch the Devil* (1995)—Lestat narrates a personal adventure, this time filled with devastating shocks and mysteries as he confronts a powerful spirit, Memnoch, claiming to be none other than the Devil of Christian lore, the fallen angel himself, who invites Lestat to journey with him to Heaven and Hell, and seeks to enlist Lestat as a helper in the Christian realm.

6. *Pandora* (1998)—Published under the series title "New Tales of the Vampires," this story is Pandora's autobiographical confession, recounting her life in the ancient Roman Empire during the time of Augustus and Tiberius, including her great and tragic love affair with the vampire Marius. Though it does recount later events, the book is principally focused on Pandora's first century as a vampire.

7. *The Vampire Armand* (1998)—Here, Armand, a profound and enigmatic presence in earlier novels, offers his autobiography to the reader, explaining his long life since the time of the Renaissance when he was kidnapped from Kiev and brought to Venice as a boy brothel slave, only to be rescued by the powerful and ancient vampire Marius. Yet another kidnapping puts Armand in the hands of the cruel and notorious Children of Satan, superstitious vampires who worship the Devil. Though Armand concludes his story in the present time and introduces new characters to the Chronicles, most of the account focuses on his earlier years.

8. *Vittorio, the Vampire* (1999)—One of the "New Tales of the Vampires," this is the autobiography of Vittorio of Tuscany, who becomes a member of the Undead during the Renaissance. This character does not appear elsewhere in the Vampire Chronicles, but he is of the same tribe and does share the same cosmology.

9. *Merrick* (2000)—Told by David Talbot, this story is centered on Merrick, a Creole woman of color from an old New Orleans family and a member of the Talamasca, who seeks to become a vampire during the last years of the twentieth century. This is a hybrid novel, involving a glimpse of a few characters from another series of books devoted to the history of the Mayfair Witches of New Orleans to whom Merrick is related, but it principally focuses on Merrick's involvement with the Undead, including Louis de Pointe du Lac.

10. *Blood and Gold* (2001)—Another in the series of vampire memoirs, this time written by the ancient Roman Marius, explaining much about his two thousand years amongst the Undead and the challenges he faced in protecting the mystery of "Those Who Must Be Kept," the ancient parents of the tribe, Akasha and Enkil. Marius offers his side of the story of his love affair with Armand and his conflicts with other vampires. This novel concludes in the present but is principally focused on the past.

11. *Blackwood Farm* (2002)—A hybrid novel narrated by Quinn Blackwood recounting his personal history and involvement with the Talamasca, the Undead, and the Mayfair Witches of New Orleans, who figure in another book series. Set in a brief period of time in the early twenty-first century.

12. *Blood Canticle* (2003)—A hybrid novel, narrated by Lestat, recounting his adventures with Quinn Blackwood and with the Mayfair Witches from another series of books. This story focuses on a brief period of time in the twenty-first century.

13. *Prince Lestat* (2014)—The return of Lestat after years of silence. Many voices and points of view reveal the crises of the worldwide tribe of the Undead.